# Selected I from a Stoic

*Seneca*

SELECTED LETTERS FROM A STOIC *by* Seneca

ALL RIGHTS RESERVED. No part of this book may be reproduced in a retrieval system or transmitted in any form or by any means electronic, mechanical, photocopying, recording and or without permission of the publisher.

Published by

MAPLE PRESS PRIVATE LIMITED
office: A-63, Sector 58, Noida 201301, U.P., India
phone: +91 120 455 3581, 455 3583
email: info@maplepress.co.in
website: www.maplepress.co.in

Printed 2021 in India

# Contents

| | |
|---|---|
| Letter 1 : On Saving Time | 5 |
| Letter 2 : On Discursiveness in Reading | 7 |
| Letter 3 : On True and False Friendship | 9 |
| Letter 4 : On the Terrors of Death | 11 |
| Letter 5 : On the Philosopher's Mean | 14 |
| Letter 6 : On Sharing Knowledge | 16 |
| Letter 7 : On Crowds | 18 |
| Letter 8 : On the Philosopher's Seclusion | 21 |
| Letter 9 : On Philosophy and Friendship | 24 |
| Letter 10 : On Living to Oneself | 29 |
| Letter 11 : On the Blush of Modesty | 31 |
| Letter 12 : On Old Age | 33 |
| Letter 13 : On Groundless Fears | 36 |
| Letter 14 : On the Reasons for Withdrawing from the World | 40 |
| Letter 15 : On Philosophy, the Guide of Life | 44 |
| Letter 16 : On Festivals and Fasting | 46 |
| Letter 17 : On Worldliness and Retirement | 49 |
| Letter 18 : On Practicing what you Preach | 52 |
| Letter 19 : On the Renown which My Writings will Bring you | 55 |
| Letter 20 : On the Futility of Half-Way Measures | 58 |
| Letter 21 : On the True Joy which Comes from Philosophy | 62 |
| Letter 22 : On Despising Death | 65 |
| Letter 23 : On Reformation | 71 |
| Letter 24 : On the Good which Abides | 73 |
| Letter 25 : On Travel as a Cure for Discontent | 75 |
| Letter 26 : On Conquering the Conqueror | 77 |
| Letter 27 : On Progress | 81 |
| Letter 28 : On the Futility of Learning Maxims | 83 |
| Letter 29 : On a Promising Pupil | 86 |
| Letter 30 : On Allegiance to Virtue | 87 |
| Letter 31 : On Noble Aspirations | 89 |
| Letter 32 : On the Proper Style for a Philosopher's Discourse | 91 |
| Letter 33 : On the God within Us | 94 |

| | |
|---|---:|
| Letter 34 : On Values | 96 |
| Letter 35 : On Sophistical Argumentation | 98 |
| Letter 36 : On the Shortness of Life | 101 |
| Letter 37 : On Choosing our Teachers | 104 |
| Letter 38 : On Quiet and Study | 107 |
| Letter 39 : On Being | 110 |
| Letter 40 : On Pleasure and Joy | 118 |
| Letter 41 : On Meeting Death Cheerfully | 123 |
| Letter 42 : On the Philosopher's Task | 124 |
| Letter 43 : On Ill-Health and Endurance of Suffering | 126 |
| Letter 44 : On Rest and Restlessness | 129 |
| Letter 45 : On the Supreme Good | 131 |
| Letter 46 : On Philosophers and Kings | 139 |
| Letter 47 : On Virtue as a Refuge from Worldly Distractions | 143 |
| Letter 48 : On the Diseases of the Soul | 151 |
| Letter 49 : On Learning Wisdom in Old Age | 155 |
| Letter 50 : On Taking One's Own Life | 163 |
| Letter 51 : On the Healing Power of the Mind | 168 |
| Letter 52 : On the Rewards of Scientific Discovery | 175 |
| Letter 53 : On Worldly Deceptions | 179 |
| Letter 54 : On Liberal and Vocational Studies | 182 |
| Letter 55 : On the Happy Life | 192 |
| Letter 56 : On the Quality, as Contrasted with the Length, of Life | 200 |
| Letter 57 : On the Usefulness of Basic Principles | 203 |
| Letter 58 : On Facing Hardships | 219 |
| Letter 59 : On the Fickleness of Fortune | 221 |
| Letter 60 : On Consolation to the Bereaved | 225 |
| Letter 61 : On the Futility of Planning Ahead | 232 |
| Letter 62 : On the Intimations of our Immortality | 236 |
| Letter 63 : On Care of Health and Peace of Mind | 243 |
| Letter 64 : On Facing the World with Confidence | 251 |
| Letter 65 : On Obedience to the Universal Will | 253 |
| Letter 66 : On the Fellowship of Wise Men | 256 |
| Letter 67 : On True and False Riches | 260 |
| Letter 68 : On Reforming Hardened Sinners | 265 |
| Letter 69 : On the Vanity of the Soul and Its Attributes | 266 |
| Letter 70 : On Style as a Mirror of Character | 272 |
| Letter 71 : On Self-Control | 279 |

# Letter 1
# On Saving Time

Greetings from Seneca to his friend, Lucilius.

Continue to act thus, my dear Lucilius—set yourself free for your own sake; gather and save your time, which till lately has been forced from you, or filched away, or has merely slipped from your hands. Make yourself believe the truth of my words—that certain moments are torn from us, that some are gently removed, and that others glide beyond our reach. The most disgraceful kind of loss, however, is that due to carelessness. Furthermore, if you will pay close heed to the problem, you will find that the largest portion of our life passes while we are doing ill, a goodly share while we are doing nothing, and the whole while we are doing that which is not to the purpose.

What man can you show me who places any value on his time, who reckons the worth of each day, who understands that he is dying daily? For we are mistaken when we look forward to death; the major portion of death has already passed. Whatever years be behind us are in death's hands.

Therefore, Lucilius, do as you write me that you are doing: hold every hour in your grasp. Lay hold of today's task, and you will not need to depend so much upon tomorrow's. While we are postponing, life speeds by.

Nothing, Lucilius, is ours, except time. We were entrusted by nature with the ownership of this single thing, so fleeting and slippery that anyone who will can oust us from possession. What fools these mortals be! They allow the cheapest and most useless things, which can easily be replaced, to be charged in the reckoning, after they have acquired them; but they never regard themselves as in debt when they have received some of that precious commodity—time! And yet time is the one loan which even a grateful recipient cannot repay.

You may desire to know how I, who preach to you so freely, am practicing. I confess frankly: my expense account balances, as you would expect from one who is free-handed but careful. I cannot boast that I waste nothing, but I can at least tell you what I am wasting, and the cause and manner of the loss; I can give you the reasons why I am a poor man. My situation, however, is the same as that of many who are reduced to slender means through no fault of their own: every one forgives them, but no one comes to their rescue.

What is the state of things, then? It is this: I do not regard a man as poor, if the little which remains is enough for him. I advise you, however, to keep what is really yours; and you cannot begin too early. For, as our ancestors believed, it is too late to spare when you reach the dregs of the cask. Of that which remains at the bottom, the amount is slight, and the quality is vile. Farewell.

# Letter 2
# On Discursiveness in Reading

Judging by what you write me, and by what I hear, I am forming a good opinion regarding your future. You do not run hither and thither and distract yourself by changing your abode; for such restlessness is the sign of a disordered spirit. The primary indication, to my thinking, of a well-ordered mind is a man's ability to remain in one place and linger in his own company.

Be careful, however, lest this reading of many authors and books of every sort may tend to make you discursive and unsteady. You must linger among a limited number of master thinkers, and digest their works, if you would derive ideas which shall win firm hold in your mind. Everywhere means nowhere. When a person spends all his time in foreign travel, he ends by having many acquaintances, but no friends. And the same thing must hold true of men who seek intimate acquaintance with no single author, but visit them all in a hasty and hurried manner.

Food does no good and is not assimilated into the body if it leaves the stomach as soon as it is eaten; nothing hinders a cure so much as frequent change of medicine; no wound will heal when one salve is tried after another; a plant which is often moved can never grow strong. There is nothing so efficacious that it can be helpful while it is being shifted about. And in reading of many books is distraction.

Accordingly, since you cannot read all the books which you may possess, it is enough to possess only as many books as you can read.

"But," you reply, "I wish to dip first into one book and then into another." I tell you that it is the sign of an overnice appetite to toy with many dishes; for when they are manifold and varied, they cloy but do not nourish. So you should always read standard authors; and when you crave a change, fall back upon those whom you read before. Each day acquire something that will fortify you against poverty, against death, indeed against other misfortunes as well; and after you have run over many thoughts, select one to be thoroughly digested that day.

This is my own custom; from the many things which I have read, I claim some one part for myself.

The thought for today is one which I discovered in Epicurus; for I am wont to cross over even into the enemy's camp—not as a deserter, but as a scout.

He says: "Contented poverty is an honourable estate." Indeed, if it be contented, it is not poverty at all. It is not the man who has too little, but the man who craves more, that is poor. What does it matter how much a man has laid up in his safe, or in his warehouse, how large are his flocks and how fat his dividends, if he covets his neighbour's property, and reckons, not his past gains, but his hopes of gains to come? Do you ask what is the proper limit to wealth? It is, first, to have what is necessary, and, second, to have what is enough. Farewell.

# Letter 3
# On True and False Friendship

You have sent a letter to me through the hand of a "friend" of yours, as you call him. And in your very next sentence you warn me not to discuss with him all the matters that concern you, saying that even you yourself are not accustomed to do this; in other words, you have in the same letter affirmed and denied that he is your friend.

Now if you used this word of ours in the popular sense, and called him "friend" in the same way in which we speak of all candidates for election as "honourable gentlemen," and as we greet all men whom we meet casually, if their names slip us for the moment, with the salutation "my dear sir"—so be it. But if you consider any man a friend whom you do not trust as you trust yourself, you are mightily mistaken and you do not sufficiently understand what true friendship means. Indeed, I would have you discuss everything with a friend; but first of all discuss the man himself. When friendship is settled, you must trust; before friendship is formed, you must pass judgment. Those persons indeed put last first and confound their duties, who, violating the rules of Theophrastus, judge a man after they have made him their friend, instead of making him their friend after they have judged him. Ponder for a long time whether you shall admit a given person to your friendship; but when you have decided to admit him, welcome him with all your heart and soul. Speak as boldly with him as with yourself.

As to yourself, although you should live in such a way that you trust your own self with nothing which you could not entrust even to your enemy, yet, since certain matters occur which convention keeps secret, you should share with a friend at least all your worries and reflections. Regard him as loyal, and you will make him loyal. Some, for example, fearing to be deceived, have taught men to deceive; by their suspicions they have given their friend the right to do wrong. Why need I keep back any words in the presence of my friend? Why should I not regard myself as alone when in his company?

There is a class of men who communicate, to anyone whom they meet, matters which should be revealed to friends alone, and unload upon the chance listener whatever irks them. Others, again, fear to confide in their closest intimates; and if it were possible, they would not trust even themselves, burying their secrets deep in their hearts. But we should do neither. It is equally faulty to trust everyone and to trust no one. Yet the former fault is, I should say, the more ingenuous, the latter the more safe.

In like manner you should rebuke these two kinds of men—both those who always lack repose, and those who are always in repose. For love of bustle is not industry—it is only the restlessness of a hunted mind. And true repose does not consist in condemning all motion as merely vexation; that kind of repose is slackness and inertia.

Therefore, you should note the following saying, taken from my reading in Pomponius: "Some men shrink into dark corners, to such a degree that they see darkly by day." No, men should combine these tendencies, and he who reposes should act and he who acts should take repose. Discuss the problem with Nature; she will tell you that she has created both day and night. Farewell.

# Letter 4
# On the Terrors of Death

Keep on as you have begun, and make all possible haste, so that you may have longer enjoyment of an improved mind, one that is at peace with itself. Doubtless you will derive enjoyment during the time when you are improving your mind and setting it at peace with itself; but quite different is the pleasure which comes from contemplation when one's mind is so cleansed from every stain that it shines.

You remember, of course, what joy you felt when you laid aside the garments of boyhood and donned the man's toga, and were escorted to the forum; nevertheless, you may look for a still greater joy when you have laid aside the mind of boyhood and when wisdom has enrolled you among men. For it is not boyhood that still stays with us, but something worse—boyishness. And this condition is all the more serious because we possess the authority of old age, together with the follies of boyhood, yea, even the follies of infancy. Boys fear trifles, children fear shadows, we fear both.

All you need to do is to advance; you will thus understand that some things are less to be dreaded, precisely because they inspire us with great fear. No evil is great which is the last evil of all. Death arrives; it would be a thing to dread, if it could remain with you. But death must either not come at all, or else must come and pass away.

"It is difficult, however," you say, "to bring the mind to a point where it can scorn life." But do you not see what trifling reasons impel men to scorn life? One hangs himself before the door of his mistress; another hurls himself from the house-top that he may no longer be compelled to bear the taunts of a bad-tempered master; a third, to be saved from arrest after running away, drives a sword into his vitals. Do you not suppose that virtue will be as efficacious as excessive fear? No man can have a peaceful life who thinks too much about lengthening it, or believes that living through many consulships is a great blessing.

Rehearse this thought every day, that you may be able to depart from life contentedly; for many men clutch and cling to life, even as those who are carried down a rushing stream clutch and cling to briars and sharp rocks.

Most men ebb and flow in wretchedness between the fear of death and the hardships of life; they are unwilling to live, and yet they do not know how to die.

For this reason, make life as a whole agreeable to yourself by banishing all worry about it. No good thing renders its possessor happy, unless his mind is reconciled to the possibility of loss; nothing, however, is lost with less discomfort than that which, when lost, cannot be missed. Therefore, encourage and toughen your spirit against the mishaps that afflict even the most powerful.

For example, the fate of Pompey was settled by a boy and a eunuch, that of Crassus by a cruel and insolent Parthian. Gaius Caesar ordered Lepidus to bare his neck for the axe of the tribune Dexter; and he himself offered his own throat to Chaerea. No man has ever been so far advanced by Fortune that she did not threaten him as greatly as she had previously indulged him. Do not trust her seeming calm; in a moment the sea is moved to its depths. The very day the ships have made a brave show in the games, they are engulfed.

Reflect that a highwayman or an enemy may cut your throat; and, though he is not your master, every slave wields the power of life and death over you. Therefore I declare to you: he is lord of your life that scorns his own. Think of those who have perished through plots in their own home, slain either openly or by guile; you will that just as many have been killed by angry slaves as by angry kings. What matter, therefore, how powerful he be whom you fear, when everyone possesses the power which inspires your fear?

"But," you will say, "if you should chance to fall into the hands of the enemy, the conqueror will command that you be led away,"—yes, whither you are already being led. Why do you voluntarily deceive yourself and require to be told now for the first time what fate it is that you have long been labouring under? Take my word for it: since the day you were born you are being led thither. We must ponder this thought, and thoughts of the like nature, if we desire to be calm as we await that last hour, the fear of which makes all previous hours uneasy.

But I must end my letter. Let me share with you the saying which pleased me today. It, too, is culled from another man's Garden: "Poverty brought into conformity with the law of nature, is great wealth." Do you know what limits that law of nature ordains for us? Merely to avert hunger, thirst, and cold. In order to banish hunger and thirst, it is not necessary for you to pay court at the doors of the purse-proud, or to submit to the stern frown, or to the kindness that humiliates; nor is it necessary for you to scour the seas, or go campaigning; nature's needs are easily provided and ready to hand.

It is the superfluous things for which men sweat—the superfluous things that wear our togas threadbare, that force us to grow old in camp, that dash us upon foreign shores. That which is enough is ready to our hands. He who has made a fair compact with poverty is rich. Farewell.

# Letter 5
# On the Philosopher's Mean

I commend you and rejoice in the fact that you are persistent in your studies, and that, putting all else aside, you make it each day your endeavour to become a better man. I do not merely exhort you to keep at it; I actually beg you to do so. I warn you, however, not to act after the fashion of those who desire to be conspicuous rather than to improve, by doing things which will rouse comment as regards your dress or general way of living.

Repellent attire, unkempt hair, slovenly beard, open scorn of silver dishes, a couch on the bare earth, and any other perverted forms of self-display, are to be avoided. The mere name of philosophy, however quietly pursued, is an object of sufficient scorn; and what would happen if we should begin to separate ourselves from the customs of our fellow-men? Inwardly, we ought to be different in all respects, but our exterior should conform to society.

Do not wear too fine, nor yet too frowzy, a toga. One needs no silver plate, encrusted and embossed in solid gold; but we should not believe the lack of silver and gold to be proof of the simple life. Let us try to maintain a higher standard of life than that of the multitude, but not a contrary standard; otherwise, we shall frighten away and repel the very persons whom we are trying to improve. We also bring it about that they are unwilling to imitate us in anything, because they are afraid lest they might be compelled to imitate us in everything.

The first thing which philosophy undertakes to give is fellow-feeling with all men; in other words, sympathy and sociability. We part company with our promise if we are unlike other men. We must see to it that the means by which we wish to draw admiration be not absurd and odious. Our motto, as you know, is "Live according to Nature"; but it is quite contrary to nature to torture the body, to hate unlaboured elegance, to be dirty on purpose, to eat food that is not only plain, but disgusting and forbidding.

Just as it is a sign of luxury to seek out dainties, so it is madness to avoid that which is customary and can be purchased at no great price. Philosophy calls for plain living, but not for penance; and we may perfectly well be plain and neat at the same time. This is the mean of which I approve; our life should observe a happy medium between the ways of a sage and the ways of the world at large; all men should admire it, but they should understand it also.

"Well then, shall we act like other men? Shall there be no distinction between ourselves and the world?" Yes, a very great one; let men find that we are unlike the common herd, if they look closely. If they visit us at home, they should admire us, rather than our household appointments. He is a great man who uses earthenware dishes as if they were silver; but he is equally great who uses silver as if it were earthenware. It is the sign of an unstable mind not to be able to endure riches.

But I wish to share with you today's profit also. I find in the writings of our Hecato that the limiting of desires helps also to cure fears: "Cease to hope," he says, "and you will cease to fear." "But how," you will reply, "can things so different go side by side?" In this way, my dear Lucilius: though they do seem at variance, yet they are really united. Just as the same chain fastens the prisoner and the soldier who guards him, so hope and fear, dissimilar as they are, keep step together; fear follows hope.

I am not surprised that they proceed in this way; each alike belongs to a mind that is in suspense, a mind that is fretted by looking forward to the future. But the chief cause of both these ills is that we do not adapt ourselves to the present, but send our thoughts a long way ahead. And so foresight, the noblest blessing of the human race, becomes perverted.

Beasts avoid the dangers which they see, and when they have escaped them are free from care; but we men torment ourselves over that which is to come as well as over that which is past. Many of our blessings bring bane to us; for memory recalls the tortures of fear, while foresight anticipates them. The present alone can make no man wretched. Farewell.

# Letter 6
# On Sharing Knowledge

I feel, my dear Lucilius, that I am being not only reformed, but transformed. I do not yet, however, assure myself, or indulge the hope, that there are no elements left in me which need to be changed. Of course there are many that should be made more compact, or made thinner, or be brought into greater prominence. And indeed this very fact is proof that my spirit is altered into something better—that it can see its own faults, of which it was previously ignorant. In certain cases sick men are congratulated because they themselves have perceived that they are sick.

I therefore wish to impart to you this sudden change in myself; I should then begin to place a surer trust in our friendship—the true friendship which hope and fear and self-interest cannot sever, the friendship in which and for the sake of which men meet death.

I can show you many who have lacked, not a friend, but a friendship; this, however, cannot possibly happen when souls are drawn together by identical inclinations into an alliance of honourable desires. And why can it not happen? Because in such cases men know that they have all things in common, especially their troubles. You cannot conceive what distinct progress I notice that each day brings to me.

And when you say: "Give me also a share in these gifts which you have found so helpful," I reply that I am anxious to heap all these privileges upon you, and that I am glad to learn in order that I may teach. Nothing will ever please me, no matter how excellent or beneficial, if I must retain the knowledge of it to myself. And if wisdom were given me under the express condition that it must be kept hidden and not uttered, I should refuse it. No good thing is pleasant to possess, without friends to share it.

I shall therefore send to you the actual books; and in order that you may not waste time in searching here and there for profitable topics, I shall mark certain passages, so that you can turn at once to those which I approve and admire. Of course, however, the living voice and the intimacy of a common life will help you more than the written word.

You must go to the scene of action, first, because men put more faith in their eyes than in their ears, and second, because the way is long if one follows precepts, but short and helpful, if one follows patterns.

Cleanthes could not have been the express image of Zeno, if he had merely heard his lectures; he shared in his life, saw into his hidden purposes, and watched him to see whether he lived according to his own rules. Plato, Aristotle, and the whole throng of sages who were destined to go each his different way, derived more benefit from the character than from the words of Socrates. It was not the class-room of Epicurus, but living together under the same roof, that made great men of Metrodorus, Hermarchus, and Polyaenus. Therefore I summon you, not merely that you may derive benefit, but that you may confer benefit; for we can assist each other greatly.

Meanwhile, I owe you my little daily contribution; you shall be told what pleased me today in the writings of Hecato; it is these words: "What progress, you ask, have I made? I have begun to be a friend to myself." That was indeed a great benefit; such a person can never be alone. You may be sure that such a man is a friend to all mankind. Farewell.

# Letter 7
# On Crowds

Do you ask me what you should regard as especially to be avoided? I say, crowds; for as yet you cannot trust yourself to them with safety. I shall admit my own weakness, at any rate; for I never bring back home the same character that I took abroad with me. Something of that which I have forced to be calm within me is disturbed; some of the foes that I have routed return again. Just as the sick man, who has been weak for a long time, is in such a condition that he cannot be taken out of the house without suffering a relapse, so we ourselves are affected when our souls are recovering from a lingering disease.

To consort with the crowd is harmful; there is no person who does not make some vice attractive to us, or stamp it upon us, or taint us unconsciously therewith. Certainly, the greater the mob with which we mingle, the greater the danger.

But nothing is so damaging to good character as the habit of lounging at the games; for then it is that vice steals subtly upon one through the avenue of pleasure.

What do you think I mean? I mean that I come home more greedy, more ambitious, more voluptuous, and even more cruel and inhuman, because I have been among human beings. By chance I attended a midday exhibition, expecting some fun, wit, and relaxation—an exhibition at which men's eyes have respite from the slaughter of their fellow-men. But it was quite the reverse. The previous combats were the essence of compassion; but now all the trifling is put aside and it is pure murder. The men have no defensive armour. They are exposed to blows at all points, and no one ever strikes in vain.

Many persons prefer this programme to the usual pairs and to the bouts "by request." Of course they do; there is no helmet or shield to deflect the weapon. What is the need of defensive armour, or of skill? All these mean delaying death. In the morning they throw men to the lions and the bears; at noon, they throw them to the spectators. The spectators demand that the slayer shall face the man who is to slay him in his turn; and they always reserve the latest conqueror for another butchering. The outcome of every fight is death, and the means are fire and sword. This sort of thing goes on while the arena is empty.

You may retort: "But he was a highway robber; he killed a man!" And what of it? Granted that, as a murderer, he deserved this punishment, what crime have you committed, poor fellow, that you should deserve to sit and see this show? In the morning they cried "Kill him! Lash him! Burn him! Why does he meet the sword in so cowardly a way? Why does he strike so feebly? Why doesn't he die game? Whip him to meet his wounds! Let them receive blow for blow, with chests bare and exposed to the stroke!" And when the games stop for the intermission, they announce: "A little throatcutting in the meantime, so that there may still be something going on!"

Come now; do you not understand even this truth, that a bad example reacts on the agent? Thank the immortal gods that you are teaching cruelty to a person who cannot learn to be cruel.

The young character, which cannot hold fast to righteousness, must be rescued from the mob; it is too easy to side with the majority. Even Socrates, Cato, and Laelius might have been shaken in their moral strength by a crowd that was unlike them; so true it is that none of us, no matter how much he cultivates his abilities, can withstand the shock of faults that approach, as it were, with so great a retinue.

Much harm is done by a single case of indulgence or greed; the familiar friend, if he be luxurious, weakens and softens us imperceptibly; the neighbour, if he be rich, rouses our covetousness; the companion, if he be slanderous, rubs off some of his rust upon us, even though we be spotless and sincere. What then do you think the effect will be on character, when the world at large assaults it! You must either imitate or loathe the world.

But both courses are to be avoided; you should not copy the bad simply because they are many, nor should you hate the many because they are unlike you. Withdraw into yourself, as far as you can. Associate with those who will make a better man of you. Welcome those whom you yourself can improve. The process is mutual; for men learn while they teach.

There is no reason why pride in advertising your abilities should lure you into publicity, so that you should desire to recite or harangue before the general public. Of course I should be willing for you to do so if you had a stock-in-trade that suited such a mob; as it is, there is not a man of them who can understand you. One or two individuals will perhaps come in your way, but even these will have to be molded and trained by you so that they will understand you. You may say: "For what purpose did I learn all these things?" But you need not fear that you have wasted your efforts; it was for yourself that you learned them.

In order, however, that I may not today have learned exclusively for myself, I shall share with you three excellent sayings, of the same general purport, which have come to my attention. This letter will give you one of them as payment of my debt; the other two you may accept as a contribution in advance. Democritus says: "One man means as much to me as a multitude, and a multitude only as much as one man."

The following also was nobly spoken by someone or other, for it is doubtful who the author was; they asked him what was the object of all this study applied to an art that would reach but very few. He replied: "I am content with few, content with one, content with none at all." The third saying—and a noteworthy one, too—is by Epicurus, written to one of the partners of his studies: "I write this not for the many, but for you; each of us is enough of an audience for the other."

Lay these words to heart, Lucilius, that you may scorn the pleasure which comes from the applause of the majority. Many men praise you; but have you any reason for being pleased with yourself, if you are a person whom the many can understand? Your good qualities should face inwards. Farewell.

# Letter 8
# On the Philosopher's Seclusion

"Do you bid me," you say, "shun the throng, and withdraw from men, and be content with my own conscience? Where are the counsels of your school, which order a man to die in the midst of active work?" As to the course which I seem to you to be urging on you now and then, my object in shutting myself up and locking the door is to be able to help a greater number. I never spend a day in idleness; I appropriate even a part of the night for study. I do not allow time for sleep but yield to it when I must, and when my eyes are wearied with waking and ready to fall shut, I keep them at their task.

I have withdrawn not only from men, but from affairs, especially from my own affairs; I am working for later generations, writing down some ideas that may be of assistance to them. There are certain wholesome counsels, which may be compared to prescriptions of useful drugs; these I am putting into writing; for I have found them helpful in ministering to my own sores, which, if not wholly cured, have at any rate ceased to spread.

I point other men to the right path, which I have found late in life, when wearied with wandering. I cry out to them: "Avoid whatever pleases the throng: avoid the gifts of Chance! Halt before every good which Chance brings to you, in a spirit of doubt and fear; for it is the dumb animals and fish that are deceived by tempting hopes. Do you call these things the 'gifts' of Fortune? They are snares. And any man among you who wishes to live a life of safety will avoid, to the utmost of his power, these limed twigs of her favour, by which we mortals, most wretched in this respect also, are deceived; for we think that we hold them in our grasp, but they hold us in theirs.

Such a career leads us into precipitous ways, and life on such heights ends in a fall. Moreover, we cannot even stand up against prosperity when she begins to drive us to leeward; nor can we go down, either, 'with the ship at least on her course,' or once for all; Fortune does not capsize us—she plunges our bows under and dashes us on the rocks.

"Hold fast, then, to this sound and wholesome rule of life—that you indulge the body only so far as is needful for good health. The body should be treated more rigorously, that it may not be disobedient to the mind. Eat merely to relieve your hunger; drink merely to quench your thirst; dress merely to keep out the cold; house yourself merely as a protection against personal discomfort. It matters little whether the house be built of turf, or of variously coloured imported marble; understand that a man is sheltered just as well by a thatch as by a roof of gold. Despise everything that useless toil creates as an ornament and an object of beauty. And reflect that nothing except the soul is worthy of wonder; for to the soul, if it be great, naught is great."

When I commune in such terms with myself and with future generations, do you not think that I am doing more good than when I appear as counsel in court, or stamp my seal upon a will, or lend my assistance in the senate, by word or action, to a candidate? Believe me, those who seem to be busied with nothing are busied with the greater tasks; they are dealing at the same time with things mortal and things immortal.

But I must stop, and pay my customary contribution, to balance this letter. The payment shall not be made from my own property; for I am still conning Epicurus. I read today, in his works, the following sentence: "If you would enjoy real freedom, you must be the slave of Philosophy." The man who submits and surrenders himself to her is not kept waiting; he is emancipated on the spot. For the very service of Philosophy is freedom.

It is likely that you will ask me why I quote so many of Epicurus's noble words instead of words taken from our own school. But is there any reason why you should regard them as sayings of Epicurus and not common property? How many poets give forth ideas that have been uttered, or may be uttered, by philosophers! I need not touch upon the tragedians and our writers of national drama; for these last are also somewhat serious, and stand half-way between comedy and tragedy. What a quantity of sagacious verses lie buried in the mime! How many of Publilius's lines are worthy of being spoken by buskin-clad actors, as well as by wearers of the slipper!

I shall quote one verse of his, which concerns philosophy, and particularly that phase of it which we were discussing a moment ago, wherein he says that the gifts of Chance are not to be regarded as part of our possessions:

> *Still alien is whatever you have gained*
> *By coveting.*

I recall that you yourself expressed this idea much more happily and concisely:

> *What Chance has made yours is not really yours.*

And a third, spoken by you still more happily, shall not be omitted:

> *The good that could be given, can be removed.*

I shall not charge this up to the expense account, because I have given it to you from your own stock. Farewell.

# Letter 9
# On Philosophy and Friendship

You desire to know whether Epicurus is right when, in one of his letters, he rebukes those who hold that the wise man is self-sufficient and for that reason does not stand in need of friendships. This is the objection raised by Epicurus against Stilbo and those who believe that the Supreme Good is a soul which is insensible to feeling.

We are bound to meet with a double meaning if we try to express the Greek term "lack of feeling" summarily, in a single word, rendering it by the Latin word *impatientia*. For it may be understood in the meaning the opposite to that which we wish it to have. What we mean to express is, a soul which rejects any sensation of evil; but people will interpret the idea as that of a soul which can endure no evil. Consider, therefore, whether it is not better to say "a soul that cannot be harmed," or "a soul entirely beyond the realm of suffering."

There is this difference between ourselves and the other school: our ideal wise man feels his troubles, but overcomes them; their wise man does not even feel them. But we and they alike hold this idea—that the wise man is self-sufficient. Nevertheless, he desires friends, neighbours, and associates, no matter how much he is sufficient unto himself.

And mark how self-sufficient he is; for on occasion he can be content with a part of himself. If he lose a hand through disease or war, or if some accident puts out one or both of his eyes, he will be satisfied with what is left, taking as much pleasure in his impaired and maimed body as he took when it was sound. But while he does not pine for these parts if they are missing, he prefers not to lose them.

In this sense the wise man is self-sufficient, that he can do without friends, not that he desires to do without them. When I say "can," I mean this: he endures the loss of a friend with equanimity.

But he need never lack friends, for it lies in his own control how soon he shall make good a loss. Just as Phidias, if he lose a statue, can straightway carve another, even so our master in the art of making friendships can fill the place of a friend he has lost.

If you ask how one can make oneself a friend quickly, I will tell you, provided we are agreed that I may pay my debt at once and square the account, so far as this letter is concerned. Hecato, says: "I can show you a philtre, compounded without drugs, herbs, or any witch's incantation: 'If you would be loved, love.'" Now there is great pleasure, not only in maintaining old and established friendships, but also in beginning and acquiring new ones.

There is the same difference between winning a new friend and having already won him, as there is between the farmer who sows and the farmer who reaps. The philosopher Attalus used to say: "It is more pleasant to make than to keep a friend, as it is more pleasant to the artist to paint than to have finished painting." When one is busy and absorbed in one's work, the very absorption affords great delight; but when one has withdrawn one's hand from the completed masterpiece, the pleasure is not so keen. Henceforth it is the fruits of his art that he enjoys; it was the art itself that he enjoyed while he was painting. In the case of our children, their young manhood yields the more abundant fruits, but their infancy was sweeter.

Let us now return to the question. The wise man, I say, self-sufficient though he be, nevertheless desires friends if only for the purpose of practicing friendship, in order that his noble qualities may not lie dormant. Not, however, for the purpose mentioned by Epicurus in the letter quoted above: "That there may be someone to sit by him when he is ill, to help him when he is in prison or in want;" but that he may have someone by whose sick-bed he himself may sit, someone a prisoner in hostile hands whom he himself may set free. He who regards himself only, and enters upon friendships for this reason, reckons wrongly. The end will be like the beginning: he has made friends with one who might assist him out of bondage; at the first rattle of the chain such a friend will desert him.

These are the so-called "fair-weather" friendships; one who is chosen for the sake of utility will be satisfactory only so long as he is useful. Hence prosperous men are blockaded by troops of friends; but those who have failed stand amid vast loneliness their friends fleeing from the very crisis which is to test their worth. Hence, also, we notice those many shameful cases of persons who, through fear, desert or betray.

The beginning and the end cannot but harmonize. He who begins to be your friend because it pays will also cease because it pays. A man will be attracted by some reward offered in exchange for his friendship, if he be attracted by aught in friendship other than friendship itself.

For what purpose, then, do I make a man my friend? In order to have someone for whom I may die, whom I may follow into exile, against whose death I may stake my own life, and pay the pledge, too. The friendship which you portray is a bargain and not a friendship; it regards convenience only, and looks to the results.

Beyond question the feeling of a lover has in it something akin to friendship; one might call it friendship run mad. But, though this is true, does anyone love for the sake of gain, or promotion, or renown? Pure love, careless of all other things, kindles the soul with desire for the beautiful object, not without the hope of a return of the affection. What then? Can a cause which is more honourable produce a passion that is base?

You may retort: "We are now discussing the question whether friendship is to be cultivated for its own sake." On the contrary, nothing more urgently requires demonstration; for if friendship is to be sought for its own sake, he may seek it who is self-sufficient. "How, then," you ask, "does he seek it?" Precisely as he seeks an object of great beauty, not attracted to it by desire for gain, nor yet frightened by the instability of Fortune. One who seeks friendship for favourable occasions, strips it of all its nobility.

"The wise man is self-sufficient." This phrase, my dear Lucilius, is incorrectly explained by many; for they withdraw the wise man from the world, and force him to dwell within his own skin. But we must mark with care what this sentence signifies and how far it applies; the wise man is sufficient unto himself for a happy existence, but not for mere existence. For he needs many helps towards mere existence; but for a happy existence he needs only a sound and upright soul, one that despises Fortune.

I should like also to state to you one of the distinctions of Chrysippus, who declares that the wise man is in want of nothing, and yet needs many things. "On the other hand," he says, "nothing is needed by the fool, for he does not understand how to use anything, but he is in want of everything." The wise man needs hands, eyes, and many things that are necessary for his daily use; but he is in want of nothing. For want implies a necessity, and nothing is necessary to the wise man.

Therefore, although he is self-sufficient, yet he has need of friends. He craves as many friends as possible, not, however, that he may live happily; for he will live happily even without friends. The Supreme Good calls for no practical aids from outside; it is developed at home, and arises entirely within itself. If the good seeks any portion of itself from without, it begins to be subject to the play of Fortune.

People may say: "But what sort of existence will the wise man have, if he be left friendless when thrown into prison, or when stranded in some foreign nation, or when delayed on a long voyage, or when out upon a lonely shore?" His life will be like that of Jupiter, who, amid the dissolution of the world, when the gods are confounded together and Nature rests for a space from her work, can retire into himself and give himself over to his own thoughts. In some such way as this the sage will act; he will retreat into himself, and live with himself.

As long as he is allowed to order his affairs according to his judgment, he is self-sufficient—and marries a wife; he is self-sufficient—and brings up children; he is self-sufficient—and yet could not live if he had to live without the society of man. Natural promptings, and not his own selfish needs, draw him into Friendships. For just as other things have for us an inherent attractiveness, so has friendship. As we hate solitude and crave society, as nature draws men to each other, so in this matter also there is an attraction which makes us desirous of friendship.

Nevertheless, though the sage may love his friends dearly, often comparing them with himself, and putting them ahead of himself, yet all the good will be limited to his own being, and he will speak the words which were spoken by the very Stilbo whom Epicurus criticizes in his letter. For Stilbo, after his country was captured and his children and his wife lost, as he emerged from the general desolation alone and yet happy, spoke as follows to Demetrius, called Sacker of Cities because of the destruction he brought upon them, in answer to the question whether he had lost anything: "I have all my goods with me!"

There is a brave and stout-hearted man for you! The enemy conquered, but Stilbo conquered his conqueror. "I have lost nothing!" Aye, he forced Demetrius to wonder whether he himself had conquered after all. "My goods are all with me!" In other words, he deemed nothing that might be taken from him to be a good.

We marvel at certain animals because they can pass through fire and suffer no bodily harm; but how much more marvellous is a man who has marched forth unhurt and unscathed through fire and sword and devastation! Do you understand now how much easier it is to conquer a whole tribe than to conquer one *man*? This saying of Stilbo makes common ground with Stoicism; the Stoic also can carry his goods unimpaired through cities that have been burned to ashes; for he is self-sufficient. Such are the bounds which he sets to his own happiness.

But you must not think that our school alone can utter noble words; Epicurus himself, the reviler of Stilbo, spoke similar language; put it down to my credit, though I have already wiped out my debt for the present day. He says: "Whoever does not regard what he has as most ample wealth, is unhappy, though he be master of the whole world." Or, if the following seems to you a more suitable phrase—for we must try to render the meaning and not the mere words: "A man may rule the world and still be unhappy, if he does not feel that he is supremely happy."

In order, however, that you may know that these sentiments are universal, suggested, of course, by Nature, you will find in one of the comic poets this verse;

*Unblest is he who thinks himself unblest.*

or what does your condition matter, if it is bad in your own eyes?

You may say; "What then? If yonder man, rich by base means, and yonder man, lord of many but slave of more, shall call themselves happy, will their own opinion make them happy?" It matters not what one says, but what one feels; also, not how one feels on one particular day, but how one feels at all times. There is no reason, however, why you should fear that this great privilege will fall into unworthy hands; only the wise man is pleased with his own. Folly is ever troubled with weariness of itself. Farewell.

# Letter 10
## On Living to Oneself

Yes, I do not change my opinion: avoid the many, avoid the few, avoid even the individual. I know of no one with whom I should be willing to have you shared. And see what an opinion of you I have; for I dare to trust you with your own self. Crates, they say, the disciple of the very Stilbo whom I mentioned in a former letter, noticed a young man walking by himself, and asked him what he was doing all alone. "I am communing with myself," replied the youth. "Pray be careful, then," said Crates, "and take good heed; you are communing with a bad man!"

When persons are in mourning, or fearful about something, we are accustomed to watch them that we may prevent them from making a wrong use of their loneliness. No thoughtless person ought to be left alone; in such cases he only plans folly, and heaps up future dangers for himself or for others; he brings into play his base desires; the mind displays what fear or shame used to repress; it whets his boldness, stirs his passions, and goads his anger. And finally, the only benefit that solitude confers—the habit of trusting no man, and of fearing no witnesses—is lost to the fool; for he betrays himself.

Mark therefore what my hopes are for you—nay, rather, what I am promising myself, inasmuch as hope is merely the title of an uncertain blessing: I do not know any person with whom I should prefer you to associate rather than yourself.

I remember in what a great-souled way you hurled forth certain phrases, and how full of strength they were! I immediately congratulated myself and said: "These words did not come from the edge of the lips; these utterances have a solid foundation. This man is not one of the many; he has regard for his real welfare."

Speak, and live, in this way; see to it that nothing keeps you down. As for your former prayers, you may dispense the gods from answering them; offer new prayers; pray for a sound mind and for good health, first of soul and then of body. And of course you should offer those prayers frequently. Call boldly upon God; you will not be asking him for that which belongs to another.

But I must, as is my custom, send a little gift along with this letter. It is a true saying which I have found in Athenodorus: "Know that thou art freed from all desires when thou hast reached such a point that thou prayest to God for nothing except what thou canst pray for openly." But how foolish men are now! They whisper the basest of prayers to heaven; but if anyone listens, they are silent at once. That which they are unwilling for men to know, they communicate to God. Do you not think, then, that some such wholesome advice as this could be given you: "Live among men as if God beheld you; speak with God as if men were listening"? Farewell.

# Letter 11
# On the Blush of Modesty

Your friend and I have had a conversation. He is a man of ability; his very first words showed what spirit and understanding he possesses, and what progress he has already made. He gave me a foretaste, and he will not fail to answer thereto. For he spoke not from forethought, but was suddenly caught off his guard. When he tried to collect himself, he could scarcely banish that hue of modesty, which is a good sign in a young man; the blush that spread over his face seemed so to rise from the depths. And I feel sure that his habit of blushing will stay with him after he has strengthened his character, stripped off all his faults, and become wise. For by no wisdom can natural weaknesses of the body be removed. That which is implanted and inborn can be toned down by training, but not overcome.

The steadiest speaker, when before the public, often breaks into a perspiration, as if he had wearied or over-heated himself; some tremble in the knees when they rise to speak; I know of some whose teeth chatter, whose tongues falter, whose lips quiver. Training and experience can never shake off this habit; nature exerts her own power and through such a weakness makes her presence known even to the strongest.

I know that the blush, too, is a habit of this sort, spreading suddenly over the faces of the most dignified men. It is, indeed more prevalent in youth, because of the warmer blood and the sensitive countenance; nevertheless, both seasoned men and aged men are affected by it. Some are most dangerous when they redden, as if they were letting all their sense of shame escape.

Sulla, when the blood mantled his cheeks, was in his fiercest mood. Pompey had the most sensitive cast of countenance; he always blushed in the presence of a gathering, and especially at a public assembly. Fabianus also, I remember, reddened when he appeared as a witness before the senate; and his embarrassment became him to a remarkable degree.

Such a habit is not due to mental weakness, but to the novelty of a situation; an inexperienced person is not necessarily confused, but is usually affected, because he slips into this habit by natural tendency of the body. Just as certain men are full-blooded, so others are of a quick and mobile blood, that rushes to the face at once.

As I remarked, Wisdom can never remove this habit; for if she could rub out all our faults, she would be mistress of the universe. Whatever is assigned to us by the terms of our birth and the blend in our constitutions, will stick with us, no matter how hard or how long the soul may have tried to master itself. And we cannot forbid these feelings any more than we can summon them.

Actors in the theatre, who imitate the emotions, who portray fear and nervousness, who depict sorrow, imitate bashfulness by hanging their heads, lowering their voices, and keeping their eyes fixed and rooted upon the ground. They cannot, however, muster a blush; for the blush cannot be prevented or acquired. Wisdom will not assure us of a remedy, or give us help against it; it comes or goes unbidden, and is a law unto itself.

But my letter calls for its closing sentence. Hear and take to heart this useful and wholesome motto: "Cherish some man of high character, and keep him ever before your eyes, living as if he were watching you, and ordering all your actions as if he beheld them."

Such, my dear Lucilius, is the counsel of Epicurus; he has quite properly given us a guardian and an attendant. We can get rid of most sins, if we have a witness who stands near us when we are likely to go wrong. The soul should have someone whom it can respect—one by whose authority it may make even its inner shrine more hallowed. Happy is the man who can make others better, not merely when he is in their company, but even when he is in their thoughts! And happy also is he who can so revere a man as to calm and regulate himself by calling him to mind! One who can so revere another, will soon be himself worthy of reverence.

Choose therefore a Cato; or, if Cato seems too severe a model, choose some Laelius, a gentler spirit. Choose a master whose life, conversation, and soul-expressing face have satisfied you; picture him always to yourself as your protector or your pattern. For we must indeed have someone according to whom we may regulate our characters; you can never straighten that which is crooked unless you use a ruler. Farewell.

# Letter 12
# On Old Age

Wherever I turn, I see evidences of my advancing years. I visited lately my country-place, and protested against the money which was spent on the tumble-down building. My bailiff maintained that the flaws were not due to his own carelessness; "he was doing everything possible, but the house was old." And this was the house which grew under my own hands! What has the future in store for me, if stones of my own age are already crumbling?

I was angry, and I embraced the first opportunity to vent my spleen in the bailiff's presence. "It is clear," I cried, "that these plane-trees are neglected; they have no leaves. Their branches are so gnarled and shrivelled; the boles are so rough and unkempt! This would not happen, if someone loosened the earth at their feet, and watered them." The bailiff swore by my protecting deity that "he was doing everything possible, and never relaxed his efforts, but those trees were old." Between you and me, I had planted those trees myself, I had seen them in their first leaf.

Then I turned to the door and asked: "Who is that broken-down dotard? You have done well to place him at the entrance; for he is outward bound. Where did you get him? What pleasure did it give you to take up for burial some other man's dead?" But the slave said: "Don't you know me, sir? I am Felicio; you used to bring me little images. My father was Philositus the steward, and I am your pet slave." "The man is clean crazy," I remarked. "Has my pet slave become a little boy again? But it is quite possible; his teeth are just dropping out."

I owe it to my country-place that my old age became apparent whithersoever I turned. Let us cherish and love old age; for it is full of pleasure if one knows how to use it. Fruits are most welcome when almost over; youth is most charming at its close; the last drink delights the toper, the glass which souses him and puts the finishing touch on his drunkenness.

Each pleasure reserves to the end the greatest delights which it contains. Life is most delightful when it is on the downward slope, but has not yet reached the abrupt decline. And I myself believe that the period which stands, so to speak, on the edge of the roof, possesses pleasures of its own. Or else the very fact of our not wanting pleasures has taken the place of the pleasures themselves. How comforting it is to have tired out one's appetites, and to have done with them!

"But," you say, "it is a nuisance to be looking death in the face!" Death, however, should be looked in the face by young and old alike. We are not summoned according to our rating on the censor's list. Moreover, no one is so old that it would be improper for him to hope for another day of existence. And one day, mind you, is a stage on life's journey.

Our span of life is divided into parts; it consists of large circles enclosing smaller. One circle embraces and bounds the rest; it reaches from birth to the last day of existence. The next circle limits the period of our young manhood. The third confines all of childhood in its circumference. Again, there is, in a class by itself, the year; it contains within itself all the divisions of time by the multiplication of which we get the total of life. The month is bounded by a narrower ring. The smallest circle of all is the day; but even a day has its beginning and its ending, its sunrise and its sunset.

Hence Heraclitus, whose obscure style gave him his surname, remarked: "One day is equal to every day." Different persons have interpreted the saying in different ways. Some hold that days are equal in number of hours, and this is true; for if by "day" we mean twenty-four hours' time, all days must be equal, inasmuch as the night acquires what the day loses. But others maintain that one day is equal to all days through resemblance, because the very longest space of time possesses no element which cannot be found in a single day—namely, light and darkness—and even to eternity day makes these alternations more numerous, not different when it is shorter and different again when it is longer.

Hence, every day ought to be regulated as if it closed the series, as if it rounded out and completed our existence.

Pacuvius, who by long occupancy made Syria his own, used to hold a regular burial sacrifice in his own honour, with wine and the usual funeral feasting, and then would have himself carried from the dining room to his chamber, while eunuchs applauded and sang in Greek to a musical accompaniment: "He has lived his life, he has lived his life!"

Thus Pacuvius had himself carried out to burial every day. Let us, however, do from a good motive what he used to do from a debased motive; let us go to our sleep with joy and gladness; let us say:

*I have lived; the course which Fortune set for me Is finished.*

And if God is pleased to add another day, we should welcome it with glad hearts. That man is happiest, and is secure in his own possession of himself, who can await the morrow without apprehension. When a man has said: "I have lived!", every morning he arises he receives a bonus.

But now I ought to close my letter. "What?" you say; "shall it come to me without any little offering?" "Be not afraid; it brings something—nay, more than something, a great deal. For what is more noble than the following saying of which I make this letter the bearer: "It is wrong to live under constraint; but no man is constrained to live under constraint." Of course not. On all sides lie many short and simple paths to freedom; and let us thank God that no man can be kept in life. We may spurn the very constraints that hold us

"Epicurus," you reply, "uttered these words; what are you doing with another's property?" Any truth, I maintain, is my own property. And I shall continue to heap quotations from Epicurus upon you, so that all persons who swear by the words of another, and put a value upon the speaker and not upon the thing spoken, may understand that the best ideas are common property. Farewell.

# Letter 13
# On Groundless Fears

I know that you have plenty of spirit; for even before you began to equip yourself with maxims which were wholesome and potent to overcome obstacles, you were taking pride in your contest with Fortune; and this is all the more true, now that you have grappled with Fortune and tested your powers. For our powers can never inspire in us implicit faith in ourselves except when many difficulties have confronted us on this side and on that, and have occasionally even come to close quarters with us. It is only in this way that the true spirit can be tested—the spirit that will never consent to come under the jurisdiction of things external to ourselves.

This is the touchstone of such a spirit; no prizefighter can go with high spirits into the strife if he has never been beaten black and blue; the only contestant who can confidently enter the lists is the man who has seen his own blood, who has felt his teeth rattle beneath his opponent's fist, who has been tripped and felt the full force of his adversary's charge, who has been downed in body but not in spirit, one who, as often as he falls, rises again with greater defiance than ever.

So then, to keep up my figure, Fortune has often in the past got the upper hand of you, and yet you have not surrendered, but have leaped up and stood your ground still more eagerly. For manliness gains much strength by being challenged; nevertheless, if you approve, allow me to offer some additional safeguards by which you may fortify yourself.

There are more things, Lucilius, likely to frighten us than there are to crush us; we suffer more often in imagination than in reality. I am not speaking with you in the Stoic strain but in my milder style. For it is our Stoic fashion to speak of all those things, which provoke cries and groans, as unimportant and beneath notice; but you and I must drop such great-sounding words, although, heaven knows, they are true enough. What I advise you to do is, not to be unhappy before the crisis comes; since it may be that the dangers before which you paled as if they were threatening you, will never come upon you; they certainly have not yet come.

Accordingly, some things torment us more than they ought; some torment us before they ought; and some torment us when they ought not to torment us at all. We are in the habit of exaggerating, or imagining, or anticipating, sorrow.

The first of these three faults may be postponed for the present, because the subject is under discussion and the case is still in court, so to speak. That which I should call trifling, you will maintain to be most serious; for of course I know that some men laugh while being flogged, and that others wince at a box on the ear. We shall consider later whether these evils derive their power from their own strength, or from our own weakness.

Do me the favour, when men surround you and try to talk you into believing that you are unhappy, to consider not what you hear but what you yourself feel, and to take counsel with your feelings and question yourself independently, because you know your own affairs better than anyone else does. Ask: "Is there any reason why these persons should condole with me? Why should they be worried or even fear some infection from me, as if troubles could be transmitted? Is there any evil involved, or is it a matter merely of ill report, rather than an evil?" Put the question voluntarily to yourself: "Am I tormented without sufficient reason, am I morose, and do I convert what is not an evil into what is an evil?"

You may retort with the question: "How am I to know whether my sufferings are real or imaginary?" Here is the rule for such matters: we are tormented either by things present, or by things to come, or by both. As to things present, the decision is easy. Suppose that your person enjoys freedom and health, and that you do not suffer from any external injury. As to what may happen to it in the future, we shall see later on. Today there is nothing wrong with it.

"But," you say, "something will happen to it." First of all, consider whether your proofs of future trouble are sure. For it is more often the case that we are troubled by our apprehensions, and that we are mocked by that mocker, rumour, which is wont to settle wars, but much more often settles individuals. Yes, my dear Lucilius; we agree too quickly with what people say. We do not put to the test those things which cause our fear; we do not examine into them; we blench and retreat just like soldiers who are forced to abandon their camp because of a dust-cloud raised by stampeding cattle, or are thrown into a panic by the spreading of some unauthenticated rumour.

And somehow or other it is the idle report that disturbs us most. For truth has its own definite boundaries, but that which arises from uncertainty is delivered over to guesswork and the irresponsible license of a frightened mind. That is why no fear is so ruinous and so uncontrollable as panic fear. For other fears are groundless, but this fear is witless.

Let us, then, look carefully into the matter. It is likely that some troubles will befall us; but it is not a present fact. How often has the unexpected happened! How often has the expected never come to pass! And even though it is ordained to be, what does it avail to run out to meet your suffering? You will suffer soon enough, when it arrives; so look forward meanwhile to better things.

What shall you gain by doing this? Time. There will be many happenings meanwhile which will serve to postpone, or end, or pass on to another person, the trials which are near or even in your very presence. A fire has opened the way to flight. Men have been let down softly by a catastrophe. Sometimes the sword has been checked even at the victim's throat. Men have survived their own executioners. Even bad fortune is fickle. Perhaps it will come, perhaps not; in the meantime it is not. So look forward to better things.

The mind at times fashions for itself false shapes of evil when there are no signs that point to any evil; it twists into the worst construction some word of doubtful meaning; or it fancies some personal grudge to be more serious than it really is, considering not how angry the enemy is, but to what lengths he may go if he is angry. But life is not worth living, and there is no limit to our sorrows, if we indulge our fears to the greatest possible extent; in this matter, let prudence help you, and contemn with a resolute spirit even when it is in plain sight. If you cannot do this, counter one weakness with another, and temper your fear with hope. There is nothing so certain among these objects of fear that it is not more certain still that things we dread sink into nothing and that things we hope for mock us.

Accordingly, weigh carefully your hopes as well as your fears, and whenever all the elements are in doubt, decide in your own favour; believe what you prefer. And if fear wins a majority of the votes, incline in the other direction anyhow, and cease to harass your soul, reflecting continually that most mortals, even when no troubles are actually at hand or are certainly to be expected in the future, become excited and disquieted. No one calls a halt on himself, when he begins to be urged ahead; nor does he regulate his alarm according to the truth. No one says; "The author of the story is a fool, and he who has believed it is a fool, as well as he who fabricated it." We let ourselves drift with every breeze; we are frightened at uncertainties, just as if they were certain. We observe no moderation. The slightest thing turns the scales and throws us forthwith into a panic.

But I am ashamed either to admonish you sternly or to try to beguile you with such mild remedies. Let another say. "Perhaps the worst will not happen." You yourself must say. "Well, what if it does happen? Let us see who wins! Perhaps it happens for my best interests; it may be that such a death will shed credit upon my life." Socrates was ennobled by the hemlock draught. Wrench from Cato's hand his sword, the vindicator of liberty, and you deprive him of the greatest share of his glory.

I am exhorting you far too long, since you need reminding rather than exhortation. The path on which I am leading you is not different from that on which your nature leads you; you were born to such conduct as I describe. Hence there is all the more reason why you should increase and beautify the good that is in you.

But now, to close my letter, I have only to stamp the usual seal upon it, in other words, to commit thereto some noble message to be delivered to you: "The fool, with all his other faults, has this also, he is always getting ready to live." Reflect, my esteemed Lucilius, what this saying means, and you will see how revolting is the fickleness of men who lay down every day new foundations of life, and begin to build up fresh hopes even at the brink of the grave.

Look within your own mind for individual instances; you will think of old men who are preparing themselves at that very hour for a political career, or for travel, or for business. And what is baser than getting ready to live when you are already old? I should not name the author of this motto, except that it is somewhat unknown to fame and is not one of those popular sayings of Epicurus which I have allowed myself to praise and to appropriate. Farewell.

## Letter 14
# On the Reasons for Withdrawing from the World

I confess that we all have an inborn affection for our body; I confess that we are entrusted with its guardianship. I do not maintain that the body is not to be indulged at all; but I maintain that we must not be slaves to it. He will have many masters who makes his body his master, who is over-fearful in its behalf, who judges everything according to the body.

We should conduct ourselves not as if we ought to live for the body, but as if we could not live without it. Our too great love for it makes us restless with fears, burdens us with cares, and exposes us to insults. Virtue is held too cheap by the man who counts his body too dear. We should cherish the body with the greatest care; but we should also be prepared, when reason, self-respect, and duty demand the sacrifice, to deliver it even to the flames.

Let us, however, in so far as we can, avoid discomforts as well as dangers, and withdraw to safe ground, by thinking continually how we may repel all objects of fear. If I am not mistaken, there are three main classes of these: we fear want, we fear sickness, and we fear the troubles which result from the violence of the stronger.

And of all these, that which shakes us most is the dread which hangs over us from our neighbour's ascendancy; for it is accompanied by great outcry and uproar. But the natural evils which I have mentioned—want and sickness, steal upon us silently with no shock of terror to the eye or to the ear. The other kind of evil comes, so to speak, in the form of a huge parade. Surrounding it is a retinue of swords and fire and chains and a mob of beasts to be let loose upon the disembowelled entrails of men.

Picture to yourself under this head the prison, the cross, the rack, the hook, and the stake which they drive straight through a man until it protrudes from his throat. Think of human limbs torn apart by chariots driven in opposite directions, of the terrible shirt smeared and interwoven with inflammable materials, and of all the other contrivances devised by cruelty, in addition to those which I have mentioned!

It is not surprising, then, if our greatest terror is of such a fate; for it comes in many shapes and its paraphernalia are terrifying. For just as the torturer accomplishes more in proportion to the number of instruments which he displays—indeed, the spectacle overcomes those who would have patiently withstood the suffering—similarly, of all the agencies which coerce and master our minds, the most effective are those which can make a display. Those other troubles are of course not less serious; I mean hunger, thirst, ulcers of the stomach, and fever that parches our very bowels. They are, however, secret; they have no bluster and no heralding; but these, like huge arrays of war, prevail by virtue of their display and their equipment.

Let us, therefore, see to it that we abstain from giving offence. It is sometimes the people that we ought to fear; or sometimes a body of influential oligarchs in the Senate, if the method of governing the State is such that most of the business is done by that body; and sometimes individuals equipped with power by the people and against the people. It is burdensome to keep the friendship of all such persons; it is enough not to make enemies of them. So the wise man will never provoke the anger of those in power; nay, he will even turn his course, precisely as he would turn from a storm if he were steering a ship.

When you travelled to Sicily, you crossed the Straits. The reckless pilot scorned the blustering South Wind—the wind which roughens the Sicilian Sea and forces it into choppy currents; he sought not the shore on the left, but the strand hard by the place where Charybdis throws the seas into confusion. Your more careful pilot, however, questions those who know the locality as to the tides and the meaning of the clouds; he holds his course far from that region notorious for its swirling waters. Our wise man does the same he shuns a strong man who may be injurious to him, making a point of not seeming to avoid him, because an important part of one's safety lies in not seeking safety openly; for what one avoids, one condemns.

We should therefore look about us, and see how we may protect ourselves from the mob. And first of all, we should have no cravings like theirs; for rivalry results in strife. Again, let us possess nothing that can be snatched from us to the great profit of a plotting foe. Let there be as little booty as possible on your person. No one sets out to shed the blood of his fellow-men for the sake of bloodshed—at any rate very few. More murderers speculate on their profits than give vent to hatred. If you are empty-handed, the highwayman passes you by: even along an infested road, the poor may travel in peace.

Next, we must follow the old adage and avoid three things with special care: hatred, jealousy, and scorn. And wisdom alone can show you how this may be done. It is hard to observe a mean; we must be chary of letting the fear of jealousy lead us into becoming objects of scorn, lest, when we choose not to stamp others down, we let them think that they can stamp us down. The power to inspire fear has caused many men to be in fear. Let us withdraw ourselves in every way; for it is as harmful to be scorned as to be admired.

One must therefore take refuge in philosophy; this pursuit, not only in the eyes of good men, but also in the eyes of those who are even moderately bad, is a sort of protecting emblem. For speechmaking at the bar, or any other pursuit that claims the people's attention, wins enemies for a man; but philosophy is peaceful and minds her own business. Men cannot scorn her; she is honoured by every profession, even the vilest among them. Evil can never grow so strong, and nobility of character can never be so plotted against, that the name of philosophy shall cease to be worshipful and sacred.

Philosophy itself, however should be practiced with calmness and moderation.

"Very well, then," you retort, "do you regard the philosophy of Marcus Cato as moderate? Cato's voice strove to check a civil war. Cato parted the swords of maddened chieftains. When some fell foul of Pompey and others fell foul of Caesar, Cato defied both parties at once!"

Nevertheless, one may well question whether, in those days, a wise man ought to have taken any part in public affairs, and ask: "What do you mean, Marcus Cato? It is not now a question of freedom; long since has freedom gone to rack and ruin. The question is, whether it is Caesar or Pompey who controls the State. Why, Cato, should you take sides in that dispute? It is no business of yours; a tyrant is being selected. What does it concern you who conquers? The better man may win; but the winner is bound to be the worse man." I have referred to Cato's final rôle. But even in previous years the wise man was not permitted to intervene in such plundering of the state; for what could Cato do but raise his voice and utter unavailing words? At one time he was "bustled" by the mob and spat upon and forcibly removed from the forum and marked for exile; at another, he was taken straight to prison from the senate-chamber.

However, we shall consider later whether the wise man ought to give his attention to politics; meanwhile, I beg you to consider those Stoics who, shut out from public life, have withdrawn into privacy for the purpose of improving men's existence and framing laws for the human race without incurring the displeasure of those in power. The wise man will not upset the customs of the people, nor will he invite the attention of the populace by any novel ways of living.

"What then? Can one who follows out this Plan be safe in any case?" I cannot guarantee you this any more than I can guarantee good health in the case of a man who observes moderation; although, as a matter of fact, good health results from such moderation. Sometimes a vessel perishes in harbour; but what do you think happens on the open sea? And how much more beset with danger that man would be, who even in his leisure is not secure, if he were busily working at many things! Innocent persons sometimes perish; who would deny that? But the guilty perish more frequently. A soldier's skill is not at fault if he receives the death-blow through his armour.

And finally, the wise man regards the reason for all his actions, but not the results. The beginning is in our own power; fortune decides the issue, but I do not allow her to pass sentence upon myself. You may say: "But she can inflict a measure of suffering and of trouble." The highwayman does not pass sentence when he slays.

Now you are stretching forth your hand for the daily gift. Golden indeed will be the gift with which I shall load you; and, inasmuch as we have mentioned gold, let me tell you how its use and enjoyment may bring you greater pleasure. "He who needs riches least, enjoys riches most." "Author's name, please!" you say. Now, to show you how generous I am, it is my intent to praise the dicta of other schools. The phrase belongs to Epicurus, or Metrodorus, or some one of that particular thinking-shop.

But what difference does it make who spoke the words? They were uttered for the world. He who craves riches feels fear on their account. No man, however, enjoys a blessing that brings anxiety; he is always trying to add a little more. While he puzzles over increasing his wealth, he forgets how to use it. He collects his accounts, he wears out the pavement in the forum, he turns over his ledger—in short, he ceases to be master and becomes a steward. Farewell.

# Letter 15
# On Philosophy, the Guide of Life

It is clear to you, I am sure, Lucilius, that no man can live a happy life, or even a supportable life, without the study of wisdom; you know also that a happy life is reached when our wisdom is brought to completion, but that life is at least endurable even when our wisdom is only begun. This idea, however, clear though it is, must be strengthened and implanted more deeply by daily reflection; it is more important for you to keep the resolutions you have already made than to go on and make noble ones. You must persevere, must develop new strength by continuous study, until that which is only a good inclination becomes a good settled purpose.

Hence you no longer need to come to me with much talk and protestations; I know that you have made great progress. I understand the feelings which prompt your words; they are not feigned or specious words. Nevertheless I shall tell you what I think—that at present I have hopes for you, but not yet perfect trust. And I wish that you would adopt the same attitude towards yourself; there is no reason why you should put confidence in yourself too quickly and readily. Examine yourself; scrutinize and observe yourself in divers ways; but mark, before all else, whether it is in philosophy or merely in life itself that you have made progress.

Philosophy is no trick to catch the public; it is not devised for show. It is a matter, not of words, but of facts. It is not pursued in order that the day may yield some amusement before it is spent, or that our leisure may be relieved of a tedium that irks us. It moulds and constructs the soul; it orders our life, guides our conduct, shows us what we should do and what we should leave undone; it sits at the helm and directs our course as we waver amid uncertainties. Without it, no one can live fearlessly or in peace of mind. Countless things that happen every hour call for advice; and such advice is to be sought in philosophy.

Perhaps someone will say: "How can philosophy help me, if Fate exists? Of what avail is philosophy, if God rules the universe? Of what avail is it, if Chance governs everything? For not only is it impossible to change things that are determined, but it is also impossible to plan beforehand against what is undetermined; either God has forestalled my plans, and decided what I am to do, or else Fortune gives no free play to my plans."

Whether the truth, Lucilius, lies in one or in all of these views, we must be philosophers; whether Fate binds us down by an inexorable law, or whether God as arbiter of the universe has arranged everything, or whether Chance drives and tosses human affairs without method, philosophy ought to be our defence. She will encourage us to obey God cheerfully, but Fortune defiantly; she will teach us to follow God and endure Chance.

But it is not my purpose now to be led into a discussion as to what is within our own control—if foreknowledge is supreme, or if a chain of fated events drags us along in its clutches, or if the sudden and the unexpected play the tyrant over us; I return now to my warning and my exhortation, that you should not allow the impulse of your spirit to weaken and grow cold. Hold fast to it and establish it firmly, in order that what is now impulse may become a habit of the mind.

If I know you well, you have already been trying to find out, from the very beginning of my letter, what little contribution it brings to you. Sift the letter, and you will find it. You need not wonder at any genius of mine; for as yet I am lavish only with other men's property. But why did I say "other men"? Whatever is well said by anyone is mine. This also is a saying of Epicurus: "If you live according to nature, you will never be poor; if you live according to opinion, you will never be rich."

Nature's wants are slight; the demands of opinion are boundless. Suppose that the property of many millionaires is heaped up in your possession. Assume that fortune carries you far beyond the limits of a private income, decks you with gold, clothes you in purple, and brings you to such a degree of luxury and wealth that you can bury the earth under your marble floors; that you may not only possess, but tread upon, riches. Add statues, paintings, and whatever any art has devised for the luxury; you will only learn from such things to crave still greater.

Natural desires are limited; but those which spring from false opinion can have no stopping-point. The false has no limits. When you are travelling on a road, there must be an end; but when astray, your wanderings are limitless. Recall your steps, therefore, from idle things, and when you would know whether that which you seek is based upon a natural or upon a misleading desire, consider whether it can stop at any definite point. If you find, after having travelled far, that there is a more distant goal always in view, you may be sure that this condition is contrary to nature. Farewell.

# Letter 16
# On Festivals and Fasting

It is the month of December, and yet the city is at this very moment in a sweat. License is given to the general merrymaking. Everything resounds with mighty preparations—as if the Saturnalia differed at all from the usual business day! So true it is that the difference is nil, that I regard as correct the remark of the man who said: "Once December was a month; now it is a year."

If I had you with me, I should be glad to consult you and find out what you think should be done—whether we ought to make no change in our daily routine, or whether, in order not to be out of sympathy with the ways of the public, we should dine in gayer fashion and doff the toga. As it is now, we Romans have changed our dress for the sake of pleasure and holiday-making, though in former times that was only customary when the State was disturbed and had fallen on evil days.

I am sure that, if I know you aright, playing the part of an umpire you would have wished that we should be neither like the liberty-capped throng in all ways, nor in all ways unlike them; unless, perhaps, this is just the season when we ought to lay down the law to the soul, and bid it be alone in refraining from pleasures just when the whole mob has let itself go in pleasures; for this is the surest proof which a man can get of his own constancy, if he neither seeks the things which are seductive and allure him to luxury, nor is led into them.

It shows much more courage to remain dry and sober when the mob is drunk and vomiting; but it shows greater self-control to refuse to withdraw oneself and to do what the crowd does, but in a different way—thus neither making oneself conspicuous nor becoming one of the crowd. For one may keep holiday without extravagance.

I am so firmly determined, however, to test the constancy of your mind that, drawing from the teachings of great men, I shall give you also a lesson: Set aside a certain number of days, during which you shall be content with the scantiest and cheapest fare, with coarse and rough dress, saying to yourself the while: "Is this the condition that I feared?"

It is precisely in times of immunity from care that the soul should toughen itself beforehand for occasions of greater stress, and it is while Fortune is kind that it should fortify itself against her violence. In days of peace the soldier performs manoeuvres, throws up earthworks with no enemy in sight, and wearies himself by gratuitous toil, in order that he may be equal to unavoidable toil. If you would not have a man flinch when the crisis comes, train him before it comes. Such is the course which those men have followed who, in their imitation of poverty, have every month come almost to want, that they might never recoil from what they had so often rehearsed.

You need not suppose that I mean meals like Timon's, or "paupers' huts," or any other device which luxurious millionaires use to beguile the tedium of their lives. Let the pallet be a real one, and the coarse cloak; let the bread be hard and grimy. Endure all this for three or four days at a time, sometimes for more, so that it may be a test of yourself instead of a mere hobby. Then, I assure you, my dear Lucilius, you will leap for joy when filled with a pennyworth of food, and you will understand that a man's peace of mind does not depend upon Fortune; for, even when angry she grants enough for our needs.

There is no reason, however, why you should think that you are doing anything great; for you will merely be doing what many thousands of slaves and many thousands of poor men are doing every day. But you may credit yourself with this item—that you will not be doing it under compulsion, and that it will be as easy for you to endure it permanently as to make the experiment from time to time. Let us practice our strokes on the "dummy"; let us become intimate with poverty, so that Fortune may not catch us off our guard. We shall be rich with all the more comfort, if we once learn how far poverty is from being a burden.

Even Epicurus, the teacher of pleasure, used to observe stated intervals, during which he satisfied his hunger in niggardly fashion; he wished to see whether he thereby fell short of full and complete happiness, and, if so, by what amount he fell short, and whether this amount was worth purchasing at the price of great effort. At any rate, he makes such a statement in the well known letter written to Polyaenus in the archonship of Charinus. Indeed, he boasts that he himself lived on less than a penny, but that Metrodorus, whose progress was not yet so great, needed a whole penny.

Do you think that there can be fullness on such fare? Yes, and there is pleasure also—not that shifty and fleeting Pleasure which needs a fillip now and then, but a pleasure that is steadfast and sure. For though water, barley-meal, and crusts of barley-bread, are not a cheerful diet, yet it is the highest kind of Pleasure to be able to derive pleasure from this sort of food, and to have reduced one's needs to that modicum which no unfairness of Fortune can snatch away.

Even prison fare is more generous; and those who have been set apart for capital punishment are not so meanly fed by the man who is to execute them. Therefore, what a noble soul must one have, to descend of one's own free will to a diet which even those who have been sentenced to death have not to fear! This is indeed forestalling the spearthrusts of Fortune.

So begin, my dear Lucilius, to follow the custom of these men, and set apart certain days on which you shall withdraw from your business and make yourself at home with the scantiest fare. Establish business relations with poverty.

*Dare, O my friend, to scorn the sight of wealth,*
*And mould thyself to kinship with thy God.*

For he alone is in kinship with God who has scorned wealth. Of course I do not forbid you to possess it, but I would have you reach the point at which you possess it dauntlessly; this can be accomplished only by persuading yourself that you can live happily without it as well as with it, and by regarding riches always as likely to elude you.

But now I must begin to fold up my letter. "Settle your debts first," you cry. Here is a draft on Epicurus; he will pay down the sum: "Ungoverned anger begets madness." You cannot help knowing the truth of these words, since you have had not only slaves, but also enemies.

But indeed this emotion blazes out against all sorts of persons; it springs from love as much as from hate, and shows itself not less in serious matters than in jest and sport. And it makes no difference how important the provocation may be, but into what kind of soul it penetrates. Similarly with fire; it does not matter how great is the flame, but what it falls upon. For solid timbers have repelled a very great fire; conversely, dry and easily inflammable stuff nourishes the slightest spark into a conflagration. So it is with anger, my dear Lucilius; the outcome of a mighty anger is madness, and hence anger should be avoided, not merely that we may escape excess, but that we may have a healthy mind. Farewell.

# Letter 17

## On Worldliness and Retirement

I leap for joy whenever I receive letters from you. For they fill me with hope; they are now not mere assurances concerning you, but guarantees. And I beg and pray you to proceed in this course; for what better request could I make of a friend than one which is to be made for his own sake? If possible, withdraw yourself from all the business of which you speak; and if you cannot do this, tear yourself away. We have dissipated enough of our time already—let us in old age begin to pack up our baggage.

Surely there is nothing in this that men can begrudge us. We have spent our lives on the high seas; let us die in harbour. Not that I would advise you to try to win fame by your retirement; one's retirement should neither be paraded nor concealed. Not concealed, I say, for I shall not go so far in urging you as to expect you to condemn all men as mad and then seek out for yourself a hiding-place and oblivion; rather make this your business, that your retirement be not conspicuous, though it should be obvious.

In the second place, while those whose choice is unhampered from the start will deliberate on that other question, whether they wish to pass their lives in obscurity, in your case there is not a free choice. Your ability and energy have thrust you into the work of the world; so have the charm of your writings and the friendships you have made with famous and notable men.

Renown has already taken you by storm. You may sink yourself into the depths of obscurity and utterly hide yourself; yet your earlier acts will reveal you.

You cannot keep lurking in the dark; much of the old gleam will follow you wherever you fly.

Peace you can claim for yourself without being disliked by anyone, without any sense of loss, and without any pangs of spirit. For what will you leave behind you that you can imagine yourself reluctant to leave? Your clients? But none of these men courts you for yourself; they merely court something from you. People used to hunt friends, but now they hunt pelf; if a lonely old man changes his will, the morning-caller transfers himself to another door. Great things cannot be bought for small sums; so reckon up whether it is preferable to leave your own true self, or merely some of your belongings.

Would that you had had the privilege of growing old amid the limited circumstances of your origin, and that fortune had not raised you to such heights! You were removed far from the sight of wholesome living by your swift rise to prosperity, by your province, by your position as procurator, and by all that such things promise; you will next acquire more important duties and after them still more. And what will be the result?

Why wait until there is nothing left for you to crave? That time will never come. We hold that there is a succession of causes, from which fate is woven; similarly, you may be sure, there is a succession in our desires; for one begins where its predecessor ends. You have been thrust into an existence which will never of itself put an end to your wretchedness and your slavery. Withdraw your chafed neck from the yoke; it is better that it should be cut off once for all, than galled for ever.

If you retreat to privacy, everything will be on a smaller scale, but you will be satisfied abundantly; in your present condition, however, there is no satisfaction in the plenty which is heaped upon you on all sides. Would you rather be poor and sated, or rich and hungry? Prosperity is not only greedy, but it also lies exposed to the greed of others. And as long as nothing satisfies you, you yourself cannot satisfy others.

"But," you say, "how can I take my leave?" Any way you please. Reflect how many hazards you have ventured for the sake of money, and how much toil you have undertaken for a title! You must dare something to gain leisure, also—or else grow old amid the worries of procuratorships abroad and subsequently of civil duties at home, living in turmoil and in ever fresh floods of responsibilities, which no man has ever succeeded in avoiding by unobtrusiveness or by seclusion of life. For what bearing on the case has your personal desire for a secluded life? Your position in the world desires the opposite! What if, even now, you allow that position to grow greater? But all that is added to your successes will be added to your fears.

At this point I should like to quote a saying of Maecenas, who spoke the truth when he stood on the very summit: "There's thunder even on the loftiest peaks." If you ask me in what book these words are found, they occur in the volume entitled *Prometheus*. He simply meant to say that these lofty peaks have their tops surrounded with thunder-storms. But is any power worth so high a price that a man like you would ever, in order to obtain it, adopt a style so debauched as that? Maecenas was indeed a man of parts, who would have left a great pattern for Roman oratory to follow, had his good fortune not made him effeminate—nay, had it not emasculated him! An end like his awaits you also, unless you forthwith shorten sail and—as Maecenas was not willing to do until it was too late—hug the shore!

This saying of Maecenas's might have squared my account with you; but I feel sure, knowing you, that you will get out an injunction against me, and that you will be unwilling to accept payment of my debt in such crude and debased currency. However that may be, I shall draw on the account of Epicurus. He says: "You must reflect carefully beforehand with whom you are to eat and drink, rather than what you are to eat and drink. For a dinner of meats without the company of a friend is like the life of a lion or a wolf."

This privilege will not be yours unless you withdraw from the world; otherwise, you will have as guests only those whom your slave-secretary sorts out from the throng of callers. It is, however, a mistake to select your friend in the reception-hall or to test him at the dinner-table. The most serious misfortune for a busy man who is overwhelmed by his possessions is, that he believes men to be his friends when he himself is not a friend to them, and that he deems his favours to be effective in winning friends, although, in the case of certain men, the more they owe, the more they hate. A trifling debt makes a man your debtor; a large one makes him an enemy.

"What," you say, "do not kindnesses establish friendships?" They do, if one has had the privilege of choosing those who are to receive them, and if they are placed judiciously, instead of being scattered broadcast.

Therefore, while you are beginning to call your mind your own, meantime apply this maxim of the wise: consider that it is more important who receives a thing, than what it is he receives. Farewell.

# Letter 18
# On Practicing what you Preach

If you are in good health and if you think yourself worthy of becoming at last your own master, I am glad. For the credit will be mine, if I can drag you from the floods in which you are being buffeted without hope of emerging. This, however, my dear Lucilius, I ask and beg of you, on your part, that you let wisdom sink into your soul, and test your progress, not by mere speech or writings, but by stoutness of heart and decrease of desire. Prove your words by your deeds.

Far different is the purpose of those who are speech-making and trying to win the approbation of a throng of hearers, far different that of those who allure the ears of young men and idlers by many-sided or fluent argumentation; philosophy teaches us to act, not to speak; it exacts of every man that he should live according to his own standards, that his life should not be out of harmony with his words, and that, further, his inner life should be of one hue and not out of harmony with all his activities. This, I say, is the highest duty and the highest proof of wisdom—that deed and word should be in accord, that a man should be equal to himself under all conditions, and always the same.

"But," you reply, "who can maintain this standard?" Very few, to be sure; but there are some. It is indeed a hard undertaking, and I do not say that the philosopher can always keep the same pace. But he can always travel the same path.

Observe yourself, then, and see whether your dress and your house are inconsistent, whether you treat yourself lavishly and your family meanly, whether you eat frugal dinners and yet build luxurious houses. You should lay hold, once for all, upon a single norm to live by, and should regulate your whole life according to this norm. Some men restrict themselves at home, but strut with swelling port before the public; such discordance is a fault, and it indicates a wavering mind which cannot yet keep its balance.

And I can tell you, further, whence arise this unsteadiness and disagreement of action and purpose; it is because no man resolves upon what he wishes, and, even if he has done so, he does not persist in it, but jumps the track; not only does he change, but he returns and slips back to the conduct which he has abandoned and abjured.

Therefore, to omit the ancient definitions of wisdom and to include the whole manner of human life, I can be satisfied with the following: "What is wisdom? Always desiring the same things, and always refusing the same things." You may be excused from adding the little proviso—that what you wish, should be right; since no man can always be satisfied with the same thing, unless it is right.

For this reason men do not know what they wish, except at the actual moment of wishing; no man ever decided once and for all to desire or to refuse. Judgment varies from day to day, and changes to the opposite, making many a man pass his life in a kind of game. Press on, therefore, as you have begun; perhaps you will be led to perfection, or to a point which you alone understand is still short of perfection.

"But what," you say, "will become of my crowded household without a household income?" If you stop supporting that crowd, it will support itself; or perhaps you will learn by the bounty of poverty what you cannot learn by your own bounty. Poverty will keep for you your true and tried friends; you will be rid of the men who were not seeking you for yourself, but for something which you have. Is it not true, however, that you should love poverty, if only for this single reason—that it will show you those by whom you are loved? O when will that time come, when no one shall tell lies to compliment you!

Accordingly, let your thoughts, your efforts, your desires, help to make you content with your own self and with the goods that spring from yourself; and commit all your other prayers to God's keeping! What happiness could come closer home to you? Bring yourself down to humble conditions, from which you cannot be ejected and in order that you may do so with greater alacrity, the contribution contained in this letter shall refer to that subject; I shall bestow it upon you forthwith.

Although you may look askance, Epicurus will once again be glad to settle my indebtedness: "Believe me, your words will be more imposing if you sleep on a cot and wear rags. For in that case you will not be merely saying them; you will be demonstrating their truth." I, at any rate, listen in a different spirit to the utterances of our friend Demetrius, after I have seen him reclining without even a cloak to cover him, and, more than this, without rugs to lie upon. He is not only a teacher of the truth, but a witness to the truth.

"May not a man, however, despise wealth when it lies in his very pocket?" Of course; he also is great-souled, who sees riches heaped up round him and, after wondering long and deeply because they have come into his possession, smiles, and hears rather than feels that they are his. It means much not to be spoiled by intimacy with riches; and he is truly great who is poor amidst riches.

"Yes, but I do not know," you say, "how the man you speak of will endure poverty, if he falls into it suddenly." Nor do I, Epicurus, know whether the poor man you speak of will despise riches, should he suddenly fall into them; accordingly, in the case of both, it is the mind that must be appraised, and we must investigate whether your man is pleased with his poverty, and whether my man is displeased with his riches. Otherwise, the cot-bed and the rags are slight proof of his good intentions, if it has not been made clear that the person concerned endures these trials not from necessity but from preference.

It is the mark, however, of a noble spirit not to precipitate oneself into such things on the ground that they are better, but to practice for them on the ground that they are thus easy to endure. And they are easy to endure, Lucilius; when, however, you come to them after long rehearsal, they are even pleasant; for they contain a sense of freedom from care—and without this nothing is pleasant.

I hold it essential, therefore, to do as I have told you in a letter that great men have often done: to reserve a few days in which we may prepare ourselves for real poverty by means of fancied poverty. There is all the more reason for doing this, because we have been steeped in luxury and regard all duties as hard and onerous. Rather let the soul be roused from its sleep and be prodded, and let it be reminded that nature has prescribed very little for us. No man is born rich. Every man, when he first sees light, is commanded to be content with milk and rags. Such is our beginning, and yet kingdoms are all too small for us! Farewell.

# Letter 19
# On the Renown which My Writings will Bring you

Do you conclude that you are having difficulties with those men about whom you wrote to me? Your greatest difficulty is with yourself; for you are your own stumbling-block. You do not know what you want. You are better at approving the right course than at following it out. You see where the true happiness lies, but you have not the courage to attain it. Let me tell you what it is that hinders you, inasmuch as you do not of yourself discern it.

You think that this condition, which you are to abandon, is one of importance, and after resolving upon that ideal state of calm into which you hope to pass, you are held back by the lustre of your present life, from which it is your intention to depart, just as if you were about to fall into a state of filth and darkness. This is a mistake, Lucilius; to go from your present life into the other is a promotion. There is the same difference between these two lives as there is between mere brightness and real light; the latter has a definite source within itself, the other borrows its radiance; the one is called forth by an illumination coming from the outside, and anyone who stands between the source and the object immediately turns the latter into a dense shadow; but the other has a glow that comes from within.

It is your own studies that will make you shine and will render you eminent. Allow me to mention the case of Epicurus.

He was writing to Idomeneus and trying to recall him from a showy existence to sure and steadfast renown. Idomeneus was at that time a minister of state who exercised a rigorous authority and had important affairs in hand. "If," said Epicurus, "you are attracted by fame, my letters will make you more renowned than all the things which you cherish and which make you cherished."

Did Epicurus speak falsely? Who would have known of Idomeneus, had not the philosopher thus engraved his name in those letters of his? All the grandees and satraps, even the king himself, who was petitioned for the title which Idomeneus sought, are sunk in deep oblivion. Cicero's letters keep the name of Atticus from perishing. It would have profited Atticus nothing to have an Agrippa for a son-in-law, a Tiberius for the husband of his grand-daughter, and a Drusus Caesar for a great-grandson; amid these mighty names his name would never be spoken, had not Cicero bound him to himself.

The deep flood of time will roll over us; some few great men will raise their heads above it, and, though destined at the last to depart into the same realms of silence, will battle against oblivion and maintain their ground for long.

That which Epicurus could promise his friend, this I promise you, Lucilius. I shall find favour among later generations; I can take with me names that will endure as long as mine. Our poet Vergil promised an eternal name to two heroes, and is keeping his promise:

> Blest heroes twain! If power my song possess,
> The record of your names shall never be
> Erased from out the book of Time, while yet
> Aeneas' tribe shall keep the Capitol,
> That rock immovable, and Roman sire
> Shall empire hold.

Whenever men have been thrust forward by fortune, whenever they have become part and parcel of another's influence, they have found abundant favour, their houses have been thronged, only so long as they themselves have kept their position; when they themselves have left it, they have slipped at once from the memory of men. But in the case of innate ability, the respect in which it is held increases, and not only does honour accrue to the man himself, but whatever has attached itself to his memory is passed on from one to another.

In order that Idomeneus may not be introduced free of charge into my letter, he shall make up the indebtedness from his own account. It was to him that Epicurus addressed the well-known saying urging him to make Pythocles rich, but not rich in the vulgar and equivocal way. "If you wish," said he, "to make Pythocles rich, do not add to his store of money, but subtract from his desires."

This idea is too clear to need explanation, and too clever to need reinforcement. There is, however, one point on which I would warn you—not to consider that this statement applies only to riches; its value will be the same, no matter how you apply it. "If you wish to make Pythocles honourable, do not add to his honours, but subtract from his desires"; "if you wish Pythocles to have pleasure for ever, do not add to his pleasures, but subtract from his desires"; "if you wish to make Pythocles an old man, filling his life to the full, do not add to his years, but subtract from his desires."

There is no reason why you should hold that these words belong to Epicurus alone; they are public property. I think we ought to do in philosophy as they are wont to do in the Senate: when someone has made a motion, of which I approve to a certain extent, I ask him to make his motion in two parts, and I vote for the part which I approve. So I am all the more glad to repeat the distinguished words of Epicurus, in order that I may prove to those who have recourse to him through a bad motive, thinking that they will have in him a screen for their own vices, that they must live honourably, no matter what school they follow.

Go to his Garden and read the motto carved there:

"Stranger, here you will do well to tarry; here our highest good is pleasure."

The care-taker of that abode, a kindly host, will be ready for you; he will welcome you with barley-meal and serve you water also in abundance, with these words: "Have you not been well entertained?" "This garden," he says, "does not whet your appetite; it quenches it. Nor does it make you more thirsty with every drink; it slakes the thirst by a natural cure, a cure that demands no fee. This is the 'pleasure' in which I have grown old."

In speaking with you, however, I refer to those desires which refuse alleviation, which must be bribed to cease. For in regard to the exceptional desires, which may be postponed, which may be chastened and checked, I have this one thought to share with you: a pleasure of that sort is according to our nature, but it is not according to our needs; one owes nothing to it; whatever is expended upon it is a free gift. The belly will not listen to advice; it makes demands, it importunes. And yet it is not a troublesome creditor; you can send it away at small cost, provided only that you give it what you owe, not merely all you are able to give. Farewell.

# Letter 20
# On the Futility of Half-Way Measures

You understand by this time that you must withdraw yourself from those showy and depraved pursuits; but you still wish to know how this may be accomplished. There are certain things which can be pointed out only by someone who is present. The physician cannot prescribe by letter the proper time for eating or bathing; he must feel the pulse. There is an old adage about gladiators—that they plan their fight in the ring; as they intently watch, something in the adversary's glance, some movement of his hand, even some slight bending of his body, gives a warning.

We can formulate general rules and commit them to writing, as to what is usually done, or ought to be done; such advice may be given, not only to our absent friends, but also to succeeding generations. In regard, however, to that second question—when or how your plan is to be carried out—no one will advise at long range; we must take counsel in the presence of the actual situation.

You must be not only present in the body, but watchful in mind, if you would avail yourself of the fleeting opportunity. Accordingly, look about you for the opportunity; if you see it, grasp it, and with all your energy and with all your strength devote yourself to this task—to rid yourself of those business duties.

Now listen carefully to the opinion which I shall offer; it is my opinion that you should withdraw either from that kind of existence, or else from existence altogether. But I likewise maintain that you should take a gentle path, that you may loosen rather than cut the knot which you have bungled so badly in tying—provided that if there shall be no other way of loosening it, you may actually cut it. No man is so faint-hearted that he would rather hang in suspense for ever than drop once for all.

Meanwhile—and this is of first importance—do not hamper yourself; be content with the business into which you have lowered yourself, or, as you prefer to have people think, have tumbled. There is no reason why you should be struggling on to something further; if you do, you will lose all grounds of excuse, and men will see that it was not a tumble. The usual explanation which men offer is wrong: "I was compelled to do it. Suppose it was against my will; I had to do it." But no one is compelled to pursue prosperity at top speed; it means something to call a halt—even if one does not offer resistance—instead of pressing eagerly after favouring fortune.

Shall you then be put out with me, if I not only come to advise you, but also call in others to advise you—wiser heads than my own, men before whom I am wont to lay any problem upon which I am pondering? Read the letter of Epicurus which appears on this matter; it is addressed to Idomeneus. The writer asks him to hasten as fast as he can, and beat a retreat before some stronger influence comes between and takes from him the liberty to withdraw.

But he also adds that one should attempt nothing except at the time when it can be attempted suitably and seasonably. Then, when the long-sought occasion comes, let him be up and doing. Epicurus forbids us to doze when we are meditating escape; he bids us hope for a safe release from even the hardest trials, provided that we are not in too great a hurry before the time, nor too dilatory when the time arrives.

Now, I suppose, you are looking for a Stoic motto also. There is really no reason why anyone should slander that school to you on the ground of its rashness; as a matter of fact, its caution is greater than its courage. You are perhaps expecting the sect to utter such words as these: "It is base to flinch under a burden. Wrestle with the duties which you have once undertaken. No man is brave and earnest if he avoids danger, if his spirit does not grow with the very difficulty of his task."

Words like these will indeed be spoken to you, if only your perseverance shall have an object that is worth while, if only you will not have to do or to suffer anything unworthy of a good man; besides, a good man will not waste himself upon mean and discreditable work or be busy merely for the sake of being busy. Neither will he, as you imagine, become so involved in ambitious schemes that he will have continually to endure their ebb and flow. Nay, when he sees the dangers, uncertainties, and hazards in which he was formerly tossed about, he will withdraw—not turning his back to the foe, but falling back little by little to a safe position.

From business, however, my dear Lucilius, it is easy to escape, if only you will despise the rewards of business. We are held back and kept from escaping by thoughts like these: "What then? Shall I leave behind me these great prospects? Shall I depart at the very time of harvest? Shall I have no slaves at my side? no retinue for my litter? no crowd in my reception room?"

Hence men leave such advantages as these with reluctance; they love the reward of their hardships, but curse the hardships themselves.

Men complain about their ambitions as they complain about their mistresses; in other words, if you penetrate their real feelings, you will find, not hatred, but bickering. Search the minds of those who cry down what they have desired, who talk about escaping from things which they are unable to do without; you will comprehend that they are lingering of their own free will in a situation which they declare they find it hard and wretched to endure.

It is so, my dear Lucilius; there are a few men whom slavery holds fast, but there are many more who hold fast to slavery.

If, however, you intend to be rid of this slavery; if freedom is genuinely pleasing in your eyes; and if you seek counsel for this one purpose—that you may have the good fortune to accomplish this purpose without perpetual annoyance—how can the whole company of Stoic thinkers fail to approve your course? Zeno, Chrysippus, and all their kind will give you advice that is temperate, honourable, and suitable.

But if you keep turning round and looking about, in order to see how much you may carry away with you, and how much money you may keep to equip yourself for the life of leisure, you will never find a way out. No man can swim ashore and take his baggage with him. Rise to a higher life, with the favour of the gods; but let it not be favour of such a kind as the gods give to men when with kind and genial faces they bestow magnificent ills, justified in so doing by the one fact that the things which irritate and torture have been bestowed in answer to prayer.

I was just putting the seal upon this letter; but it must be broken again, in order that it may go to you with its customary contribution, bearing with it some noble word. And lo, here is one that occurs to my mind; I do not know whether its truth or its nobility of utterance is the greater. "Spoken by whom?" you ask. By Epicurus; for I am still appropriating other men's belongings.

The words are: "Everyone goes out of life just as if he had but lately entered it." Take anyone off his guard, young, old, or middle-aged; you will find that all are equally afraid of death, and equally ignorant of life. No one has anything finished, because we have kept putting off into the future all our undertakings. No thought in the quotation given above pleases me more than that it taunts old men with being infants.

"No one," he says, "leaves this world in a different manner from one who has just been born." That is not true; for we are worse when we die than when we were born; but it is our fault, and not that of Nature. Nature should scold us, saying: "What does this mean? I brought you into the world without desires or fears, free from superstition, treachery and the other curses. Go forth as you were when you entered!"

A man has caught the message of wisdom, if he can die as free from care as he was at birth; but as it is we are all a-flutter at the approach of the dreaded end. Our courage fails us, our cheeks blanch; our tears fall, though they are unavailing. But what is baser than to fret at the very threshold of peace?

The reason, however is, that we are stripped of all our goods, we have jettisoned our cargo of life and are in distress; for no part of it has been packed in the hold; it has all been heaved overboard and has drifted away. Men do not care how nobly they live, but only how long, although it is within the reach of every man to live nobly, but within no man's power to live long. Farewell.

# Letter 21
# On the True Joy which Comes from Philosophy

Do you suppose that I shall write you how kindly the winter season has dealt with us—a short season and a mild one—or what a nasty spring we are having—cold weather out of season—and all the other trivialities which people write when they are at a loss for topics of conversation? No; I shall communicate something which may help both you and myself. And what shall this "something" be, if not an exhortation to soundness of mind? Do you ask what is the foundation of a sound mind? It is, not to find joy in useless things. I said that it was the foundation; it is really the pinnacle.

We have reached the heights if we know what it is that we find joy in and if we have not placed our happiness in the control of externals. The man who is goaded ahead by hope of anything, though it be within reach, though it be easy of access, and though his ambitions have never played him false, is troubled and unsure of himself.

Above all, my dear Lucilius, make this your business: learn how to feel joy.

Do you think that I am now robbing you of many pleasures when I try to do away with the gifts of chance, when I counsel the avoidance of hope, the sweetest thing that gladdens our hearts? Quite the contrary; I do not wish you ever to be deprived of gladness. I would have it born in your house; and it is born there, if only it be inside of you. Other objects of cheer do not fill a man's bosom; they merely smooth his brow and are inconstant—unless perhaps you believe that he who laughs has joy. The very soul must be happy and confident, lifted above every circumstance.

Real joy, believe me, is a stern matter. Can one, do you think, despise death with a care-free countenance, or with a "blithe and gay" expression, as our young dandies are accustomed to say? Or can one thus open his door to poverty, or hold the curb on his pleasures, or contemplate the endurance of pain? He who ponders these things in his heart is indeed full of joy; but it is not a cheerful joy. It is just this joy, however, of which I would have you become the owner; for it will never fail you when once you have found its source.

The yield of poor mines is on the surface; those are really rich whose veins lurk deep, and they will make more bountiful returns to him who delves unceasingly. So too those baubles which delight the common crowd afford but a thin pleasure, laid on as a coating, and even joy that is only plated lacks a real basis. But the joy of which I speak, that to which I am endeavouring to lead you, is something solid, disclosing itself the more fully as you penetrate into it.

Therefore I pray you, my dearest Lucilius, do the one thing that can render you really happy: cast aside and trample under foot all the things that glitter outwardly and are held out to you by another or as obtainable from another; look toward the true good, and rejoice only in that which comes from your own store. And what do I mean by "from your own store"? I mean from your very self, that which is the best part of you. The frail body, also, even though we can accomplish nothing without it, is to be regarded as necessary rather than as important; it involves us in vain pleasures, short-lived, and soon to be regretted, which, unless they are reined in by extreme self-control, will be transformed into the opposite. This is what I mean: pleasure, unless it has been kept within bounds, tends to rush headlong into the abyss of sorrow.

But it is hard to keep within bounds in that which you believe to be good. The real good may be coveted with safety.

Do you ask me what this real good is, and whence it derives? I will tell you: it comes from a good conscience, from honourable purposes, from right actions, from contempt of the gifts of chance, from an even and calm way of living which treads but one path. For men who leap from one purpose to another, or do not even leap but are carried over by a sort of hazard—how can such wavering and unstable persons possess any good that is fixed and lasting?

There are only a few who control themselves and their affairs by a guiding purpose; the rest do not proceed; they are merely swept along, like objects afloat in a river. And of these objects, some are held back by sluggish waters and are transported gently; others are torn along by a more violent current; some, which are nearest the bank, are left there as the current slackens; and others are carried out to sea by the onrush of the stream. Therefore, we should decide what we wish, and abide by the decision.

Now is the time for me to pay my debt. I can give you a saying of your friend Epicurus and thus clear this letter of its obligation. "It is bothersome always to be beginning life." Or another, which will perhaps express the meaning better: "They live ill who are always beginning to live."

You are right in asking why; the saying certainly stands in need of a commentary. It is because the life of such persons is always incomplete. But a man cannot stand prepared for the approach of death if he has just begun to live. We must make it our aim already to have lived long enough. No one deems that he has done so, if he is just on the point of planning his life.

You need not think that there are few of this kind; practically everyone is of such a stamp. Some men, indeed, only begin to live when it is time for them to leave off living. And if this seems surprising to you, I shall add that which will surprise you still more: Some men have left off living before they have begun. Farewell.

# Letter 22
# On Despising Death

You write me that you are anxious about the result of a lawsuit, with which an angry opponent is threatening you; and you expect me to advise you to picture to yourself a happier issue, and to rest in the allurements of hope. Why, indeed, is it necessary to summon trouble—which must be endured soon enough when it has once arrived, or to anticipate trouble and ruin the present through fear of the future? It is indeed foolish to be unhappy now because you may be unhappy at some future time.

But I shall conduct you to peace of mind by another route: if you would put off all worry, assume that what you fear may happen will certainly happen in any event; whatever the trouble may be, measure it in your own mind, and estimate the amount of your fear. You will thus understand that what you fear is either insignificant or short-lived.

And you need not spend a long time in gathering illustrations which will strengthen you; every epoch has produced them. Let your thoughts travel into any era of Roman or foreign history, and there will throng before you notable examples of high achievement or of high endeavour.

If you lose this case, can anything more severe happen to you than being sent into exile or led to prison? Is there a worse fate that any man may fear than being burned or being killed?

Name such penalties one by one, and mention the men who have scorned them; one does not need to hunt for them—it is simply a matter of selection.

Sentence of conviction was borne by Rutilius as if the injustice of the decision were the only thing which annoyed him. Exile was endured by Metellus with courage, by Rutilius even with gladness; for the former consented to come back only because his country called him; the latter refused to return when Sulla summoned him—and nobody in those days said "No" to Sulla! Socrates in prison discoursed, and declined to flee when certain persons gave him the opportunity; he remained there, in order to free mankind from the fear of two most grievous things, death and imprisonment.

Mucius put his hand into the fire. It is painful to be burned; but how much more painful to inflict such suffering upon oneself! Here was a man of no learning, not primed to face death and pain by any words of wisdom, and equipped only with the courage of a soldier, who punished himself for his fruitless daring; he stood and watched his own right hand falling away piecemeal on the enemy's brazier, nor did he withdraw the dissolving limb, with its uncovered bones, until his foe removed the fire. He might have accomplished something more successful in that camp, but never anything more brave. See how much keener a brave man is to lay hold of danger than a cruel man is to inflict it: Porsenna was more ready to pardon Mucius for wishing to slay him than Mucius to pardon himself for failing to slay Porsenna!

"Oh," say you, "those stories have been droned to death in all the schools; pretty soon, when you reach the topic 'On Despising Death,' you will be telling me about Cato." But why should I not tell you about Cato, how he read Plato's book on that last glorious night, with a sword laid at his pillow? He had provided these two requisites for his last moments—the first, that he might have the will to die, and the second, that he might have the means. So he put his affairs in order—as well as one could put in order that which was ruined and near its end—and thought that he ought to see to it that no one should have the power to slay or the good fortune to save Cato.

Drawing the sword—which he had kept unstained from all bloodshed against the final day, he cried: "Fortune, you have accomplished nothing by resisting all my endeavours. I have fought, till now, for my country's freedom, and not for my own, I did not strive so doggedly to be free, but only to live among the free. Now, since the affairs of mankind are beyond hope, let Cato be withdrawn to safety."

So saying, he inflicted a mortal wound upon his body. After the physicians had bound it up, Cato had less blood and less strength, but no less courage; angered now not only at Caesar but also at himself, he rallied his unarmed hands against his wound, and expelled, rather than dismissed, that noble soul which had been so defiant of all worldly power.

I am not now heaping up these illustrations for the purpose of exercising my wit, but for the purpose of encouraging you to face that which is thought to be most terrible. And I shall encourage you all the more easily by showing that not only resolute men have despised that moment when the soul breathes its last, but that certain persons, who were craven in other respects, have equalled in this regard the courage of the bravest. Take, for example, Scipio, the father-in-law of Gnaeus Pompeius: he was driven back upon the African coast by a head-wind and saw his ship in the power of the enemy. He therefore pierced his body with a sword; and when they asked where the commander was, he replied: "All is well with the commander."

These words brought him up to the level of his ancestors and suffered not the glory which fate gave to the Scipios in Africa to lose its continuity. It was a great deed to conquer Carthage, but a greater deed to conquer death. "All is well with the commander!" Ought a general to die otherwise, especially one of Cato's generals?

I shall not refer you to history, or collect examples of those men who throughout the ages have despised death; for they are very many. Consider these times of ours, whose enervation and over-refinement call forth our complaints; they nevertheless will include men of every rank, of every lot in life, and of every age, who have cut short their misfortunes by death.

Believe me, Lucilius; death is so little to be feared that through its good offices nothing is to be feared.

Therefore, when your enemy threatens, listen unconcernedly. Although your conscience makes you confident, yet, since many things have weight which are outside your case, both hope for that which is utterly just, and prepare yourself against that which is utterly unjust. Remember, however, before all else, to strip things of all that disturbs and confuses, and to see what each is at bottom; you will then comprehend that they contain nothing fearful except the actual fear.

That you see happening to boys happens also to ourselves, who are only slightly bigger boys: when those whom they love, with whom they daily associate, with whom they play, appear with masks on, the boys are frightened out of their wits. We should strip the mask, not only from men, but from things, and restore to each object its own aspect.

"Why dost thou hold up before my eyes swords, fires, and a throng of executioners raging about thee? Take away all that vain show, behind which thou lurkest and scarest fools! Ah! thou art naught but Death, whom only yesterday a manservant of mine and a maid-servant did despise! Why dost thou again unfold and spread before me, with all that great display, the whip and the rack? Why are those engines of torture made ready, one for each several member of the body, and all the other innumerable machines for tearing a man apart piecemeal? Away with all such stuff, which makes us numb with terror! And thou, silence the groans the cries, and the bitter shrieks ground out of the victim as he is torn on the rack! Forsooth thou are naught but Pain, scorned by yonder gout-ridden wretch, endured by yonder dyspeptic in the midst of his dainties, borne bravely by the girl in travail. Slight thou art, if I can bear thee; short thou art if I cannot bear thee!"

Ponder these words which you have often heard and often uttered. Moreover, prove by the result whether that which you have heard and uttered is true. For there is a very disgraceful charge often brought against our school—that we deal with the words, and not with the deeds, of philosophy.

What, have you only at this moment learned that death is hanging over your head, at this moment exile, at this moment grief? You were born to these perils. Let us think of everything that can happen as something which will happen.

I know that you have really done what I advise you to do; I now warn you not to drown your soul in these petty anxieties of yours; if you do, the soul will be dulled and will have too little vigour left when the time comes for it to arise. Remove the mind from this case of yours to the case of men in general. Say to yourself that our petty bodies are mortal and frail; pain can reach them from other sources than from wrong or the might of the stronger. Our pleasures themselves become torments; banquets bring indigestion, carousals paralysis of the muscles and palsy, sensual habits affect the feet, the hands, and every joint of the body.

I may become a poor man; I shall then be one among many. I may be exiled; I shall then regard myself as born in the place to which I shall be sent. They may put me in chains. What then? Am I free from bonds now? Behold this clogging burden of a body, to which nature has fettered me! "I shall die," you say; you mean to say "I shall cease to run the risk of sickness; I shall cease to run the risk of imprisonment; I shall cease to run the risk of death."

I am not so foolish as to go through at this juncture the arguments which Epicurus harps upon, and say that the terrors of the world below are idle—that Ixion does not whirl round on his wheel, that Sisyphus does not shoulder his stone uphill, that a man's entrails cannot be restored and devoured every day; no one is so childish as to fear Cerberus, or the shadows, or the spectral garb of those who are held together by naught but their unfleshed bones. Death either annihilates us or strips us bare. If we are then released, there remains the better part, after the burden has been withdrawn; if we are annihilated, nothing remains; good and bad are alike removed.

Allow me at this point to quote a verse of yours, first suggesting that, when you wrote it, you meant it for yourself no less than for others. It is ignoble to say one thing and mean another; and how much more ignoble to write one thing and mean another! I remember one day you were handling the well-known commonplace—that we do not suddenly fall on death, but advance towards it by slight degrees; we die every day.

For every day a little of our life is taken from us; even when we are growing, our life is on the wane. We lose our childhood, then our boyhood, and then our youth. Counting even yesterday, all past time is lost time; the very day which we are now spending is shared between ourselves and death. It is not the last drop that empties the water-clock, but all that which previously has flowed out; similarly, the final hour when we cease to exist does not of itself bring death; it merely of itself completes the death-process. We reach death at that moment, but we have been a long time on the way.

In describing this situation, you said in your customary, style (for you are always impressive, but never more pungent than when you are putting the truth in appropriate words):

*Not single is the death which comes; the death*
*Which takes us off is but the last of all.*

I prefer that you should read your own words rather than my letter; for then it will be clear to you that this death, of which we are afraid, is the last but not the only death.

I see what you are looking for; you are asking what I have packed into my letter, what inspiriting saying from some master-mind, what useful precept. So I shall send you something dealing with this very subject which has been under discussion. Epicurus upbraids those who crave, as much as those who shrink from, death: "It is absurd," he says, "to run towards death because you are tired of life, when it is your manner of life that has made you run towards death."

And in another passage: "What is so absurd as to seek death, when it is through fear of death that you have robbed your life of peace?" And you may add a third statement, of the same stamp: "Men are so thoughtless, nay, so mad, that some, through fear of death, force themselves to die."

Whichever of these ideas you ponder, you will strengthen your mind for the endurance alike of death and of life. For we need to be warned and strengthened in both directions—not to love or to hate life overmuch; even when reason advises us to make an end of it, the impulse is not to be adopted without reflection or at headlong speed.

The grave and wise man should not beat a hasty retreat from life; he should make a becoming exit. And above all, he should avoid the weakness which has taken possession of so many—the lust for death. For just as there is an unreflecting tendency of the mind towards other things, so, my dear Lucilius, there is an unreflecting tendency towards death; this often seizes upon the noblest and most spirited men, as well as upon the craven and the abject. The former despise life; the latter find it irksome.

Others also are moved by a satiety of doing and seeing the same things, and not so much by a hatred of life as because they are cloyed with it. We slip into this condition, while philosophy itself pushes us on, and we say; "How long must I endure the same things? Shall I continue to wake and sleep, be hungry and be cloyed, shiver and perspire? There is an end to nothing; all things are connected in a sort of circle; they flee and they are pursued. Night is close at the heels of day, day at the heels of night; summer ends in autumn, winter rushes after autumn, and winter softens into spring; all nature in this way passes, only to return. I do nothing new; I see nothing new; sooner or later one sickens of this, also." There are many who think that living is not painful, but superfluous. Farewell.

# Letter 23
# On Reformation

With regard to these two friends of ours, we must proceed along different lines; the faults of the one are to be corrected, the other's are to be crushed out. I shall take every liberty; for I do not love this one if I am unwilling to hurt his feelings. "What," you say, "do you expect to keep a forty-year-old ward under your tutelage? Consider his age, how hardened it now is, and past handling!

Such a man cannot be re-shaped; only young minds are moulded." I do not know whether I shall make progress; but I should prefer to lack success rather than to lack faith. You need not despair of curing sick men even when the disease is chronic, if only you hold out against excess and force them to do and submit to many things against their will. As regards our other friend I am not sufficiently confident, either, except for the fact that he still has sense of shame enough to blush for his sins. This modesty should be fostered; so long as it endures in his soul, there is some room for hope. But as for this veteran of yours, I think we should deal more carefully with him, that he may not become desperate about himself.

There is no better time to approach him than now, when he has an interval of rest and seems like one who has corrected his faults. Others have been cheated by this interval of virtue on his part, but he does not cheat me. I feel sure that these faults will return, as it were, with compound interest, for just now, I am certain, they are in abeyance but not absent. I shall devote some time to the matter, and try to see whether or not something can be done.

But do you yourself, as indeed you are doing, show me that you are stout-hearted; lighten your baggage for the march. None of our possessions is essential. Let us return to the law of nature; for then riches are laid up for us. The things which we actually need are free for all, or else cheap; nature craves only bread and water. No one is poor according to this standard; when a man has limited his desires within these bounds, he can challenge the happiness of Jove himself, as Epicurus says. I must insert in this letter one or two more of his sayings:

"Do everything as if Epicurus were watching you." There is no real doubt that it is good for one to have appointed a guardian over oneself, and to have someone whom you may look up to, someone whom you may regard as a witness of your thoughts. It is, indeed, nobler by far to live as you would live under the eyes of some good man, always at your side; but nevertheless I am content if you only act, in whatever you do, as you would act if anyone at all were looking on; because solitude prompts us to all kinds of evil.

And when you have progressed so far that you have also respect for yourself, you may send away your attendant; but until then, set as a guard over yourself the authority of some man, whether your choice be the great Cato or Scipio, or Laelius—or any man in whose presence even abandoned wretches would check their bad impulses. Meantime, you are engaged in making of yourself the sort of person in whose company you would not dare to sin. When this aim has been accomplished and you begin to hold yourself in some esteem, I shall gradually allow you to do what Epicurus, in another passage, suggests: "The time when you should most of all withdraw into yourself is when you are forced to be in a crowd."

You ought to make yourself of a different stamp from the multitude. Therefore, while it is not yet safe to withdraw into solitude, seek out certain individuals; for everyone is better off in the company of somebody or other—no matter who—than in his own company alone. "The time when you should most of all withdraw into yourself is when you are forced to be in a crowd." Yes, provided that you are a good, tranquil, and self-restrained man; otherwise, you had better withdraw into a crowd in order to get away from your self. Alone, you are too close to a rascal. Farewell.

# Letter 24
# On the Good which Abides

"What," say you, "are you giving me advice? Indeed, have you already advised yourself, already corrected your own faults? Is this the reason why you have leisure to reform other men?" No, I am not so shameless as to undertake to cure my fellow-men when I am ill myself. I am, however, discussing with you troubles which concern us both, and sharing the remedy with you, just as if we were lying ill in the same hospital. Listen to me, therefore, as you would if I were talking to myself. I am admitting you to my inmost thoughts, and am having it out with myself, merely making use of you as my pretext.

I keep crying out to myself: "Count your years, and you will be ashamed to desire and pursue the same things you desired in your boyhood days. Of this one thing make sure against your dying day—let your faults die before you die. Away with those disordered pleasures, which must be dearly paid for; it is not only those which are to come that harm me, but also those which have come and gone. Just as crimes, even if they have not been detected when they were committed, do not allow anxiety to end with them; so with guilty pleasures, regret remains even after the pleasures are over. They are not substantial, they are not trustworthy; even if they do not harm us, they are fleeting.

Cast about rather for some good which will abide. But there can be no such good except as the soul discovers it for itself within itself. Virtue alone affords everlasting and peace-giving joy; even if some obstacle arise, it is but like an intervening cloud, which floats beneath the sun but never prevails against it."

When will it be your lot to attain this joy? Thus far, you have indeed not been sluggish, but you must quicken your pace. Much toil remains; to confront it, you must yourself lavish all your waking hours, and all your efforts, if you wish the result to be accomplished. This matter cannot be delegated to someone else.

The other kind of literary activity admits of outside assistance. Within our own time there was a certain rich man named Calvisius Sabinus; he had the bank-account and the brains of a freedman. I never saw a man whose good fortune was a greater offence against propriety. His memory was so faulty that he would sometimes forget the name of Ulysses, or Achilles, or Priam—names which we know as well as we know those of our own attendants. No major-domo in his dotage, who cannot give men their right names, but is compelled to invent names for them—no such man, I say, calls off the names of his master's tribesmen so atrociously as Sabinus used to call off the Trojan and Achaean heroes. But none the less did he desire to appear learned.

So he devised this short cut to learning: he paid fabulous prices for slaves—one to know Homer by heart and another to know Hesiod; he also delegated a special slave to each of the nine lyric poets. You need not wonder that he paid high prices for these slaves; if he did not find them ready to hand he had them made to order. After collecting this retinue, he began to make life miserable for his guests; he would keep these fellows at the foot of his couch, and ask them from time to time for verses which he might repeat, and then frequently break down in the middle of a word.

Satellius Quadratus, a feeder, and consequently a fawner, upon addle-pated millionaires, and also (for this quality goes with the other two) a flouter of them, suggested to Sabinus that he should have philologists to gather up the bits. Sabinus remarked that each slave cost him one hundred thousand sesterces; Satellius replied: "You might have bought as many book-cases for a smaller sum." But Sabinus held to the opinion that what any member of his household knew, he himself knew also.

This same Satellius began to advise Sabinus to take wrestling lessons—sickly, pale, and thin as he was, Sabinus answered: "How can I? I can scarcely stay alive now." "Don't say that, I implore you," replied the other, "consider how many perfectly healthy slaves you have!" No man is able to borrow or buy a sound mind; in fact, as it seems to me, even though sound minds were for sale, they would not find buyers. Depraved minds, however, are bought and sold every day.

But let me pay off my debt and say farewell: "Real wealth is poverty adjusted to the law of Nature." Epicurus has this saying in various ways and contexts; but it can never be repeated too often, since it can never be learned too well. For some persons the remedy should be merely prescribed; in the case of others, it should be forced down their throats. Farewell.

# Letter 25
# On Travel as a Cure for Discontent

Do you suppose that you alone have had this experience? Are you surprised, as if it were a novelty, that after such long travel and so many changes of scene you have not been able to shake off the gloom and heaviness of your mind? You need a change of soul rather than a change of climate. Though you may cross vast spaces of sea, and though, as our Vergil remarks,

> Lands and cities are left astern,

your faults will follow you whithersoever you travel.

Socrates made the same remark to one who complained; he said: "Why do you wonder that globe-trotting does not help you, seeing that you always take yourself with you? The reason which set you wandering is ever at your heels." What pleasure is there in seeing new lands? Or in surveying cities and spots of interest? All your bustle is useless. Do you ask why such flight does not help you? It is because you flee along with yourself. You must lay aside the burdens of the mind; until you do this, no place will satisfy you.

Reflect that your present behaviour is like that of the prophetess whom Vergil describes: she is excited and goaded into fury, and contains within herself much inspiration that is not her own:

> The priestess raves, if haply she may shake
> The great god from her heart.

You wander hither and yon, to rid yourself of the burden that rests upon you, though it becomes more troublesome by reason of your very restlessness, just as in a ship the cargo when stationary makes no trouble, but when it shifts to this side or that, it causes the vessel to heel more quickly in the direction where it has settled. Anything you do tells against you, and you hurt yourself by your very unrest; for you are shaking up a sick man.

That trouble once removed, all change of scene will become pleasant; though you may be driven to the uttermost ends of the earth, in whatever corner of a savage land you may find yourself, that place, however forbidding, will be to you a hospitable abode. The person you are matters more than the place to which you go; for that reason we should not make the mind a bondsman to any one place. Live in this belief: "I am not born for any one corner of the universe; this whole world is my country."

If you saw this fact clearly, you would not be surprised at getting no benefit from the fresh scenes to which you roam each time through weariness of the old scenes. For the first would have pleased you in each case, had you believed it wholly yours. As it is, however, you are not journeying; you are drifting and being driven, only exchanging one place for another, although that which you seek—to live well—is found everywhere.

Can there be any spot so full of confusion as the Forum? Yet you can live quietly even there, if necessary. Of course, if one were allowed to make one's own arrangements, I should flee far from the very sight and neighbourhood of the Forum. For just as pestilential places assail even the strongest constitution, so there are some places which are also unwholesome for a healthy mind which is not yet quite sound, though recovering from its ailment.

I disagree with those who strike out into the midst of the billows and, welcoming a stormy existence, wrestle daily in hardihood of soul with life's problems. The wise man will endure all that, but will not choose it; he will prefer to be at peace rather than at war. It helps little to have cast out your own faults if you must quarrel with those of others.

Says one: "There were thirty tyrants surrounding Socrates, and yet they could not break his spirit"; but what does it matter how many masters a man has? "Slavery" has no plural; and he who has scorned it is free—no matter amid how large a mob of over-lords he stands.

It is time to stop, but not before I have paid duty. "The knowledge of sin is the beginning of salvation." This saying of Epicurus seems to me to be a noble one. For he who does not know that he has sinned does not desire correction; you must discover yourself in the wrong before you can reform yourself.

Some boast of their faults. Do you think that the man has any thought of mending his ways who counts over his vices as if they were virtues? Therefore, as far as possible, prove yourself guilty, hunt up charges against yourself; play the part, first of accuser, then of judge, last of intercessor. At times be harsh with yourself. Farewell.

# Letter 26
# On Conquering the Conqueror

I have beheld Aufidius Bassus, that noble man, shattered in health and wrestling with his years. But they already bear upon him so heavily that he cannot be raised up; old age has settled down upon him with great— yes, with its entire, weight. You know that his body was always delicate and sapless. For a long time he has kept it in hand, or, to speak more correctly, has kept it together; of a sudden it has collapsed.

Just as in a ship that springs a leak, you can always stop the first or the second fissure, but when many holes begin to open and let in water, the gaping hull cannot be saved; similarly, in an old man's body, there is a certain limit up to which you can sustain and prop its weakness. But when it comes to resemble a decrepit building, when every joint begins to spread and while one is being repaired another falls apart—then it is time for a man to look about him and consider how he may get out.

But the mind of our friend Bassus is active. Philosophy bestows this boon upon us; it makes us joyful in the very sight of death, strong and brave no matter in what state the body may be, cheerful and never failing though the body fail us. A great pilot can sail even when his canvas is rent; if his ship be dismantled, he can yet put in trim what remains of her hull and hold her to her course. This is what our friend Bassus is doing; and he contemplates his own end with the courage and countenance which you would regard as undue indifference in a man who so contemplated another's.

This is a great accomplishment, Lucilius, and one which needs long practice to learn—to depart calmly when the inevitable hour arrives. Other kinds of death contain an ingredient of hope: a disease comes to an end; a fire is quenched; falling houses have set down in safety those whom they seemed certain to crush; the sea has cast ashore unharmed those whom it had engulfed, by the same force through which it drew them down; the soldier has drawn back his sword from the very neck of his doomed foe. But those whom old age is leading away to death have nothing to hope for; old age alone grants no reprieve. No ending, to be sure, is more painless; but there is none more lingering.

Our friend Bassus seemed to me to be attending his own funeral, and laying out his own body for burial, and living almost as if he had survived his own death, and bearing with wise resignation his grief at his own departure. For he talks freely about death, trying hard to persuade us that if this process contains any element of discomfort or of fear, it is the fault of the dying person, and not of death itself; also, that there is no more inconvenience at the actual moment than there is after it is over.

"And it is just as insane," he adds, "for a man to fear what will not happen to him, as to fear what he will not feel if it does happen." Or does anyone imagine it to be possible that the agency by which feeling is removed can be itself felt? "Therefore," says Bassus, "death stands so far beyond all evil that it is beyond all fear of evils."

I know that all this has often been said and should be often repeated; but neither when I read them were such precepts so effective with me, nor when I heard them from the lips of those who were at a safe distance from the fear of the things which they declared were not to be feared. But this old man had the greatest weight with me when he discussed death and death was near.

For I must tell you what I myself think: I hold that one is braver at the very moment of death than when one is approaching death. For death, when it stands near us, gives even to inexperienced men the courage not to seek to avoid the inevitable. So the gladiator, who throughout the fight has been no matter how faint-hearted, offers his throat to his opponent and directs the wavering blade to the vital spot. But an end that is near at hand, and is bound to come, calls for tenacious courage of soul; this is a rarer thing, and none but the wise man can manifest it.

Accordingly, I listened to Bassus with the deepest pleasure; he was casting his vote concerning death and pointing out what sort of a thing it is when it is observed, so to speak, nearer at hand. I suppose that a man would have your confidence in a larger degree, and would have more weight with you, if he had come back to life and should declare from experience that there is no evil in death; and so, regarding the approach of death, those will tell you best what disquiet it brings who have stood in its path, who have seen it coming and have welcomed it.

Bassus may be included among these men; and he had no wish to deceive us. He says that it is as foolish to fear death as to fear old age; for death follows old age precisely as old age follows youth. He who does not wish to die cannot have wished to live. For life is granted to us with the reservation that we shall die; to this end our path leads. Therefore, how foolish it is to fear it, since men simply await that which is sure, but fear only that which is uncertain!

Death has its fixed rule—equitable and unavoidable. Who can complain when he is governed by terms which include everyone? The chief part of equity, however, is equality.

But it is superfluous at the present time to plead Nature's cause; for she wishes our laws to be identical with her own; she but resolves that which she has compounded, and compounds again that which she has resolved.

Moreover, if it falls to the lot of any man to be set gently adrift by old age—not suddenly torn from life, but withdrawn bit by bit, oh, verily he should thank the gods, one and all, because, after he has had his fill, he is removed to a rest which is ordained for mankind, a rest that is welcome to the weary. You may observe certain men who crave death even more earnestly than others are wont to beg for life. And I do not know which men give us greater courage—those who call for death, or those who meet it cheerfully and tranquilly—for the first attitude is sometimes inspired by madness and sudden anger, the second is the calm which results from fixed judgment. Before now men have gone to meet death in a fit of rage; but when death comes to meet him, no one welcomes it cheerfully, except the man who has long since composed himself for death.

I admit, therefore, that I have visited this dear friend of mine more frequently on many pretexts, but with the purpose of learning whether I should find him always the same, and whether his mental strength was perhaps waning in company with his bodily powers. But it was on the increase, just as the joy of the charioteer is wont to show itself more clearly when he is on the seventh round of the course, and nears the prize.

Indeed, he often said, in accord with the counsels of Epicurus: "I hope, first of all, that there is no pain at the moment when a man breathes his last; but if there is, one will find an element of comfort in its very shortness. For no great pain lasts long. And at all events, a man will find relief at the very time when soul and body are being torn asunder, even though the process be accompanied by excruciating pain, in the thought that after this pain is over he can feel no more pain. I am sure, however, that an old man's soul is on his very lips, and that only a little force is necessary to disengage it from the body. A fire which has seized upon a substance that sustains it needs water to quench it, or, sometimes, the destruction of the building itself; but the fire which lacks sustaining fuel dies away of its own accord."

I am glad to hear such words, my dear Lucilius, not as new to me, but as leading me into the presence of an actual fact. And what then? Have I not seen many men break the thread of life? I have indeed seen such men; but those have more weight with me who approach death without any loathing for life, letting death in, so to speak, and not pulling it towards them.

Bassus kept saying: "It is due to our own fault that we feel this torture, because we shrink from dying only when we believe that our end is near at hand." But who is not near death? It is ready for us in all places and at all times. "Let us consider," he went on to say, "when some agency of death seems imminent, how much nearer are other varieties of dying which are not feared by us."

A man is threatened with death by an enemy, but this form of death is anticipated by an attack of indigestion. And if we are willing to examine critically the various causes of our fear, we shall find that some exist, and others only seem to be. We do not fear death; we fear the thought of death. For death itself is always the same distance from us; wherefore, if it is to be feared at all, it is to be feared always. For what season of our life is exempt from death?

But what I really ought to fear is that you will hate this long letter worse than death itself; so I shall stop. Do you, however, always think on death in order that you may never fear it. Farewell.

# Letter 27
# On Progress

I have been asking about you, and inquiring of everyone who comes from your part of the country, what you are doing, and where you are spending your time, and with whom. You cannot deceive me; for I am with you. Live just as if I were sure to get news of your doings, nay, as if I were sure to behold them. And if you wonder what particularly pleases me that I hear concerning you, it is that I hear nothing, that most of those whom I ask do not know what you are doing.

This is sound practice—to refrain from associating with men of different stamp and different aims. And I am indeed confident that you cannot be warped, that you will stick to your purpose, even though the crowd may surround and seek to distract you. What, then, is on my mind? I am not afraid lest they work a change in you; but I am afraid lest they may hinder your progress. And much harm is done even by one who holds you back, especially since life is so short; and we make it still shorter by our unsteadiness, by making ever fresh beginnings at life, now one and immediately another. We break up life into little bits, and fritter it away.

Hasten ahead, then, dearest Lucilius, and reflect how greatly you would quicken your speed if an enemy were at your back, or if you suspected the cavalry were approaching and pressing hard upon your steps as you fled. It is true; the enemy is indeed pressing upon you; you should therefore increase your speed and escape away and reach a safe position, remembering continually what a noble thing it is to round out your life before death comes, and then await in peace the remaining portion of your time, claiming nothing for yourself, since you are in possession of the happy life; for such a life is not made happier for being longer.

O when shall you see the time when you shall know that time means nothing to you, when you shall be peaceful and calm, careless of the morrow, because you are enjoying your life to the full?

Would you know what makes men greedy for the future? It is because no one has yet found himself. Your parents, to be sure, asked other blessings for you; but I myself pray rather that you may despise all those things which your parents wished for you in abundance. Their prayers plunder many another person, simply that you may be enriched. Whatever they make over to you must be removed from someone else.

I pray that you may get such control over yourself that your mind, now shaken by wandering thoughts, may at last come to rest and be steadfast, that it may be content with itself and, having attained an understanding of what things are truly good—and they are in our possession as soon as we have this knowledge—that it may have no need of added years. He has at length passed beyond all necessities—he has won his honourable discharge and is free—who still lives after his life has been completed. Farewell.

# Letter 28
# On the Futility of Learning Maxims

You wish me to close these letters also, as I closed my former letters, with certain utterances taken from the chiefs of our school. But they did not interest themselves in choice extracts; the whole texture of their work is full of strength. There is unevenness, you know, when some objects rise conspicuous above others. A single tree is not remarkable if the whole forest rises to the same height.

Poetry is crammed with utterances of this sort, and so is history. For this reason I would not have you think that these utterances belong to Epicurus. they are common property and are emphatically our own. They are, however, more noteworthy in Epicurus, because they appear at infrequent intervals and when you do not expect them, and because it is surprising that brave words should be spoken at any time by a man who made a practice of being effeminate. For that is what most persons maintain. In my own opinion, however, Epicurus is really a brave man, even though he did wear long sleeves. Fortitude, energy, and readiness for battle are to be found among the Persians, just as much as among men who have girded themselves up high.

Therefore, you need not call upon me for extracts and quotations; such thoughts as one may extract here and there in the works of other philosophers run through the whole body of our writings. Hence we have no "show-window goods," nor do we deceive the purchaser in such a way that, if he enters our shop, he will find nothing except that which is displayed in the window. We allow the purchasers themselves to get their samples from anywhere they please.

Suppose we should desire to sort out each separate motto from the general stock; to whom shall we credit them? To Zeno, Cleanthes, Chrysippus, Panaetius, or Posidonius? We Stoics are not subjects of a despot: each of us lays claim to his own freedom. With them, on the other hand, whatever Hermarchus says or Metrodorus, is ascribed to one source. In that brotherhood, everything that any man utters is spoken under the leadership and commanding authority of one alone. We cannot, I maintain, no matter how we try, pick out anything from so great a multitude of things equally good.

*Only the poor man counts his flock.*

Wherever you direct your gaze, you will meet with something that might stand out from the rest, if the context in which you read it were not equally notable.

For this reason, give over hoping that you can skim, by means of epitomes, the wisdom of distinguished men. Look into their wisdom as a whole; study it as a whole. They are working out a plan and weaving together, line upon line, a masterpiece, from which nothing can be taken away without injury to the whole. Examine the separate parts, if you like, provided you examine them as parts of the man himself. She is not a beautiful woman whose ankle or arm is praised, but she whose general appearance makes you forget to admire her single attributes.

If you insist, however, I shall not be niggardly with you, but lavish; for there is a huge multitude of these passages; they are scattered about in profusion—they do not need to be gathered together, but merely to be picked up. They do not drip forth occasionally; they flow continuously. They are unbroken and are closely connected. Doubtless they would be of much benefit to those who are still novices and worshipping outside the shrine; for single maxims sink in more easily when they are marked off and bounded like a line of verse.

That is why we give to children a proverb, or that which the Greeks call *Chria*, to be learned by heart; that sort of thing can be comprehended by the young mind, which cannot as yet hold more. For a man, however, whose progress is definite, to chase after choice extracts and to prop his weakness by the best known and the briefest sayings and to depend upon his memory, is disgraceful; it is time for him to lean on himself. He should make such maxims and not memorize them. For it is disgraceful even for an old man, or one who has sighted old age, to have a note-book knowledge. "This is what Zeno said." But what have you yourself said? "This is the opinion of Cleanthes." But what is your own opinion? How long shall you march under another man's orders? Take command, and utter some word which posterity will remember. Put forth something from your own stock.

For this reason I hold that there is nothing of eminence in all such men as these, who never create anything themselves, but always lurk in the shadow of others, playing the rôle of interpreters, never daring to put once into practice what they have been so long in learning. They have exercised their memories on other men's material. But it is one thing to remember, another to know. Remembering is merely safeguarding something entrusted to the memory; knowing, however, means making everything your own; it means not depending upon the copy and not all the time glancing back at the master.

"Thus said Zeno, thus said Cleanthes, indeed!" Let there be a difference between yourself and your book! How long shall you be a learner? From now on be a teacher as well! "But why," one asks, "should I have to continue hearing lectures on what I can read?" "The living voice," one replies, "is a great help." Perhaps, but not the voice which merely makes itself the mouthpiece of another's words, and only performs the duty of a reporter.

Consider this fact also. Those who have never attained their mental independence begin, in the first place, by following the leader in cases where everyone has deserted the leader; then, in the second place, they follow him in matters where the truth is still being investigated. However, the truth will never be discovered if we rest contented with discoveries already made. Besides, he who follows another not only discovers nothing but is not even investigating.

What then? Shall I not follow in the footsteps of my predecessors? I shall indeed use the old road, but if I find one that makes a shorter cut and is smoother to travel, I shall open the new road. Men who have made these discoveries before us are not our masters, but our guides. Truth lies open for all; it has not yet been monopolized. And there is plenty of it left even for posterity to discover. Farewell.

# Letter 29
# On a Promising Pupil

I grow in spirit and leap for joy and shake off my years and my blood runs warm again, whenever I understand, from your actions and your letters, how far you have outdone yourself; for as to the ordinary man, you left him in the rear long ago. If the farmer is pleased when his tree develops so that it bears fruit, if the shepherd takes pleasure in the increase of his flocks, if every man regards his pupil as though he discerned in him his own early manhood—what, then, do you think are the feelings of those who have trained a mind and moulded a young idea, when they see it suddenly grown to maturity?

I claim you for myself; you are my handiwork. When I saw your abilities, I laid my hand upon you, I exhorted you, I applied the goad and did not permit you to march lazily, but roused you continually. And now I do the same; but by this time I am cheering on one who is in the race and so in turn cheers me on.

"What else do you want of me, then?" you ask; "the will is still mine." Well, the will in this case is almost everything, and not merely the half, as in the proverb "A task once begun is half done." It is more than half, for the matter of which we speak is determined by the soul. Hence it is that the larger part of goodness is the will to become good. You know what I mean by a good man? One who is complete, finished—whom no constraint or need can render bad.

I see such a person in you, if only you go steadily on and bend to your task, and see to it that all your actions and words harmonize and correspond with each other and are stamped in the same mould. If a man's acts are out of harmony, his soul is crooked. Farewell.

# Letter 30
# On Allegiance to Virtue

You have promised to be a good man; you have enlisted under oath; that is the strongest chain which will hold you to a sound understanding. Any man will be but mocking you, if he declares that this is an effeminate and easy kind of soldiering. I will not have you deceived. The word of this most honourable compact are the same as the words of that most disgraceful one, to wit: "Through burning, imprisonment, or death by the sword."

From the men who hire out their strength for the arena, who eat and drink what they must pay for with their blood, security is taken that they will endure such trials even though they be unwilling; from you, that you will endure them willingly and with alacrity. The gladiator may lower his weapon and test the pity of the people; but you will neither lower your weapon nor beg for life. You must die erect and unyielding. Moreover, what profit is it to gain a few days or a few years? There is no discharge for us from the moment we are born.

"Then how can I free myself?" you ask. You cannot escape necessities, but you can overcome them

*By force a way is made.*

And this way will be afforded you by philosophy. Betake yourself therefore to philosophy if you would be safe, untroubled, happy, in fine, if you wish to be—and that is most important—free. There is no other way to attain this end.

Folly is low, abject, mean, slavish, and exposed to many of the cruellest passions. These passions, which are heavy taskmasters, sometimes ruling by turns, and sometimes together, can be banished from you by wisdom, which is the only real freedom. There is but one path leading thither, and it is a straight path; you will not go astray. Proceed with steady step, and if you would have all things under your control, put yourself under the control of reason; if reason becomes your ruler, you will become ruler over many. You will learn from her what you should undertake, and how it should be done; you will not blunder into things.

You can show me no man who knows how he began to crave that which he craves. He has not been led to that pass by forethought; he has been driven to it by impulse. Fortune attacks us as often as we attack Fortune. It is disgraceful, instead of proceeding ahead, to be carried along, and then suddenly, amid the whirlpool of events, to ask in a dazed way: "How did I get into this condition?" Farewell.

# Letter 31
# On Noble Aspirations

I shall indeed arrange for you, in careful order and narrow compass, the notes which you request. But consider whether you may not get more help from the customary method than from that which is now commonly called a "breviary," though in the good old days, when real Latin was spoken, it was called a "summary." The former is more necessary to one who is learning a subject, the latter to one who knows it. For the one teaches, the other stirs the memory. But I shall give you abundant opportunity for both. A man like you should not ask me for this authority or that; he who furnishes a voucher for his statements argues himself unknown.

I shall therefore write exactly what you wish, but I shall do it in my own way; until then, you have many authors whose works will presumably keep your ideas sufficiently in order. Pick up the list of the philosophers; that very act will compel you to wake up, when you see how many men have been working for your benefit. You will desire eagerly to be one of them yourself, for this is the most excellent quality that the noble soul has within itself, that it can be roused to honourable things.

No man of exalted gifts is pleased with that which is low and mean; the vision of great achievement summons him and uplifts him.

Just as the flame springs straight into the air and cannot be cabined or kept down any more than it can repose in quiet, so our soul is always in motion, and the more ardent it is, the greater its motion and activity. But happy is the man who has given it this impulse toward better things! He will place himself beyond the jurisdiction of chance; he will wisely control prosperity; he will lessen adversity, and will despise what others hold in admiration.

It is the quality of a great soul to scorn great things and to prefer that which is ordinary rather than that which is too great. For the one condition is useful and life-giving; but the other does harm just because it is excessive. Similarly, too rich a soil makes the grain fall flat, branches break down under too heavy a load, excessive productiveness does not bring fruit to ripeness. This is the case with the soul also; for it is ruined by uncontrolled prosperity, which is used not only to the detriment of others, but also to the detriment of itself.

What enemy was ever so insolent to any opponent as are their pleasures to certain men? The only excuse that we can allow for the incontinence and mad lust of these men is the fact that they suffer the evils which they have inflicted upon others. And they are rightly harassed by this madness, because desire must have unbounded space for its excursions, if it transgresses nature's mean. For this has its bounds, but waywardness and the acts that spring from wilful lust are without boundaries.

Utility measures our needs; but by what standard can you check the superfluous? It is for this reason that men sink themselves in pleasures, and they cannot do without them when once they have become accustomed to them, and for this reason they are most wretched, because they have reached such a pass that what was once superfluous to them has become indispensable. And so they are the slaves of their pleasures instead of enjoying them; they even love their own ills, —and that is the worst ill of all!

Then it is that the height of unhappiness is reached, when men are not only attracted, but even pleased, by shameful things, and when there is no longer any room for a cure, now that those things which once were vices have become habits. Farewell.

# Letter 32
# On the Proper Style for a Philosopher's Discourse

I thank you for writing to me so often; for you are revealing your real self to me in the only way you can. I never receive a letter from you without being in your company forthwith. If the pictures of our absent friends are pleasing to us, though they only refresh the memory and lighten our longing by a solace that is unreal and unsubstantial, how much more pleasant is a letter, which brings us real traces, real evidences, of an absent friend! For that which is sweetest when we meet face to face is afforded by the impress of a friend's hand upon his letter—recognition.

You write me that you heard a lecture by the philosopher Serapio, when he landed at your present place of residence. "He is wont," you say, "to wrench up his words with a mighty rush, and he does not let them flow forth one by one, but makes them crowd and dash upon each other. For the words come in such quantity that a single voice is inadequate to utter them." I do not approve of this in a philosopher; his speech, like his life, should be composed; and nothing that rushes headlong and is hurried is well ordered. That is why, in Homer, the rapid style, which sweeps down without a break like a snow-squall, is assigned to the younger speaker; from the old man eloquence flows gently, sweeter than honey.

Therefore, mark my words; that forceful manner of speech, rapid and copious, is more suited to a mountebank than to a man who is discussing and teaching an important and serious subject. But I object just as strongly that he should drip out his words as that he should go at top speed; he should neither keep the ear on the stretch, nor deafen it. For that poverty-stricken and thin-spun style also makes the audience less attentive because they are weary of its stammering slowness; nevertheless, the word which has been long awaited sinks in more easily than the word which flits past us on the wing. Finally, people speak of "handing down" precepts to their pupils; but one is not "handing down" that which eludes the grasp.

Besides, speech that deals with the truth should be unadorned and plain. This popular style has nothing to do with the truth; its aim is to impress the common herd, to ravish heedless ears by its speed; it does not offer itself for discussion, but snatches itself away from discussion. But how can that speech govern others which cannot itself be governed? May I not also remark that all speech which is employed for the purpose of healing our minds, ought to sink into us? Remedies do not avail unless they remain in the system.

Besides, this sort of speech contains a great deal of sheer emptiness; it has more sound than power. My terrors should be quieted, my irritations soothed, my illusions shaken off, my indulgences checked, my greed rebuked. And which of these cures can be brought about in a hurry? What physician can heal his patient on a flying visit? May I add that such a jargon of confused and ill-chosen words cannot afford pleasure, either?

No; but just as you are well satisfied, in the majority of cases, to have seen through tricks which you did not think could possibly be done, so in the case of these word-gymnasts to have heard them once is amply sufficient. For what can a man desire to learn or to imitate in them? What is he to think of their souls, when their speech is sent into the charge in utter disorder, and cannot be kept in hand?

Just as, when you run down hill, you cannot stop at the point where you had decided to stop, but your steps are carried along by the momentum of your body and are borne beyond the place where you wished to halt; so this speed of speech has no control over itself, nor is it seemly for philosophy; since philosophy should carefully place her words, not fling them out, and should proceed step by step.

"What then?" you say; "should not philosophy sometimes take a loftier tone?" Of course she should; but dignity of character should be preserved, and this is stripped away by such violent and excessive force. Let philosophy possess great forces, but kept well under control; let her stream flow unceasingly, but never become a torrent. And I should hardly allow even to an orator a rapidity of speech like this, which cannot be called back, which goes lawlessly ahead; for how could it be followed by jurors, who are often inexperienced and untrained? Even when the orator is carried away by his desire to show off his powers, or by uncontrollable emotion, even then he should not quicken his pace and heap up words to an extent greater than the ear can endure.

You will be acting rightly, therefore, if you do not regard those men who seek how much they may say, rather than how they shall say it, and if for yourself you choose, provided a choice must be made, to speak as Publius Vinicius the stammerer does. When Asellius was asked how Vinicius spoke, he replied: "Gradually"! (It was a remark of Geminus Varius, by the way: "I don't see how you can call that man 'eloquent'; why, he can't get out three words together.") Why, then, should you not choose to speak as Vinicius does? Though of course some wag may cross your path, like the person who said, when Vinicius was dragging out his words one by one, as if he were dictating and not speaking, "Say, haven't you anything to say?" And yet that were the better choice, for the rapidity of Quintus Haterius, the most famous orator of his age, is, in my opinion, to be avoided by a man of sense. Haterius never hesitated, never paused; he made only one start, and only one stop.

However, I suppose that certain styles of speech are more or less suitable to nations also; in a Greek you can put up with the unrestrained style, but we Romans, even when writing, have become accustomed to separate our words. And our compatriot Cicero, with whom Roman oratory sprang into prominence, was also a slow pacer. The Roman language is more inclined to take stock of itself, to weigh, and to offer something worth weighing.

Fabianius, a man noteworthy because of his life, his knowledge, and, less important than either of these, his eloquence also, used to discuss a subject with dispatch rather than with haste; hence you might call it ease rather than speed. I approve this quality in the wise man; but I do not demand it; only let his speech proceed unhampered, though I prefer that it should be deliberately uttered rather than spouted.

However, I have this further reason for frightening you away from the latter malady, namely, that you could only be successful in practicing this style by losing your sense of modesty; you would have to rub all shame from your countenance, and refuse to hear yourself speak. For that heedless flow will carry with it many expressions which you would wish to criticize.

And, I repeat, you could not attain it and at the same time preserve your sense of shame. Moreover, you would need to practice every day, and transfer your attention from subject matter to words. But words, even if they came to you readily and flowed without any exertion on your part, yet would have to be kept under control. For just as a less ostentatious gait becomes a philosopher, so does a restrained style of speech, far removed from boldness. Therefore, the ultimate kernel of my remarks is this: I bid you be slow of speech. Farewell

# Letter 33
# On the God within Us

You are doing an excellent thing, one which will be wholesome for you, if, as you write me, you are persisting in your effort to attain sound understanding; it is foolish to pray for this when you can acquire it from yourself. We do not need to uplift our hands towards heaven, or to beg the keeper of a temple to let us approach his idol's ear, as if in this way our prayers were more likely to be heard. God is near you, he is with you, he is within you. This is what I mean, Lucilius: a holy spirit indwells within us, one who marks our good and bad deeds, and is our guardian. As we treat this spirit, so are we treated by it. Indeed, no man can be good without the help of God. Can one rise superior to fortune unless God helps him to rise? He it is that gives noble and upright counsel. In each good man

*A god doth dwell, but what god know we not.*

If ever you have come upon a grove that is full of ancient trees which have grown to an unusual height, shutting out a view of the sky by a veil of pleached and intertwining branches, then the loftiness of the forest, the seclusion of the spot, and your marvel at the thick unbroken shade in the midst of the open spaces, will prove to you the presence of deity. Or if a cave, made by the deep crumbling of the rocks, holds up a mountain on its arch, a place not built with hands but hollowed out into such spaciousness by natural causes, your soul will be deeply moved by a certain intimation of the existence of God. We worship the sources of mighty rivers; we erect altars at places where great streams burst suddenly from hidden sources; we adore springs of hot water as divine, and consecrate certain pools because of their dark waters or their immeasurable depth.

If you see a man who is unterrified in the midst of dangers, untouched by desires, happy in adversity, peaceful amid the storm, who looks down upon men from a higher plane, and views the gods on a footing of equality, will not a feeling of reverence for him steal over you, will you not say: "This quality is too great and too lofty to be regarded as resembling this petty body in which it dwells? A divine power has descended upon that man."

When a soul rises superior to other souls, when it is under control, when it passes through every experience as if it were of small account, when it smiles at our fears and at our prayers, it is stirred by a force from heaven. A thing like this cannot stand upright unless it be propped by the divine. Therefore, a greater part of it abides in that place from whence it came down to earth. Just as the rays of the sun do indeed touch the earth, but still abide at the source from which they are sent; even so the great and hallowed soul, which has come down in order that we may have a nearer knowledge of divinity, does indeed associate with us, but still cleaves to its origin; on that source it depends, thither it turns its gaze and strives to go, and it concerns itself with our doings only as a being superior to ourselves.

What, then, is such a soul? One which is resplendent with no external good, but only with its own. For what is more foolish than to praise in a man the qualities which come from without? And what is more insane than to marvel at characteristics which may at the next instant be passed on to someone else? A golden bit does not make a better horse. The lion with gilded mane, in process of being trained and forced by weariness to endure the decoration, is sent into the arena in quite a different way from the wild lion whose spirit is unbroken; the latter, indeed, bold in his attack, as nature wished him to be, impressive because of his wild appearance— and it is his glory that none can look upon him without fear—is favoured in preference to the other lion, that languid and gilded brute.

No man ought to glory except in that which is his own. We praise a vine if it makes the shoots teem with increase, if by its weight it bends to the ground the very poles which hold its fruit; would any man prefer to this vine one from which golden grapes and golden leaves hang down? In a vine the virtue peculiarly its own is fertility; in man also we should praise that which is his own. Suppose that he has a retinue of comely slaves and a beautiful house, that his farm is large and large his income, none of these things is in the man himself; they are all on the outside.

Praise the quality in him which cannot be given or snatched away, that which is the peculiar property of the man. Do you ask what this is? It is soul, and reason brought to perfection in the soul. For man is a reasoning animal. Therefore, man's highest good is attained, if he has fulfilled the good for which nature designed him at birth.

And what is it which this reason demands of him? The easiest thing in the world—to live in accordance with his own nature. But this is turned into a hard task by the general madness of mankind; we push one another into vice. And how can a man be recalled to salvation, when he has none to restrain him, and all mankind to urge him on? Farewell.

# Letter 34

# On Values

Has that friend of yours already made you believe that he is a good man? And yet it is impossible in so short a time for one either to become good or be known as such. Do you know what kind of man I now mean when I speak of "a good man"? I mean one of the second grade, like your friend. For one of the first class perhaps springs into existence, like the phoenix, only once in five hundred years. And it is not surprising, either, that greatness develops only at long intervals; Fortune often brings into being commonplace powers, which are born to please the mob; but she holds up for our approval that which is extraordinary by the very fact that she makes it rare.

This man, however, of whom you spoke, is still far from the state which he professes to have reached. And if he knew what it meant to be "a good man," he would not yet believe himself such; perhaps he would even despair of his ability to become good. "But," you say, "he thinks ill of evil men." Well, so do evil men themselves; and there is no worse penalty for vice than the fact that it is dissatisfied with itself and all its fellows.

"But he hates those who make an ungoverned use of great power suddenly acquired." I retort that he will do the same thing as soon as he acquires the same powers. In the case of many men, their vices, being powerless, escape notice; although, as soon as the persons in question have become satisfied with their own strength, the vices will be no less daring than those which prosperity has already disclosed.

These men simply lack the means whereby they may unfold their wickedness. Similarly, one can handle even a poisonous snake while it is stiff with cold; the poison is not lacking; it is merely numbed into inaction. In the case of many men, their cruelty, ambition, and indulgence only lack the favour of Fortune to make them dare crimes that would match the worst. That their wishes are the same you will in a moment discover, in this way: give them the power equal to their wishes.

Do you remember how, when you declared that a certain person was under your influence, I pronounced him fickle and a bird of passage, and said that you held him not by the foot but merely by a wing? Was I mistaken? You grasped him only by a feather; he left it in your hands and escaped. You know what an exhibition he afterwards made of himself before you, how many of the things he attempted were to recoil upon his own head. He did not see that in endangering others he was tottering to his own downfall. He did not reflect how burdensome were the objects which he was bent upon attaining, even if they were not superfluous.

Therefore, with regard to the objects which we pursue, and for which we strive with great effort, we should note this truth; either there is nothing desirable in them, or the undesirable is preponderant. Some objects are superfluous; others are not worth the price we pay for them. But we do not see this clearly, and we regard things as free gifts when they really cost us very dear.

Our stupidity may be clearly proved by the fact that we hold that "buying" refers only to the objects for which we pay cash, and we regard as free gifts the things for which we spend our very selves. These we should refuse to buy, if we were compelled to give in payment for them our houses or some attractive and profitable estate; but we are eager to attain them at the cost of anxiety, of danger, and of lost honour, personal freedom, and time; so true it is that each man regards nothing as cheaper than himself.

Let us therefore act, in all our plans and conduct, just as we are accustomed to act whenever we approach a huckster who has certain wares for sale; let us see how much we must pay for that which we crave. Very often the things that cost nothing cost us the most heavily; I can show you many objects the quest and acquisition of which have wrested freedom from our hands. We should belong to ourselves, if only these things did not belong to us. I would therefore have you reflect thus, not only when it is a question of gain, but also when it is a question of loss. "This object is bound to perish." Yes, it was a mere extra; you will live without it just as easily as you have lived before. If you have possessed it for a long time, you lose it after you have had your fill of it; if you have not possessed it long, then you lose it before you have become wedded to it. "You will have less money." Yes, and less trouble.

"Less influence." Yes, and less envy. Look about you and note the things that drive us mad, which we lose with a flood of tears; you will perceive that it is not the loss that troubles us with reference to these things, but a notion of loss. No one feels that they have been lost, but his mind tells him that it has been so. He that owns himself has lost nothing. But how few men are blessed with ownership of self! Farewell.

# Letter 35
# On Sophistical Argumentation

You complain that in your part of the world there is a scant supply of books. But it is quality, rather than quantity, that matters; a limited list of reading benefits; a varied assortment serves only for delight. He who would arrive at the appointed end must follow a single road and not wander through many ways. What you suggest is not travelling; it is mere tramping.

"But," you say, "I should rather have you give me advice than books." Still, I am ready to send you all the books I have, to ransack the whole storehouse. If it were possible, I should join you there myself; and were it not for the hope that you will soon complete your term of office, I should have imposed upon myself this old man's journey; no Scylla or Charybdis or their storied straits could have frightened me away. I should not only have crossed over, but should have been willing to swim over those waters, provided that I could greet you and judge in your presence how much you had grown in spirit.

Your desire, however, that I should dispatch to you my own writings does not make me think myself learned, any more than a request for my picture would flatter my beauty. I know that it is due to your charity rather than to your judgment. And even if it is the result of judgment, it was charity that forced the judgment upon you.

But whatever the quality of my works may be, read them as if I were still seeking, and were not aware of, the truth, and were seeking it obstinately, too. For I have sold myself to no man; I bear the name of no master. I give much credit to the judgment of great men; but I claim something also for my own. For these men, too, have left to us, not positive discoveries, but problems whose solution is still to be sought. They might perhaps have discovered the essentials, had they not sought the superfluous also.

They lost much time in quibbling about words and in sophistical argumentation; all that sort of thing exercises the wit to no purpose.

We tie knots and bind up words in double meanings, and then try to untie them.

Have we leisure enough for this? Do we already know how to live, or die? We should rather proceed with our whole souls towards the point where it is our duty to take heed lest things, as well as words, deceive us.

Why, pray, do you discriminate between similar words, when nobody is ever deceived by them except during the discussion? It is things that lead us astray: it is between things that you must discriminate. We embrace evil instead of good; we pray for something opposite to that which we have prayed for in the past. Our prayers clash with our prayers, our plans with our plans.

How closely flattery resembles friendship! It not only apes friendship, but outdoes it, passing it in the race; with wide-open and indulgent ears it is welcomed and sinks to the depths of the heart, and it is pleasing precisely wherein it does harm. Show me how I may be able to see through this resemblance! An enemy comes to me full of compliments, in the guise of a friend. Vices creep into our hearts under the name of virtues, rashness lurks beneath the appellation of bravery, moderation is called sluggishness, and the coward is regarded as prudent; there is great danger if we go astray in these matters. So stamp them with special labels.

Then, too, the man who is asked whether he has horns on his head is not such a fool as to feel for them on his forehead, nor again so silly or dense that you can persuade him by means of argumentation, no matter how subtle, that he does not know the facts. Such quibbles are just as harmlessly deceptive as the juggler's cup and dice, in which it is the very trickery that pleases me. But show me how the trick is done, and I have lost my interest therein. And I hold the same opinion about these tricky word-plays; for by what other name can one call such sophistries? Not to know them does no harm, and mastering them does no good.

At any rate, if you wish to sift doubtful meanings of this kind, teach us that the happy man is not he whom the crowd deems happy, namely, he into whose coffers mighty sums have flowed, but he whose possessions are all in his soul, who is upright and exalted, who spurns inconstancy, who sees no man with whom he wishes to change places, who rates men only at their value as men, who takes Nature for his teacher, conforming to her laws and living as she commands, whom no violence can deprive of his possessions, who turns evil into good, is unerring in judgment, unshaken, unafraid, who may be moved by force but never moved to distraction, whom Fortune when she hurls at him with all her might the deadliest missile in her armoury, may graze, though rarely, but never wound. For Fortune's other missiles, with which she vanquishes mankind in general, rebound from such a one, like hail which rattles on the roof with no harm to the dweller therein, and then melts away.

Why do you bore me with that which you yourself call the "liar fallacy," about which so many books have been written? Come now, suppose that my whole life is a lie; prove that to be wrong and, if you are sharp enough, bring that back to the truth. At present it holds things to be essential of which the greater part is superfluous. And even that which is not superfluous is of no significance in respect to its power of making one fortunate and blest. For if a thing be necessary, it does not follow that it is a good. Else we degrade the meaning of "good," if we apply that name to bread and barley-porridge and other commodities without which we cannot live.

The good must in every case be necessary; but that which is necessary is not in every case a good, since certain very paltry things are indeed necessary. No one is to such an extent ignorant of the noble meaning of the word "good," as to debase it to the level of these humdrum utilities.

What, then? Shall you not rather transfer your efforts to making it clear to all men that the search for the superfluous means a great outlay of time, and that many have gone through life merely accumulating the instruments of life? Consider individuals, survey men in general; there is none whose life does not look forward to the morrow.

"What harm is there in this," you ask? Infinite harm; for such persons do not live, but are preparing to live. They postpone everything. Even if we paid strict attention, life would soon get ahead of us; but as we are now, life finds us lingering and passes us by as if it belonged to another, and though it ends on the final day, it perishes every day.

But I must not exceed the bounds of a letter, which ought not to fill the reader's left hand. So I shall postpone to another day our case against the hair-splitters, those over-subtle fellows who make argumentation supreme instead of subordinate. Farewell.

# Letter 36
# On the Shortness of Life

A man is indeed lazy and careless, my dear Lucilius, if he is reminded of a friend only by seeing some landscape which stirs the memory; and yet there are times when the old familiar haunts stir up a sense of loss that has been stored away in the soul, not bringing back dead memories, but rousing them from their dormant state, just as the sight of a lost friend's favourite slave, or his cloak, or his house, renews the mourner's grief, even though it has been softened by time.

Now, lo and behold, Campania, and especially Naples and your beloved Pompeii, struck me, when I viewed them, with a wonderfully fresh sense of longing for you. You stand in full view before my eyes. I am on the point of parting from you. I see you choking down your tears and resisting without success the emotions that well up at the very moment when you try to check them. I seem to have lost you but a moment ago. For what is not "but a moment ago" when one begins to use the memory?

It was but a moment ago that I sat, as a lad, in the school of the philosopher Sotion, but a moment ago that I began to plead in the courts, but a moment ago that I lost the desire to plead, but a moment ago that I lost the ability. Infinitely swift is the flight of time, as those see more clearly who are looking backwards. For when we are intent on the present, we do not notice it, so gentle is the passage of time's headlong flight.

Do you ask the reason for this? All past time is in the same place; it all presents the same aspect to us, it lies together. Everything slips into the same abyss. Besides, an event which in its entirety is of brief compass cannot contain long intervals. The time which we spend in living is but a point, nay, even less than a point. But this point of time, infinitesimal as it is, nature has mocked by making it seem outwardly of longer duration; she has taken one portion thereof and made it infancy, another childhood, another youth, another the gradual slope, so to speak, from youth to old age, and old age itself is still another. How many steps for how short a climb!

It was but a moment ago that I saw you off on your journey; and yet this "moment ago" makes up a goodly share of our existence, which is so brief, we should reflect, that it will soon come to an end altogether. In other years time did not seem to me to go so swiftly; now, it seems fast beyond belief, perhaps, because I feel that the finish-line is moving closer to me, or it may be that I have begun to take heed and reckon up my losses.

For this reason I am all the more angry that some men claim the major portion of this time for superfluous things—time which, no matter how carefully it is guarded, cannot suffice even for necessary things. Cicero declared that if the number of his days were doubled, he should not have time to read the lyric poets. And you may rate the dialecticians in the same class; but they are foolish in a more melancholy way. The lyric poets are avowedly frivolous; but the dialecticians believe that they are themselves engaged upon serious business.

I do not deny that one must cast a glance at dialectic; but it ought to be a mere glance, a sort of greeting from the threshold, merely that one may not be deceived, or judge these pursuits to contain any hidden matters of great worth.

Why do you torment yourself and lose weight over some problem which it is more clever to have scorned than to solve? When a soldier is undisturbed and travelling at his ease, he can hunt for trifles along his way; but when the enemy is closing in on the rear, and a command is given to quicken the pace, necessity makes him throw away everything which he picked up in moments of peace and leisure.

I have no time to investigate disputed inflections of words, or to try my cunning upon them.

> *Behold the gathering clans, the fast-shut gates,*
> *And weapons whetted ready for the war.*

I need a stout heart to hear without flinching this din of battle which sounds round about.

And all would rightly think me mad if, when graybeards and women were heaping up rocks for the fortifications, when the armour-clad youths inside the gates were awaiting, or even demanding, the order for a sally, when the spears of the foemen were quivering in our gates and the very ground was rocking with mines and subterranean passages—I say, they would rightly think me mad if I were to sit idle, putting such petty posers as this: "What you have not lost, you have. But you have not lost any horns. Therefore, you have horns," or other tricks constructed after the model of this piece of sheer silliness.

And yet I may well seem in your eyes no less mad, if I spend my energies on that sort of thing; for even now I am in a state of siege. And yet, in the former case it would be merely a peril from the outside that threatened me, and a wall that sundered me from the foe; as it is now, death-dealing perils are in my very presence. I have no time for such nonsense; a mighty undertaking is on my hands. What am I to do? Death is on my trail, and life is fleeting away; teach me something with which to face these troubles. Bring it to pass that I shall cease trying to escape from death, and that life may cease to escape from me. Give me courage to meet hardships; make me calm in the face of the unavoidable. Relax the straitened limits of the time which is allotted me. Show me that the good in life does not depend upon life's length, but upon the use we make of it; also, that it is possible, or rather usual, for a man who has lived long to have lived too little. Say to me when I lie down to sleep: "You may not wake again!" And when I have waked: "You may not go to sleep again!" Say to me when I go forth from my house: "You may not return!" And when I return: "You may never go forth again!"

You are mistaken if you think that only on an ocean voyage there is a very slight space between life and death. No, the distance between is just as narrow everywhere. It is not everywhere that death shows himself so near at hand; yet everywhere he is as near at hand.

Rid me of these shadowy terrors; then you will more easily deliver to me the instruction for which I have prepared myself. At our birth nature made us teachable, and gave us reason, not perfect, but capable of being perfected.

Discuss for me justice, duty, thrift, and that twofold purity, both the purity which abstains from another's person, and that which takes care of one's own self. If you will only refuse to lead me along by-paths, I shall more easily reach the goal at which I am aiming. For, as the tragic poet says:

The language of truth is simple. We should not, therefore, make that language intricate; since there is nothing less fitting for a soul of great endeavour than such crafty cleverness. Farewell.

# Letter 37
# On Choosing our Teachers

What is this force, Lucilius, that drags us in one direction when we are aiming in another, urging us on to the exact place from which we long to withdraw? What is it that wrestles with our spirit, and does not allow us to desire anything once for all? We veer from plan to plan. None of our wishes is free, none is unqualified, none is lasting.

"But it is the fool," you say, "who is inconsistent; nothing suits him for long." But how or when can we tear ourselves away from this folly? No man by himself has sufficient strength to rise above it; he needs a helping hand, and some one to extricate him.

Epicurus remarks that certain men have worked their way to the truth without any one's assistance, carving out their own passage. And he gives special praise to these, for their impulse has come from within, and they have forged to the front by themselves. Again, he says, there are others who need outside help, who will not proceed unless someone leads the way, but who will follow faithfully. Of these, he says, Metrodorus was one; this type of man is also excellent, but belongs to the second grade. We ourselves are not of that first class, either; we shall be well treated if we are admitted into the second. Nor need you despise a man who can gain salvation only with the assistance of another; the will to be saved means a great deal, too.

You will find still another class of man—and a class not to be despised—who can be forced and driven into righteousness, who do not need a guide as much as they require someone to encourage and, as it were, to force them along. This is the third variety. If you ask me for a man of this pattern also, Epicurus tells us that Hermarchus was such. And of the two last-named classes, he is more ready to congratulate the one, but he feels more respect for the other; for although both reached the same goal, it is a greater credit to have brought about the same result with the more difficult material upon which to work.

Suppose that two buildings have been erected, unlike as to their foundations, but equal in height and in grandeur. One is built on faultless ground, and the process of erection goes right ahead. In the other case, the foundations have exhausted the building materials, for they have been sunk into soft and shifting ground and much labour has been wasted in reaching the solid rock. As one looks at both of them, one sees clearly what progress the former has made but the larger and more difficult part of the latter is hidden.

So with men's dispositions; some are pliable and easy to manage, but others have to be laboriously wrought out by hand, so to speak, and are wholly employed in the making of their own foundations. I should accordingly deem more fortunate the man who has never had any trouble with himself; but the other, I feel, has deserved better of himself, who has won a victory over the meanness of his own nature, and has not gently led himself, but has wrestled his way, to wisdom.

You may be sure that this refractory nature, which demands much toil, has been implanted in us. There are obstacles in our path; so let us fight, and call to our assistance some helpers. "Whom," you say, "shall I call upon? Shall it be this man or that?" There is another choice also open to you; you may go to the ancients; for they have the time to help you. We can get assistance not only from the living, but from those of the past.

Let us choose, however, from among the living, not men who pour forth their words with the greatest glibness, turning out commonplaces and holding. as it were, their own little private exhibitions, —not these, I say, but men who teach us by their lives, men who tell us what we ought to do and then prove it by practice, who show us what we should avoid, and then are never caught doing that which they have ordered us to avoid.

Choose as a guide one whom you will admire more when you see him act than when you hear him speak.

Of course I would not prevent you from listening also to those philosophers who are wont to hold public meetings and discussions, provided they appear before the people for the express purpose of improving themselves and others, and do not practice their profession for the sake of self-seeking. For what is baser than philosophy courting applause? Does the sick man praise the surgeon while he is operating?

In silence and with reverent awe submit to the cure. Even though you cry applause, I shall listen to your cries as if you were groaning when your sores were touched. Do you wish to bear witness that you are attentive, that you are stirred by the grandeur of the subject? You may do this at the proper time; I shall of course allow you to pass judgment and cast a vote as to the better course. Pythagoras made his pupils keep silence for five years; do you think that they had the right on that account to break out immediately into applause?

How mad is he who leaves the lecture-room in a happy frame of mind simply because of applause from the ignorant! Why do you take pleasure in being praised by men whom you yourself cannot praise? Fabianus used to give popular talks, but his audience listened with self-control. Occasionally a loud shout of praise would burst forth, but it was prompted by the greatness of his subject, and not by the sound of oratory that slipped forth pleasantly and softly.

There should be a difference between the applause of the theatre and the applause of the school; and there is a certain decency even in bestowing praise. If you mark them carefully, all acts are always significant, and you can gauge character by even the most trifling signs. The lecherous man is revealed by his gait, by a movement of the hand, sometimes by a single answer, by his touching his head with a finger, by the shifting of his eye. The scamp is shown up by his laugh; the madman by his face and general appearance. These qualities become known by certain marks; but you can tell the character of every man when you see how he gives and receives praise.

The philosopher's audience, from this corner and that, stretch forth admiring hands, and sometimes the adoring crowd almost hang over the lecturer's head. But, if you really understand, that is not praise; it is merely applause. These outcries should be left for the arts which aim to please the crowd; let philosophy be worshipped in silence.

Young men, indeed, must sometimes have free play to follow their impulses, but it should only be at times when they act from impulse, and when they cannot force themselves to be silent. Such praise as that gives a certain kind of encouragement to the hearers themselves, and acts as a spur to the youthful mind. But let them be roused to the matter, and not to the style; otherwise, eloquence does them harm, making them enamoured of itself, and not of the subject.

I shall postpone this topic for the present; it demands a long and special investigation, to show how the public should be addressed, what indulgences should be allowed to a speaker on a public occasion, and what should be allowed to the crowd itself in the presence of the speaker. There can be no doubt that philosophy has suffered a loss, now that she has exposed her charms for sale. But she can still be viewed in her sanctuary, if her exhibitor is a priest and not a pedlar. Farewell.

# Letter 38
# On Quiet and Study

Beshrew me if I think anything more requisite than silence for a man who secludes himself in order to study! Imagine what a variety of noises reverberates about my ears! I have lodgings right over a bathing establishment. So picture to yourself the assortment of sounds, which are strong enough to make me hate my very powers of hearing! When your strenuous gentleman, for example, is exercising himself by flourishing leaden weights; when he is working hard, or else pretends to be working hard, I can hear him grunt; and whenever he releases his imprisoned breath, I can hear him panting in wheezy and high-pitched tones. Or perhaps I notice some lazy fellow, content with a cheap rubdown, and hear the crack of the pummelling hand on his shoulder, varying in sound according as the hand is laid on flat or hollow. Then, perhaps, a professional comes along, shouting out the score; that is the finishing touch.

Add to this the arresting of an occasional roisterer or pickpocket, the racket of the man who always likes to hear his own voice in the bathroom, or the enthusiast who plunges into the swimming-tank with unconscionable noise and splashing. Besides all those whose voices, if nothing else, are good, imagine the hair-plucker with his penetrating, shrill voice—for purposes of advertisement—continually giving it vent and never holding his tongue except when he is plucking the armpits and making his victim yell instead. Then the cakeseller with his varied cries, the sausageman, the confectioner, and all the vendors of food hawking their wares, each with his own distinctive intonation.

So you say: "What iron nerves or deadened ears, you must have, if your mind can hold out amid so many noises, so various and so discordant, when our friend Chrysippus is brought to his death by the continual good-morrows that greet him!" But I assure you that this racket means no more to me than the sound of waves or falling water; although you will remind me that a certain tribe once moved their city merely because they could not endure the din of a Nile cataract.

Words seem to distract me more than noises; for words demand attention, but noises merely fill the ears and beat upon them. Among the sounds that din round me without distracting, I include passing carriages, a machinist in the same block, a saw-sharpener near by, or some fellow who is demonstrating with little pipes and flutes at the Trickling Fountain, shouting rather than singing.

Furthermore, an intermittent noise upsets me more than a steady one. But by this time I have toughened my nerves against all that sort of thing, so that I can endure even a boatswain marking the time in high-pitched tones for his crew. For I force my mind to concentrate, and keep it from straying to things outside itself; all outdoors may be bedlam, provided that there is no disturbance within, provided that fear is not wrangling with desire in my breast, provided that meanness and lavishness are not at odds, one harassing the other. For of what benefit is a quiet neighbourhood, if our emotions are in an uproar?

*'Twas night, and all the world was lulled to rest.*

This is not true; for no real rest can be found when reason has not done the lulling. Night brings our troubles to the light, rather than banishes them; it merely changes the form of our worries. For even when we seek slumber, our sleepless moments are as harassing as the daytime. Real tranquillity is the state reached by an unperverted mind when it is relaxed.

Think of the unfortunate man who courts sleep by surrendering his spacious mansion to silence, who, that his ear may be disturbed by no sound, bids the whole retinue of his slaves be quiet and that whoever approaches him shall walk on tiptoe; he tosses from this side to that and seeks a fitful slumber amid his frettings!

He complains that he has heard sounds, when he has not heard them at all. The reason, you ask? His soul's in an uproar; it must be soothed, and its rebellious murmuring checked. You need not suppose that the soul is at peace when the body is still. Sometimes quiet means disquiet. We must therefore rouse ourselves to action and busy ourselves with interests that are good, as often as we are in the grasp of an uncontrollable sluggishness.

Great generals, when they see that their men are mutinous, check them by some sort of labour or keep them busy with small forays. The much occupied man has no time for wantonness, and it is an obvious commonplace that the evils of leisure can be shaken off by hard work. Although people may often have thought that I sought seclusion because I was disgusted with politics and regretted my hapless and thankless position, yet, in the retreat to which apprehension and weariness have driven me, my ambition sometimes develops afresh. For it is not because my ambition was rooted out that it has abated, but because it was wearied or perhaps even put out of temper by the failure of its plans.

And so with luxury, also, which sometimes seems to have departed, and then when we have made a profession of frugality, begins to fret us and, amid our economies, seeks the pleasures which we have merely left but not condemned. Indeed, the more stealthily it comes, the greater is its force. For all unconcealed vices are less serious; a disease also is farther on the road to being cured when it breaks forth from concealment and manifests its power. So with greed, ambition, and the other evils of the mind—you may be sure that they do most harm when they are hidden behind a pretence of soundness.

Men think that we are in retirement, and yet we are not. For if we have sincerely retired, and have sounded the signal for retreat, and have scorned outward attractions, then, as I remarked above, no outward thing will distract us; no music of men or of birds can interrupt good thoughts, when they have once become steadfast and sure.

The mind which starts at words or at chance sounds is unstable and has not yet withdrawn into itself; it contains within itself an element of anxiety and rooted fear, and this makes one a prey to care, as our Vergil says:

> *I, whom of yore no dart could cause to flee,*
> *Nor Greeks, with crowded lines of infantry,*
> *Now shake at every sound, and fear the air,*
> *Both for my child and for the load I bear.*

This man in his first state is wise; he blenches neither at the brandished spear, nor at the clashing armour of the serried foe, nor at the din of the stricken city. This man in his second state lacks knowledge fearing for his own concerns, he pales at every sound; any cry is taken for the battle-shout and overthrows him; the slightest disturbance renders him breathless with fear. It is the load that makes him afraid.

Select anyone you please from among your favourites of Fortune, trailing their many responsibilities, carrying their many burdens, and you will behold a picture of Vergil's hero, "fearing both for his child and for the load he bears." You may therefore be sure that you are at peace with yourself, when no noise reaches you, when no word shakes you out of yourself, whether it be of flattery or of threat, or merely an empty sound buzzing about you with unmeaning din.

"What then?" you say, "is it not sometimes a simpler matter just to avoid the uproar?" I admit this. Accordingly, I shall change from my present quarters. I merely wished to test myself and to give myself practice. Why need I be tormented any longer, when Ulysses found so simple a cure for his comrades even against the songs of the Sirens? Farewell.

# Letter 39

# On Being

*Tim Ferriss here. Pardon the interruption, but what follows is a very strange letter. Seneca is usually concrete, relatable, and very tactical. For most people, Letter 58, titled "On Being," is none of these things.*

*Still, it's here because we want you to have the complete experience. Just be forewarned that Seneca goes a bit off the reservation. I found it jarring and wished I'd had a warning, hence this short note. You might think of Letter 58 as Seneca on mushrooms. If not your thing, feel free to skip to Letter 59. I usually do.*

*And there's another abstract letter coming up in Letter 65, titled "On The First Cause." Please feel free to skip that letter—or any letter, for that matter—that doesn't strike your fancy.*

*With all that said, enjoy.*

How scant of words our language is, nay, how poverty-stricken, I have not fully understood until today. We happened to be speaking of Plato, and a thousand subjects came up for discussion, which needed names and yet possessed none; and there were certain others which once possessed, but have since lost, their words because we were too nice about their use. But who can endure to be nice in the midst of poverty?

There is an insect, called by the Greeks *oestrus*, which drives cattle wild and scatters them all over their pasturing grounds; it used to be called *asilus* in our language, as you may believe on the authority of Vergil:

> Near Silarus groves, and eke Alburnus' shades
> Of green-clad oak-trees flits an insect, named
> Asilus *by the Romans; in the Greek*
> *The word is rendered* oestrus. *With a rough*
> *And strident sound it buzzes and drives wild*
> *The terror-stricken herds throughout the woods.*

By which I infer that the word has gone out of use. And, not to keep you waiting too long, there were certain uncompounded words current, like *cernere ferro inter se*, as will be proved again by Vergil:

> Great heroes, born in various lands, had come
> To settle matters *mutually with the sword.*

This "settling matters" we now express by *decernere*. The plain word has become obsolete.

The ancients used to say *iusso*, instead of *iussero*, in conditional clauses. You need not take my word, but you may turn again to Vergil:

> *The other soldiers shall conduct the fight*
> With me, where I shall bid.

It is not in my purpose to show, by this array of examples, how much time I have wasted on the study of language; I merely wish you to understand how many words, that were current in the works of Ennius and Accius, have become mouldy with age; while even in the case of Vergil, whose works are explored daily, some of his words have been filched away from us.

You will say, I suppose: "What is the purpose and meaning of this preamble?" I shall not keep you in the dark; I desire, if possible, to say the word *essentia* to you and obtain a favourable hearing. If I cannot do this, I shall risk it even though it put you out of humour. I have Cicero, as authority for the use of this word, and I regard him as a powerful authority. If you desire testimony of a later date, I shall cite Fabianus, careful of speech, cultivated, and so polished in style that he will suit even our nice tastes. For what can we do, my dear Lucilius? How otherwise can we find a word for that which the Greeks call οὐσία, something that is indispensable, something that is the natural substratum of everything? I beg you accordingly to allow me to use this word *essentia*. I shall nevertheless take pains to exercise the privilege, which you have granted me, with as sparing a hand as possible; perhaps I shall be content with the mere right.

Yet what good will your indulgence do me, if, lo and behold, I can in no wise express in Latin the meaning of the word which gave me the opportunity to rail at the poverty of our language? And you will condemn our narrow Roman limits even more, when you find out that there is a word of one syllable which I cannot translate. "What is this?" you ask. It is the word ὄν. You think me lacking in facility; you believe that the word is ready to hand, that it might be translated by *quod est*. I notice, however, a great difference; you are forcing me to render a noun by a verb.

But if I must do so, I shall render it by *quod est*. There are six ways in which Plato expresses this idea, according to a friend of ours, a man of great learning, who mentioned the fact today. And I shall explain all of them to you, if I may first point out that there is something called *genus* and something called *species*.

For the present, however, we are seeking the primary idea of *genus*, on which the others, the different *species*, depend, which is the source of all classification, the term under which universal ideas are embraced. And the idea of *genus* will be reached if we begin to reckon back from particulars; for in this way we shall be conducted back to the primary notion.

Now "man" is a *species*, as Aristotle says; so is "horse," or "dog." We must therefore discover some common bond for all these terms, one which embraces them and holds them subordinate to itself. And what is this? It is "animal." And so there begins to be a *genus* "animal," including all these terms, "man," "horse," and "dog."

But there are certain things which have life (*anima*) and yet are not "animals." For it is agreed that plants and trees possess life, and that is why we speak of them as living and dying. Therefore the term "living things" will occupy a still higher place, because both animals and plants are included in this category. Certain objects, however, lack life—such as rocks. There will therefore be another term to take precedence over "living things," and that is "substance." I shall classify "substance" by saying that all substances are either animate or inanimate.

But there is still something superior to "substance"; for we speak of certain things as possessing substance, and certain things as lacking substance. What, then, will be the term from which these things are derived? It is that to which we lately gave an inappropriate name, "that which exists." For by using this term they will be divided into *species*, so that we can say: that which exists either possesses, or lacks, substance.

This, therefore, is what *genus* is—the primary, original, and (to play upon the word) "general." Of course there are the other *genera*: but they are "special" *genera*: "man" being, for example, a *genus*. For "man" comprises species: by nations—Greek, Roman, Parthian; by colours—white, black, yellow. The term comprises individuals also: Cato, Cicero, Lucretius. So "man" falls into the category *genus*, in so far as it includes many kinds; but in so far as it is subordinate to another term, it falls into the category *species*. But the *genus* "that which exists" is general, and has no term superior to it. It is the first term in the classification of things, and all things are included under it.

The Stoics would set ahead of this still another *genus*, even more primary; concerning which I shall immediately speak, after proving that the *genus* which has been discussed above, has rightly been placed first, being, as it is, capable of including everything.

I therefore distribute "that which exists" into these two species—things with, and things without, substance. There is no third class. And how do I distribute "substance"? By saying that it is either animate or inanimate. And how do I distribute the "animate"? By saying: "Certain things have mind, while others have only life." Or the idea may be expressed as follows: "Certain things have the power of movement, of progress, of change of position, while others are rooted in the ground; they are fed and they grow only through their roots." Again, into what species do I divide "animals"? They are either perishable or imperishable.

Certain of the Stoics regard the primary *genus* as the "something." I shall add the reasons they give for their belief; they say: "in the order of nature some things exist, and other things do not exist. And even the things that do not exist are really part of the order of nature. What these are will readily occur to the mind, for example centaurs, giants, and all other figments of unsound reasoning, which have begun to have a definite shape, although they have no bodily consistency."

But I now return to the subject which I promised to discuss for you, namely, how it is that Plato divides all existing things in six different ways. The first class of "that which exists" cannot be grasped by the sight or by the touch, or by any of the senses; but it can be grasped by the thought. Any generic conception, such as the generic idea "man," does not come within the range of the eyes; but "man" in particular does; as, for example, Cicero, Cato. The term "animal" is not seen; it is grasped by thought alone. A particular animal, however, is seen, for example, a horse, a dog.

The second class of "things which exist," according to Plato, is that which is prominent and stands out above everything else; this, he says, exists in a pre-eminent degree. The word "poet" is used indiscriminately, for this term is applied to all writers of verse; but among the Greeks it has come to be the distinguishing mark of a single individual. You know that Homer is meant when you hear men say "the poet." What, then, is this pre-eminent Being? God, surely, one who is greater and more powerful than anyone else.

The third class is made up of those things which exist in the proper sense of the term; they are countless in number, but are situated beyond our sight. "What are these?" you ask. They are Plato's own furniture, so to speak; he calls them "ideas," and from them all visible things are created, and according to their pattern all things are fashioned. They are immortal, unchangeable, inviolable.

And this "idea," or rather, Plato's conception of it, is as follows: "The 'idea' is the everlasting pattern of those things which are created by nature." I shall explain this definition, in order to set the subject before you in a clearer light: Suppose that I wish to make a likeness of you; I possess in your own person the pattern of this picture, wherefrom my mind receives a certain outline, which it is to embody in its own handiwork. That outward appearance, then, which gives me instruction and guidance, this pattern for me to imitate, is the "idea." Such patterns, therefore, nature possesses in infinite number—of men, fish, trees, according to whose model everything that nature has to create is worked out.

In the fourth place we shall put "form." And if you would know what "form" means, you must pay close attention, calling Plato, and not me, to account for the difficulty of the subject. However, we cannot make fine distinctions without encountering difficulties. A moment ago I made use of the artist as an illustration. When the artist desired to reproduce Vergil in colours he would gaze upon Vergil himself. The "idea" was Vergil's outward appearance, and this was the pattern of the intended work. That which the artist draws from this "idea" and has embodied in his own work, is the "form."

Do you ask me where the difference lies? The former is the pattern; while the latter is the shape taken from the pattern and embodied in the work. Our artist follows the one, but the other he creates. A statue has a certain external appearance; this external appearance of the statue is the "form." And the pattern itself has a certain external appearance, by gazing upon which the sculptor has fashioned his statue; this is the "idea." If you desire a further distinction, I will say that the "form" is in the artist's work, the "idea" outside his work, and not only outside it, but prior to it.

The fifth class is made up of the things which exist in the usual sense of the term. These things are the first that have to do with us; here we have all such things as men, cattle, and things. In the sixth class goes all that which has a fictitious existence, like void, or time.

Whatever is concrete to the sight or touch, Plato does not include among the things which he believes to be existent in the strict sense of the term. These things are the first that have to do with us: here we have all such things as men, cattle, and things. For they are in a state of flux, constantly diminishing or increasing. None of us is the same man in old age that he was in youth; nor the same on the morrow as on the day preceding. Our bodies are burned along like flowing waters; every visible object accompanies time in its flight; of the things which we see, nothing is fixed. Even I myself as I comment on this change, am changed myself.

This is just what Heraclitus says: "We go down twice into the same river, and yet into a different river." For the stream still keeps the same name, but the water has already flowed past. Of course this is much more evident in rivers than in human beings. Still, we mortals are also carried past in no less speedy a course; and this prompts me to marvel at our madness in cleaving with great affection to such a fleeting thing as the body, and in fearing lest some day we may die, when every instant means the death of our previous condition. Will you not stop fearing lest that may happen once which really happens every day?

So much for man—a substance that flows away and falls, exposed to every influence; but the universe, too, immortal and enduring as it is, changes and never remains the same. For though it has within itself all that it has had, it has it in a different way from that in which it has had it; it keeps changing its arrangement.

"Very well," say you, "what good shall I get from all this fine reasoning?" None, if you wish me to answer your question. Nevertheless, just as an engraver rests his eyes when they have long been under a strain and are weary, and calls them from their work, and "feasts" them, as the saying is; so we at times should slacken our minds and refresh them with some sort of entertainment. But let even your entertainment be work; and even from these various forms of entertainment you will select, if you have been watchful, something that may prove wholesome.

That is my habit, Lucilius: I try to extract and render useful some element from every field of thought, no matter how far removed it may be from philosophy. Now what could be less likely to reform character than the subjects which we have been discussing? And how can I be made a better man by the "ideas" of Plato? What can I draw from them that will put a check on my appetites? Perhaps the very thought, that all these things which minister to our senses, which arouse and excite us, are by Plato denied a place among the things that really exist.

Such things are therefore imaginary, and though they for the moment present a certain external appearance, yet they are in no case permanent or substantial; none the less, we crave them as if they were always to exist, or as if we were always to possess them.

We are weak, watery beings standing in the midst of unrealities; therefore let us turn our minds to the things that are everlasting. Let us look up to the ideal outlines of all things, that flit about on high, and to the God who moves among them and plans how he may defend from death that which he could not make imperishable because its substance forbade, and so by reason may overcome the defects of the body.

For all things abide, not because they are everlasting, but because they are protected by the care of him who governs all things; but that which was imperishable would need no guardian. The Master Builder keeps them safe, overcoming the weakness of their fabric by his own power. Let us despise everything that is so little an object of value that it makes us doubt whether it exists at all.

Let us at the same time reflect, seeing that Providence rescues from its perils the world itself, which is no less mortal than we ourselves, that to some extent our petty bodies can be made to tarry longer upon earth by our own providence, if only we acquire the ability to control and check those pleasures whereby the greater portion of mankind perishes.

Plato himself, by taking pains, advanced to old age. To be sure, he was the fortunate possessor of a strong and sound body (his very name was given him because of his broad chest ); but his strength was much impaired by sea voyages and desperate adventures. Nevertheless, by frugal living, by setting a limit upon all that rouses the appetites, and by painstaking attention to himself, he reached that advanced age in spite of many hindrances.

You know, I am sure, that Plato had the good fortune, thanks to his careful living, to die on his birthday, after exactly completing his eighty-first year. For this reason wise men of the East, who happened to be in Athens at that time, sacrificed to him after his death, believing that his length of days was too full for a mortal man, since he had rounded out the perfect number of nine times nine. I do not doubt that he would have been quite willing to forgo a few days from this total, as well as the sacrifice.

Frugal living can bring one to old age; and to my mind old age is not to be refused any more than is to be craved. There is a pleasure in being in one's own company as long as possible, when a man has made himself worth enjoying. The question, therefore, on which we have to record our judgment is, whether one should shrink from extreme old age and should hasten the end artificially, instead of waiting for it to come. A man who sluggishly awaits his fate is almost a coward, just as he is immoderately given to wine who drains the jar dry and sucks up even the dregs.

But we shall ask this question also: "Is the extremity of life the dregs, or is it the clearest and purest part of all, provided only that the mind is unimpaired, and the senses, still sound, give their support to the spirit, and the body is not worn out and dead before its time?" For it makes a great deal of difference whether a man is lengthening his life or his death.

But if the body is useless for service, why should one not free the struggling soul? Perhaps one ought to do this a little before the debt is due, lest, when it falls due, he may be unable to perform the act. And since the danger of living in wretchedness is greater than the danger of dying soon, he is a fool who refuses to stake a little time and win a hazard of great gain.

Few have lasted through extreme old age to death without impairment, and many have lain inert, making no use of themselves: How much more cruel, then, do you suppose it really is to have lost a portion of your life, than to have lost your right to end that life?

Do not hear me with reluctance, as if my statement applied directly to you, but weigh what I have to say. It is this, that I shall not abandon old age, if old age preserves me intact for myself, and intact as regards the better part of myself; but if old age begins to shatter my mind, and to pull its various faculties to pieces, if it leaves me, not life, but only the breath of life, I shall rush out of a house that is crumbling and tottering.

I shall not avoid illness by seeking death, as long as the illness is curable and does not impede my soul. I shall not lay violent hands upon myself just because I am in pain; for death under such circumstances is defeat. But if I find out that the pain must always be endured, I shall depart, not because of the pain but because it will be a hindrance to me as regards all my reasons for living. He who dies just because he is in pain is a weakling, a coward; but he who lives merely to brave out this pain, is a fool.

But I am running on too long; and, besides, there is matter here to fill a day. And how can a man end his life, if he cannot end a letter? So farewell. This last word you will read with greater pleasure than all my deadly talk about death. Farewell.

# Letter 40
# On Pleasure and Joy

I received great pleasure from your letter; kindly allow me to use these words in their everyday meaning, without insisting upon their Stoic import. For we Stoics hold that pleasure is a vice. Very likely it is a vice; but we are accustomed to use the word when we wish to indicate a happy state of mind.

I am aware that if we test words by our formula, even pleasure is a thing of ill repute, and joy can be attained only by the wise. For "joy" is an elation of spirit, of a spirit which trusts in the goodness and truth of its own possessions. The common usage, however, is that we derive great "joy" from a friend's position as consul, or from his marriage, or from the birth of his child; but these events, so far from being matters of joy, are more often the beginnings of sorrow to come. No, it is a characteristic of real joy that it never ceases, and never changes into its opposite.

Accordingly, when our Vergil speaks of

*The evil joys of the mind,*

his words are eloquent, but not strictly appropriate. For no "joy" can be evil. He has given the name "joy" to pleasures, and has thus expressed his meaning. For he has conveyed the idea that men take delight in their own evil.

Nevertheless, I was not wrong in saying that I received great "pleasure" from your letter; for although an ignorant man may derive "joy" if the cause be an honourable one, yet, since his emotion is wayward, and is likely soon to take another direction, I call it "pleasure"; for it is inspired by an opinion concerning a spurious good; it exceeds control and is carried to excess.

But, to return to the subject, let me tell you what delighted me in your letter. You have your words under control. You are not carried away by your language, or borne beyond the limits which you have determined upon.

Many writers are tempted by the charm of some alluring phrase to some topic other than that which they had set themselves to discuss. But this has not been so in your case; all your words are compact, and suited to the subject, You say all that you wish, and you mean still more than you say. This is a proof of the importance of your subject matter, showing that your mind, as well as your words, contains nothing superfluous or bombastic.

I do, however, find some metaphors, not, indeed, daring ones, but the kind which have stood the test of use. I find similes also; of course, if anyone forbids us to use them, maintaining that poets alone have that privilege, he has not, apparently, read any of our ancient prose writers, who had not yet learned to affect a style that should win applause. For those writers, whose eloquence was simple and directed only towards proving their case, are full of comparisons; and I think that these are necessary, not for the same reason which makes them necessary for the poets, but in order that they may serve as props to our feebleness, to bring both speaker and listener face to face with the subject under discussion.

For example, I am at this very moment reading Sextius; he is a keen man, and a philosopher who, though he writes in Greek, has the Roman standard of ethics. One of his similes appealed especially to me, that of an army marching in hollow square, in a place where the enemy might be expected to appear from any quarter, ready for battle. "This," said he, "is just what the wise man ought to do; he should have all his fighting qualities deployed on every side, so that wherever the attack threatens, there his supports may be ready to hand and may obey the captain's command without confusion." This is what we notice in armies which serve under great leaders; we see how all the troops simultaneously understand their general's orders, since they are so arranged that a signal given by one man passes down the ranks of cavalry and infantry at the same moment.

This, he declares, is still more necessary for men like ourselves; for soldiers have often feared an enemy without reason, and the march which they thought most dangerous has in fact been most secure; but folly brings no repose, fear haunts it both in the van and in the rear of the column, and both flanks are in a panic. Folly is pursued, and confronted, by peril. It blenches at everything; it is unprepared; it is frightened even by auxiliary troops. But the wise man is fortified against all inroads; he is alert; he will not retreat before the attack of poverty, or of sorrow, or of disgrace, or of pain. He will walk undaunted both against them and among them.

We human beings are fettered and weakened by many vices; we have wallowed in them for a long time and it is hard for us to be cleansed. We are not merely defiled; we are dyed by them. But, to refrain from passing from one figure to another, I will raise this question, which I often consider in my own heart: why is it that folly holds us with such an insistent grasp? It is, primarily, because we do not combat it strongly enough, because we do not struggle towards salvation with all our might; secondly, because we do not put sufficient trust in the discoveries of the wise, and do not drink in their words with open hearts; we approach this great problem in too trifling a spirit.

But how can a man learn, in the struggle against his vices, an amount that is enough, if the time which he gives to learning is only the amount left over from his vices? None of us goes deep below the surface. We skim the top only, and we regard the smattering of time spent in the search for wisdom as enough and to spare for a busy man.

What hinders us most of all is that we are too readily satisfied with ourselves; if we meet with someone who calls us good men, or sensible men, or holy men, we see ourselves in his description, not content with praise in moderation, we accept everything that shameless flattery heaps upon us, as if it were our due. We agree with those who declare us to be the best and wisest of men, although we know that they are given to much lying. And we are so self-complacent that we desire praise for certain actions when we are especially addicted to the very opposite. Yonder person hears himself called "most gentle" when he is inflicting tortures, or "most generous" when he is engaged in looting, or "most temperate" when he is in the midst of drunkenness and lust. Thus it follows that we are unwilling to be reformed, just because we believe ourselves to be the best of men.

Alexander was roaming as far as India, ravaging tribes that were but little known, even to their neighbours. During the blockade of a certain city, while he was reconnoitring the walls and hunting for the weakest spot in the fortifications, he was wounded by an arrow. Nevertheless, he long continued the siege, intent on finishing what he had begun. The pain of his wound, however, as the surface became dry and as the flow of blood was checked, increased; his leg gradually became numb as he sat his horse; and finally, when he was forced to withdraw, he exclaimed: "All men swear that I am the son of Jupiter, but this wound cries out that I am mortal."

Let us also act in the same way. Each man, according to his lot in life, is stultified by flattery. We should say to him who flatters us: "You call me a man of sense, but I understand how many of the things which I crave are useless, and how many of the things which I desire will do me harm. I have not even the knowledge, which satiety teaches to animals, of what should be the measure of my food or my drink. I do not yet know how much I can hold."

I shall now show you how you may know that you are not wise. The wise man is joyful, happy and calm, unshaken, he lives on a plane with the gods. Now go, question yourself; if you are never downcast, if your mind is not harassed by my apprehension, through anticipation of what is to come, if day and night your soul keeps on its even and unswerving course, upright and content with itself, then you have attained to the greatest good that mortals can possess. If, however, you seek pleasures of all kinds in all directions, you must know that you are as far short of wisdom as you are short of joy. Joy is the goal which you desire to reach, but you are wandering from the path, if you expect to reach your goal while you are in the midst of riches and official titles—in other words, if you seek joy in the midst of cares, these objects for which you strive so eagerly, as if they would give you happiness and pleasure, are merely causes of grief.

All men of this stamp, I maintain, are pressing on in pursuit of joy, but they do not know where they may obtain a joy that is both great and enduring. One person seeks it in feasting and self-indulgence; another, in canvassing for honours and in being surrounded by a throng of clients; another, in his mistress; another, in idle display of culture and in literature that has no power to heal; all these men are led astray by delights which are deceptive and short-lived—like drunkenness for example, which pays for a single hour of hilarious madness by a sickness of many days, or like applause and the popularity of enthusiastic approval which are gained, and atoned for, at the cost of great mental disquietude.

Reflect, therefore, on this, that the effect of wisdom is a joy that is unbroken and continuous. The mind of the wise man is like the ultra-lunar firmament; eternal calm pervades that region. You have, then, a reason for wishing to be wise, if the wise man is never deprived of joy. This joy springs only from the knowledge that you possess the virtues. None but the brave, the just, the self-restrained, can rejoice.

And when you query: "What do you mean? Do not the foolish and the wicked also rejoice?" I reply, no more than lions who have caught their prey. When men have wearied themselves with wine and lust, when night fails them before their debauch is done, when the pleasures which they have heaped upon a body that is too small to hold them begin to fester, at such times they utter in their wretchedness those lines of Vergil:

*Thou knowest how, amid false-glittering joys.*
*We spent that last of nights.*

Pleasure-lovers spend every night amid false-glittering joys, and just as if it were their last. But the joy which comes to the gods, and to those who imitate the gods, is not broken off, nor does it cease; but it would surely cease were it borrowed from without. Just because it is not in the power of another to bestow, neither is it subject to another's whims. That which Fortune has not given, she cannot take away. Farewell.

# Letter 41
# On Meeting Death Cheerfully

Let us cease to desire that which we have been desiring. I, at least, am doing this: in my old age I have ceased to desire what I desired when a boy. To this single end my days and my nights are passed; this is my task, this the object of my thoughts—to put an end to my chronic ills. I am endeavouring to live every day as if it were a complete life. I do not indeed snatch it up as if it were my last; I do regard it, however, as if it might even be my last.

The present letter is written to you with this in mind as if death were about to call me away in the very act of writing. I am ready to depart, and I shall enjoy life just because I am not over-anxious as to the future date of my departure.

Before I became old I tried to live well; now that I am old, I shall try to die well; but dying well means dying gladly. See to it that you never do anything unwillingly.

That which is bound to be a necessity if you rebel, is not a necessity if you desire it. This is what I mean: he who takes his orders gladly, escapes the bitterest part of slavery—doing what one does not want to do. The man who does something under orders is not unhappy; he is unhappy who does something against his will. Let us therefore so set our minds in order that we may desire whatever is demanded of us by circumstances, and above all that we may reflect upon our end without sadness.

We must make ready for death before we make ready for life. Life is well enough furnished, but we are too greedy with regard to its furnishings; something always seems to us lacking, and will always seem lacking. To have lived long enough depends neither upon our years nor upon our days, but upon our minds. I have lived, my dear friend Lucilius, long enough. I have had my fill; I await death. Farewell.

# Letter 42
# On the Philosopher's Task

Yesterday you were with us. You might complain if I said "yesterday" merely. This is why I have added "with us." For, so far as I am concerned, you are always with me. Certain friends had happened in, on whose account a somewhat brighter fire was laid—not the kind that generally bursts from the kitchen chimneys of the rich and scares the watch, but the moderate blaze which means that guests have come.

Our talk ran on various themes, as is natural at a dinner; it pursued no chain of thought to the end, but jumped from one topic to another. We then had read to us a book by Quintus Sextius the Elder. He is a great man, if you have any confidence in my opinion, and a real Stoic, though he himself denies it. Ye Gods, what strength and spirit one finds in him! This is not the case with all philosophers; there are some men of illustrious name whose writings are sapless. They lay down rules, they argue, and they quibble; they do not infuse spirit simply because they have no spirit. But when you come to read Sextius you will say: "He is alive; he is strong; he is free; he is more than a man; he fills me with a mighty confidence before I close his book."

I shall acknowledge to you the state of mind I am in when I read his works: I want to challenge every hazard; I want to cry: "Why keep me waiting, Fortune? Enter the lists! Behold, I am ready for you!" I assume the spirit of a man who seeks where he may make trial of himself where he may show his worth:

> And fretting 'mid the unwarlike flocks he prays
> Some foam-flecked boar may cross his path, or else
> A tawny lion stalking down the hills.

I want something to overcome, something on which I may test my endurance. For this is another remarkable quality that Sextius possesses: he will show you the grandeur of the happy life and yet will not make you despair of attaining it; you will understand that it is on high, but that it is accessible to him who has the will to seek it.

And virtue herself will have the same effect upon you, of making you admire her and yet hope to attain her. In my own case, at any rate the very contemplation of wisdom takes much of my time; I gaze upon her with bewilderment, just as I sometimes gaze upon the firmament itself, which I often behold as if I saw it for the first time.

Hence I worship the discoveries of wisdom and their discoverers; to enter, as it were, into the inheritance of many predecessors is a delight. It was for me that they laid up this treasure; it was for me that they toiled. But we should play the part of a careful householder; we should increase what we have inherited. This inheritance shall pass from me to my descendants larger than before. Much still remains to do, and much will always remain, and he who shall be born a thousand ages hence will not be barred from his opportunity of adding something further.

But even if the old masters have discovered everything, one thing will be always new—the application and the scientific study and classification of the discoveries made by others. Assume that prescriptions have been handed down to us for the healing of the eyes; there is no need of my searching for others in addition; but for all that, these prescriptions must be adapted to the particular disease and to the particular stage of the disease. Use this prescription to relieve granulation of the eyelids, that to reduce the swelling of the lids, this to prevent sudden pain or a rush of tears, that to sharpen the vision. Then compound these several prescriptions, watch for the right time of their application, and supply the proper treatment in each case.

The cures for the spirit also have been discovered by the ancients; but it is our task to learn the method and the time of treatment.

Our predecessors have worked much improvement, but have not worked out the problem. They deserve respect, however, and should be worshipped with a divine ritual. Why should I not keep statues of great men to kindle my enthusiasm, and celebrate their birthdays? Why should I not continually greet them with respect and honour? The reverence which I owe to my own teachers I owe in like measure to those teachers of the human race, the source from which the beginnings of such great blessings have flowed.

If I meet a consul or a practor, I shall pay him all the honour which his post of honour is wont to receive: I shall dismount, uncover, and yield the road. What, then? Shall I admit into my soul with less than the highest marks of respect Marcus Cato, the Elder and the Younger, Laelius the Wise, Socrates and Plato, Zeno and Cleanthes? I worship them in very truth, and always rise to do honour to such noble names. Farewell.

# Letter 43
# On Ill-Health and Endurance of Suffering

If I may begin with a commonplace remark, spring is gradually disclosing itself; but though it is rounding into summer, when you would expect hot weather, it has kept rather cool, and one cannot yet be sure of it. For it often slides back into winter weather. Do you wish to know how uncertain it still is? I do not yet trust myself to a bath which is absolutely cold; even at this time I break its chill. You may say that this is no way to show the endurance either of heat or of cold; very true, dear Lucilius, but at my time of life one is at length contented with the natural chill of the body. I can scarcely thaw out in the middle of summer. Accordingly, I spend most of the time bundled up; and I thank old age for keeping me fastened to my bed. Why should I not thank old age on this account? That which I ought not to wish to do, I lack the ability to do. Most of my converse is with books. Whenever your letters arrive, I imagine that I am with you, and I have the feeling that I am about to speak my answer, instead of writing it. Therefore let us together investigate the nature of this problem of yours, just as if we were conversing with one another.

You ask me whether every good is desirable. You say: "If it is a good to be brave under torture, to go to the stake with a stout heart, to endure illness with resignation, it follows that these things are desirable. But I do not see that any of them is worth praying for. At any rate I have as yet known of no man who has paid a vow by reason of having been cut to pieces by the rod, or twisted out of shape by the gout, or made taller by the rack."

My dear Lucilius, you must distinguish between these cases; you will then comprehend that there is something in them that is to be desired. I should prefer to be free from torture; but if the time comes when it must be endured, I shall desire that I may conduct myself therein with bravery, honour, and courage. Of course I prefer that war should not occur; but if war does occur, I shall desire that I may nobly endure the wounds, the starvation, and all that the exigency of war brings. Nor am I so mad as to crave illness; but if I must suffer illness, I shall desire that I may do nothing which shows lack of restraint, and nothing that is unmanly. The conclusion is, not that hardships are desirable, but that virtue is desirable, which enables us patiently to endure hardships.

Certain of our school, think that, of all such qualities, a stout endurance is not desirable—though not to be deprecated either—because we ought to seek by prayer only the good which is unalloyed, peaceful, and beyond the reach of trouble. Personally, I do not agree with them. And why? First, because it is impossible for anything to be good without being also desirable. Because, again, if virtue is desirable, and if nothing that is good lacks virtue, then everything good is desirable. And, lastly, because a brave endurance even under torture is desirable.

At this point I ask you: is not bravery desirable? And yet bravery despises and challenges danger. The most beautiful and most admirable part of bravery is that it does not shrink from the stake, advances to meet wounds, and sometimes does not even avoid the spear, but meets it with opposing breast. If bravery is desirable, so is patient endurance of torture; for this is a part of bravery. Only sift these things, as I have suggested; then there will be nothing which can lead you astray. For it is not mere endurance of torture, but brave endurance, that is desirable. I therefore desire that "brave" endurance; and this is virtue.

"But," you say, "who ever desired such a thing for himself?" Some prayers are open and outspoken, when the requests are offered specifically; other prayers are indirectly expressed, when they include many requests under one title. For example, I desire a life of honour. Now a life of honour includes various kinds of conduct; it may include the chest in which Regulus was confined, or the wound of Cato which was torn open by Cato's own hand, or the exile of Rutilius, or the cup of poison which removed Socrates from gaol to heaven. Accordingly, in praying for a life of honour, I have prayed also for those things without which, on some occasions, life cannot be honourable

> *O thrice and four times blest were they*
> *Who underneath the lofty walls of Troy*
> *Met happy death before their parents' eyes!*

What does it matter whether you offer this prayer for some individual, or admit that it was desirable in the past?

Decius sacrificed himself for the State; he set spurs to his horse and rushed into the midst of the foe, seeking death. The second Decius, rivalling his father's valour, reproducing the words which had become sacred and already household words, dashed into the thickest of the fight, anxious only that his sacrifice might bring omen of success, and regarding a noble death as a thing to be desired. Do you doubt, then, whether it is best to die glorious and performing some deed of valour?

When one endures torture bravely, one is using all the virtues. Endurance may perhaps be the only virtue that is on view and most manifest; but bravery is there too, and endurance and resignation and long-suffering are its branches. There, too, is foresight; for without foresight no plan can be undertaken; it is foresight that advises one to bear as bravely as possible the things one cannot avoid. There also is steadfastness, which cannot be dislodged from its position, which the wrench of no force can cause to abandon its purpose. There is the whole inseparable company of virtues; every honourable act is the work of one single virtue, but it is in accordance with the judgment of the whole council. And that which is approved by all the virtues, even though it seems to be the work of one alone, is desirable.

What? Do you think that those things only are desirable which come to us amid pleasure and ease, and which we bedeck our doors to welcome? There are certain goods whose features are forbidding. There are certain prayers which are offered by a throng, not of men who rejoice, but of men who bow down reverently and worship. Was it not in this fashion, think you, that Regulus prayed that he might reach Carthage? Clothe yourself with a hero's courage, and withdraw for a little space from the opinions of the common man. Form a proper conception of the image of virtue, a thing of exceeding beauty and grandeur; this image is not to be worshipped by us with incense or garlands, but with sweat and blood.

Behold Marcus Cato, laying upon that hallowed breast his unspotted hands, and tearing apart the wounds which had not gone deep enough to kill him! Which, pray, shall you say to him: "I hope all will be as you wish," and "I am grieved," or shall it be "Good fortune in your undertaking!"?

In this connexion I think of our friend Demetrius, who calls an easy existence, untroubled by the attacks of Fortune, a "Dead Sea." If you have nothing to stir you up and rouse you to action, nothing which will test your resolution by its threats and hostilities; if you recline in unshaken comfort, it is not tranquillity; it is merely a flat calm. The Stoic Attalus was wont to say: "I should prefer that Fortune keep me in her camp rather than in the lap of luxury. If I am tortured, but bear it bravely, all is well; if I die, but die bravely, it is also well." Listen to Epicurus; he will tell you that it is actually pleasant. I myself shall never apply an effeminate word to an act so honourable and austere. If I go to the stake, I shall go unbeaten.

Why should I not regard this as desirable—not because the fire, burns me, but because it does not overcome me? Nothing is more excellent or more beautiful than virtue; whatever we do in obedience to her orders is both good and desirable. Farewell.

# Letter 44
# On Rest and Restlessness

I do not like you to change your headquarters and scurry about from one place to another. My reasons are—first, that such frequent flitting means an unsteady spirit. And the spirit cannot through retirement grow into unity unless it has ceased from its inquisitiveness and its wanderings. To be able to hold your spirit in check, you must first stop the runaway flight of the body.

My second reason is, that the remedies which are most helpful are those which are not interrupted. You should not allow your quiet, or the oblivion to which you have consigned your former life, to be broken into. Give your eyes time to unlearn what they have seen, and your ears to grow accustomed to more wholesome words. Whenever you stir abroad you will meet, even as you pass from one place to another, things that will bring back your old cravings.

Just as he who tries to be rid of an old love must avoid every reminder of the person once held dear (for nothing grows again so easily as love), similarly, he who would lay aside his desire for all the things which he used to crave so passionately, must turn away both eyes and ears from the objects which he has abandoned. The emotions soon return to the attack; at every turn they will notice before their eyes an object worth their attention. There is no evil that does not offer inducements. Avarice promises money; luxury, a varied assortment of pleasures; ambition, a purple robe and applause, and the influence which results from applause, and all that influence can do.

Vices tempt you by the rewards which they offer; but in the life of which I speak, you must live without being paid. Scarcely will a whole life-time suffice to bring our vices into subjection and to make them accept the yoke, swollen as they are by long-continued indulgence; and still less, if we cut into our brief span by any interruptions. Even constant care and attention can scarcely bring any one undertaking to full completion.

If you will give ear to my advice, ponder and practice this— how to welcome death, or even, if circumstances commend that course, to invite it. There is no difference whether death comes to us, or whether we go to death. Make yourself believe that all ignorant men are wrong when they say: "It is a beautiful thing to die one's own death." But there is no man who does not die his own death. What is more, you may reflect on this thought: No one dies except on his own day. You are throwing away none of your own time; for what you leave behind does not belong to you. Farewell.

# Letter 45
# On the Supreme Good

You are continually referring special questions to me, forgetting that a vast stretch of sea sunders us. Since, however, the value of advice depends mostly on the time when it is given, it must necessarily result that by the time my opinion on certain matters reaches you, the opposite opinion is the better. For advice conforms to circumstances; and our circumstances are carried along, or rather whirled along. Accordingly, advice should be produced at short notice; and even this is too late; it should "grow while we work," as the saying is. And I propose to show you how you may discover the method.

As often as you wish to know what is to be avoided or what is to be sought, consider its relation to the Supreme Good, to the purpose of your whole life. For whatever we do ought to be in harmony with this; no man can set in order the details unless he has already set before himself the chief purpose of his life. The artist may have his colours all prepared, but he cannot produce a likeness unless he has already made up his mind what he wishes to paint. The reason we make mistakes is because we all consider the parts of life, but never life as a whole.

The archer must know what he is seeking to hit; then he must aim and control the weapon by his skill. Our plans miscarry because they have no aim. When a man does not know what harbour he is making for, no wind is the right wind. Chance must necessarily have great influence over our lives, because we live by chance.

It is the case with certain men, however, that they do not know that they know certain things. Just as we often go searching for those who stand beside us, so we are apt to forget that the goal of the Supreme Good lies near us.

To infer the nature of this Supreme Good, one does not need many words or any round-about discussion; it should be pointed out with the forefinger, so to speak, and not be dissipated into many parts. For what good is there in breaking it up into tiny bits, when you can say: the

Supreme Good is that which is honourable? Besides (and you may be still more surprised at this), that which is honourable is the only good; all other goods are alloyed and debased.

If you once convince yourself of this, and if you come to love virtue devotedly (for mere loving is not enough), anything that has been touched by virtue will be fraught with blessing and prosperity for you, no matter how it shall be regarded by others. Torture, if only, as you lie suffering, you are more calm in mind than your very torturer; illness, if only you curse not Fortune and yield not to the disease—in short, all those things which others regard as ills will become manageable and will end in good, if you succeed in rising above them.

Let this once be clear, that there is nothing good except that which is honourable, and all hardships will have a just title to the name of "goods," when once virtue has made them honourable.

Many think that we Stoics are holding out expectations greater than our human lot admits of; and they have a right to think so. For they have regard to the body only. But let them turn back to the soul, and they will soon measure man by the standard of God. Rouse yourself, most excellent Lucilius, and leave off all this word-play of the philosophers, who reduce a most glorious subject to a matter of syllables, and lower and wear out the soul by teaching fragments; then you will become like the men who discovered these precepts, instead of those who by their teaching do their best to make philosophy seem difficult rather than great.

Socrates, who recalled the whole of philosophy to rules of conduct, and asserted that the highest wisdom consisted in distinguishing between good and evil, said: "Follow these rules, if my words carry weight with you, in order that you may be happy; and let some men think you even a fool. Allow any man who so desires to insult you and work you wrong; but if only virtue dwells with you, you will suffer nothing. If you wish to be happy, if you would be in good faith a good man let one person or another despise you." No man can accomplish this unless he has come to regard all goods as equal, for the reason that no good exists without that which is honourable, and that which is honourable is in every case equal.

You may say: "What then? Is there no difference between Cato's being elected praetor and his failure at the polls? Or whether Cato is conquered or conqueror in the battle-line of Pharsalia? And when Cato could not be defeated, though his party met defeat, was not this goodness of his equal to that which would have been his if he had returned victorious to his native land and arranged a peace?" Of course it was; for it is by the same virtue that evil fortune is overcome and good fortune is controlled. Virtue however, cannot be increased or decreased; its stature is uniform.

"But," you will object, "Gnaeus Pompey will lose his army; the patricians, those noblest patterns of the State's creation, and the front-rank men of Pompey's party, a senate under arms, will be routed in a single engagement; the ruins of that great oligarchy will be scattered all over the world; one division will fall in Egypt, another in Africa, and another in Spain! And the poor State will not be allowed even the privilege of being ruined once for all!"

Yes, all this may happen; Juba's familiarity with every position in his own kingdom may be of no avail to him, of no avail the resolute bravery of his people when fighting for their king; even the men of Utica, crushed by their troubles, may waver in their allegiance; and the good fortune which ever attended men of the name of Scipio may desert Scipio in Africa. But long ago destiny "saw to it that Cato should come to no harm."

"He was conquered in spite of it all!" Well, you may include this among Cato's "failures"; Cato will bear with an equally stout heart anything that thwarts him of his victory, as he bore that which thwarted him of his praetorship. The day whereon he failed of election, he spent in play; the night wherein he intended to die, he spent in reading. He regarded in the same light both the loss of his praetorship and the loss of his life; he had convinced himself that he ought to endure anything which might happen.

Why should he not suffer, bravely and calmly, a change in the government? For what is free from the risk of change? Neither earth, nor sky, nor the whole fabric of our universe, though it be controlled by the hand of God. It will not always preserve its present order; it will be thrown from its course in days to come.

All things move in accord with their appointed times, they are destined to be born, to grow, and to be destroyed. The stars which you see moving above us, and this seemingly immovable earth to which we cling and on which we are set, will be consumed and will cease to exist. There is nothing that does not have its old age; the intervals are merely unequal at which Nature sends forth all these things towards the same goal. Whatever is will cease to be, and yet it will not perish, but will be resolved into its elements.

To our minds, this process means perishing, for we behold only that which is nearest; our sluggish mind, under allegiance to the body, does not penetrate to bournes beyond. Were it not so, the mind would endure with greater courage its own ending and that of its possessions, if only it could hope that life and death, like the whole universe about us, go by turns, that whatever has been put together is broken up again, that whatever has been broken up is put together again, and that the eternal craftsmanship of God, who controls all things is working at this task.

Therefore the wise man will say just what a Marcus Cato would say, after reviewing his past life: "The whole race of man, both that which is and that which is to be, is condemned to die. Of all the cities that at any time have held sway over the world, and of all that have been the splendid ornaments of empires not their own, men shall some day ask where they were, and they shall be swept away by destructions of various kinds; some shall be ruined by wars, others shall be wasted away by inactivity and by the kind of peace which ends in sloth, or by that vice which is fraught with destruction even for mighty dynasties—luxury. All these fertile plains shall be buried out of sight by a sudden overflowing of the sea, or a slipping of the soil, as it settles to lower levels, shall draw them suddenly into a yawning chasm. Why then should I be angry or feel sorrow, if I precede the general destruction by a tiny interval of time?"

Let great souls comply with God's wishes, and suffer unhesitatingly whatever fate the law of the universe ordains; for the soul at death is either sent forth into a better life, destined to dwell with deity amid greater radiance and calm, or else, at least, without suffering any harm to itself, it will be mingled with nature again, and will return to the universe.

Therefore Cato's honourable death was no less a good than his honourable life, since virtue admits of no stretching. Socrates used to say that verity and virtue were the same. Just as truth does not grow, so neither does virtue grow; for it has its due proportions and is complete.

You need not, therefore, wonder that goods are equal, both those which are to be deliberately chosen, and those which circumstances have imposed. For if you once adopt the view that they are unequal, deeming, for instance, a brave endurance of torture as among the lesser goods, you will be including it among the evils also; you will pronounce Socrates unhappy in his prison, Cato unhappy when he reopens his wounds with more courage than he allowed in inflicting them, and Regulus the most ill-starred of all when he pays the penalty for keeping his word even with his enemies. And yet no man, even the most effeminate person in the world, has ever dared to maintain such an opinion. For though such persons deny that a man like Regulus is happy, yet for all that they also deny that he is wretched.

The earlier Academics do indeed admit that a man is happy even amid such tortures, but do not admit that he is completely or fully happy. With this view we cannot in any wise agree; for unless a man is happy, he has not attained the Supreme Good; and the good which is supreme admits of no higher degree, if only virtue exists within this man, and if adversity does not impair his virtue, and if, though the body be injured, the virtue abides unharmed. And it does abide. For I understand virtue to be high-spirited and exalted, so that it is aroused by anything that molests it.

This spirit, which young men of noble breeding often assume, when they are so deeply stirred by the beauty of some honourable object that they despise all the gifts of chance, is assuredly infused in us and communicated to us by wisdom. Wisdom will bring the conviction that there is but one good—that which is honourable; that this can neither be shortened nor extended, any more than a carpenter's rule, with which straight lines are tested, can be bent. Any change in the rule means spoiling the straight line.

Applying, therefore, this same figure to virtue, we shall say: virtue also is straight, and admits of no bending. What can be made more tense than a thing which is already rigid? Such is virtue, which passes judgment on everything, but nothing passes judgment on virtue. And if this rule, virtue, cannot itself be made more straight, neither can the things created by virtue be in one case straighter and in another less straight. For they must necessarily correspond to virtue; hence they are equal.

"What," you say, "do you call reclining at a banquet and submitting to torture equally good?" Does this seem surprising to you? You may be still more surprised at the following—that reclining at a banquet is an evil, while reclining on the rack is a good, if the former act is done in a shameful, and the latter in an honourable manner. It is not the material that makes these actions good or bad; it is the virtue. All acts in which virtue has disclosed itself are of the same measure and value.

At this moment the man who measures the souls of all men by his own is shaking his fist in my face because I hold that there is a parity between the goods involved in the case of one who passes sentence honourably, and of one who suffers sentence honourably; or because I hold that there is a parity between the goods of one who celebrates a triumph, and of one who, unconquered in spirit, is carried before the victor's chariot. For such critics think that whatever they themselves cannot do, is not done; they pass judgment on virtue in the light of their own weaknesses.

Why do you marvel if it helps a man, and on occasion even pleases him, to be burned, wounded, slain, or bound in prison? To a luxurious man, a simple life is a penalty; to a lazy man, work is punishment; the dandy pities the diligent man; to the slothful, studies are torture. Similarly, we regard those things with respect to which we are all infirm of disposition, as hard and beyond endurance, forgetting what a torment it is to many men to abstain from wine or to be routed from their beds at break of day. These actions are not essentially difficult; it is we ourselves that are soft and flabby.

We must pass judgment concerning great matters with greatness of soul; otherwise, that which is really our fault will seem to be their fault. So it is that certain objects which are perfectly straight, when sunk in water appear to the onlooker as bent or broken off. It matters not only what you see, but with what eyes you see it; our souls are too dull of vision to perceive the truth.

But give me an unspoiled and sturdy-minded young man; he will pronounce more fortunate one who sustains on unbending shoulders the whole weight of adversity, who stands out superior to Fortune. It is not a cause for wonder that one is not tossed about when the weather is calm; reserve your wonderment for cases where a man is lifted up when all others sink, and keeps his footing when all others are prostrate.

What element of evil is there in torture and in the other things which we call hardships? It seems to me that there is this evil—that the mind sags, and bends, and collapses. But none of these things can happen to the sage; he stands erect under any load. Nothing can subdue him; nothing that must be endured annoys him. For he does not complain that he has been struck by that which can strike any man. He knows his own strength; he knows that he was born to carry burdens.

I do not withdraw the wise man from the category of man, nor do I deny to him the sense of pain as though he were a rock that has no feelings at all. I remember that he is made up of two parts: the one part is irrational—it is this that may be bitten, burned, or hurt; the other part is rational—it is this which holds resolutely to opinions, is courageous, and unconquerable. In the latter is situated man's Supreme Good. Before this is completely attained, the mind wavers in uncertainty; only when it is fully achieved is the mind fixed and steady.

And so when one has just begun, or is on one's way to the heights and is cultivating virtue, or even if one is drawing near the perfect good but has not yet put the finishing touch upon it, one will retrograde at times and there will be a certain slackening of mental effort. For such a man has not yet traversed the doubtful ground; he is still standing in slippery places. But the happy man, whose virtue is complete, loves himself most of all when his bravery has been submitted to the severest test, and when he not only, endures but welcomes that which all other men regard with fear, if it is the price which he must pay for the performance of a duty which honour imposes, and he greatly prefers to have men say of him: "how much more noble!" rather than "how much more lucky!"

And now I have reached the point to which your patient waiting summons me. You must not think that our human virtue transcends nature; the wise man will tremble, will feel pain, will turn pale, For all these are sensations of the body. Where, then, is the abode of utter distress, of that which is truly an evil? In the other part of us, no doubt, if it is the mind that these trials drag down, force to a confession of its servitude, and cause to regret its existence.

The wise man, indeed, overcomes Fortune by his virtue, but many who profess wisdom are sometimes frightened by the most unsubstantial threats. And at this stage it is a mistake on our part to make the same demands upon the wise man and upon the learner. I still exhort myself to do that which I recommend; but my exhortations are not yet followed. And even if this were the case, I should not have these principles so ready for practice, or so well trained, that they would rush to my assistance in every crisis.

Just as wool takes up certain colours at once, while there are others which it will not absorb unless it is soaked and steeped in them many times; so other systems of doctrine can be immediately applied by men's minds after once being accepted, but this system of which I speak, unless it has gone deep and has sunk in for a long time, and has not merely coloured but thoroughly permeated the soul, does not fulfil any of its promises.

The matter can be imparted quickly and in very few words: "Virtue is the only good; at any rate there is no good without virtue; and virtue itself is situated in our nobler part, that is, the rational part." And what will this virtue be? A true and never-swerving judgment. For therefrom will spring all mental impulses, and by its agency every external appearance that stirs our impulses will be clarified.

It will be in keeping with this judgment to judge all things that have been coloured by virtue as goods, and as equal goods.

Bodily goods are, to be sure, good for the body; but they are not absolutely good. There will indeed be some value in them; but they will possess no genuine merit, for they will differ greatly; some will be less, others greater.

And we are constrained to acknowledge that there are great differences among the very followers of wisdom. One man has already made so much progress that he dares to raise his eyes and look Fortune in the face, but not persistently, for his eyes soon drop, dazzled by her overwhelming splendour; another has made so much progress that he is able to match glances with her—that is, unless he has already reached the summit and is full of confidence.

That which is short of perfection must necessarily be unsteady, at one time progressing, at another slipping or growing faint; and it will surely slip back unless it keeps struggling ahead; for if a man slackens at all in zeal and faithful application, he must retrograde. No one can resume his progress at the point where he left off.

Therefore let us press on and persevere. There remains much more of the road than we have put behind us; but the greater part of progress is the desire to progress.

I fully understand what this task is. It is a thing which I desire, and I desire it with all my heart. I see that you also have been aroused and are hastening with great zeal towards infinite beauty. Let us, then, hasten; only on these terms will life be a boon to us; otherwise, there is delay, and indeed disgraceful delay, while we busy ourselves with revolting things. Let us see to it that all time belongs to us. This, however, cannot be unless first of all our own selves begin to belong to us.

And when will it be our privilege to despise both kinds of fortune? When will it be our privilege, after all the passions have been subdued and brought under our own control, to utter the words "I have conquered!"? Do you ask me whom I have conquered? Neither the Persians, nor the far-off Medes, nor any warlike race that lies beyond the Dahae; not these, but greed, ambition, and the fear of death that has conquered the conquerors of the world. Farewell.

# Letter 46
# On Philosophers and Kings

It seems to me erroneous to believe that those who have loyally dedicated themselves to philosophy are stubborn and rebellious, scorners of magistrates or kings or of those who control the administration of public affairs. For, on the contrary, no class of man is so popular with the philosopher as the ruler is; and rightly so, because rulers bestow upon no men a greater privilege than upon those who are allowed to enjoy peace and leisure.

Hence, those who are greatly profited, as regards their purpose of right living, by the security of the State, must needs cherish as a father the author of this good; much more so, at any rate, than those restless persons who are always in the public eye, who owe much to the ruler, but also expect much from him, and are never so generously loaded with favours that their cravings, which grow by being supplied, are thoroughly satisfied. And yet he whose thoughts are of benefits to come has forgotten the benefits received; and there is no greater evil in covetousness than its ingratitude.

Besides, no man in public life thinks of the many whom he has outstripped; he thinks rather of those by whom he is outstripped. And these men find it less pleasing to see many behind them than annoying to see anyone ahead of them. That is the trouble with every sort of ambition; it does not look back. Nor is it ambition alone that is fickle, but also every sort of craving, because it always begins where it ought to end.

But that other man, upright and pure, who has left the senate and the bar and all affairs of state, that he may retire to nobler affairs, cherishes those who have made it possible for him to do this in security; he is the only person who returns spontaneous thanks to them, the only person who owes them a great debt without their knowledge. Just as a man honours and reveres his teachers, by whose aid he has found release from his early wanderings, so the sage honours these men, also, under whose guardianship he can put his good theories into practice.

But you answer: "Other men too are protected by a king's personal power." Perfectly true. But just as, out of a number of persons who have profited by the same stretch of calm weather, a man deems that his debt to Neptune is greater if his cargo during that voyage has been more extensive and valuable, and just as the vow is paid with more of a will by the merchant than by the passenger, and just as, from among the merchants themselves, heartier thanks are uttered by the dealer in spices, purple fabrics, and objects worth their weight in gold, than by him who has gathered cheap merchandise that will be nothing but ballast for his ship; similarly, the benefits of this peace, which extends to all, are more deeply appreciated by those who make good use of it.

For there are many of our toga-clad citizens to whom peace brings more trouble than war. Or do those, think you, owe as much as we do for the peace they enjoy, who spend it in drunkenness, or in lust, or in other vices which it were worth even a war to interrupt? No, not unless you think that the wise man is so unfair as to believe that as an individual he owes nothing in return for the advantages which he enjoys with all the rest. I owe a great debt to the sun and to the moon; and yet they do not rise for me alone. I am personally beholden to the seasons and to the god who controls them, although in no respect have they been apportioned for my benefit.

The foolish greed of mortals makes a distinction between possession and ownership, and believes that it has ownership in nothing in which the general public has a share. But our philosopher considers nothing more truly his own than that which he shares in partnership with all mankind. For these things would not be common property, as indeed they are, unless every individual had his quota; even a joint interest based upon the slightest share makes one a partner.

Again, the great and true goods are not divided in such a manner that each has but a slight interest; they belong in their entirety to each individual. At a distribution of grain men receive only the amount that has been promised to each person; the banquet and the meat-dole, or all else that a man can carry away with him, are divided into parts. These goods, however, are indivisible—I mean peace and liberty—and they belong in their entirety to all men just as much as they belong to each individual.

Therefore the philosopher thinks of the person who makes it possible for him to use and enjoy these things, of the person who exempts him when the state's dire need summons to arms, to sentry duty, to the defence of the walls, and to the manifold exactions of war; and he gives thanks to the helmsman of his state. This is what philosophy teaches most of all—honourably to avow the debt of benefits received, and honourably to pay them; sometimes, however, the acknowledgment itself constitutes payment.

Our philosopher will therefore acknowledge that he owes a large debt to the ruler who makes it possible, by his management and foresight, for him to enjoy rich leisure, control of his own time, and a tranquillity uninterrupted by public employments.

> Shepherd! a god this leisure gave to me,
> For he shall be my god eternally.

And if even such leisure as that of our poet owes a great debt to its author, though its greatest boon is this:

> As thou canst see,
> He let me turn my cattle out to feed,
> And play what fancy pleased on rustic reed;

how highly are we to value this leisure of the philosopher, which is spent among the gods, and makes us gods?

Yes, this is what I mean, Lucilius; and I invite you to heaven by a short cut.

Sextius used to say that Jupiter had no more power than the good man. Of course, Jupiter has more gifts which he can offer to mankind; but when you are choosing between two good men, the richer is not necessarily the better, any more than, in the case of two pilots of equal skill in managing the tiller, you would call him the better whose ship is larger and more imposing.

In what respect is Jupiter superior to our good man? His goodness lasts longer; but the wise man does not set a lower value upon himself, just because his virtues are limited by a briefer span. Or take two wise men; he who has died at a greater age is not happier than he whose virtue has been limited to fewer years: similarly, a god has no advantage over a wise man in point of happiness, even though he has such an advantage in point of years. That virtue is not greater which lasts longer.

Jupiter possesses all things, but he has surely given over the possession of them to others; the only use of them which belongs to him is this: he is the cause of their use to all men. The wise man surveys and scorns all the possessions of others as calmly as does Jupiter, and regards himself with the greater esteem because, while Jupiter cannot make use of them, he, the wise man, does not wish to do so.

Let us therefore believe Sextius when he shows us the path of perfect beauty, and cries: "This is 'the way to the stars' ; this is the way, by observing thrift, self-restraint, and courage!"

The gods are not disdainful or envious; they open the door to you; they lend a hand as you climb.

Do you marvel that man goes to the gods? God comes to men; nay, he comes nearer—he comes into men. No mind that has not God, is good. Divine seeds are scattered throughout our mortal bodies; if a good husbandman receives them, they spring up in the likeness of their source and of a parity with those from which they came. If, however, the husbandman be bad, like a barren or marshy soil, he kills the seeds, and causes tares to grow up instead of wheat. Farewell.

# Letter 47
# On Virtue as a Refuge from Worldly Distractions

Your letter has given me pleasure, and has roused me from sluggishness. It has also prompted my memory, which has been for some time slack and nerveless.

You are right, of course, my dear Lucilius, in deeming the chief means of attaining the happy life to consist in the belief that the only good lies in that which is honourable. For anyone who deems other things to be good, puts himself in the power of Fortune, and goes under the control of another; but he who has in every case defined the good by the honourable, is happy with an inward happiness.

One man is saddened when his children die; another is anxious when they become ill; a third is embittered when they do something disgraceful, or suffer a taint in their reputation. One man, you will observe, is tortured by passion for his neighbour's wife, another by passion for his own. You will find men who are completely upset by failure to win an election, and others who are actually plagued by the offices which they have won.

But the largest throng of unhappy men among the host of mortals are those whom the expectation of death, which threatens them on every hand, drives to despair. For there is no quarter from which death may not approach. Hence, like soldiers scouting in the enemy's country, they must look about in all directions, and turn their heads at every sound; unless the breast be rid of this fear, one lives with a palpitating heart.

You will readily recall those who have been driven into exile and dispossessed of their property. You will also recall (and this is the most serious kind of destitution) those who are poor in the midst of their riches. You will recall men who have suffered shipwreck, or those whose sufferings resemble shipwreck; for they were untroubled and at ease, when the anger or perhaps the envy of the populace—a missile most deadly to those in high places —dismantled them like a storm which is wont to rise when one is most confident of continued calm, or like a sudden stroke of lightning which even causes the region round about it to tremble. For just as anyone who stands near the bolt is stunned and resembles one who is struck so in these sudden and violent mishaps, although but one person is overwhelmed by the disaster, the rest are overwhelmed by fear, and the possibility that they may suffer makes them as downcast as the actual sufferer.

Every man is troubled in spirit by evils that come suddenly upon his neighbour. Like birds, who cower even at the whirr of an empty sling, we are distracted by mere sounds as well as by blows. No man therefore can be happy if he yields himself up to such foolish fancies. For nothing brings happiness unless it also brings calm; it is a bad sort of existence that is spent in apprehension.

Whoever has largely surrendered himself to the power of Fortune has made for himself a huge web of disquietude, from which he cannot get free; if one would win a way to safety, there is but one road—to despise externals and to be contented with that which is honourable. For those who regard anything as better than virtue, or believe that there is any good except virtue, are spreading their arms to gather in that which Fortune tosses abroad, and are anxiously awaiting her favours.

Picture now to yourself that Fortune is holding a festival, and is showering down honours, riches, and influence upon this mob of mortals; some of these gifts have already been torn to pieces in the hands of those who try to snatch them, others have been divided up by treacherous partnerships, and still others have been seized to the great detriment of those into whose possession they have come. Certain of these favours have fallen to men while they were absent-minded; others have been lost to their seekers because they were snatching too eagerly for them, and, just because they are greedily seized upon, have been knocked from their hands. There is not a man among them all, however—even he who has been lucky in the booty which has fallen to him—whose joy in his spoil has lasted until the morrow.

The most sensible man, therefore, as soon as he sees the dole being brought in, runs from the theatre; for he knows that one pays a high price for small favours. No one will grapple with him on the way out, or strike him as he departs; the quarrelling takes place where the prizes are.

Similarly with the gifts which Fortune tosses down to us; wretches that we are, we become excited, we are torn asunder, we wish that we had many hands, we look back now in this direction and now in that. All too slowly, as it seems, are the gifts thrown in our direction; they merely excite our cravings, since they can reach but few and are awaited by all.

We are keen to intercept them as they fall down. We rejoice if we have laid hold of anything; and some have been mocked by the idle hope of laying hold; we have either paid a high price for worthless plunder with some disadvantage to ourselves, or else have been defrauded and are left in the lurch. Let us therefore withdraw from a game like this, and give way to the greedy rabble; let them gaze after such "goods," which hang suspended above them, and be themselves still more in suspense.

Whoever makes up his mind to be happy should conclude that the good consists only in that which is honourable. For if he regards anything else as good, he is, in the first place, passing an unfavourable judgment upon Providence because of the fact that upright men often suffer misfortunes, and that the time which is allotted to us is but short and scanty, if you compare it with the eternity which is allotted to the universe.

It is a result of complaints like these that we are unappreciative in our comments upon the gifts of heaven; we complain because they are not always granted to us, because they are few and unsure and fleeting. Hence we have not the will either to live or to die; we are possessed by hatred of life, by fear of death. Our plans are all at sea, and no amount of prosperity can satisfy us. And the reason for all this is that we have not yet attained to that good which is immeasurable and unsurpassable, in which all wishing on our part must cease, because there is no place beyond the highest.

Do you ask why virtue needs nothing? Because it is pleased with what it has, and does not lust after that which it has not. Whatever is enough is abundant in the eyes of virtue.

Dissent from this judgment, and duty and loyalty will not abide. For one who desires to exhibit these two qualities must endure much that the world calls evil; we must sacrifice many things to which we are addicted, thinking them to be goods.

Gone is courage, which should be continually testing itself; gone is greatness of soul, which cannot stand out clearly unless it has learned to scorn as trivial everything that the crowd covets as supremely important; and gone is kindness and the repaying of kindness, if we fear toil, if we have acknowledged anything to be more precious than loyalty, if our eyes are fixed upon anything except the best.

But to pass these questions by: either these so-called goods are not goods, or else man is more fortunate than God, because God has no enjoyment of the things which are given to us. For lust pertains not to God, nor do elegant banquets, nor wealth, nor any of the things that allure mankind and lead him on through the influence of degrading pleasure. Therefore, it is, either not incredible that there are goods which God does not possess, or else the very fact that God does not possess them is in itself a proof that these things are not goods. Besides, many things which are wont to be regarded as goods are granted to animals in fuller measure than to men. Animals eat their food with better appetite, are not in the same degree weakened by sexual indulgence, and have a greater and more uniform constancy in their strength. Consequently, they are much more fortunate than man. For there is no wickedness, no injury to themselves, in their way of living. They enjoy their pleasures and they take them more often and more easily, without any of the fear that results from shame or regret.

This being so, you should consider whether one has a right to call anything good in which God is outdone by man. Let us limit the Supreme Good to the soul; it loses its meaning if it is taken from the best part of us and applied to the worst, that is, if it is transferred to the senses; for the senses are more active in dumb beasts. The sum total of our happiness must not be placed in the flesh; the true goods are those which reason bestows, substantial and eternal; they cannot fall away, neither can they grow less or be diminished.

Other things are goods according to opinion, and though they are called by the same name as the true goods, the essence of goodness is not in them. Let us therefore call them "advantages," and, to use our technical term, "preferred" things. Let us, however, recognize that they are our chattels, not parts of ourselves; and let us have them in our possession, but take heed to remember that they are outside ourselves. Even though they are in our possession, they are to be reckoned as things subordinate and poor, the possession of which gives no man a right to plume himself. For what is more foolish than being self-complacent about something which one has not accomplished by one's own efforts?

Let everything of this nature be added to us, and not stick fast to us, so that, if it is withdrawn, it may come away without tearing off any part of us. Let us use these things, but not boast of them, and let us use them sparingly, as if they were given for safe-keeping and will be withdrawn. Anyone who does not employ reason in his possession of them never keeps them long; for prosperity of itself, if uncontrolled by reason, overwhelms itself. If anyone has put his trust in goods that are most fleeting, he is soon bereft of them, and, to avoid being bereft, he suffers distress. Few men have been permitted to lay aside prosperity gently. The rest all fall, together with the things amid which they have come into eminence, and they are weighted down by the very things which had before exalted them.

For this reason foresight must be brought into play, to insist upon a limit or upon frugality in the use of these things, since license overthrows and destroys its own abundance. That which has no limit has never endured, unless reason, which sets limits, has held it in check. The fate of many cities will prove the truth of this; their sway has ceased at the very prime because they were given to luxury, and excess has ruined all that had been won by virtue. We should fortify ourselves against such calamities. But no wall can be erected against Fortune which she cannot take by storm; let us strengthen our inner defences. If the inner part be safe, man can be attacked, but never captured.

Do you wish to know what this weapon of defence is?

It is the ability to refrain from chafing over whatever happens to one, of knowing that the very agencies which seem to bring harm are working for the preservation of the world, and are a part of the scheme for bringing to fulfilment the order of the universe and its functions. Let man be pleased with whatever has pleased God; let him marvel at himself and his own resources for this very reason, that he cannot be overcome, that he has the very powers of evil subject to his control, and that he brings into subjection chance and pain and wrong by means of that strongest of powers—reason.

Love reason! The love of reason will arm you against the greatest hardships. Wild beasts dash against the hunter's spear through love of their young, and it is their wildness and their unpremeditated onrush that keep them from being tamed; often a desire for glory has stirred the mind of youth to despise both sword and stake; the mere vision and semblance of virtue impel certain men to a self-imposed death. In proportion as reason is stouter and steadier than ally of these emotions, so much the more forcefully will she make her way through the midst of utter terrors and dangers.

Men say to us: "You are mistaken if you maintain that nothing is a good except that which is honourable; a defence like this will not make you safe from Fortune and free from her assaults. For you maintain that dutiful children, and a well-governed country, and good parents, are to be reckoned as goods; but you cannot see these dear objects in danger and be yourself at ease. Your calm will be disturbed by a siege conducted against your country, by the death of your children, or by the enslaving of your parents."

I will first state what we Stoics usually reply to these objectors, and then will add what additional answer should, in my opinion, be given.

The situation is entirely different in the case of goods whose loss entails some hardship substituted in their place; for example, when good health is impaired there is a change to ill-health; when the eye is put out, we are visited with blindness; we not only lose our speed when our leg-muscles are cut, but infirmity takes the place of speed. But no such danger is involved in the case of the goods to which we referred a moment ago. And why if I have lost a good friend, I have no false friend whom I must endure in his place; nor if I have buried a dutiful son, must I face in exchange unfilial conduct.

In the second place, this does not mean to me the taking-off of a friend or of a child; it is the mere taking-off of their bodies. But a good can be lost in only one way, by changing into what is bad; and this is impossible according to the law of nature, because every virtue, and every work of virtue, abides uncorrupted. Again, even if friends have perished, or children of approved goodness who fulfil their father's prayers for them, there is something that can fill their place. Do you ask what this is? It is that which had made them good in the first place, namely, virtue.

Virtue suffers no space in us to be unoccupied; it takes possession of the whole soul and removes all sense of loss. It alone is sufficient; for the strength and beginnings of all goods exist in virtue herself. What does it matter if running water is cut off and flows away, as long as the fountain from which it has flowed is unharmed? You will not maintain that a man's life is more just if his children are unharmed than if they have passed away, nor yet better appointed, nor more intelligent, nor more honourable; therefore, no better, either. The addition of friends does not make one wiser, nor does their taking away make one more foolish; therefore, not happier or more wretched, either. As long is your virtue is unharmed, you will not feel the loss of anything that has been withdrawn from you.

You may say, "Come now; is not a man happier when girt about with a large company of friends and children?" Why should this be so? For the Supreme Good is neither impaired nor increased thereby; it abides within its own limits, no matter how Fortune has conducted herself. Whether a long old age falls to one's lot, or whether the end comes on this side of old age—the measure of the Supreme Good is unvaried, in spite of the difference in years.

Whether you draw a larger or a smaller circle, its size affects its area, not its shape. One circle may remain as it is for a long time while you may contract the other forthwith, or even merge it completely with the sand in which it was drawn; yet each circle has had the same shape. That which is straight is not judged by its size, or by its number, or by its duration; it can no more be made longer than it can be made shorter. Scale down the honourable life as much as you like from the full hundred years, and reduce it to a single day; it is equally honourable.

Sometimes virtue is widespread, governing kingdoms, cities, and provinces, creating laws, developing friendships, and regulating the duties that hold good between relatives and children; at other times it is limited by the narrow bounds of poverty, exile, or bereavement. But it is no smaller when it is reduced from prouder heights to a private station, from a royal palace to a humble dwelling, or when from a general and broad jurisdiction it is gathered into the narrow limits of a private house or a tiny corner.

Virtue is just as great, even when it has retreated within itself and is shut in on all sides. For its spirit is no less great and upright, its sagacity no less complete, its justice no less inflexible. It is, therefore, equally happy. For happiness has its abode in one place only, namely, in the mind itself, and is noble, steadfast, and calm; and this state cannot be attained without a knowledge of things divine and human.

The other answer, which I promised to make to your objection, follows from this reasoning. The wise man is not distressed by the loss of children or of friends. For he endures their death in the same spirit in which he awaits his own. And he fears the one as little as he grieves for the other. For the underlying principle of virtue is conformity; all the works of virtue are in harmony and agreement with virtue itself. But this harmony is lost if the soul, which ought to be uplifted, is cast down by grief or a sense of loss. It is ever a dishonour for a man to be troubled and fretted, to be numbed when there is any call for activity. For that which is honourable is free from care and untrammelled, is unafraid, and stands girt for action.

"What," you ask, "will the wise man experience no emotion like disturbance of spirit? Will not his features change colour, his countenance be agitated, and his limbs grow cold? And there are other things which we do, not under the influence of the will, but unconsciously and as the result of a sort of natural impulse." I admit that this is true; but the sage will retain the firm belief that none of these things is evil, or important enough to make a healthy mind break down.

Whatever shall remain to be done virtue can do with courage and readiness. For anyone would admit that it is a mark of folly to do in a slothful and rebellious spirit whatever one has to do, or to direct the body in one direction and the mind in another, and thus to be torn between utterly conflicting emotions. For folly is despised precisely because of the things for which she vaunts and admires herself, and she does not do gladly even those things in which she prides herself. But if folly fears some evil, she is burdened by it in the very moment of awaiting it, just as if it had actually come—already suffering in apprehension whatever she fears she may suffer.

Just as in the body symptoms of latent ill-health precede the disease—there is, for example, a certain weak sluggishness, a lassitude which is not the result of any work, a trembling, and a shivering that pervades the limbs—so the feeble spirit is shaken by its ills a long time before it is overcome by them. It anticipates them, and totters before its time.

But what is greater madness than to be tortured by the future and not to save your strength for the actual suffering, but to invite and bring on wretchedness? If you cannot be rid of it, you ought at least to postpone it.

Will you not understand that no man should be tormented by the future? The man who has been told that he will have to endure torture fifty years from now is not disturbed thereby, unless he has leaped over the intervening years, and has projected himself into the trouble that is destined to arrive a generation later. In the same way, souls that enjoy being sick and that seize upon excuses for sorrow are saddened by events long past and effaced from the records. Past and future are both absent; we feel neither of them. But there can be no pain except as the result of what you feel. Farewell.

# Letter 48
# On the Diseases of the Soul

You have been complaining that my letters to you are rather carelessly written. Now who talks carefully unless he also desires to talk affectedly? I prefer that my letters should be just what my conversation would be if you and I were sitting in one another's company or taking walks together, spontaneous and easy; for my letters have nothing strained or artificial about them.

If it were possible, I should prefer to show, rather than speak, my feelings. Even if I were arguing a point, I should not stamp my foot, or toss my arms about, or raise my voice; but I should leave that sort of thing to the orator, and should be content to have conveyed my feelings to you without having either embellished them or lowered their dignity.

I should like to convince you entirely of this one fact—that I feel whatever I say, that I not only feel it, but am wedded to it. It is one sort of kiss which a man gives his mistress and another which he gives his children; yet in the father's embrace also, holy and restrained as it is, plenty of affection is disclosed.

I prefer, however, that our conversation on matters so important should not be meagre and dry; for even philosophy does not renounce the company of cleverness. One should not, however, bestow very much attention upon mere words.

Let this be the kernel of my idea: let us say what we feel, and feel what we say; let speech harmonize with life. That man has fulfilled his promise who is the same person both when you see him and when you hear him.

We shall not fail to see what sort of man he is and how large a man he is, if only he is one and the same. Our words should aim not to please, but to help. If, however, you can attain eloquence without painstaking, and if you either are naturally gifted or can gain eloquence at slight cost, make the most of it and apply it to the noblest uses. But let it be of such a kind that it displays facts rather than itself. It and the other arts are wholly concerned with cleverness; but our business here is the soul.

A sick man does not call in a physician who is eloquent; but if it so happens that the physician who can cure him likewise discourses elegantly about the treatment which is to be followed, the patient will take it in good part. For all that, he will not find any reason to congratulate himself on having discovered a physician who is eloquent. For the case is no different from that of a skilled pilot who is also handsome.

Why do you tickle my ears? Why do you entertain me? There is other business at hand; I am to be cauterized, operated upon, or put on a diet. That is why you were summoned to treat me!

You are required to cure a disease that is chronic and serious—one which affects the general weal. You have as serious a business on hand as a physician has during a plague. Are you concerned about words? Rejoice this instant if you can cope with *things*. When shall you learn all that there is to learn? When shall you so plant in your mind that which you have learned, that it cannot escape? When shall you put it all into practice? For it is not sufficient merely to commit these things to memory, like other matters; they must be practically tested. He is not happy who only knows them, but he who does them.

You reply: "What? Are there no degrees of happiness below your 'happy' man? Is there a sheer descent immediately below wisdom?" I think not. For though he who makes progress is still numbered with the fools, yet he is separated from them by a long interval. Among the very persons who are making progress there are also great spaces intervening. They fall into three classes, as certain philosophers believe.

First come those who have not yet attained wisdom but have already gained a place near by. Yet even that which is not far away is still outside. These, if you ask me, are men who have already laid aside all passions and vices, who have learned what things are to be embraced; but their assurance is not yet tested. They have not yet put their good into practice, yet from now on they cannot slip back into the faults which they have escaped. They have already arrived at a point from which there is no slipping back, but they are not yet aware of the fact; as I remember writing in another letter, "They are ignorant of their knowledge." It has now been vouchsafed to them to enjoy their good, but not yet to be sure of it.

Some define this class, of which I have been speaking—a class of men who are making progress—as having escaped the diseases of the mind, but not yet the passions, and as still standing upon slippery ground;

because no one is beyond the dangers of evil except him who has cleared himself of it wholly. But no one has so cleared himself except the man who has adopted wisdom in its stead.

I have often before explained the difference between the diseases of the mind and its passions. And I shall remind you once more: the diseases are hardened and chronic vices, such as greed and ambition; they have enfolded the mind in too close a grip, and have begun to be permanent evils thereof. To give a brief definition: by "disease" we mean a persistent perversion of the judgment, so that things which are mildly desirable are thought to be highly desirable. Or, if you prefer, we may define it thus: to be too zealous in striving for things which are only mildly desirable or not desirable at all, or to value highly things which ought to be valued but slightly or valued not at all.

"Passions" are objectionable impulses of the spirit, sudden and vehement; they have come so often, and so little attention has been paid to them, that they have caused a state of disease; just as a catarrh, when there has been but a single attack and the catarrh has not yet become habitual, produces a cough, but causes consumption when it has become regular and chronic. Therefore we may say that those who have made most progress are beyond the reach of the "diseases"; but they still feel the "passions" even when very near perfection.

The second class is composed of those who have laid aside both the greatest ills of the mind and its passions, but yet are not in assured possession of immunity. For they can still slip back into their former state.

The third class are beyond the reach of many of the vices and particularly of the great vices, but not beyond the reach of all. They have escaped avarice, for example, but still feel anger; they no longer are troubled by lust, but are still troubled by ambition; they no longer have desire, but they still have fear. And just because they fear, although they are strong enough to withstand certain things, there are certain things to which they yield; they scorn death, but are in terror of pain.

Let us reflect a moment on this topic. It will be well with us if we are admitted to this class. The second stage is gained by great good fortune with regard to our natural gifts and by great and unceasing application to study. But not even the third type is to be despised. Think of the host of evils which you see about you; behold how there is no crime that is not exemplified, how far wickedness advances every day, and how prevalent are sins in home and commonwealth. You will see, therefore, that we are making a considerable gain, if we are not numbered among the basest.

"But as for me," you say, "I hope that it is in me to rise to a higher rank than that!" I should pray, rather than promise, that we may attain this; we have been forestalled. We hasten towards virtue while hampered by vices. I am ashamed to say it; but we worship that which is honourable only in so far as we have time to spare. But what a rich reward awaits us if only we break off the affairs which forestall us and the evils that cling to us with utter tenacity!

Then neither desire nor fear shall rout us. Undisturbed by fears, unspoiled by pleasures, we shall be afraid neither of death nor of the gods; we shall know that death is no evil and that the gods are not powers of evil. That which harms has no greater power than that which receives harm, and things which are utterly good have no power at all to harm.

There await us, if ever we escape from these low dregs to that sublime and lofty height, peace of mind and, when all error has been driven out, perfect liberty. You ask what this freedom is? It means not fearing either men or gods; it means not craving wickedness or excess; it means possessing supreme power over oneself And it is a priceless good to be master of oneself. Farewell.

# Letter 49

# On Learning Wisdom in Old Age

You have been threatening me with your enmity, if I do not keep you informed about all my daily actions. But see, now, upon what frank terms you and I live: for I shall confide even the following fact to your ears. I have been hearing the lectures of a philosopher; four days have already passed since I have been attending his school and listening to the harangue, which begins at two o'clock. "A fine time of life for that!" you say. Yes, fine indeed! Now what is more foolish than refusing to learn, simply because one has not been learning for a long time?

"What do you mean? Must I follow the fashion set by the fops and youngsters?" But I am pretty well off if this is the only thing that discredits my declining years. Men of all ages are admitted to this class-room. You retort: "Do we grow old merely in order to tag after the youngsters?" But if I, an old man, go to the theatre, and am carried to the races, and allow no duel in the arena to be fought to a finish without my presence, shall I blush to attend a philosopher's lecture?

You should keep learning as long as you are ignorant—even to the end of your life, if there is anything in the proverb. And the proverb suits the present case as well as any: "As long as you live, keep learning how to live." For all that, there is also something which I can teach in that school. You ask, do you, what I can teach? That even an old man should keep learning.

But I am ashamed of mankind, as often as I enter the lecture hall. On my way to the house of Metronax I am compelled to go, as you know, right past the Neapolitan Theatre. The building is jammed; men are deciding, with tremendous zeal, who is entitled to be called a good flute-player; even the Greek piper and the herald draw their crowds. But in the other place, where the question discussed is: "What is a good man?" and the lesson which we learn is "How to be a good man," very few are in attendance, and the majority think that even these few are engaged in no good business; they have the name of being empty-headed idler. I hope I may be blessed with that kind of mockery; for one should listen in an unruffled spirit to the railings of the ignorant; when one is marching toward the goal of honour, one should scorn scorn itself.

Proceed, then, Lucilius, and hasten, lest you yourself be compelled to learn in your old age, as is the case with me. Nay, you must hasten all the more, because for a long time you have not approached the subject, which is one that you can scarcely learn thoroughly when you are old. "How much progress shall I make?" you ask. Just as much as you try to make.

Why do you wait? Wisdom comes haphazard to no man. Money will come of its own accord; titles will be given to you; influence and authority will perhaps be thrust upon you; but virtue will not fall upon you by chance. Either is knowledge thereof to be won by light effort or small toil; but toiling is worth while when one is about to win all goods at a single stroke.

For there is but a single good—namely, that which is honourable; in all those other things of which the general opinion approves, you will find no truth or certainty. Why it is, however, that there is but one good, namely, that which is honourable, I shall now tell you, inasmuch as you judge that in my earlier letter I did not carry the discussion far enough, and think that this theory was commended to you rather than proved. I shall also compress the remarks of other authors into narrow compass.

Everything is estimated by the standard of its own good. The vine is valued for its productiveness and the flavour of its wine, the stag for his speed. We ask, with regard to beasts of burden, how sturdy of back they are; for their only use is to bear burdens. If a dog is to find the trail of a wild beast, keenness of scent is of first importance; if to catch his quarry, swiftness of foot; if to attack and harry it, courage. In each thing that quality should be best for which the thing is brought into being and by which it is judged.

And what quality is best in man? It is reason; by virtue of reason he surpasses the animals, and is surpassed only by the gods. Perfect reason is therefore the good peculiar to man; all other qualities he shares in some degree with animals and plants. Man is strong; so is the lion. Man is comely; so is the peacock. Man is swift; so is the horse. I do not say that man is surpassed in all these qualities. I am not seeking to find that which is greatest in him, but that which is peculiarly his own. Man has body; so also have trees. Man has the power to act and to move at will;

so have beasts and worms. Man has a voice; but how much louder is the voice of the dog, how much shriller that of the eagle, how much deeper that of the bull, how much sweeter and more melodious that of the nightingale!

What then is peculiar to man? Reason. When this is right and has reached perfection, man's felicity is complete. Hence, if everything is praiseworthy and has arrived at the end intended by its nature, when it has brought its peculiar good to perfection, and if man's peculiar good is reason; then, if a man has brought his reason to perfection, he is praiseworthy and has reached the end suited to his nature. This perfect reason is called virtue, and is likewise that which is honourable.

Hence that in man is alone a good which alone belongs to man. For we are not now seeking to discover what is a good, but what good is man's. And if there is no other attribute which belongs peculiarly to man except reason, then reason will be his one peculiar good, but a good that is worth all the rest put together. If any man is bad, he will, I suppose, be regarded with disapproval; if good, I suppose he will be regarded with approval. Therefore, that attribute of man whereby he is approved or disapproved is his chief and only good.

You do not doubt whether this is a good; you merely doubt whether it is the sole good. If a man possess all other things, such as health, riches, pedigree, a crowded reception-hall, but is confessedly bad, you will disapprove of him. Likewise, if a man possess none of the things which I have mentioned, and lacks money, or an escort of clients, or rank and a line of grandfathers and great-grandfathers, but is confessedly good, you will approve of him. Hence, this is man's one peculiar good, and the possessor of it is to be praised even if he lacks other things; but he who does not possess it, though he possess everything else in abundance is condemned and rejected.

The same thing holds good regarding men as regarding things. A ship is said to be good not when it is decorated with costly colours, nor when its prow is covered with silver or gold or its figure-head embossed in ivory, nor when it is laden with the imperial revenues or with the wealth of kings, but when it is steady and staunch and taut, with seams that keep out the water, stout enough to endure the buffeting of the waves' obedient to its helm, swift and caring naught for the winds.

You will speak of a sword as good, not when its sword-belt is of gold, or its scabbard studded with gems, but when its edge is fine for cutting and its point will pierce any armour. Take the carpenter's rule: we do not ask how beautiful it is, but how straight it is. Each thing is praised in regard to that attribute which is taken as its standard, in regard to that which is its peculiar quality.

Therefore in the case of man also, it is not pertinent to the question to know how many acres he ploughs, how much money he has out at interest, how many callers attend his receptions, how costly is the couch on which he lies, how transparent are the cups from which he drinks, but how good he is. He is good, however, if his reason is well-ordered and right and adapted to that which his nature has willed.

It is this that is called virtue; this is what we mean by "honourable"; it is man's unique good. For since reason alone brings man to perfection, reason alone, when perfected, makes man happy. This, moreover, is man's only good, the only means by which he is made happy. We do indeed say that those things also are goods which are furthered and brought together by virtue—that is, all the works of virtue; but virtue itself is for this reason the only good, because there is no good without virtue.

If every good is in the soul, then whatever strengthens, uplifts, and enlarges the soul, is a good; virtue, however, does make the soul stronger, loftier, and larger. For all other things, which arouse our desires, depress the soul and weaken it, and when we think that they are uplifting the soul, they are merely puffing it up and cheating it with much emptiness. Therefore, that alone is good which will make the soul better.

All the actions of life, taken as a whole, are controlled by the consideration of what is honourable or base; it is with reference to these two things that our reason is governed in doing or not doing a particular thing. I shall explain what I mean: A good man will do what he thinks it will be honourable for him to do, even if it involves toil; he will do it even if it involves harm to him; he will do it even if it involves peril; again, he will not do that which will be base, even if it brings him money, or pleasure, or power. Nothing will deter him from that which is honourable, and nothing will tempt him into baseness.

Therefore, if he is determined invariably to follow that which is honourable, invariably to avoid baseness, and in every act of his life to have regard for these two things, deeming nothing else good except that which is honourable, and nothing else bad except that which is base; if virtue alone is unperverted in him and by itself keeps its even course, then virtue is that man's only good, and nothing can thenceforth happen to it which may make it anything else than good. It has escaped all risk of change; folly may creep upwards towards wisdom, but wisdom never slips back into folly.

You may perhaps remember my saying that the things which have been generally desired and feared have been trampled down by many a man in moments of sudden passion. There have been found men who would place their hands in the flames, men whose smiles could not be stopped by the torturer, men who would shed not a tear at the funeral of their children, men who would meet death unflinchingly. It is love, for example, anger, lust, which have challenged dangers. If a momentary stubbornness can accomplish all this when roused by some goad that pricks the spirit, how much more can be accomplished by virtue, which does not act impulsively or suddenly, but uniformly and with a strength that is lasting!

It follows that the things which are often scorned by the men who are moved with a sudden passion, and are always scorned by the wise, are neither goods nor evils. Virtue itself is therefore the only good; she marches proudly between the two extremes of fortune, with great scorn for both.

If, however, you accept the view that there is anything good besides that which is honourable, all the virtues will suffer. For it will never be possible for any virtue to be won and held, if there is anything outside itself which virtue must take into consideration. If there is any such thing, then it is at variance with reason, from which the virtues spring, and with truth also, which cannot exist without reason. Any opinion, however, which is at variance with truth, is wrong.

A good man, you will admit, must have the highest sense of duty toward the gods. Hence he will endure with an unruffled spirit whatever happens to him; for he will know that it has happened as a result of the divine law, by which the whole creation moves. This being so, there will be for him one good, and only one, namely, that which is honourable; for one of its dictates is that we shall obey the gods and not blaze forth in anger at sudden misfortunes or deplore our lot, but rather patiently accept fate and obey its commands.

If anything except the honourable is good, we shall be hounded by greed for life, and by greed for the things which provide life with its furnishings—an intolerable state, subject to no limits, unstable. The only good, therefore, is that which is honourable, that which is subject to bounds.

I have declared that man's life would be more blest than that of the gods, if those things which the gods do not enjoy are goods—such as money and offices of dignity. There is this further consideration: if only it is true that our souls, when released from the body, still abide, a happier condition is in store for them than is theirs while they dwell in the body. And yet, if those things are goods which we make use of for our bodies' sake, our souls will be worse off when set free; and that is contrary to our belief, to say that the soul is happier when it is cabined and confined than when it is free and has betaken itself to the universe.

I also said that if those things which dumb animals possess equally with man are goods, then dumb animals also will lead a happy life; which is of course impossible. One must endure all things in defence of that which is honourable; but this would not be necessary if there existed any other good besides that which is honourable.

Although this question was discussed by me pretty extensively in a previous letter, I have discussed it summarily and briefly run through the argument.

But an opinion of this kind will never seem true to you unless you exalt your mind and ask yourself whether, at the call of duty, you would be willing to die for your country, and buy the safety of all your fellow-citizens at the price of your own; whether you would offer your neck not only with patience, but also with gladness. If you would do this, there is no other good in your eyes. For you are giving up everything in order to acquire this good. Consider how great is the power of that which is honourable: you will die for your country, even at a moment's notice, when you know that you ought to do so.

Sometimes, as a result of noble conduct, one wins great joy even in a very short and fleeting space of time; and though none of the fruits of a deed that has been done will accrue to the doer after he is dead and removed from the sphere of human affairs, yet the mere contemplation of a deed that is to be done is a delight, and the brave and upright man, picturing to himself the guerdons of his death—guerdons such as the freedom of his country and the deliverance of all those for whom he is paying out his life—partakes of the greatest pleasure and enjoys the fruit of his own peril.

But that man also who is deprived of this joy, the joy which is afforded by the contemplation of some last noble effort, will leap to his death without a moment's hesitation, content to act rightly and dutifully. Moreover, you may confront him with many discouragements; you may say: "Your deed will speedily be forgotten," or "Your fellow-citizens will offer you scant thanks." He will answer: "All these matters lie outside my task. My thoughts are on the deed itself. I know that this is honourable. Therefore, whithersoever I am led and summoned by honour, I will go."

This, therefore, is the only good, and not only is every soul that has reached perfection aware of it, but also every soul that is by nature noble and of right instincts; all other goods are trivial and mutable. For this reason we are harassed if we possess them. Even though, by the kindness of Fortune, they have been heaped together, they weigh heavily upon their owners, always pressing them down and sometimes crushing them.

None of those whom you behold clad in purple is happy, any more than one of these actors upon whom the play bestows a sceptre and a cloak while on the stage; they strut their hour before a crowded house, with swelling port and buskined foot; but when once they make their exit the foot gear is removed and they return to their proper stature. None of those who have been raised to a loftier height by riches and honours is really great. Why then does he seem great to you? It is because you are measuring the pedestal along with the man. A dwarf is not tall, though he stand upon a mountain-top; a colossal statue will still be tall, though you place it in a well.

This is the error under which we labour; this is the reason why we are imposed upon: we value no man at what he is, but add to the man himself the trappings in which he is clothed. But when you wish to inquire into a man's true worth, and to know what manner of man he is, look at him when he is naked; make him lay aside his inherited estate, his titles, and the other deceptions of fortune; let him even strip off his body. Consider his soul, its quality and its stature, and thus learn whether its greatness is borrowed, or its own.

If a man can behold with unflinching eyes the flash of a sword, if he knows that it makes no difference to him whether his soul takes flight through his mouth or through a wound in his throat, you may call him happy; you may also call him happy if, when he is threatened with bodily torture, whether it be the result of accident or of the might of the stronger, he can without concern hear talk of chains, or of exile, or of all the idle fears that stir men's minds, and can say:

> "O maiden, no new sudden form of toil
> Springs up before my eyes; within my soul
> I have forestalled and surveyed everything.

Today it is you who threaten me with these terrors; but I have always threatened myself with them, and have prepared myself as a man to meet man's destiny.

If an evil has been pondered beforehand, the blow is gentle when it comes. To the fool, however, and to him who trusts in fortune, each event as it arrives "comes in a new and sudden form," and a large part of evil, to the inexperienced, consists in its novelty. This is proved by the fact that men endure with greater courage, when they have once become accustomed to them, the things which they had at first regarded as hardships.

Hence, the wise man accustoms himself to coming trouble, lightening by long reflection the evils which others lighten by long endurance. We sometimes hear the inexperienced say: "I knew that this was in store for me." But the wise man knows that all things are in store for him. Whatever happens, he says: "I knew it." Farewell.

# Letter 50
# On Taking One's Own Life

Suddenly there came into our view today the "Alexandrian" ships—I mean those which are usually sent ahead to announce the coming of the fleet; they are called "mail-boats." The Campanians are glad to see them; all the rabble of Puteoli stand on the docks, and can recognize the "Alexandrian" boats, no matter how great the crowd of vessels, by the very trim of their sails. For they alone may keep spread their topsails, which all ships use when out at sea, because nothing sends a ship along so well as its upper canvas; that is where most of the speed is obtained. So when the breeze has stiffened and becomes stronger than is comfortable, they set their yards lower; for the wind has less force near the surface of the water. Accordingly, when they have made Capreae and the headland whence

*Tall Pallas watches on the stormy peak,*

all other vessels are bidden to be content with the mainsail, and the topsail stands out conspicuously on the "Alexandrian" mail-boats.

While everybody was bustling about and hurrying to the water-front, I felt great pleasure in my laziness, because, although I was soon to receive letters from my friends, I was in no hurry to know how my affairs were progressing abroad, or what news the letters were bringing; for some time now I have had no losses, nor gains either. Even if I were not an old man, I could not have helped feeling pleasure at this; but as it is, my pleasure was far greater. For, however small my possessions might be, I should still have left over more travelling-money than journey to travel, especially since this journey upon which we have set out is one which need not be followed to the end.

An expedition will be incomplete if one stops half-way, or anywhere on this side of one's destination; but life is not incomplete if it is honourable. At whatever point you leave off living, provided you leave off nobly, your life is a whole. Often, however, one must leave off bravely, and our reasons therefore need not be momentous; for neither are the reasons momentous which hold us here.

Tullius Marcellinus, a man whom you knew very well, who in youth was a quiet soul and became old prematurely, fell ill of a disease which was by no means hopeless; but it was protracted and troublesome, and it demanded much attention; hence he began to think about dying. He called many of his friends together. Each one of them gave Marcellinus advice—the timid friend urging him to do what he had made up his mind to do; the flattering and wheedling friend giving counsel which he supposed would be more pleasing to Marcellinus when he came to think the matter over; but our Stoic friend, a rare man, and, to praise him in language which he deserves, a man of courage and vigour admonished him best of all, as it seems to me. For he began as follows: "Do not torment yourself, my dear Marcellinus, as if the question which you are weighing were a matter of importance. It is not an important matter to live; all your slaves live, and so do all animals; but it is important to die honourably, sensibly, bravely. Reflect how long you have been doing the same thing: food, sleep, lust—this is one's daily round. The desire to die may be felt, not only by the sensible man or the brave or unhappy man, but even by the man who is merely surfeited."

Marcellinus did not need someone to urge him, but rather someone to help him; his slaves refused to do his bidding. The Stoic therefore removed their fears, showing them that there was no risk involved for the household except when it was uncertain whether the master's death was self-sought or not; besides, it was as bad a practice to kill one's master as it was to prevent him forcibly from killing himself.

Then he suggested to Marcellinus himself that it would be a kindly act to distribute gifts to those who had attended him throughout his whole life, when that life was finished, just as, when a banquet is finished, the remaining portion is divided among the attendants who stand about the table. Marcellinus was of a compliant and generous disposition, even when it was a question of his own property; so he distributed little sums among his sorrowing slaves, and comforted them besides.

No need had he of sword or of bloodshed; for three days he fasted and had a tent put up in his very bedroom. Then a tub was brought in; he lay in it for a long time, and, as the hot water was continually poured over him, he gradually passed away, not without a feeling of pleasure, as he himself remarked—such a feeling as a slow dissolution is wont to give. Those of us who have ever fainted know from experience what this feeling is.

This little anecdote into which I have digressed will not be displeasing to you. For you will see that your friend departed neither with difficulty nor with suffering. Though he committed suicide, yet he withdrew most gently, gliding out of life. The anecdote may also be of some use; for often a crisis demands just such examples. There are times when we ought to die and are unwilling; sometimes we die and are unwilling.

No one is so ignorant as not to know that we must at some time die; nevertheless, when one draws near death, one turns to flight, trembles, and laments. Would you not think him an utter fool who wept because he was not alive a thousand years ago? And is he not just as much of a fool who weeps because he will not be alive a thousand years from now? It is all the same; you will not be, and you were not. Neither of these periods of time belongs to you.

You have been cast upon this point of time; if you would make it longer, how much longer shall you make it? Why weep? Why pray? You are taking pains to no purpose.

> Give over thinking that your prayers can bend
> Divine decrees from their predestined end.

These decrees are unalterable and fixed; they are governed by a mighty and everlasting compulsion. Your goal will be the goal of all things. What is there strange in this to you? You were born to be subject to this law; this fate befell your father, your mother, your ancestors, all who came before you; and it will befall all who shall come after you. A sequence which cannot be broken or altered by any power binds all things together and draws all things in its course.

Think of the multitudes of men doomed to death who will come after you, of the multitudes who will go with you! You would die more bravely, I suppose, in the company of many thousands; and yet there are many thousands, both of men and of animals, who at this very moment, while you are irresolute about death, are breathing their last, in their several ways. But you—did you believe that you would not some day reach the goal towards which you have always been travelling? No journey but has its end.

You think, I suppose, that it is now in order for me to cite some examples of great men. No, I shall cite rather the case of a boy. The story of the Spartan lad has been preserved: taken captive while still a stripling, he kept crying in his Doric dialect, "I will not be a slave!" and he made good his word; for the very first time he was ordered to perform a menial and degrading service—and the command was to fetch a chamber-pot—he dashed out his brains against the wall.

So near at hand is freedom, and is anyone still a slave? Would you not rather have your own son die thus than reach old age by weakly yielding? Why therefore are you distressed, when even a boy can die so bravely? Suppose that you refuse to follow him; you will be led. Take into your own control that which is now under the control of another. Will you not borrow that boy's courage, and say: "I am no slave!"? Unhappy fellow, you are a slave to men, you are a slave to your business, you are a slave to life. For life, if courage to die be lacking, is slavery.

Have you anything worth waiting for? Your very pleasures, which cause you to tarry and hold you back, have already been exhausted by you. None of them is a novelty to you, and there is none that has not already become hateful because you are cloyed with it. You know the taste of wine and cordials. It makes no difference whether a hundred or a thousand measures pass through your bladder; you are nothing but a wine-strainer. You are a connoisseur in the flavour of the oyster and of the mullet; your luxury has not left you anything untasted for the years that are to come; and yet these are the things from which you are torn away unwillingly.

What else is there which you would regret to have taken from you? Friends? But who can be a friend to you? Country? What? Do you think enough of your country to be late to dinner? The light of the sun? You would extinguish it, if you could; for what have you ever done that was fit to be seen in the light? Confess the truth; it is not because you long for the senate chamber or the forum, or even for the world of nature, that you would fain put off dying; it is because you are loth to leave the fish-market, though you have exhausted its stores.

You are afraid of death; but how can you scorn it in the midst of a mushroom supper? You wish to live; well, do you know how to live? You are afraid to die. But come now: is this life of yours anything but death? Gaius Caesar was passing along the Via Latina, when a man stepped out from the ranks of the prisoners, his grey beard hanging down even to his breast, and begged to be put to death. "What!" said Caesar, "are you alive now?" That is the answer which should be given to men to whom death would come as a relief. "You are afraid to die; what! are you alive now?"

"But," says one, "I wish to live, for I am engaged in many honourable pursuits. I am loth to leave life's duties, which I am fulfilling with loyalty and zeal." Surely you are aware that dying is also one of life's duties? You are deserting no duty; for there is no definite number established which you are bound to complete.

There is no life that is not short. Compared with the world of nature, even Nestor's life was a short one, or Sattia's, the woman who bade carve on her tombstone that she had lived ninety and nine years. Some persons, you see, boast of their long lives; but who could have endured the old lady if she had had the luck to complete her hundredth year? It is with life as it is with a play   it matters not how long the action is spun out, but how good the acting is. It makes no difference at what point you stop. Stop whenever you choose; only see to it that the closing period is well turned. Farewell.

# Letter 51
# On the Healing Power of the Mind

That you are frequently troubled by the snuffling of catarrh and by short attacks of fever which follow after long and chronic catarrhal seizures, I am sorry to hear; particularly because I have experienced this sort of illness myself, and scorned it in its early stages. For when I was still young, I could put up with hardships and show a bold front to illness. But I finally succumbed, and arrived at such a state that I could do nothing but snuffle, reduced as I was to the extremity of thinness.

I often entertained the impulse of ending my life then and there; but the thought of my kind old father kept me back. For I reflected, not how bravely I had the power to die, but how little power he had to bear bravely the loss of me. And so I commanded myself to live. For sometimes it is an act of bravery even to live.

Now I shall tell you what consoled me during those days, stating at the outset that these very aids to my peace of mind were as efficacious as medicine. Honourable consolation results in a cure; and whatever has uplifted the soul helps the body also. My studies were my salvation. I place it to the credit of philosophy that I recovered and regained my strength. I owe my life to philosophy, and that is the least of my obligations!

My friends, too, helped me greatly toward good health; I used to be comforted by their cheering words, by the hours they spent at my bedside, and by their conversation. Nothing, my excellent Lucilius, refreshes and aids a sick man so much as the affection of his friends; nothing so steals away the expectation and the fear of death. In fact, I could not believe that, if they survived me, I should be dying at all. Yes, I repeat, it seemed to me that I should continue to live, not with them, but through them. I imagined myself not to be yielding up my soul, but to be making it over to them.

All these things gave me the inclination to succour myself and to endure any torture; besides, it is a most miserable state to have lost one's zest for dying, and to have no zest in living.

These, then, are the remedies to which you should have recourse. The physician will prescribe your walks and your exercise; he will warn you not to become addicted to idleness, as is the tendency of the inactive invalid; he will order you to read in a louder voice and to exercise your lungs the passages and cavity of which are affected; or to sail and shake up your bowels by a little mild motion; he will recommend the proper food, and the suitable time for aiding your strength with wine or refraining from it in order to keep your cough from being irritated and hacking. But as for me, my counsel to you is this—and it is a cure, not merely of this disease of yours, but of your whole life—"Despise death." There is no sorrow in the world, when we have escaped from the fear of death.

There are these three serious elements in every disease: fear of death, bodily pain, and interruption of pleasures. Concerning death enough has been said, and I shall add only a word: this fear is not a fear of disease, but a fear of nature. Disease has often postponed death, and a vision of dying has been many a man's salvation. You will die, not because you are ill, but because you are alive; even when you have been cured, the same end awaits you; when you have recovered, it will be not death, but ill-health, that you have escaped.

Let us now return to the consideration of the characteristic disadvantage of disease: it is accompanied by great suffering. The suffering, however, is rendered endurable by interruptions; for the strain of extreme pain must come to an end. No man can suffer both severely and for a long time; Nature, who loves us most tenderly, has so constituted us as to make pain either endurable or short.

The severest pains have their seat in the most slender parts of our body; nerves, joints, and any other of the narrow passages, hurt most cruelly when they have developed trouble within their contracted spaces. But these parts soon become numb, and by reason of the pain itself lose the sensation of pain, whether because the life-force, when checked in its natural course and changed for the worse, loses the peculiar power through which it thrives and through which it warns us, or because the diseased humours of the body, when they cease to have a place into which they may flow, are thrown back upon themselves, and deprive of sensation the parts where they have caused congestion.

So gout, both in the feet and in the hands, and all pain in the vertebrae and in the nerves, have their intervals of rest at the times when they have dulled the parts which they before had tortured; the first twinges, in all such cases, are what cause the distress, and their onset is checked by lapse of time, so that there is an end of pain when numbness has set in. Pain in the teeth, eyes, and ears is most acute for the very reason that it begins among the narrow spaces of the body—no less acute, indeed, than in the head itself. But if it is more violent than usual, it turns to delirium and stupor.

This is, accordingly, a consolation for excessive pain—that you cannot help ceasing to feel it if you feel it to excess. The reason, however, why the inexperienced are impatient when their bodies suffer is, that they have not accustomed themselves to be contented in spirit. They have been closely associated with the body Therefore a high-minded and sensible man divorces soul from body, and dwells much with the better or divine part, and only as far as he must with this complaining and frail portion.

"But it is a hardship," men say, "to do without our customary pleasures—to fast, to feel thirst and hunger." These are indeed serious when one first abstains from them. Later the desire dies down, because the appetites themselves which lead to desire are wearied and forsake us; then the stomach becomes petulant, then the food which we craved before becomes hateful. Our very wants die away. But there is no bitterness in doing without that which you have ceased to desire.

Moreover, every pain sometimes stops, or at any rate slackens; moreover, one may take precautions against its return, and, when it threatens, may check it by means of remedies. Every variety of pain has its premonitory symptoms; this is true, at any rate, of pain that is habitual and recurrent. One can endure the suffering which disease entails, if one has come to regard its results with scorn.

But do not of your own accord make your troubles heavier to bear and burden yourself with complaining. Pain is slight if opinion has added nothing to it; but if, on the other hand, you begin to encourage yourself and say, "It is nothing—a trifling matter at most; keep a stout heart and it will soon cease"; then in thinking it slight, you will make it slight. Everything depends on opinion; ambition, luxury, greed, hark back to opinion. It is according to opinion that we suffer.

A man is as wretched as he has convinced himself that he is. I hold that we should do away with complaint about past sufferings and with all language like this: "None has ever been worse off than I. What sufferings, what evils have I endured! No one has thought that I shall recover. How often have my family bewailed me, and the physicians given me over! Men who are placed on the rack are not torn asunder with such agony!"

However, even if all this is true, it is over and gone. What benefit is there in reviewing past sufferings, and in being unhappy, just because once you were unhappy? Besides, every one adds much to his own ills, and tells lies to himself. And that which was bitter to bear is pleasant to have borne; it is natural to rejoice at the ending of one's ills.

Two elements must therefore be rooted out once for all—the fear of future suffering, and the recollection of past suffering; since the latter no longer concerns me, and the former concerns me not yet.

But when set in the very midst of troubles one should say:

*Perchance some day the memory of this sorrow*
*Will even bring delight.*

Let such a man fight against them with all his might: if he once gives way, he will be vanquished; but if he strives against his sufferings, he will conquer. As it is, however, what most men do is to drag down upon their own heads a falling ruin which they ought to try to support. If you begin to withdraw your support from that which thrusts toward you and totters and is ready to plunge, it will follow you and lean more heavily upon you; but if you hold your ground and make up your mind to push against it, it will be forced back.

What blows do athletes receive on their faces and all over their bodies! Nevertheless, through their desire for fame they endure every torture, and they undergo these things not only because they are fighting but in order to be able to fight. Their very training means torture. So let us also win the way to victory in all our struggles—for the reward is not a garland or a palm or a trumpeter who calls for silence at the proclamation of our names, but rather virtue, steadfastness of soul, and a peace that is won for all time, if fortune has once been utterly vanquished in any combat. You say, "I feel severe pain."

What then; are you relieved from feeling it, if you endure it like a woman? Just as an enemy is more dangerous to a retreating army, so every trouble that fortune brings attacks us all the harder if we yield and turn our backs. "But the trouble is serious." What? Is it for this purpose that we are strong—that we may have light burdens to bear? Would you have your illness long-drawn-out, or would you have it quick and short? If it is long, it means a respite, allows you a period for resting yourself, bestows upon you the boon of time in plenty; as it arises, so it must also subside. A short and rapid illness will do one of two things: it will quench or be quenched. And what difference does it make whether it is not or I am not? In either case there is an end of pain.

This, too, will help—to turn the mind aside to thoughts of other things and thus to depart from pain. Call to mind what honourable or brave deeds you have done; consider the good side of your own life. Run over in your memory those things which you have particularly admired. Then think of all the brave men who have conquered pain: of him who continued to read his book as he allowed the cutting out of varicose veins; of him who did not cease to smile, though that very smile so enraged his torturers that they tried upon him every instrument of their cruelty. If pain can be conquered by a smile, will it not be conquered by reason?

You may tell me now of whatever you like—of colds, bad coughing-spells that bring up parts of our entrails, fever that parches our very vitals, thirst, limbs so twisted that the joints protrude in different directions; yet worse than these are the stake, the rack, the red-hot plates, the instrument that reopens wounds while the wounds themselves are still swollen and that drives their imprint still deeper. Nevertheless there have been men who have not uttered a moan amid these tortures. "More yet!" says the torturer; but the victim has not begged for release. "More yet!" he says again; but no answer has come. "More yet!" the victim has smiled, and heartily, too. Can you not bring yourself, after an example like this, to make a mock at pain?

"But," you object, "my illness does not allow me to be doing anything; it has withdrawn me from all my duties." It is your body that is hampered by ill-health, and not your soul as well. It is for this reason that it clogs the feet of the runner and will hinder the handiwork of the cobbler or the artisan; but if your soul be habitually in practice, you will plead and teach, listen and learn, investigate and meditate. What more is necessary? Do you think that you are doing nothing if you possess self-control in your illness? You will be showing that a disease can be overcome, or at any rate endured.

There is, I assure you, a place for virtue even upon a bed of sickness. It is not only the sword and the battle-line that prove the soul alert and unconquered by fear; a man can display bravery even when wrapped in his bed-clothes. You have something to do: wrestle bravely with disease. If it shall compel you to nothing, beguile you to nothing, it is a notable example that you display. O what ample matter were there for renown, if we could have spectators of our sickness! Be your own spectator; seek your own applause.

Again, there are two kinds of pleasures. Disease checks the pleasures of the body, but does not do away with them. Nay, if the truth is to be considered, it serves to excite them; for the thirstier a man is, the more he enjoys a drink; the hungrier he is, the more pleasure he takes in food. Whatever falls to one's lot after a period of abstinence is welcomed with greater zest. The other kind, however, the pleasures of the mind, which are higher and less uncertain, no physician can refuse to the sick man. Whoever seeks these and knows well what they are, scorns all the blandishments of the senses.

Men say, "Poor sick fellow!" But why? Is it because he does not mix snow with his wine, or because he does not revive the chill of his drink—mixed as it is in a good-sized bowl—by chipping ice into it? Or because he does not have Lucrine oysters opened fresh at his table? Or because there is no din of cooks about his dining-hall, as they bring in their very cooking apparatus along with their viands? For luxury has already devised this fashion—of having the kitchen accompany the dinner, so that the food may not grow luke-warm, or fail to be hot enough for a palate which has already become hardened.

"Poor sick fellow!"—he will eat as much as he can digest. There will be no boar lying before his eyes, banished from the table as if it were a common meat; and on his sideboard there will be heaped together no breast-meat of birds, because it sickens him to see birds served whole. But what evil has been done to you? You will dine like a sick man, nay, sometimes like a sound man.

All these things, however, can be easily endured—gruel, warm water, and anything else that seems insupportable to a fastidious man, to one who is wallowing in luxury, sick in soul rather than in body—if only we cease to shudder at death. And we shall cease, if once we have gained a knowledge of the limits of good and evil; then, and then only, life will not weary us, neither will death make us afraid.

For surfeit of self can never seize upon a life that surveys all the things which are manifold, great, divine; only idle leisure is wont to make men hate their lives. To one who roams through the universe, the truth can never pall; it will be the untruths that will cloy.

And, on the other hand, if death comes near with its summons, even though it be untimely in its arrival, though it cut one off in one's prime, a man has had a taste of all that the longest life can give. Such a man has in great measure come to understand the universe. He knows that honourable things do not depend on time for their growth; but any life must seem short to those who measure its length by pleasures which are empty and for that reason unbounded.

Refresh yourself with such thoughts as these, and meanwhile reserve some hours for our letters. There will come a time when we shall be united again and brought together; however short this time may be, we shall make it long by knowing how to employ it. For, as Posidonius says: "A single day among the learned lasts longer than the longest life of the ignorant."

Meanwhile, hold fast to this thought, and grip it close: yield not to adversity; trust not to prosperity; keep before your eyes the full scope of Fortune's power, as if she would surely do whatever is in her power to do. That which has been long expected comes more gently. Farewell.

# Letter 52
# On the Rewards of Scientific Discovery

I have been awaiting a letter from you, that you might inform me what new matter was revealed to you during your trip round Sicily, and especially that you might give me further information regarding Charybdis itself. I know very well that Scylla is a rock—and indeed a rock not dreaded by mariners; but with regard to Charybdis I should like to have a full description, in order to see whether it agrees with the accounts in mythology; and, if you have by chance investigated it (for it is indeed worthy of your investigation), please enlighten me concerning the following: Is it lashed into a whirlpool by a wind from only one direction, or do all storms alike serve to disturb its depths? Is it true that objects snatched downwards by the whirlpool in that strait are carried for many miles under water, and then come to the surface on the beach near Tauromenium?

If you will write me a full account of these matters, I shall then have the boldness to ask you to perform another task—also to climb Aetna at my special request. Certain naturalists have inferred that the mountain is wasting away and gradually settling, because sailors used to be able to see it from a greater distance. The reason for this may be, not that the height of the mountain is decreasing, but because the flames have become dim and the eruptions less strong and less copious, and because for the same reason the smoke also is less active by day. However, either of these two things is possible to believe: that on the one hand the mountain is growing smaller because it is consumed from day to day, and that, on the other hand, it remains the same in size because the mountain is not devouring itself, but instead of this the matter which seethes forth collects in some subterranean valley and is fed by other material, finding in the mountain itself not the food which it requires, but simply a passage-way out.

There is a well-known place in Lycia—called by the inhabitants "Hephaestion" —where the ground is full of holes in many places and is surrounded by a harmless fire, which does no injury to the plants that grow there. Hence the place is fertile and luxuriant with growth, because the flames do not scorch but merely shine with a force that is mild and feeble.

But let us postpone this discussion, and look into the matter when you have given me a description just how far distant the snow lies from the crater—I mean the snow which does not melt even in summer, so safe is it from the adjacent fire. But there is no ground for your charging this work to my account; for you were about to gratify your own craze for fine writing, without a commission from anyone at all.

Nay, what am I to offer you *not* merely to describe Aetna in your poem, and *not* to touch lightly upon a topic which is a matter of ritual for all poets? Ovid could not be prevented from using this theme simply because Vergil had already fully covered it; nor could either of these writers frighten off Cornelius Severus. Besides, the topic has served them all with happy results, and those who have gone before seem to me not to have forestalled all what could be said, but merely to have opened the way.

It makes a great deal of difference whether you approach a subject that has been exhausted, or one where the ground has merely been broken; in the latter case, the topic grows day by day, and what is already discovered does not hinder new discoveries. Besides, he who writes last has the best of the bargain; he finds already at hand words which, when marshalled in a different way, show a new face. And he is not pilfering them, as if they belonged to someone else, when he uses them, for they are common property. Now if Aetna does not make your mouth water, I am mistaken in you. You have for some time been desirous of writing something in the grand style and on the level of the older school. For your modesty does not allow you to set your hopes any higher; this quality of yours is so pronounced that, it sees to me, you are likely to curb the force of your natural ability, if there should be any danger of outdoing others; so greatly do you reverence the old masters.

Wisdom has this advantage, among others—that no man can be outdone by another, except during the climb. But when you have arrived at the top, it is a draw; there is no room for further ascent, the game is over. Can the sun add to his size? Can the moon advance beyond her usual fullness? The seas do not increase in bulk. The universe keeps the same character, the same limits.

Things which have reached their full stature cannot grow higher. Men who have attained wisdom will therefore be equal and on the same footing. Each of them will possess his own peculiar gifts —one will be more affable, another more facile, another more ready of speech, a fourth more eloquent; but as regards the quality under discussion—the element that produces happiness—it is equal in them all.

I do not know whether this Aetna of yours can collapse and fall in ruins, whether this lofty summit, visible for many miles over the deep sea, is wasted by the incessant power of the flames; but I do know that virtue will not be brought down to a lower plane either by flames or by ruins. Hers is the only greatness that knows no lowering; there can be for her no further rising or sinking. Her stature, like that of the stars in the heavens, is fixed. Let us therefore strive to raise ourselves to this altitude.

Already much of the task is accomplished; nay, rather, if I can bring myself to confess the truth, not much. For goodness does not mean merely being better than the lowest. Who that could catch but a mere glimpse of the daylight would boast his powers of vision? One who sees the sun shining through a mist may be contented meanwhile that he has escaped darkness, but he does not yet enjoy the blessing of light.

Our souls will not have reason to rejoice in their lot until, freed from this darkness in which they grope, they have not merely glimpsed the brightness with feeble vision, but have absorbed the full light of day and have been restored to their place in the sky—until, indeed, they have regained the place which they held at the allotment of their birth. The soul is summoned upward by its very origin. And it will reach that goal even before it is released from its prison below, as soon as it has cast off sin and, in purity and lightness, has leaped up into celestial realms of thought.

I am glad, beloved Lucilius, that we are occupied with this ideal, that we pursue it with all our might, even though few know it, or none. Fame is the shadow of virtue; it will attend virtue even against her will. But, as the shadow sometimes precedes and sometimes follows or even lags behind, so fame sometimes goes before us and shows herself in plain sight, and sometimes is in the rear, and is all the greater in proportion as she is late in coming, when once envy has beaten a retreat.

How long did men believe Democritus to be mad! Glory barely came to Socrates. And how long did our state remain in ignorance of Cato! They rejected him, and did not know his worth until they had lost him. If Rutilius had not resigned himself to wrong, his innocence and virtue would have escaped notice; the hour of his suffering was the hour of his triumph. Did he not give thanks for his lot, and welcome his exile with open arms? I have mentioned thus far those to whom Fortune has brought renown at the very moment of persecution; but how many there are whose progress toward virtue has come to light only after their death! And how many have been ruined, not rescued, by their reputation?

There is Epicurus, for example; mark how greatly he is admired, not only by the more cultured, but also by this ignorant rabble. This man, however, was unknown to Athens itself, near which he had hidden himself away. And so, when he had already survived by many years his friend Metrodorus, he added in a letter these last words, proclaiming with thankful appreciation the friendship that had existed between them: "So greatly blest were Metrodorus and I that it has been no harm to us to be unknown, and almost unheard of, in this well-known land of Greece."

Is it not true, therefore, that men did not discover him until after he had ceased to be? Has not his renown shone forth, for all that? Metrodorus also admits this fact in one of his letters: that Epicurus and he were not well known to the public; but he declares that after the lifetime of Epicurus and himself any man who might wish to follow in their footsteps would win great and ready-made renown.

Virtue is never lost to view; and yet to have been lost to view is no loss. There will come a day which will reveal her, though hidden away or suppressed by the spite of her contemporaries. That man is born merely for a few, who thinks only of the people of his own generation. Many thousands of years and many thousands of peoples will come after you; it is to these that you should have regard. Malice may have imposed silence upon the mouths of all who were alive in your day; but there will come men who will judge you without prejudice and without favour. If there is any reward that virtue receives at the hands of fame, not even this can pass away. We ourselves, indeed, shall not be affected by the talk of posterity; nevertheless, posterity will cherish and celebrate us even though we are not conscious thereof.

Virtue has never failed to reward a man, both during his life and after his death, provided he has followed her loyally, provided he has not decked himself out or painted himself up, but has been always the same, whether he appeared before men's eyes after being announced, or suddenly and without preparation. Pretence accomplishes nothing. Few are deceived by a mask that is easily drawn over the face. Truth is the same in every part. Things which deceive us have no real substance. Lies are thin stuff; they are transparent, if you examine them with care. Farewell.

# Letter 53
# On Worldly Deceptions

Today I have some free time, thanks not so much to myself as to the games, which have attracted all the bores to the boxing-match. No one will interrupt me or disturb the train of my thoughts, which go ahead more boldly as the result of my very confidence. My door has not been continually creaking on its hinges nor will my curtain be pulled aside; my thoughts may march safely on—and that is all the more necessary for one who goes independently and follows out his own path. Do I then follow no predecessors? Yes, but I allow myself to discover something new, to alter, to reject. I am not a slave to them, although I give them my approval.

And yet that was a very bold word which I spoke when I assured myself that I should have some quiet, and some uninterrupted retirement. For lo, a great cheer comes from the stadium, and while it does not drive me distracted, yet it shifts my thought to a contrast suggested by this very noise. How many men, I say to myself, train their bodies, and how few train their minds! What crowds flock to the games, spurious as they are and arranged merely for pastime—and what a solitude reigns where the good arts are taught! How feather-brained are the athletes whose muscles and shoulders we admire!

The question which I ponder most of all is this: if the body can be trained to such a degree of endurance that it will stand the blows and kicks of several opponents at once and to such a degree that a man can last out the day and resist the scorching sun in the midst of the burning dust, drenched all the while with his own blood—if this can be done, how much more easily might the mind be toughened so that it could receive the blows of Fortune and not be conquered, so that it might struggle to its feet again after it has been laid low, after it has been trampled under foot?

For although the body needs many things in order to be strong, yet the mind grows from within, giving to itself nourishment and exercise.

Yonder athletes must have copious food, copious drink, copious quantities of oil, and long training besides; but you can acquire virtue without equipment and without expense. All that goes to make you a good man lies within yourself.

And what do you need in order to become good? To wish it. But what better thing could you wish for than to break away from this slavery, a slavery that oppresses us all, a slavery which even chattels of the lowest estate, born amid such degradation, strive in every possible way to strip off? In exchange for freedom they pay out the savings which they have scraped together by cheating their own bellies; shall *you* not be eager to attain liberty at any price, seeing that you claim it as your birthright?

Why cast glances toward your strong-box? Liberty cannot be bought. It is therefore useless to enter in your ledger the item of "Freedom," for freedom is possessed neither by those who have bought it, nor by those who have sold it. You must give this good to yourself, and seek it from yourself.

First of all, free yourself from the fear of death, for death puts the yoke about our necks; then free yourself from the fear of poverty. If you would know how little evil there is in poverty, compare the faces of the poor with those of the rich; the poor man smiles more often and more genuinely; his troubles do not go deep down; even if any anxiety comes upon him, it passes like a fitful cloud. But the merriment of those whom men call happy is feigned, while their sadness is heavy and festering, and all the heavier because they may not meanwhile display their grief, but must act the part of happiness in the midst of sorrows that eat out their very hearts.

I often feel called upon to use the following illustration, and it seems to me that none expresses more effectively this drama of human life, wherein we are assigned the parts which we are to play so badly. Yonder is the man who stalks upon the stage with swelling port and head thrown back, and says:

> Lo, I am he whom Argos hails as lord,
> Whom Pelops left the heir of lands that spread
> From Hellespont and from th' Ionian sea
> E'en to the Isthmian straits.

And who is this fellow? He is but a slave; his wage is five measures of grain and five denarii.

Yon other who, proud and wayward and puffed up by confidence in his power, declaims:

*Peace, Menelaus, or this hand shall slay thee!*

receives a daily pittance and sleeps on rags. You may speak in the same way about all these dandies whom you see riding in litters above the heads of men and above the crowd; in every case their happiness is put on like the actor's mask. Tear it off, and you will scorn them.

When you buy a horse, you order its blanket to be removed; you pull off the garments from slaves that are advertised for sale, so that no bodily flaws may escape your notice; if you judge a man, do you judge him when he is wrapped in a disguise? Slave dealers hide under some sort of finery any defect which may give offence, and for that reason the very trappings arouse the suspicion of the buyer. If you catch sight of a leg or an arm that is bound up in cloths, you demand that it be stripped and that the body itself be revealed to you.

Do you see yonder Scythian or Sarmatian king, his head adorned with the badge of his office? If you wish to see what he amounts to, and to know his full worth, take off his diadem; much evil lurks beneath it. But why do I speak of others? If you wish to set a value on yourself, put away your money, your estates, your honours, and look into your own soul. At present, you are taking the word of others for what you are. Farewell.

# Letter 54
# On Liberal and Vocational Studies

You have been wishing to know my views with regard to liberal studies. My answer is this: I respect no study, and deem no study good, which results in money-making. Such studies are profit-bringing occupations, useful only in so far as they give the mind a preparation and do not engage it permanently. One should linger upon them only so long as the mind can occupy itself with nothing greater; they are our apprenticeship, not our real work.

Hence you see why "liberal studies" are so called; it is because they are studies worthy of a free-born gentleman. But there is only one really liberal study—that which gives a man his liberty. It is the study of wisdom, and that is lofty, brave, and great-souled. All other studies are puny and puerile. You surely do not believe that there is good in any of the subjects whose teachers are, as you see, men of the most ignoble and base stamp? We ought not to be learning such things; we should have done with learning them.

Certain persons have made up their minds that the point at issue with regard to the liberal studies is whether they make men good; but they do not even profess or aim at a knowledge of this particular subject.

The scholar busies himself with investigations into language, and if it be his desire to go farther afield, he works on history, or, if he would extend his range to the farthest limits, on poetry. But which of these paves the way to virtue? Pronouncing syllables, investigating words, memorizing plays, or making rules for the scansion of poetry, what is there in all this that rids one of fear, roots out desire, or bridles the passions?

The question is: do such men teach virtue, or not? If they do not teach it, then neither do they transmit it. If they do teach it, they are philosophers. Would you like to know how it happens that they have not taken the chair for the purpose of teaching virtue? See how unlike their subjects are; and yet their subjects would resemble each other if they taught the same thing.

It may be, perhaps, that they make you believe that Homer was a philosopher, although they disprove this by the very arguments through which they seek to prove it. For sometimes they make of him a Stoic, who approves nothing but virtue, avoids pleasures, and refuses to relinquish honour even at the price of immortality; sometimes they make him an Epicurean, praising the condition of a state in repose, which passes its days in feasting and song; sometimes a Peripatetic, classifying goodness in three ways; sometimes an Academic, holding that all things are uncertain. It is clear, however, that no one of these doctrines is to be fathered upon Homer, just because they are all there; for they are irreconcilable with one another. We may admit to these men, indeed, that Homer was a philosopher; yet surely he became a wise man before he had any knowledge of poetry. So let us learn the particular things that made Homer wise.

It is no more to the point, of course, for me to investigate whether Homer or Hesiod was the older poet, than to know why Hecuba, although younger than Helen, showed her years so lamentably. What, in your opinion, I say, would be the point in trying to determine the respective ages of Achilles and Patroclus?

Do you raise the question, "Through what regions did Ulysses stray?" instead of trying to prevent ourselves from going astray at all times? We have no leisure to hear lectures on the question whether he was sea-tost between Italy and Sicily, or outside our known world (indeed, so long a wandering could not possibly have taken place within its narrow bounds); we ourselves encounter storms of the spirit, which toss us daily, and our depravity drives us into all the ills which troubled Ulysses. For us there is never lacking the beauty to tempt our eyes, or the enemy to assail us; on this side are savage monsters that delight in human blood, on that side the treacherous allurements of the ear, and yonder is shipwreck and all the varied category of misfortunes. Show me rather, by the example of Ulysses, how I am to love my country, my wife, my father, and how, even after suffering shipwreck, I am to sail toward these ends, honourable as they are.

Why try to discover whether Penelope was a pattern of purity, or whether she had the laugh on her contemporaries? Or whether she suspected that the man in her presence was Ulysses, before she knew it was he? Teach me rather what purity is, and how great a good we have in it, and whether it is situated in the body or in the soul.

Now I will transfer my attention to the musician. You, sir, are teaching me how the treble and the bass are in accord with one another, and how, though the strings produce different notes, the result is a harmony; rather bring my soul into harmony with itself, and let not my purposes be out of tune. You are showing me what the doleful keys are; show me rather how, in the midst of adversity, I may keep from uttering a doleful note.

The mathematician teaches me how to lay out the dimensions of my estates; but I should rather be taught how to lay out what is enough for a man to own. He teaches me to count, and adapts my fingers to avarice; but I should prefer him to teach me that there is no point in such calculations, and that one is none the happier for tiring out the book-keepers with his possessions—or rather, how useless property is to any man who would find it the greatest misfortune if he should be required to reckon out, by his own wits, the amount of his holdings.

What good is there for me in knowing how to parcel out a piece of land, if I know not how to share it with my brother? What good is there in working out to a nicety the dimensions of an acre, and in detecting the error if a piece has so much as escaped my measuring-rod, if I am embittered when an ill-tempered neighbour merely scrapes off a bit of my land? The mathematician teaches me how I may lose none of my boundaries; I, however, seek to learn how to lose them all with a light heart.

"But," comes the reply, "I am being driven from the farm which my father and grandfather owned!" Well? Who owned the land before your grandfather? Can you explain what people (I will not say what person) held it originally? You did not enter upon it as a master, but merely as a tenant. And whose tenant are you? If your claim is successful, you are tenant of the heir. The lawyers say that public property cannot be acquired privately by possession; what you hold and call your own is public property—indeed, it belongs to mankind at large.

O what marvellous skill! You know how to measure the circle; you find the square of any shape which is set before you; you compute the distances between the stars; there is nothing which does not come within the scope of your calculations. But if you are a real master of your profession, measure me the mind of man! Tell me how great it is, or how puny! You know what a straight line is; but how does it benefit you if you do not know what is straight in this life of ours?

I come next to the person who boasts his knowledge of the heavenly bodies, who knows

> Whither the chilling star of Saturn hides,
> And through what orbit Mercury doth stray.

Of what benefit will it be to know this? That I shall be disturbed because Saturn and Mars are in opposition, or when Mercury sets at eventide in plain view of Saturn, rather than learn that those stars, wherever they are, are propitious, and that they are not subject to change?

They are driven along by an unending round of destiny, on a course from which they cannot swerve. They return at stated seasons; they either set in motion, or mark the intervals of the whole world's work. But if they are responsible for whatever happens, how will it help you to know the secrets of the immutable? Or if they merely give indications, what good is there in foreseeing what you cannot escape? Whether you know these things or not, they will take place.

> Behold the fleeting sun,
> The stars that follow in his train, and thou
> Shalt never find the morrow play thee false,
> Or be misled by nights without a cloud.

It has, however, been sufficiently and fully ordained that I shall be safe from anything that may mislead me.

"What," you say, "does the 'morrow never play me false'? Whatever happens without my knowledge plays me false." I, for my part, do not know what is to be, but I do know what may come to be. I shall have no misgivings in this matter; I await the future in its entirety; and if there is any abatement in its severity, I make the most of it. If the morrow treats me kindly, it is a sort of deception; but it does not deceive me even at that. For just as I know that all things can happen, so I know, too, that they will not happen in every case. I am ready for favourable events in every case, but I am prepared for evil.

In this discussion you must bear with me if I do not follow the regular course. For I do not consent to admit painting into the list of liberal arts, any more than sculpture, marble-working, and other helps toward luxury. I also debar from the liberal studies wrestling and all knowledge that is compounded of oil and mud; otherwise, I should be compelled to admit perfumers also, and cooks, and all others who lend their wits to the service of our pleasures.

For what "liberal" element is there in these ravenous takers of emetics, whose bodies are fed to fatness while their minds are thin and dull? Or do we really believe that the training which they give is "liberal" for the young men of Rome, who used to be taught by our ancestors to stand straight and hurl a spear, to wield a pike, to guide a horse, and to handle weapons? Our ancestors used to teach their children nothing that could be learned while lying down. But neither the new system nor the old teaches or nourishes virtue. For what good does it do us to guide a horse and control his speed with the curb, and then find that our own passions, utterly uncurbed, bolt with us? Or to beat many opponents in wrestling or boxing, and then to find that we ourselves are beaten by anger?

"What then," you say, "do the liberal studies contribute nothing to our welfare?" Very much in other respects, but nothing at all as regards virtue. For even these arts of which I have spoken, though admittedly of a low grade—depending as they do upon handiwork—contribute greatly toward the equipment of life, but nevertheless have nothing to do with virtue. And if you inquire, "Why, then, do we educate our children in the liberal studies?" it is not because they can bestow virtue, but because they prepare the soul for the reception of virtue. Just as that "primary course," as the ancients called it, in grammar, which gave boys their elementary training, does not teach them the liberal arts, but prepares the ground for their early acquisition of these arts, so the liberal arts do not conduct the soul all the way to virtue, but merely set it going in that direction.

Posidonius divides the arts into four classes: first we have those which are common and low, then those which serve for amusement, then those which refer to the education of boys, and, finally, the liberal arts. The common sort belong to workmen and are mere hand-work; they are concerned with equipping life; there is in them no pretence to beauty or honour.

The arts of amusement are those which aim to please the eye and the ear. To this class you may assign the stage-machinists, who invent scaffolding that goes aloft of its own accord, or floors that rise silently into the air, and many other surprising devices, as when objects that fit together then fall apart, or objects which are separate then join together automatically, or objects which stand erect then gradually collapse. The eye of the inexperienced is struck with amazement by these things; for such persons marvel at everything that takes place without warning, because they do not know the causes.

The arts which belong to the education of boys, and are somewhat similar to the liberal arts, are those which the Greeks call the "cycle of studies," but which we Romans call the "liberal." However, those alone are really liberal—or rather, to give them a truer name, "free"—whose concern is virtue.

"But," one will say, "just as there is a part of philosophy which has to do with nature, and a part which has to do with ethics, and a part which has to do with reasoning, so this group of liberal arts also claims for itself a place in philosophy. When one approaches questions that deal with nature, a decision is reached by means of a word from the mathematician. Therefore mathematics is a department of that branch which it aids."

But many things aid us and yet are not parts of ourselves. Nay, if they were, they would not aid us. Food is an aid to the body, but is not a part of it. We get some help from the service which mathematics renders; and mathematics is as indispensable to philosophy as the carpenter is to the mathematician. But carpentering is not a part of mathematics, nor is mathematics a part of philosophy.

Moreover, each has its own limits; for the wise man investigates and learns the causes of natural phenomena, while the mathematician follows up and computes their numbers and their measurements. The wise man knows the laws by which the heavenly bodies persist, what powers belong to them, and what attributes; the astronomer merely notes their comings and goings, the rules which govern their settings and their risings, and the occasional periods during which they seem to stand still, although as a matter of fact no heavenly body can stand still.

The wise man will know what causes the reflection in a mirror; but, the mathematician can merely tell you how far the body should be from the reflection, and what shape of mirror will produce a given reflection. The philosopher will demonstrate that the sun is a large body, while the astronomer will compute just how large, progressing in knowledge by his method of trial and experiment; but in order to progress, he must summon to his aid certain principles. No art, however, is sufficient unto itself, if the foundation upon which it rests depends upon mere favour.

Now philosophy asks no favours from any other source; it builds everything on its own soil; but the science of numbers is, so to speak, a structure built on another man's land—it builds on everything on alien soil; It accepts first principles, and by their favour arrives at further conclusions. If it could march unassisted to the truth, if it were able to understand the nature of the universe, I should say that it would offer much assistance to our minds; for the mind grows by contact with things heavenly and draws into itself something from on high. There is but one thing that brings the soul to perfection—the unalterable knowledge of good and evil. But there is no other art which investigates good and evil.

I should like to pass in review the several virtues.

Bravery is a scorner of things which inspire fear; it looks down upon, challenges, and crushes the powers of terror and all that would drive our freedom under the yoke. But do "liberal studies" strengthen this virtue? Loyalty is the holiest good in the human heart; it is forced into betrayal by no constraint, and it is bribed by no rewards. Loyalty cries: "Burn me, slay me, kill me! I shall not betray my trust; and the more urgently torture shall seek to find my secret, the deeper in my heart will I bury it!" Can the "liberal arts" produce such a spirit within us? Temperance controls our desires; some it hates and routs, others it regulates and restores to a healthy measure, nor does it ever approach our desires for their own sake. Temperance knows that the best measure of the appetites is not what you want to take, but what you ought to take.

Kindliness forbids you to be over-bearing towards your associates, and it forbids you to be grasping. In words and in deeds and in feelings it shows itself gentle and courteous to all men. It counts no evil as another's solely. And the reason why it loves its own good is chiefly because it will some day be the good of another. Do "liberal studies" teach a man such character as this? No; no more than they teach simplicity, moderation and self-restraint, thrift and economy, and that kindliness which spares a neighbour's life as if it were one's own and knows that it is not for man to make wasteful use of his fellow-man.

"But," one says, "since you declare that virtue cannot be attained without the 'liberal studies,' how is it that you deny that they offer any assistance to virtue?" Because you cannot attain virtue without food, either; and yet food has nothing to do with virtue. Wood does not offer assistance to a ship, although a ship cannot be built except of wood. There is no reason, I say, why you should think that anything is made by the assistance of that without which it cannot be made.

We might even make the statement that it is possible to attain wisdom without the "liberal studies"; for although virtue is a thing that must be learned, yet it is not learned by means of these studies.

What reason have I, however, for supposing that one who is ignorant of letters will never be a wise man, since wisdom is not to be found in letters? Wisdom communicates facts and not words; and it may be true that the memory is more to be depended upon when it has no support outside itself.

Wisdom is a large and spacious thing. It needs plenty of free room. One must learn about things divine and human, the past and the future, the ephemeral and the eternal; and one must learn about Time. See how many questions arise concerning time alone: in the first place, whether it is anything in and by itself; in the second place, whether anything exists prior to time and without time; and again, did time begin along with the universe, or, because there was something even before the universe began, did time also exist then?

There are countless questions concerning the soul alone: whence it comes, what is its nature, when it begins to exist, and how long it exists; whether it passes from one place to another and changes its habitation, being transferred successively from one animal shape to another, or whether it is a slave but once, roaming the universe after it is set free; whether it is corporeal or not; what will become of it when it ceases to use us as its medium; how it will employ its freedom when it has escaped from this present prison; whether it will forget all its past, and at that moment begin to know itself when, released from the body, it has withdrawn to the skies.

Thus, whatever phase of things human and divine you have apprehended, you will be wearied by the vast number of things to be answered and things to be learned. And in order that these manifold and mighty subjects may have free entertainment in your soul, you must remove therefrom all superfluous things. Virtue will not surrender herself to these narrow bounds of ours; a great subject needs wide space in which to move. Let all other things be driven out, and let the breast be emptied to receive virtue.

"But it is a pleasure to be acquainted with many arts." Therefore let us keep only as much of them as is essential. Do you regard that man as blameworthy who puts superfluous things on the same footing with useful things, and in his house makes a lavish display of costly objects, but do not deem him blameworthy who has allowed himself to become engrossed with the useless furniture of learning? This desire to know more than is sufficient is a sort of intemperance.

Why? Because this unseemly pursuit of the liberal arts makes men troublesome, wordy, tactless, self-satisfied bores, who fail to learn the essentials just because they have learned the non-essentials. Didymus the scholar wrote four thousand books. I should feel pity for him if he had only read the same number of superfluous volumes. In these books he investigates Homer's birthplace, who was really the mother of Aeneas, whether Anacreon was more of a rake or more of a drunkard, whether Sappho was a bad lot, and other problems the answers to which, if found, were forthwith to be forgotten. Come now, do not tell me that life is long!

Nay, when you come to consider our own countrymen also, I can show you many works which ought to be cut down with the axe.

It is at the cost of a vast outlay of time and of vast discomfort to the ears of others that we win such praise as this: "What a learned man you are!" Let us be content with this recommendation, less citified though it be: "What a good man you are!"

Do I mean this? Well, would you have me unroll the annals of the world's history and try to find out who first wrote poetry? Or, in the absence of written records, shall I make an estimate of the number of years which lie between Orpheus and Homer? Or shall I make a study of the absurd writings of Aristarchus, wherein he branded the text of other men's verses, and wear my life away upon syllables? Shall I then wallow in the geometrician's dust? Have I so far forgotten that useful saw "Save your time"? Must I know these things? And what may I choose not to know?

Apion, the scholar, who drew crowds to his lectures all over Greece in the days of Gaius Caesar and was acclaimed a Homerid by every state, used to maintain that Homer, when he had finished his two poems, the *Iliad* and the *Odyssey*, added a preliminary poem to his work, wherein he embraced the whole Trojan war. The argument which Apion adduced to prove this statement was that Homer had purposely inserted in the opening line two letters which contained a key to the number of his books.

A man who wishes to know many things must know such things as these, and must take no thought of all the time which one loses by ill-health, public duties, private duties, daily duties, and sleep. Apply the measure to the years of your life; they have no room for all these things.

I have been speaking so far of liberal studies; but think how much superfluous and unpractical matter the philosophers contain! Of their own accord they also have descended to establishing nice divisions of syllables, to determining the true meaning of conjunctions and prepositions; they have been envious of the scholars, envious of the mathematicians. They have taken over into their own art all the superfluities of these other arts; the result is that they know more about careful speaking than about careful living.

Let me tell you what evils are due to over-nice exactness, and what an enemy it is of truth! Protagoras declares that one can take either side on any question and debate it with equal success—even on this very question, whether every subject can be debated from either point of view. Nausiphanes holds that in things which seem to exist, there is no difference between existence and non-existence.

Parmenides maintains that nothing exists of all this which seems to exist, except the universe alone. Zeno of Elea removed all the difficulties by removing one; for he declares that nothing exists. The Pyrrhonean, Megarian, Eretrian, and Academic schools are all engaged in practically the same task; they have introduced a new knowledge, non-knowledge.

You may sweep all these theories in with the superfluous troops of "liberal" studies; the one class of men give me a knowledge that will be of no use to me, the other class do away with any hope of attaining knowledge. It is better, of course, to know useless things than to know nothing. One set of philosophers offers no light by which I may direct my gaze toward the truth; the other digs out my very eyes and leaves me blind. If I cleave to Protagoras, there is nothing in the scheme of nature that is not doubtful; if I hold with Nausiphanes, I am sure only of this—that everything is unsure; if with Parmenides, there is nothing except the One; if with Zeno, there is not even the One.

What are we, then? What becomes of all these things that surround us, support us, sustain us? The whole universe is then a vain or deceptive shadow. I cannot readily say whether I am more vexed at those who would have it that we know nothing, or with those who would not leave us even this privilege. Farewell.

# Letter 55
# On the Happy Life

You and I will agree, I think, that outward things are sought for the satisfaction of the body, that the body is cherished out of regard for the soul, and that in the soul there are certain parts which minister to us, enabling us to move and to sustain life, bestowed upon us just for the sake of the primary part of us. In this primary part there is something irrational, and something rational. The former obeys the latter, while the latter is the only thing that is not referred back to another, but rather refers all things to itself. For the divine reason also is set in supreme command over all things, and is itself subject to none; and even this reason which we possess is the same, because it is derived from the divine reason.

Now if we are agreed on this point, it is natural that we shall be agreed on the following also—namely, that the happy life depends upon this and this alone: our attainment of perfect reason. For it is naught but this that keeps the soul from being bowed down, that stands its ground against Fortune; whatever the condition of their affairs may be, it keeps men untroubled. And that alone is a good which is never subject to impairment. That man, I declare, is happy whom nothing makes less strong than he is; he keeps to the heights, leaning upon none but himself; for one who sustains himself by any prop may fall. If the case is otherwise, then things which do not pertain to us will begin to have great influence over us. But who desires Fortune to have the upper hand, or what sensible man prides himself upon that which is not his own?

What is the happy life? It is peace of mind, and lasting tranquillity. This will be yours if you possess greatness of soul; it will be yours if you possess the steadfastness that resolutely clings to a good judgment just reached. How does a man reach this condition? By gaining a complete view of truth, by maintaining, in all that he does, order, measure, fitness, and a will that is inoffensive and kindly, that is intent upon reason and never departs therefrom, that commands at the same time love and admiration. In short, to give you the principle in brief compass, the wise man's soul ought to be such as would be proper for a god.

What more can one desire who possesses all honourable things? For if dishonourable things can contribute to the best estate, then there will be the possibility of a happy life under conditions which do not include an honourable life. And what is more base or foolish than to connect the good of a rational soul with things irrational?

Yet there are certain philosophers who hold that the Supreme Good admits of increase because it is hardly complete when the gifts of fortune are adverse. Even Antipater, one of the great leaders of this school, admits that he ascribes some influence to externals, though only a very slight influence. You see, however, what absurdity lies in not being content with the daylight unless it is increased by a tiny fire. What importance can a spark have in the midst of this clear sunlight?

If you are not contented with only that which is honourable, it must follow that you desire in addition either the kind of quiet which the Greeks call "undisturbedness," or else pleasure. But the former may be attained in any case. For the mind is free from disturbance when it is fully free to contemplate the universe, and nothing distracts it from the contemplation of nature. The second, pleasure, is simply the good of cattle. We are but adding the irrational to the rational, the dishonourable to the honourable. A pleasant physical sensation affects this life of ours why, therefore, do you hesitate to say that all is well with a man just because all is well with his appetite? And do you rate, I will not say among heroes, but among men, the person whose Supreme Good is a matter of flavours and colours and sounds? Nay, let him withdraw from the ranks of this, the noblest class of living beings, second only to the gods; let him herd with the dumb brutes—an animal whose delight is in fodder!

The irrational part of the soul is twofold: the one part is spirited, ambitious, uncontrolled; its seat is in the passions; the other is lowly, sluggish, and devoted to pleasure. Philosophers have neglected the former, which, though unbridled, is yet better, and is certainly more courageous and more worthy of a man, and have regarded the latter, which is nerveless and ignoble, as indispensable to the happy life.

They have ordered reason to serve this latter; they have made the Supreme Good of the noblest living being an abject and mean affair, and a monstrous hybrid, too, composed of various members which harmonize but ill. For as our Vergil, describing Scylla, says

> *Above, a human face and maiden's breast,*
> *A beauteous breast—below, a monster huge*

*Of bulk and shapeless, with a dolphin's tail*
*Joined to a wolf-like belly.*

And yet to this Scylla are tacked on the forms of wild animals, dreadful and swift; but from what monstrous shapes have these wiseacres compounded wisdom!

Man's primary art is virtue itself; there is joined to this the useless and fleeting flesh, fitted only for the reception of food, as Posidonius remarks. This divine virtue ends in foulness, and to the higher parts, which are worshipful and heavenly, there is fastened a sluggish and flabby animal. As for the second desideratum— quiet—although it would indeed not of itself be of any benefit to the soul, yet it would relieve the soul of hindrances; pleasure, on the contrary, actually destroys the soul and softens all its vigour. What elements so inharmonious as these can be found united? To that which is most vigorous is joined that which is most sluggish, to that which is austere that which is far from serious, to that which is most holy that which is unrestrained even to the point of impurity.

"What, then," comes the retort, "if good health, rest, and freedom from pain are not likely to hinder virtue, shall you not seek all these?" Of course I shall seek them, but not because they are goods—I shall seek them because they are according to nature and because they will be acquired through the exercise of good judgment on my part. What, then, will be good in them? This alone—that it is a good thing to choose them. For when I don suitable attire, or walk as I should, or dine as I ought to dine, it is not my dinner, or my walk, or my dress that are goods, but the deliberate choice which I show in regard to them, as I observe, in each thing I do, a mean that conforms with reason.

Let me also add that the choice of neat clothing is a fitting object of a man's efforts; for man is by nature a neat and well-groomed animal. Hence the choice of neat attire, and not neat attire in itself, is a good; since the good is not in the thing selected, but in the quality of the selection. Our actions are honourable, but not the actual things which we do.

And you may assume that what I have said about dress applies also to the body. For nature has surrounded our soul with the body as with a sort of garment; the body is its cloak. But who has ever reckoned the value of clothes by the wardrobe which contained them? The scabbard does not make the sword good or bad. Therefore, with regard to the body I shall return the same answer to you—that, if I have the choice, I shall choose health and strength, but that the good involved will be my judgment regarding these things, and not the things themselves.

Another retort is: "Granted that the wise man is happy; nevertheless, he does not attain the Supreme Good which we have defined, unless the means also which nature provides for its attainment are at his call. So, while one who possesses virtue cannot be unhappy, yet one cannot be perfectly happy if one lacks such natural gifts as health, or soundness of limb."

But in saying this, you grant the alternative which seems the more difficult to believe—that the man who is in the midst of unremitting and extreme pain is not wretched, nay, is even happy; and you deny that which is much less serious—that he is completely happy. And yet, if virtue can keep a man from being wretched, it will be an easier task for it to render him completely happy. For the difference between happiness and complete happiness is less than that between wretchedness and happiness. Can it be possible that a thing which is so powerful as to snatch a man from disaster, and place him among the happy, cannot also accomplish what remains, and render him supremely happy? Does its strength fail at the very top of the climb?

There are in life things which are advantageous and disadvantageous—both beyond our control. If a good man, in spite of being weighed down by all kinds of disadvantages, is not wretched, how is he not supremely happy, no matter if he does lack certain advantages? For as he is not weighted down to wretchedness by his burden of disadvantages, so he is not withdrawn from supreme happiness through lack of any advantages; nay, he is just as supremely happy without the advantages as he is free from wretchedness though under the load of his disadvantages. Otherwise, if his good can be impaired, it can be snatched from him altogether.

A short space above, I remarked that a tiny fire does not add to the sun's light. For by reason of the sun's brightness any light that shines apart from the sunlight is blotted out. "But," one may say, "there are certain objects that stand in the way even of the sunlight." The sun, however, is unimpaired even in the midst of obstacles, and, though an object may intervene and cut off our view thereof, the sun sticks to his work and goes on his course. Whenever he shines forth from amid the clouds, he is no smaller, nor less punctual either, than when he is free from clouds; since it makes a great deal of difference whether there is merely something in the way of his light or something which interferes with his shining.

Similarly, obstacles take nothing away from virtue; it is no smaller, but merely shines with less brilliancy. In our eyes, it may perhaps be less visible and less luminous than before; but as regards itself it is the same and, like the sun when he is eclipsed, is still, though in secret, putting forth its strength. Disasters, therefore, and losses, and wrongs, have only the same power over virtue that a cloud has over the sun.

We meet with one person who maintains that a wise man who has met with bodily misfortune is neither wretched nor happy. But he also is in error, for he is putting the results of chance upon a parity with the virtues, and is attributing only the same influence to things that are honourable as to things that are devoid of honour. But what is more detestable and more unworthy than to put contemptible things in the same class with things worthy of reverence! For reverence is due to justice, duty, loyalty, bravery, and prudence; on the contrary, those attributes are worthless with which the most worthless men are often blessed in fuller measure—such as a sturdy leg, strong shoulders, good teeth, and healthy and solid muscles.

Again, if the wise man whose body is a trial to him shall be regarded as neither wretched nor happy, but shall be left in a sort of half-way position, his life also will be neither desirable nor undesirable. But what is so foolish as to say that the wise man's life is not desirable? And what is so far beyond the bounds of credence as the opinion that any life is neither desirable nor undesirable? Again, if bodily ills do not make a man wretched, they consequently allow him to be happy. For things which have no power to change his condition for the worse, have not the power, either, to disturb that condition when it is at its best.

"But," someone will say, "we know what is cold and what is hot; a lukewarm temperature lies between. Similarly, A is happy, and B is wretched, and C is neither happy nor wretched." I wish to examine this figure, which is brought into play against us. If I add to your lukewarm water a larger quantity of cold water, the result will be cold water. But if I pour in a larger quantity of hot water, the water will finally become hot. In the case, however, of your man who is neither wretched nor happy, no matter how much I add to his troubles, he will not be unhappy, according to your argument; hence your figure offers no analogy.

Again, suppose that I set before you a man who is neither miserable nor happy. I add blindness to his misfortunes; he is not rendered unhappy. I cripple him; he is not rendered unhappy. I add afflictions which are unceasing and severe; he is not rendered unhappy. Therefore, one whose life is not changed to misery by all these ills is not dragged by them, either, from his life of happiness.

Then if, as you say, the wise man cannot fall from happiness to wretchedness, he cannot fall into non-happiness. For how, if one has begun to slip, can one stop at any particular place? That which prevents him from rolling to the bottom, keeps him at the summit. Why, you urge, may not a happy life possibly be destroyed? It cannot even be disjointed; and for that reason virtue is itself of itself sufficient for the happy life.

"But," it is said, "is not the wise man happier if he has lived longer and has been distracted by no pain, than one who has always been compelled to grapple with evil fortune?" Answer me now—is he any better or more honourable? If he is not, then he is not happier either. In order to live more happily, he must live more rightly; if he cannot do that, then he cannot live more happily either. Virtue cannot be strained tighter, and therefore neither can the happy life, which depends on virtue. For virtue is so great a good that it is not affected by such insignificant assaults upon it as shortness of life, pain, and the various bodily vexations. For pleasure does not deserve that virtue should even glance at it.

Now what is the chief thing in virtue? It is the quality of not needing a single day beyond the present, and of not reckoning up the days that are ours; in the slightest possible moment of time virtue completes an eternity of good. These goods seem to us incredible and transcending man's nature; for we measure its grandeur by the standard of our own weakness, and we call our vices by the name of virtue. Furthermore, does it not seem just as incredible that any man in the midst of extreme suffering should say, "I am happy"? And yet this utterance was heard in the very factory of pleasure, when Epicurus said: "Today and one other day have been the happiest of all!" although in the one case he was tortured by strangury, and in the other by the incurable pain of an ulcerated stomach.

Why, then, should those goods which virtue bestows be incredible in the sight of us, who cultivate virtue, when they are found even in those who acknowledge pleasure as their mistress? These also, ignoble and base-minded as they are, declare that even in the midst of excessive pain and misfortune the wise man will be neither wretched nor happy. And yet this also is incredible—nay, still more incredible, than the other case. For I do not understand how, if virtue falls from her heights, she can help being hurled all the way to the bottom. She either must preserve one in happiness, or, if driven from this position, she will not prevent us from becoming unhappy. If virtue only stands her ground, she cannot be driven from the field; she must either conquer or be conquered.

But some say: "Only to the immortal gods is given virtue and the happy life; we can attain but the shadow, as it were, and semblance of such goods as theirs. We approach them, but we never reach them." Reason, however, is a common attribute of both gods and men; in the gods it is already perfected, in us it is capable of being perfected.

But it is our vices that bring us to despair; for the second class of rational being, man, is of an inferior order—a guardian, as it were, who is too unstable to hold fast to what is best, his judgment still wavering and uncertain. He may require the faculties of sight and hearing, good health, a bodily exterior that is not loathsome, and, besides, greater length of days conjoined with an unimpaired constitution.

Though by means of reason he can lead a life which will not bring regrets, yet there resides in this imperfect creature, man, a certain power that makes for badness, because he possesses a mind which is easily moved to perversity. Suppose, however, the badness which is in full view, and has previously been stirred to activity, to be removed; the man is still not a good man, but he is being moulded to goodness. One, however, in whom there is lacking any quality that makes for goodness, is bad.

But

> *He in whose body virtue dwells, and spirit*
> *E'er present*

is equal to the gods; mindful of his origin, he strives to return thither. No man does wrong in attempting to regain the heights from which he once came down. And why should you not believe that something of divinity exists in one who is a part of God? All this universe which encompasses us is one, and it is God; we are associates of God; we are his members. Our soul has capabilities, and is carried thither, if vices do not hold it down. Just as it is the nature of our bodies to stand erect and look upward to the sky, so the soul, which may reach out as far as it will, was framed by nature to this end, that it should desire equality with the gods. And if it makes use of its powers and stretches upward into its proper region it is by no alien path that it struggles toward the heights.

It would be a great task to journey heavenwards; the soul but returns thither. When once it has found the road, it boldly marches on, scornful of all things. It casts, no backward glance at wealth; gold and silver—things which are fully worthy of the gloom in which they once lay—it values not by the sheen which smites the eyes of the ignorant, but by the mire of ancient days, whence our greed first detached and dug them out.

The soul, I affirm, knows that riches are stored elsewhere than in men's heaped-up treasure-houses; that it is the soul, and not the strong-box, which should be filled. It is the soul that men may set in dominion over all things, and may install as owner of the universe, so that it may limit its riches only by the boundaries of East and West, and, like the gods, may possess all things; and that it may, with its own vast resources, look down from on high upon the wealthy, no one of whom rejoices as much in his own wealth as he resents the wealth of another.

When the soul has transported itself to this lofty height, it regards the body also, since it is a burden which must be borne, not as a thing to love, but as a thing to oversee; nor is it subservient to that over which it is set in mastery. For no man is free who is a slave to his body. Indeed, omitting all the other masters which are brought into being by excessive care for the body, the sway which the body itself exercises is captious and fastidious.

Forth from this body the soul issues, now with unruffled spirit, now with exultation, and, when once it has gone forth, asks not what shall be the end of the deserted day. No; just as we do not take thought for the clippings of the hair and the beard, even so that divine soul, when it is about to issue forth from the mortal man, regards the destination of its earthly vessel—whether it be consumed by fire, or shut in by a stone, or buried in the earth, or torn by wild beasts—as being of no more concern to itself than is the afterbirth to a child just born. And whether this body shall be cast out and plucked to pieces by birds, or devoured when

> *thrown to the sea-dogs as prey,*

how does that concern him who is nothing?

Nay even when it is among the living, the soul fears nothing that may happen to the body after death; for though such things may have been threats, they were not enough to terrify the soul previous to the moment of death. It says: "I am not frightened by the executioner's hook, nor by the revolting mutilation of the corpse which is exposed to the scorn of those who would witness the spectacle. I ask no man to perform the last rites for me; I entrust my remains to none. Nature has made provision that none shall go unburied. Time will lay away one whom cruelty has cast forth." Those were eloquent words which Maecenas uttered:

> *I want no tomb; for Nature doth provide*
> *For outcast bodies burial.*

You would imagine that this was the saying of a man of strict principles. He was indeed a man of noble and robust native gifts, but in prosperity he impaired these gifts by laxness. Farewell.

# Letter 56
# On the Quality, as Contrasted with the Length, of Life

While reading the letter in which you were lamenting the death of the philosopher Metronax as if he might have, and indeed ought to have, lived longer, I missed the spirit of fairness which abounds in all your discussions concerning men and things, but is lacking when you approach one single subject—as is indeed the case with us all. In other words, I have noticed many who deal fairly with their fellow-men, but none who deals fairly with the gods. We rail every day at Fate, saying "Why has A. been carried off in the very middle of his career? Why is not B. carried off instead? Why should he prolong his old age, which is a burden to himself as well as to others?"

But tell me, pray, do you consider it fairer that you should obey Nature, or that Nature should obey you? And what difference does it make how soon you depart from a place which you must depart from sooner or later? We should strive, not to live long, but to live rightly; for to achieve long life you have need of Fate only, but for right living you need the soul. A life is really long if it is a full life; but fullness is not attained until the soul has rendered to itself its proper Good, that is, until it has assumed control over itself.

What benefit does this older man derive from the eighty years he has spent in idleness? A person like him has not lived; he has merely tarried awhile in life. Nor has he died late in life; he has simply been a long time dying. He has lived eighty years, has he? That depends upon the date from which you reckon his death! Your other friend, however, departed in the bloom of his manhood.

But he had fulfilled all the duties of a good citizen, a good friend, a good son; in no respect had he fallen short. His age may have been incomplete, but his life was complete. The other man has lived eighty years, has he? Nay, he has existed eighty years, unless perchance you mean by "he has lived" what we mean when we say that a tree "lives."

Pray, let us see to it, my dear Lucilius, that our lives, like jewels of great price, be noteworthy not because of their width but because of their weight. Let us measure them by their performance, not by their duration. Would you know wherein lies the difference between this hardy man who, despising Fortune, has served through every campaign of life and has attained to life's Supreme Good, and that other person over whose head many years have passed? The former exists even after his death; the latter has died even before he was dead.

We should therefore praise, and number in the company of the blest, that man who has invested well the portion of time, however little, that has been allotted to him; for such a one has seen the true light. He has not been one of the common herd. He has not only lived, but flourished. Sometimes he enjoyed fair skies; sometimes, as often happens, it was only through the clouds that there flashed to him the radiance of the mighty star. Why do you ask: "How long did he live?" He still lives! At one bound he has passed over into posterity and has consigned himself to the guardianship of memory.

And yet I would not on that account decline for myself a few additional years; although, if my life's space be shortened, I shall not say that I have lacked aught that is essential to a happy life. For I have not planned to live up to the very last day that my greedy hopes had promised me; nay, I have looked upon every day as if it were my last. Why ask the date of my birth, or whether I am still enrolled on the register of the younger men? What I have is my own.

Just as one of small stature can be a perfect man, so a life of small compass can be a perfect life. Age ranks among the external things. How long I am to exist is not mine to decide, but how long I shall go on existing in my present way is in my own control. This is the only thing you have the right to require of me—that I shall cease to measure out an inglorious age as it were in darkness, and devote myself to living instead of being carried along past life.

And what, you ask, is the fullest span of life? It is living until you possess wisdom. He who has attained wisdom has reached, not the furthermost, but the most important, goal. Such a one may indeed exult boldly and give thanks to the gods—aye, and to himself also—and he may count himself Nature's creditor for having lived. He will indeed have the right to do so, for he has paid her back a better life than he has received. He has set up the pattern of a good man, showing the quality and the greatness of a good man. Had another year been added, it would merely have been like the past.

And yet how long are we to keep living? We have had the joy of learning the truth about the universe. We know from what beginnings Nature arises; how she orders the course of the heavens; by what successive changes she summons back the year; how she has brought to an end all things that ever have been, and has established herself as the only end of her own being. We know that the stars move by their own motion, and that nothing except the earth stands still, while all the other bodies run on with uninterrupted swiftness. We know how the moon outstrips the sun; why it is that the slower leaves the swifter behind; in what manner she receives her light, or loses it again; what brings on the night, and what brings back the day. To that place you must go where you are to have a closer view of all these things.

"And yet," says the wise man, "I do not depart more valiantly because of this hope—because I judge the path lies clear before me to my own gods. I have indeed earned admission to their presence, and in fact have already been in their company; I have sent my soul to them as they had previously sent theirs to me. But suppose that I am utterly annihilated, and that after death nothing mortal remains; I have no less courage, even if, when I depart, my course leads—nowhere."

"But," you say, "he has not lived as many years as he might have lived."

There are books which contain very few lines, admirable and useful in spite of their size; and there are also the *Annals of Tanusius* —you know how bulky the book is, and what men say of it. This is the case with the long life of certain persons—a state which resembles the *Annals of Tanusius*!

Do you regard as more fortunate the fighter who is slain on the last day of the games than one who goes to his death in the middle of the festivities? Do you believe that anyone is so foolishly covetous of life that he would rather have his throat cut in the dressing-room than in the amphitheatre? It is by no longer an interval than this that we precede one another. Death visits each and all; the slayer soon follows the slain. It is an insignificant trifle, after all, that people discuss with so much concern. And anyhow, what does it matter for how long a time you avoid that which you cannot escape? Farewell.

# Letter 57
# On the Usefulness of Basic Principles

You keep asking me to explain without postponement a topic which I once remarked should be put off until the proper time, and to inform you by letter whether this department of philosophy which the Greeks call *paraenetic*, and we Romans call the "preceptorial," is enough to give us perfect wisdom. Now I know that you will take it in good part if I refuse to do so. But I accept your request all the more willingly, and refuse to let the common saying lose its point:

*Don't ask for what you'll wish you hadn't got.*

For sometimes we seek with effort that which we should decline if offered voluntarily. Call that fickleness or call it pettishness —we must punish the habit by ready compliance. There are many things that we would have men think that we wish, but that we really do not wish. A lecturer sometimes brings upon the platform a huge work of research, written in the tiniest hand and very closely folded; after reading off a large portion, he says: "I shall stop, if you wish;" and a shout arises: "Read on, read on!" from the lips of those who are anxious for the speaker to hold his peace then and there. We often want one thing and pray for another, not telling the truth even to the gods, while the gods either do not hearken, or else take pity on us.

But I shall without pity avenge myself and shall load a huge letter upon your shoulders; for your part, if you read it with reluctance, you may say: "I brought this burden upon myself," and may class yourself among those men whose too ambitious wives drive them frantic, or those whom riches harass, earned by extreme sweat of the brow, or those who are tortured with the titles which they have sought by every sort of device and toil, and all others who are responsible for their own misfortunes.

But I must stop this preamble and approach the problem under consideration. Men say: "The happy life consists in upright conduct; precepts guide one to upright conduct; therefore precepts are sufficient for attaining the happy life." But they do not always guide us to upright conduct; this occurs only when the will is receptive; and sometimes they are applied in vain, when wrong opinions obsess the soul.

Furthermore, a man may act rightly without knowing that he is acting rightly. For nobody, except he be trained from the start and equipped with complete reason, can develop to perfect proportions, understanding when he should do certain things, and to what extent, and in whose company, and how, and why. Without such training a man cannot strive with all his heart after that which is honourable, or even with steadiness or gladness, but will ever be looking back and wavering.

It is also said: "If honourable conduct results from precepts, then precepts are amply sufficient for the happy life; but the first of these statements is true; therefore the second is true also." We shall reply to these words that honourable conduct is, to be sure, brought about by precepts, but not by precepts alone.

"Then," comes the reply, "if the other arts are content with precepts, wisdom will also be content therewith; for wisdom itself is an art of living. And yet the pilot is made by precepts which tell him thus and so to turn the tiller, set his sails, make use of a fair wind, tack, make the best of shifting and variable breezes—all in the proper manner. Other craftsmen also are drilled by precepts; hence precepts will be able to accomplish the same result in the case of our craftsman in the art of living."

Now all these arts are concerned with the tools of life, but not with life as a whole. Hence there is much to clog these arts from without and to complicate them—such as hope, greed, fear. But that art which professes to teach the art of life cannot be forbidden by any circumstance from exercising its functions; for it shakes off complications and pierces through obstacles. Would you like to know how unlike its status is to the other arts? In the case of the latter, it is more pardonable to err voluntarily rather than by accident; but in the case of wisdom the worst fault is to commit sin wilfully.

I mean something like this: A scholar will blush for shame, not if he makes a grammatical blunder intentionally, but if he makes it unintentionally; if a physician does not recognize that his patient is failing, he is a much poorer practitioner than if he recognizes the fact and conceals his knowledge. But in this art of living a voluntary mistake is the more shameful.

Furthermore, many arts, aye and the most liberal of them all, have their special doctrine, and not mere precepts of advice—the medical profession, for example. There are the different schools of Hippocrates, of Asclepiades, of Themison.

And besides, no art that concerns itself with theories can exist without its own doctrines; the Greeks call them *dogmas*, while we Romans may use the term "doctrines," or "tenets," or "adopted principles" —such as you will find in geometry or astronomy. But philosophy is both theoretic and practical; it contemplates and at the same time acts. You are indeed mistaken if you think that philosophy offers you nothing but worldly assistance; her aspirations are loftier than that. She cries: "I investigate the whole universe, nor am I content, keeping myself within a mortal dwelling, to give you favourable or unfavourable advice. Great matters invite and such as are set far above you. In the words of Lucretius:

> To thee shall I reveal the ways of heaven
> And the gods, spreading before thine eyes
> The atoms—whence all things are brought to birth,
> Increased, and fostered by creative power,
> And eke their end when Nature casts them off.

Philosophy, therefore, being theoretic, must have her doctrines.

And why? Because no man can duly perform right actions except one who has been entrusted with reason, which will enable him, in all cases, to fulfil all the categories of duty. These categories he cannot observe unless he receives precepts for every occasion, and not for the present alone. Precepts by themselves are weak and, so to speak, rootless if they be assigned to the parts and not to the whole. It is the doctrines which will strengthen and support us in peace and calm, which will include simultaneously the whole of life and the universe in its completeness. There is the same difference between philosophical doctrines and precepts as there is between elements and members; the latter depend upon the former, while the former are the source both of the latter and of all things.

People say: "The old-style wisdom advised only what one should do and avoid; and yet the men of former days were better men by far. When savants have appeared, sages have become rare. For that frank, simple virtue has changed into hidden and crafty knowledge; we are taught how to debate, not how to live."

Of course, as you say, the old-fashioned wisdom, especially in its beginnings, was crude; but so were the other arts, in which dexterity developed with progress. Nor indeed in those days was there yet any need for carefully-planned cures. Wickedness had not yet reached such a high point, or scattered itself so broadcast. Plain vices could be treated by plain cures; now, however, we need defences erected with all the greater care, because of the stronger powers by which we are attacked.

Medicine once consisted of the knowledge of a few simples, to stop the flow of blood, or to heal wounds; then by degrees it reached its present stage of complicated variety. No wonder that in early days medicine had less to do! Men's bodies were still sound and strong; their food was light and not spoiled by art and luxury, whereas when they began to seek dishes not for the sake of removing, but of rousing, the appetite, and devised countless sauces to whet their gluttony—then what before was nourishment to a hungry man became a burden to the full stomach.

Thence come paleness, and a trembling of wine-sodden muscles, and a repulsive thinness, due rather to indigestion than to hunger. Thence weak tottering steps, and a reeling gait just like that of drunkenness. Thence dropsy, spreading under the entire skin, and the belly growing to a paunch through an ill habit of taking more than it can hold. Thence yellow jaundice, discoloured countenances, and bodies that rot inwardly, and fingers that grow knotty when the joints stiffen, and muscles that are numbed and without power of feeling, and palpitation of the heart with its ceaseless pounding.

Why need I mention dizziness? Or speak of pain in the eye and in the ear, itching and aching in the fevered brain, and internal ulcers throughout the digestive system? Besides these, there are countless kinds of fever, some acute in their malignity, others creeping upon us with subtle damage, and still others which approach us with chills and severe ague.

Why should I mention the other innumerable diseases, the tortures that result from high living?

Men used to be free from such ills, because they had not yet slackened their strength by indulgence, because they had control over themselves, and supplied their own needs. They toughened their bodies by work and real toil, tiring themselves out by running or hunting or tilling the earth. They were refreshed by food in which only a hungry man could take pleasure. Hence, there was no need for all our mighty medical paraphernalia, for so many instruments and pill-boxes. For plain reasons they enjoyed plain health; it took elaborate courses to produce elaborate diseases.

Mark the number of things—all to pass down a single throat— that luxury mixes together, after ravaging land and sea. So many different dishes must surely disagree; they are bolted with difficulty and are digested with difficulty, each jostling against the other. And no wonder, that diseases which result from ill-assorted food are variable and manifold; there must be an overflow when so many unnatural combinations are jumbled together. Hence there are as many ways of being ill as there are of living.

The illustrious founder of the guild and profession of medicine remarked that women never lost their hair or suffered from pain in the feet; and yet nowadays they run short of hair and are afflicted with gout. This does not mean that woman's physique has changed, but that it has been conquered; in rivalling male indulgences they have also rivalled the ills to which men are heirs.

They keep just as late hours, and drink just as much liquor; they challenge men in wrestling and carousing; they are no less given to vomiting from distended stomachs and to thus discharging all their wine again; nor are they behind the men in gnawing ice, as a relief to their fevered digestions. And they even match the men in their passions, although they were created to feel love passively (may the gods and goddesses confound them!). They devise the most impossible varieties of unchastity, and in the company of men they play the part of men. What wonder, then, that we can trip up the statement of the greatest and most skilled physician, when so many women are gouty and bald! Because of their vices, women have ceased to deserve the privileges of their sex; they have put off their womanly nature and are therefore condemned to suffer the diseases of men.

Physicians of old time knew nothing about prescribing frequent nourishment and propping the feeble pulse with wine; they did not understand the practice of blood-letting and of easing chronic complaints with sweat-baths; they did not understand how, by bandaging ankles and arms, to recall to the outward parts the hidden strength which had taken refuge in the centre. They were not compelled to seek many varieties of relief, because the varieties of suffering were very few in number.

Nowadays, however, to what a stage have the evils of ill-health advanced! This is the interest which we pay on pleasures which we have coveted beyond what is reasonable and right. You need not wonder that diseases are beyond counting: count the cooks! All intellectual interests are in abeyance; those who follow culture lecture to empty rooms, in out-of-the-way places. The halls of the professor and the philosopher are deserted; but what a crowd there is in the cafés! How many young fellows besiege the kitchens of their gluttonous friends!

I shall not mention the troops of luckless boys who must put up with other shameful treatment after the banquet is over. I shall not mention the troops of catamites, rated according to nation and colour, who must all have the same smooth skin, and the same amount of youthful down on their cheeks, and the same way of dressing their hair, so that no boy with straight locks may get among the curly-heads. Nor shall I mention the medley of bakers, and the numbers of waiters who at a given signal scurry to carry in the courses. Ye gods! How many men are kept busy to humour a single belly!

What? Do you imagine that those mushrooms, the epicure's poison, work no evil results in secret, even though they have had no immediate effect? What? Do you suppose that your summer snow does not harden the tissue of the liver? What? Do you suppose that those oysters, a sluggish food fattened on slime, do not weigh one down with mud-begotten heaviness? What? Do you not think that the so-called "Sauce from the Provinces," the costly extract of poisonous fish, burns up the stomach with its salted putrefaction? What? Do you judge that the corrupted dishes which a man swallows almost burning from the kitchen fire, are quenched in the digestive system without doing harm? How repulsive, then, and how unhealthy are their belchings, and how disgusted men are with themselves when they breathe forth the fumes of yesterday's debauch! You may be sure that their food is not being digested, but is rotting.

I remember once hearing gossip about a notorious dish into which everything over which epicures love to dally had been heaped together by a cookshop that was fast rushing into bankruptcy; there were two kinds of mussels, and oysters trimmed round at the line where they are edible, set off at intervals by sea-urchins; the whole was flanked by mullets cut up and served without the bones.

In these days we are ashamed of separate foods; people mix many flavours into one. The dinner table does work which the stomach ought to do. I look forward next to food being served masticated! And how little we are from it already when we pick out shells and bones and the cook performs the office of the teeth!

They say: "It is too much trouble to take our luxuries one by one; let us have everything served at the same time and blended into the same flavour. Why should I help myself to a single dish? Let us have many coming to the table at once; the dainties of various courses should be combined and confounded.

Those who used to declare that this was done for display and notoriety should understand that it is not done for show, but that it is an oblation to our sense of duty! Let us have at one time, drenched in the same sauce, the dishes that are usually served separately. Let there be no difference: let oysters, sea-urchins, shell-fish, and mullets be mixed together and cooked in the same dish." No vomited food could be jumbled up more helter-skelter.

And as the food itself is complicated, so the resulting diseases are complex, unaccountable, manifold, variegated; medicine has begun to campaign against them in many ways and by many rules of treatment.

Now I declare to you that the same statement applies to philosophy. It was once more simple because men's sins were on a smaller scale, and could be cured with but slight trouble; in the face, however, of all this moral topsy-turvy men must leave no remedy untried. And would that this pest might so at last be overcome!

We are mad, not only individually, but nationally. We check manslaughter and isolated murders; but what of war and the much-vaunted crime of slaughtering whole peoples? There are no limits to our greed, none to our cruelty. And as long as such crimes are committed by stealth and by individuals, they are less harmful and less portentous; but cruelties are practiced in accordance with acts of senate and popular assembly, and the public is bidden to do that which is forbidden to the individual.

Deeds that would be punished by loss of life when committed in secret, are praised by us because uniformed generals have carried them out. Man, naturally the gentlest class of being, is not ashamed to revel in the blood of others, to wage war, and to entrust the waging of war to his sons, when even dumb beasts and wild beasts keep the peace with one another.

Against this overmastering and widespread madness philosophy has become a matter of greater effort, and has taken on strength in proportion to the strength which is gained by the opposition forces.

It used to be easy to scold men who were slaves to drink and who sought out more luxurious food; it did not require a mighty effort to bring the spirit back to the simplicity from which it had departed only slightly. But now

*One needs the rapid hand, the master-craft.*

Men seek pleasure from every source. No vice remains within its limits; luxury is precipitated into greed. We are overwhelmed with forgetfulness of that which is honourable. Nothing that has an attractive value, is base. Man, an object of reverence in the eyes of man, is now slaughtered for jest and sport; and those whom it used to be unholy to train for the purpose of inflicting and enduring wounds, are thrust forth exposed and defenceless; and it is a satisfying spectacle to see a man made a corpse.

Amid this upset condition of morals, something stronger than usual is needed—something which will shake off these chronic ills; in order to root out a deep-seated belief in wrong ideas, conduct must be regulated by doctrines. It is only when we add precepts, consolation, and encouragement to these, that they can prevail; by themselves they are ineffective.

If we would hold men firmly bound and tear them away from the ills which clutch them fast, they must learn what is evil and what is good. They must know that everything except virtue changes its name and becomes now good and now bad. Just as the soldier's primary bond of union is his oath of allegiance and his love for the flag, and a horror of desertion, and just as, after this stage, other duties can easily be demanded of him, and trusts given to him when once the oath has been administered; so it is with those whom you would bring to the happy life: the first foundations must be laid, and virtue worked into these men. Let them be held by a sort of superstitious worship of virtue; let them love her; let them desire to live with her, and refuse to live without her.

"But what, then," people say, "have not certain persons won their way to excellence without complicated training? Have they not made great progress by obeying bare precepts alone?" Very true; but their temperaments were propitious, and they snatched salvation as it were by the way. For just as the immortal gods did not learn virtue having been born with virtue complete, and containing in their nature the essence of goodness—even so certain men are fitted with unusual qualities and reach without a long apprenticeship that which is ordinarily a matter of teaching, welcoming honourable things as soon as they hear them.

Hence come the choice minds which seize quickly upon virtue, or else produce it from within themselves. But your dull, sluggish fellow, who is hampered by his evil habits, must have this soul-rust incessantly rubbed off.

Now, as the former sort, who are inclined towards the good, can be raised to the heights more quickly: so the weaker spirits will be assisted and freed from their evil opinions if we entrust to them the accepted principles of philosophy; and you may understand how essential these principles are in the following way. Certain things sink into us, rendering us sluggish in some ways, and hasty in others. These two qualities, the one of recklessness and the other of sloth, cannot be respectively checked or roused unless we remove their causes, which are mistaken admiration and mistaken fear. As long as we are obsessed by such feelings, you may say to us: "You owe this duty to your father, this to your children, this to your friends, this to your guests"; but greed will always hold us back, no matter how we try. A man may know that he should fight for his country, but fear will dissuade him. A man may know that he should sweat forth his last drop of energy on behalf of his friends, but luxury will forbid. A man may know that keeping a mistress is the worst kind of insult to his wife, but lust will drive him in the opposite direction.

It will therefore be of no avail to give precepts unless you first remove the conditions that are likely to stand in the way of precepts; it will do no more good than to place weapons by your side and bring yourself near the foe without having your hands free to use those weapons. The soul, in order to deal with the precepts which we offer, must first be set free.

Suppose that a man is acting as he should; he cannot keep it up continuously or consistently, since he will not know the reason for so acting. Some of his conduct will result rightly because of luck or practice; but there will be in his hand no rule by which he may regulate his acts, and which he may trust to tell him whether that which he has done is right. One who is good through mere chance will not give promise of retaining such a character for ever.

Furthermore, precepts will perhaps help you to do what should be done; but they will not help you to do it in the proper way; and if they do not help you to this end, they do not conduct you to virtue. I grant you that, if warned, a man will do what he should; but that is not enough, since the credit lies, not in the actual deed, but in the way it is done.

What is more shameful than a costly meal which eats away the income even of a knight? Or what so worthy of the censor's condemnation as to be always indulging oneself and one's "inner man," if I may speak as the gluttons do? And yet often has an inaugural dinner cost the most careful man a cool million! The very sum that is called disgraceful if spent on the appetite, is beyond reproach if spent for official purposes! For it is not luxury but an expenditure sanctioned by custom.

A mullet of monstrous size was presented to the Emperor Tiberius. They say it weighed four and one half pounds (and why should I not tickle the palates of certain epicures by mentioning its weight?). Tiberius ordered it to be sent to the fish-market and put up for sale, remarking: "I shall be taken entirely by surprise, my friends, if either Apicius or P. Octavius does not buy that mullet." The guess came true beyond his expectation: the two men bid, and Octavius won, thereby acquiring a great reputation among his intimates because he had bought for five thousand sesterces a fish which the Emperor had sold, and which even Apicius did not succeed in buying. To pay such a price was disgraceful for Octavius, but not for the individual who purchased the fish in order to present it to Tiberius—though I should be inclined to blame the latter as well; but at any rate he admired a gift of which he thought Caesar worthy.

When people sit by the bedsides of their sick friends, we honour their motives.

But when people do this for the purpose of attaining a legacy, they are like vultures waiting for carrion. The same act may be either shameful or honourable: the purpose and the manner make all the difference. Now each of our acts will be honourable if we declare allegiance to honour and judge honour and its results to be the only good that can fall to man's lot; for other things are only temporarily good.

I think, then, that there should be deeply implanted a firm belief which will apply to life as a whole: this is what I call a "doctrine." And as this belief is, so will be our acts and our thoughts. As our acts and our thoughts are, so will our lives be. It is not enough, when a man is arranging his existence as a whole, to give him advice about details.

Marcus Brutus, in the book which he has entitled *Concerning Duty*, gives many precepts to parents, children, and brothers; but no one will do his duty as he ought, unless he has some principle to which he may refer his conduct. We must set before our eyes the goal of the Supreme Good, towards which we may strive, and to which all our acts and words may have reference—just as sailors must guide their course according to a certain star.

Life without ideals is erratic: as soon as an ideal is to be set up, doctrines begin to be necessary. I am sure you will admit that there is nothing more shameful than uncertain and wavering conduct, than the habit of timorous retreat. This will be our experience in all cases unless we remove that which checks the spirit and clogs it, and keeps it from making an attempt and trying with all its might.

Precepts are commonly given as to how the gods should be worshipped. But let us forbid lamps to be lighted on the Sabbath, since the gods do not need light, neither do men take pleasure in soot. Let us forbid men to offer morning salutation and to throng the doors of temples; mortal ambitions are attracted by such ceremonies, but God is worshipped by those who truly know Him. Let us forbid bringing towels and flesh-scrapers to Jupiter, and proffering mirrors to Juno; for God seeks no servants. Of course not; he himself does service to mankind, everywhere and to all he is at hand to help.

Although a man hear what limit he should observe in sacrifice, and how far he should recoil from burdensome superstitions, he will never make sufficient progress until he has conceived a right idea of God—regarding Him as one who possesses all things, and allots all things, and bestows them without price.

And what reason have the Gods for doing deeds of kindness? It is their nature. One who thinks that they are unwilling to do harm, is wrong; they cannot do harm. They cannot receive or inflict injury; for doing harm is in the same category as suffering harm. The universal nature, all-glorious and all-beautiful, has rendered incapable of inflicting ill those whom it has removed from the danger of ill.

The first way to worship the gods is to believe in the gods; the next to acknowledge their majesty, to acknowledge their goodness without which there is no majesty. Also, to know that they are supreme commanders in the universe, controlling all things by their power and acting as guardians of the human race, even though they are sometimes unmindful of the individual. They neither give nor have evil but they do chasten and restrain certain persons and impose penalties, and sometimes punish by bestowing that which seems good outwardly. Would you win over the gods? Then be a good man. Whoever imitates them, is worshipping them sufficiently.

Then comes the second problem—how to deal with men. What is our purpose? What precepts do we offer? Should we bid them refrain from bloodshed? What a little thing it is not to harm one whom you ought to help! It is indeed worthy of great praise, when man treats man with kindness! Shall we advise stretching forth the hand to the shipwrecked sailor, or pointing out the way to the wanderer, or sharing a crust with the starving? Yes, if I can only tell you first everything which ought to be afforded or withheld; meantime, I can lay down for mankind a rule, in short compass, for our duties in human relationships: all that you behold, that which comprises both god and man, is one—we are the parts of one great body. Nature produced us related to one another, since she created us from the same source and to the same end. She engendered in us mutual affection, and made us prone to friendships. She established fairness and justice; according to her ruling, it is more wretched to commit than to suffer injury. Through her orders, let our hands be ready for all that needs to be helped.

Let this verse be in your heart and on your lips:

*I am a man; and nothing in man's lot*
*Do I deem foreign to me.*

Let us possess things in common; for birth is ours in common. Our relations with one another are like a stone arch, which would collapse if the stones did not mutually support each other, and which is upheld in this very way.

Next, after considering gods and men, let us see how we should make use of things. It is useless for us to have mouthed out precepts, unless we begin by reflecting what opinion we ought to hold concerning everything—concerning poverty, riches, renown, disgrace, citizenship, exile. Let us banish rumour and set a value upon each thing, asking what it is and not what it is called.

Now let us turn to a consideration of the virtues. Some persons will advise us to rate prudence very high, to cherish bravery, and to cleave more closely, if possible, to justice than to all other qualities. But this will do us no good if we do not know what virtue is, whether it is simple or compound, whether it is one or more than one, whether its parts are separate or interwoven with one another; whether he who has one virtue possesses the other virtues also; and just what are the distinctions between them.

The carpenter does not need to inquire about his art in the light of its origin or of its function, any more than a pantomime need inquire about the art of dancing; if these arts understand themselves, nothing is lacking, for they do not refer to life as a whole. But virtue means the knowledge of other things besides herself: if we would learn virtue we must learn all about virtue.

Conduct will not be right unless the will to act is right; for this is the source of conduct. Nor, again, can the will be right without a right attitude of mind; for this is the source of the will. Furthermore, such an attitude of mind will not be found even in the best of men unless he has learned the laws of life as a whole and has worked out a proper judgment about everything, and unless he has reduced facts to a standard of truth. Peace of mind is enjoyed only by those who have attained a fixed and unchanging standard of judgment; the rest of mankind continually ebb and flow in their decisions, floating in a condition where they alternately reject things and seek them.

And what is the reason for this tossing to and fro? It is because nothing is clear to them, because they make use of a most unsure criterion—rumour. If you would always desire the same things, you must desire the truth. But one cannot attain the truth without doctrines; for doctrines embrace the whole of life. Things good and evil, honourable and disgraceful, just and unjust, dutiful and undutiful, the virtues and their practice, the possession of comforts, worth and respect, health, strength, beauty, keenness of the senses—all these qualities call for one who is able to appraise them. One should be allowed to know at what value every object is to be rated on the list; for sometimes you are deceived and believe that certain things are worth more than their real value; in fact, so badly are you deceived that you will find you should value at a mere pennyworth those things which we men regard as worth most of all—for example, riches, influence, and power.

You will never understand this unless you have investigated the actual standard by which such conditions are relatively rated. As leaves cannot flourish by their own efforts, but need a branch to which they may cling and from which they may draw sap, so your precepts, when taken alone, wither away; they must be grafted upon a school of philosophy.

Moreover, those who do away with doctrines do not understand that these doctrines are proved by the very arguments through which they seem to disprove them. For what are these men saying? They are saying that precepts are sufficient to develop life, and that the doctrines of wisdom (in other words, dogmas) are superfluous. And yet this very utterance of theirs is a doctrine just as if I should now remark that one must dispense with precepts on the ground that they are superfluous, that one must make use of doctrines, and that our studies should be directed solely towards this end; thus, by my very statement that precepts should not be taken seriously, I should be uttering a precept.

There are certain matters in philosophy which need admonition; there are others which need proof, and a great deal of proof, too, because they are complicated and can scarcely be made clear with the greatest care and the greatest dialectic skill. If proofs are necessary, so are doctrines; for doctrines deduce the truth by reasoning. Some matters are clear, and others are vague: those which the senses and the memory can embrace are clear; those which are outside their scope are vague.

But reason is not satisfied by obvious facts; its higher and nobler function is to deal with hidden things. Hidden things need proof; proof cannot come without doctrines; therefore, doctrines are necessary.

That which leads to a general agreement, and likewise to a perfect one, is an assured belief in certain facts; but if, lacking this assurance, all things are adrift in our minds, then doctrines are indispensable; for they give to our minds the means of unswerving decision.

Furthermore, when we advise a man to regard his friends as highly as himself, to reflect that an enemy may become a friend, to stimulate love in the friend, and to check hatred in the enemy, we add: "This is just and honourable." Now the just and honourable element in our doctrines is embraced by reason; hence reason is necessary; for without it the doctrines cannot exist, either.

But let us unite the two. For indeed branches are useless without their roots, and the roots themselves are strengthened by the growths which they have produced. Everyone can understand how useful the hands are; they obviously help us. But the heart, the source of the hands growth and power and motion, is hidden. And I can say the same thing about precepts: they are manifest, while the doctrines of wisdom are concealed. And as only the initiated know the more hallowed portion of the rites, so in philosophy the hidden truths are revealed only to those who are members and have been admitted to the sacred rites. But precepts and other such matters are familiar even to the uninitiated.

Posidonius holds that not only precept-giving (there is nothing to prevent my using this word), but even persuasion, consolation, and encouragement, are necessary. To these he adds *the investigation of causes* (but I fail to see why I should not dare to call it *aetiology*, since the scholars who mount guard over the Latin language thus use the term as having the right to do so). He remarks that it will also be useful to illustrate each particular virtue; this science Posidonius calls *ethology*, while others call it *characterization*. It gives the signs and marks which belong to each virtue and vice, so that by them distinction may be drawn between like things.

Its function is the same as that of precept. For he who utters precepts says: "If you would have self-control, act thus and so!" He who illustrates, says "The man who acts thus and so, and refrains from certain other things, possesses self-control." If you ask what the difference here is, I say that the one gives the precepts of virtue, the other its embodiment. These illustrations, or, to use a commercial term, these *samples*, have, I confess, a certain utility; just put them up for exhibition well recommended, and you will find men to copy them.

Would you, for instance, deem it a useful thing to have evidence given you by which you may recognize a thoroughbred horse, and not be cheated in your purchase or waste your time over a low-bred animal? But how much more useful it is to know the marks of a surpassingly fine soul—marks which one may appropriate from another for oneself!

> *Straightway the foal of the high-bred drove nursed up in the pastures,*
> *Marches with spirited step, and treads with a delicate motion;*
> *First on the dangerous pathway and into the threatening river,*
> *Trusting himself to the unknown bridge, without fear at its creakings,*
> *Neck thrown high in the air, and clear-cut head, and a belly*
> *Spare, back rounded, and breast abounding in courage and muscle.*
> *He, when the clashing of weapons is heard to resound in the distance,*
> *Leaps from his place, and pricks up his ears, and all in a tremble*
> *Pours forth the pent-up fire that lay close-shut in his nostrils.*

Vergil's description, though referring to something else, might perfectly well be the portrayal of a brave man; at any rate, I myself should select no other simile for a hero. If I had to describe Cato, who was unterrified amid the din of civil war, who was first to attack the armies that were already making for the Alps, who plunged face-forward into the civil conflict, this is exactly the sort of expression and attitude which I should give him.

Surely none could "march with more spirited step" than one who rose against Caesar and Pompey at the same time and, when some were supporting Caesar's party and others that of Pompey, issued a challenge to both leaders, thus showing that the republic also had some backers. For it is not enough to say of Cato "without fear at its creakings." Of course he is not afraid! He does not quail before real and imminent noises; in the face of ten legions, Gallic auxiliaries, and a motley host of citizens and foreigners, he utters words fraught with freedom, encouraging the Republic not to fail in the struggle for freedom, but to try all hazards; he declares that it is more honourable to fall into servitude than to fall in line with it.

What force and energy are his! What confidence he displays amid the general panic! He knows that he is the only one whose standing is not in question, and that men do not ask whether Cato is free, but whether he is still among the free. Hence his contempt for danger and the sword. What a pleasure it is to say, in admiration of the unflinching steadiness of a hero who did not totter when the whole state was in ruins:

*A breast abounding in courage and muscle!*

It will be helpful not only to state what is the usual quality of good men, and to outline their figures and features, but also to relate and set forth what men there have been of this kind. We might picture that last and bravest wound of Cato's, through which Freedom breathed her last; or the wise Laelius and his harmonious life with his friend Scipio; or the noble deeds of the Elder Cato at home and abroad; or the wooden couches of Tubero, spread at a public feast, goatskins instead of tapestry, and vessels of earthenware set out for the banquet before the very shrine of Jupiter! What else was this except consecrating poverty on the Capitol? Though I know no other deed of his for which to rank him with the Catos, is this one not enough? It was a censorship, not a banquet.

How lamentably do those who covet glory fail to understand what glory is, or in what way it should be sought! On that day the Roman populace viewed the furniture of many men; it marvelled only at that of one! The gold and silver of all the others has been broken up and melted down times without number; but Tubero's earthenware will endure throughout eternity. Farewell.

# Letter 58
# On Facing Hardships

Spite of all do you still chafe and complain, not understanding that, in all the evils to which you refer, there is really only one—the fact that you *do* chafe and complain? If you ask me, I think that for a *man* there is no misery unless there be something in the universe which he thinks miserable. I shall not endure myself on that day when I find anything unendurable.

I am ill; but that is a part of my lot. My slaves have fallen sick, my income has gone off, my house is rickety, I have been assailed by losses, accidents, toil, and fear; this is a common thing. Nay, that was an understatement; it was an inevitable thing.

Such affairs come by order, and not by accident. If you will believe me, it is my inmost emotions that I am just now disclosing to you: when everything seems to go hard and uphill, I have trained myself not merely to obey God, but to agree with His decisions. I follow Him because my soul wills it, and not because I must. Nothing will ever happen to me that I shall receive with ill humour or with a wry face. I shall pay up all my taxes willingly. Now all the things which cause us to groan or recoil, are part of the tax of life.—things, my dear Lucilius, which you should never hope and never seek to escape.

It was disease of the bladder that made you apprehensive; downcast letters came from you; you were continually getting worse; I will touch the truth more closely, and say that you feared for your life. But come, did you not know, when you prayed for long life, that this was what you were praying for? A long life includes all these troubles, just as a long journey includes dust and mud and rain.

"But," you cry, "I wished to live, and at the same time to be immune from all ills." Such a womanish cry does no credit to a man. Consider in what attitude you shall receive this prayer of mine (I offer it not only in a good, but in a noble spirit): "May gods and goddesses alike forbid that Fortune keep you in luxury!"

Ask yourself voluntarily which you would choose if some god gave you the choice—a life in a café or life in a camp.

And yet life, Lucilius, is really a battle. For this reason those who are tossed about at sea, who proceed uphill and downhill over toilsome crags and heights, who go on campaigns that bring the greatest danger, are heroes and front-rank fighters; but persons who live in rotten luxury and ease while others toil, are mere turtle-doves safe only because men despise them. Farewell.

# Letter 59
# On the Fickleness of Fortune

You need never believe that anyone who depends upon happiness is happy! It is a fragile support—this delight in adventitious things; the joy which entered from without will some day depart. But that joy which springs wholly from oneself is leal and sound; it increases and attends us to the last; while all other things which provoke the admiration of the crowd are but temporary Goods. You may reply: "What do you mean? Cannot such things serve both for utility and for delight?" Of course. But only if they depend on us, and not we on them.

All things that Fortune looks upon become productive and pleasant, only if he who possesses them is in possession also of himself, and is not in the power of that which belongs to him. For men make a mistake, my dear Lucilius, if they hold that anything good, or evil either, is bestowed upon us by Fortune; it is simply the raw material of Goods and Ills that she gives to us—the sources of things which, in our keeping, will develop into good or ill. For the soul is more powerful than any sort of Fortune; by its own agency it guides its affairs in either direction, and of its own power it can produce a happy life, or a wretched one.

A bad man makes everything bad—even things which had come with the appearance of what is best; but the upright and honest man corrects the wrongs of Fortune, and softens hardship and bitterness because he knows how to endure them; he likewise accepts prosperity with appreciation and moderation, and stands up against trouble with steadiness and courage. Though a man be prudent, though he conduct all his interests with well-balanced judgment, though he attempt nothing beyond his strength, he will not attain the Good which is unalloyed and beyond the reach of threats, unless he is sure in dealing with that which is unsure.

For whether you prefer to observe other men (and it is easier to make up one's mind when judging the affairs of others), or whether you observe yourself, with all prejudice laid aside, you will perceive and acknowledge that there is no utility in all these desirable and beloved things, unless you equip yourself in opposition to the fickleness of chance and its consequences, and unless you repeat to yourself often and uncomplainingly, at every mishap, the words: "Heaven decreed it otherwise!"

Nay rather, to adopt a phrase which is braver and nearer the truth—one on which you may more safely prop your spirit—say to yourself, whenever things turn out contrary to your expectation: "Heaven decreed *better!*"

If you are thus poised, nothing will affect you and a man will be thus poised if he reflects on the possible ups and downs in human affairs before he feels their force, and if he comes to regard children, or wife, or property, with the idea that he will not necessarily possess them always and that he will not be any more wretched just because he ceases to possess them.

It is tragic for the soul to be apprehensive of the future and wretched in anticipation of wretchedness, consumed with an anxious desire that the objects which give pleasure may remain in its possession to the very end. For such a soul will never be at rest; in waiting for the future it will lose the present blessings which it might enjoy. And there is no difference between grief for something lost and the fear of losing it.

But I do not for this reason advise you to be indifferent. Rather do you turn aside from you whatever may cause fear. Be sure to foresee whatever can be foreseen by planning. Observe and avoid, long before it happens, anything that is likely to do you harm. To effect this your best assistance will be a spirit of confidence and a mind strongly resolved to endure all things. He who can bear Fortune, can also beware of Fortune. At any rate, there is no dashing of billows when the sea is calm. And there is nothing more wretched or foolish than premature fear. What madness it is to anticipate one's troubles!

In fine, to express my thoughts in brief compass and portray to you those busybodies and self-tormentors—they are as uncontrolled in the midst of their troubles as they are before them. He suffers more than is necessary, who suffers before it is necessary; such men do not weigh the amount of their suffering, by reason of the same failing which prevents them from being ready for it; and with the same lack of restraint they fondly imagine that their luck will last for ever, and fondly imagine that their gains are bound to increase as well as merely continue. They forget this spring-board on which mortal things are tossed, and they guarantee for themselves exclusively a steady continuance of the gifts of chance.

For this very reason I regard as excellent the saying of Metrodorus, in a letter of consolation to his sister on the loss of her son, a lad of great promise: "All the Good of mortals is mortal." He is referring to those Goods towards which men rush in shoals. For the real Good does not perish; it is certain and lasting and it consists of wisdom and virtue; it is the only immortal thing that falls to mortal lot.

But men are so wayward, and so forgetful of their goal and of the point toward which every day jostles them, that they are surprised at losing anything, although some day they are bound to lose everything. Anything of which you are entitled the owner is in your possession but is not your own; for there is no strength in that which is weak, nor anything lasting and invincible in that which is frail. We must lose our lives as surely as we lose our property, and this, if we understand the truth, is itself a consolation. Lose it with equanimity; for you must lose your life also.

What resource do we find, then, in the face of these losses? Simply this—to keep in memory the things we have lost, and not to suffer the enjoyment which we have derived from them to pass away along with them. To have may be taken from us, to have had, never. A man is thankless in the highest degree if, after losing something, he feels no obligation for having received it. Chance robs us of the thing, but leaves us its use and its enjoyment—and we have lost this if we are so unfair as to regret.

Just say to yourself: "Of all these experiences that seem so frightful, none is insuperable. Separate trials have been overcome by many: fire by Mucius, crucifixion by Regulus, poison by Socrates, exile by Rutilius, and a sword-inflicted death by Cato; therefore, let us also overcome something."

Again, those objects which attract the crowd under the appearance of beauty and happiness, have been scorned by many men and on many occasions. Fabricius when he was general refused riches, and when he was censor branded them with disapproval. Tubero deemed poverty worthy both of himself and of the deity on the Capitol when, by the use of earthenware dishes at a public festival, he showed that man should be satisfied with that which the gods could still use. The elder Sextius rejected the honours of office; he was born with an obligation to take part in public affairs, and yet would not accept the broad stripe even when the deified Julius offered it to him. For he understood that what can be given can also be taken away.

Let us also, therefore, carry out some courageous act of our own accord; let us be included among the ideal types of history.

Why have we been slack? Why do we lose heart? That which could be done, can be done, if only we purify our souls and follow Nature; for when one strays away from Nature one is compelled to crave, and fear, and be a slave to the things of chance. We may return to the true path; we may be restored to our proper state; let us therefore be so, in order that we may be able to endure pain, in whatever form it attacks our bodies, and say to Fortune: "You have to deal with a man; seek someone whom you can conquer!"

By these words, and words of a like kind, the malignity of the ulcer is quieted down; and I hope indeed that it can be reduced, and either cured or brought to a stop, and grow old along with the patient himself. I am, however, comfortable in my mind regarding him; what we are now discussing is our own loss—the taking-off of a most excellent old man. For he himself has lived a full life, and anything additional may be craved by him, not for his own sake, but for the sake of those who need his services.

In continuing to live, he deals generously. Some other person might have put an end to these sufferings; but our friend considers it no less base to flee from death than to flee towards death. "But," comes the answer, "if circumstances warrant, shall he not take his departure?" Of course, if he can no longer be of service to anyone, if all his business will be to deal with pain.

This, my dear Lucilius, is what we mean by studying philosophy while applying it, by practicing it on truth—note what courage a prudent man possesses against death, or against pain, when the one approaches and the other weighs heavily. What ought to be done must be learned from one who does it.

Up to now we have dealt with arguments—whether any man can resist pain, or whether the approach of death can cast down even great souls. Why discuss it further? Here is an immediate fact for us to tackle—death does not make our friend braver to face pain, nor pain to face death. Rather does he trust himself in the face of both; he does not suffer with resignation because he hopes for death, nor does he die gladly because he is tired of suffering. Pain he endures, death he awaits. Farewell.

## Letter 60
## On Consolation to the Bereaved

I enclose a copy of the letter which I wrote to Marullus at the time when he had lost his little son and was reported to be rather womanish in his grief—a letter in which I have not observed the usual form of condolence: for I did not believe that he should be handled gently, since in my opinion he deserved criticism rather than consolation. When a man is stricken and is finding it most difficult to endure a grievous wound, one must humour him for a while; let him satisfy his grief or at any rate work off the first shock; but those who have assumed an indulgence in grief should be rebuked forthwith, and should learn that there are certain follies even in tears.

Is it solace that you look for? Let me give you a scolding instead! You are like a woman in the way you take your son's death; what would you do if you had lost an intimate friend? A son, a little child of unknown promise, is dead; a fragment of time has been lost.

We hunt out excuses for grief; we would even utter unfair complaints about Fortune, as if Fortune would never give us just reason for complaining! But I had really thought that you possessed spirit enough to deal with concrete troubles, to say nothing of the shadowy troubles over which men make moan through force of habit. Had you lost a friend (which is the greatest blow of all), you would have had to endeavour rather to rejoice because you had possessed him than to mourn because you had lost him.

"But many men fail to count up how manifold their gains have been, how great their rejoicings. Grief like yours has this among other evils: it is not only useless, but thankless. Has it then all been for nothing that you have had such a friend? During so many years, amid such close associations, after such intimate communion of personal interests, has nothing been accomplished? Do you bury friendship along with a friend? And why lament having lost him, if it be of no avail to have possessed him? Believe me, a great part of those we have loved, though chance has removed their persons, still abides with us. The past is ours, and there is nothing more secure for us than that which has been.

We are ungrateful for past gains, because we hope for the future, as if the future—if so be that any future is ours—will not be quickly blended with the past. People set a narrow limit to their enjoyments if they take pleasure only in the present; both the future and the past serve for our delight—the one with anticipation, and the other with memories but the one is contingent and may not come to pass, while the other must have been.

"What madness it is, therefore, to lose our grip on that which is the surest thing of all? Let us rest content with the pleasures we have quaffed in past days, if only, while we quaffed them, the soul was not pierced like a sieve, only to lose again whatever it had received.

There are countless cases of men who have without tears buried sons in the prime of manhood—men who have returned from the funeral pyre to the Senate chamber, or to any other official duties, and have straightway busied themselves with something else. And rightly; for in the first place it is idle to grieve if you get no help from grief. In the second place, it is unfair to complain about what has happened to one man but is in store for all. Again, it is foolish to lament one's loss, when there is such a slight interval between the lost and the loser. Hence we should be more resigned in spirit, because we follow closely those whom we have lost.

"Note the rapidity of Time—that swiftest of things; consider the shortness of the course along which we hasten at top speed; mark this throng of humanity all straining toward the same point with briefest intervals between them—even when they seem longest; he whom you count as passed away has simply posted on ahead. And what is more irrational than to bewail your predecessor, when you yourself must travel on the same journey?

Does a man bewail an event which he knew would take place? Or, if he did not think of death as man's lot, he has but cheated himself. Does a man bewail an event which he has been admitting to be unavoidable? Whoever complains about the death of anyone, is complaining that he was a man. Everyone is bound by the same terms: he who is privileged to be born, is destined to die.

Periods of time separate us, but death levels us. The period which lies between our first day and our last is shifting and uncertain: if you reckon it by its troubles, it is long even to a lad, if by its speed, it is scanty even to a greybeard. Everything is slippery, treacherous, and more shifting than any weather. All things are tossed about and shift into their opposites at the bidding of Fortune; amid such a turmoil of mortal affairs nothing but death is surely in store for anyone. And yet all men complain about the one thing wherein none of them is deceived.

'But he died in boyhood.' I am not yet prepared to say that he who quickly comes to the end of his life has the better of the bargain; let us turn to consider the case of him who has grown to old age. How very little is he superior to the child! Place before your mind's eye the vast spread of time's abyss, and consider the universe; and then contrast our so-called human life with infinity: you will then see how scant is that for which we pray, and which we seek to lengthen.

How much of this time is taken up with weeping, how much with worry! How much with prayers for death before death arrives, how much with our health, how much with our fears! How much is occupied by our years of inexperience or of useless endeavour! And half of all this time is wasted in sleeping. Add, besides, our toils, our griefs, our dangers—and you will comprehend that even in the longest life real living is the least portion thereof.

Nevertheless, who will make such an admission as: 'A man is not better off who is allowed to return home quickly, whose journey is accomplished before he is wearied out'? Life is neither a Good nor an Evil; it is simply the place where good and evil exist. Hence this little boy has lost nothing except a hazard where loss was more assured than gain. He might have turned out temperate and prudent; he might, with your fostering care, have been moulded to a better standard; but (and this fear is more reasonable) he might have become just like the many.

Note the youths of the noblest lineage whose extravagance has flung them into the arena; note those men who cater to the passions of themselves and others in mutual lust, whose days never pass without drunkenness or some signal act of shame; it will thus be clear to you that there was more to fear than to hope for.

For this reason you ought not to invite excuses for grief or aggravate slight burdens by getting indignant.

I am not exhorting you to make an effort and rise to great heights; for my opinion of you is not so low as to make me think that it is necessary for you to summon every bit of your virtue to face this trouble. Yours is not pain; it is a mere sting—and it is you yourself who are turning it into pain.

Of a surety philosophy has done you much service if you can bear courageously the loss of a boy who was as yet better known to his nurse than to his father!

And what, then? Now, at this time, am I advising you to be hard-hearted, desiring you to keep your countenance unmoved at the very funeral ceremony, and not allowing your soul even to feel the pinch of pain? By no means. That would mean lack of feeling rather than virtue—to behold the burial ceremonies of those near and dear to you with the same expression as you beheld their living forms, and to show no emotion over the first bereavement in your family. But suppose that I forbade you to show emotion; there are certain feelings which claim their own rights. Tears fall, no matter how we try to check them, and by being shed they ease the soul.

What, then, shall we do? Let us allow them to fall, but let us not command them do so; let us according as emotion floods our eyes, but not as as mere imitation shall demand. Let us, indeed, add nothing to natural grief, nor augment it by following the example of others. The display of grief makes more demands than grief itself: how few men are sad in their own company! They lament the louder for being heard; persons who are reserved and silent when alone are stirred to new paroxysms of tears when they behold others near them! At such times they lay violent hands upon their own persons—though they might have done this more easily if no one were present to check them; at such times they pray for death; at such times they toss themselves from their couches. But their grief slackens with the departure of onlookers.

In this matter, as in others also, we are obsessed by this fault—conforming to the pattern of the many, and regarding convention rather than duty. We abandon nature and surrender to the mob—who are never good advisers in anything, and in this respect as in all others are most inconsistent. People see a man who bears his grief bravely: they call him undutiful and savage-hearted; they see a man who collapses and clings to his dead: they call him womanish and weak.

Everything, therefore, should be referred to reason. But nothing is more foolish than to court a reputation for sadness and to sanction tears; for I hold that with a wise man some tears fall by consent, others by their own force.

I shall explain the difference as follows: When the first news of some bitter loss has shocked us, when we embrace the form that will soon pass from our arms to the funeral flames—then tears are wrung from us by the necessity of Nature, and the life-force, smitten by the stroke of grief, shakes both the whole body, and the eyes also, from which it presses out and causes to flow the moisture that lies within.

Tears like these fall by a forcing-out process, against our will; but different are the tears which we allow to escape when we muse in memory upon those whom we have lost. And there is in them a certain sweet sadness when we remember the sound of a pleasant voice, a genial conversation, and the busy duties of yore; at such a time the eyes are loosened, as it were, with joy. This sort of weeping we indulge; the former sort overcomes us.

There is, then, no reason why, just because a group of persons is standing in your presence or sitting at your side, you should either check or pour forth your tears; whether restrained or outpoured, they are never so disgraceful as when feigned. Let them flow naturally. But it is possible for tears to flow from the eyes of those who are quiet and at peace. They often flow without impairing the influence of the wise man—with such restraint that they show no want either of feeling or of self-respect.

We may, I assure you, obey Nature and yet maintain our dignity. I have seen men worthy of reverence, during the burial of those near and dear, with countenances upon which love was written clear even after the whole apparatus of mourning was removed, and who showed no other conduct than that which was allowed to genuine emotion. There is a comeliness even in grief. This should be cultivated by the wise man; even in tears, just as in other matters also, there is a certain sufficiency; it is with the unwise that sorrows, like joys, gush over.

Accept in an unruffled spirit that which is inevitable. What can happen that is beyond belief? Or what that is new? How many men at this very moment are making arrangements for funerals! How many are purchasing grave-clothes! How many are mourning, when you yourself have finished mourning! As often as you reflect that your boy has ceased to be, reflect also upon man, who has no sure promise of anything, whom Fortune does not inevitably escort to the confines of old age, but lets him go at whatever point she sees fit.

You may, however, speak often concerning the departed, and cherish his memory to the extent of your power. This memory will return to you all the more often if you welcome its coming without bitterness; for no man enjoys converse with one who is sorrowful, much less with sorrow itself. And whatever words, whatever jests of his, no matter how much of a child he was, may have given you pleasure to hear—these I would have you recall again and again; assure yourself confidently that he might have fulfilled the hopes which you, his father, had entertained.

Indeed, to forget the beloved dead, to bury their memory along with their bodies, to bewail them bounteously and afterwards think of them but scantily—this is the mark of a soul below that of man. For that is the way in which birds and beasts love their young; their affection is quickly roused and almost reaches madness, but it cools away entirely when its object dies. This quality does not befit a man of sense; he should continue to remember, but should cease to mourn.

And in no wise do I approve of the remark of Metrodorus—that there is a certain pleasure akin to sadness, and that one should give chase thereto at such times as these. I am quoting the actual words of Metrodorus.

I have no doubt what your feelings will be in these matters; for what is baser than to 'chase after' pleasure in the very midst of mourning—nay rather by means of mourning—and even amid one's tears to hunt out that which will give pleasure? These are the men who accuse us of too great strictness, slandering our precepts because of supposed harshness—because (say they) we declare that grief should either not be given place in the soul at all, or else should be driven out forthwith. But which is the more incredible or inhuman—to feel no grief at the loss of one's friend, or to go a-hawking after pleasure in the midst of grief?

That which we Stoics advise, is honourable; when emotion has prompted a moderate flow of tears, and has, so to speak, ceased to effervesce, the soul should not be surrendered to grief. But what do you mean, Metrodorus, by saying that with our very grief there should be a blending of pleasure? That is the sweetmeat method of pacifying children; that is the way we still the cries of infants, by pouring milk down their throats!

Even at the moment when your son's body is on the pyre, or your friend breathing his last, will you not suffer your pleasure to cease, rather than tickle your very grief with pleasure? Which is the more honourable—to remove grief from your soul, or to admit pleasure even into the company of grief? Did I say 'admit'? Nay, I mean 'chase after,' and from the hands, too, of grief itself.

Metrodorus says: 'There is a certain pleasure which is related to sadness.' We Stoics may say that, but you may not. The only Good which you recognize, is pleasure, and the only Evil, pain; and what relationship can there be between a Good and an Evil? But suppose that such a relationship does exist; now, of all times, is it to be rooted out? Shall we examine grief also, and see with what elements of delight and pleasure it is surrounded?

Certain remedies, which are beneficial for some parts of the body, cannot be applied to other parts because these are, in a way, revolting and unfit; and that which in certain cases would work to a good purpose without any loss to one's self-respect, may become unseemly because of the situation of the wound. Are you not, similarly, ashamed to cure sorrow by pleasure? No, this sore spot must be treated in a more drastic way. This is what you should preferably advise: that no sensation of evil can reach one who is dead; for if it can reach him, he is not dead.

And I say that nothing can hurt him who is as naught; for if a man can be hurt, he is alive. Do you think him to be badly off because he is no more, or because he still exists as somebody? And yet no torment can come to him from the fact that he is no more—for what feeling can belong to one who does not exist?— nor from the fact that he exists; for he has escaped the greatest disadvantage that death has in it—namely, non-existence.

Let us say this also to him who mourns and misses the untimely dead: that all of us, whether young or old, live, in comparison with eternity, on the same level as regards our shortness of life. For out of all time there comes to us less than what any one could call least, since 'least' is at any rate some part; but this life of ours is next to nothing, and yet (fools that we are!), we marshal it in broad array!

"These words I have written to you, not with the idea that you should expect a cure from me at such a late date—for it is clear to me that you have told yourself everything that you will read in my letter—but with the idea that I should rebuke you even for the slight delay during which you lapsed from your true self, and should encourage you for the future, to rouse your spirit against Fortune and to be on the watch for all her missiles, not as if they might possibly come, but as if they were bound to come." Farewell.

# Letter 61
# On the Futility of Planning Ahead

Every day and every hour reveal to us what a nothing we are, and remind us with some fresh evidence that we have forgotten our weakness; then, as we plan for eternity, they compel us to look over our shoulders at Death.

Do you ask me what this preamble means? It refers to Cornelius Senecio, a distinguished and capable Roman knight, whom you knew: from humble beginnings he had advanced himself to fortune, and the rest of the path already lay downhill before him. For it is easier to grow in dignity than to make a start; and money is very slow to come where there is poverty; until it can creep out of that, it goes halting. Senecio was already bordering upon wealth, helped in that direction by two very powerful assets—knowing how to make money and how to keep it also; either one of these gifts might have made him a rich man.

Here was a person who lived most simply, careful of health and wealth alike. He had, as usual, called upon me early in the morning, and had then spent the whole day, even up to nightfall, at the bedside of a friend who was seriously and hopelessly ill. After a comfortable dinner, he was suddenly seized with an acute attack of quinsy, and, with the breath clogged tightly in his swollen throat, barely lived until daybreak. So within a very few hours after the time when he had been performing all the duties of a sound and healthy man, he passed away.

He who was venturing investments by land and sea, who had also entered public life and left no type of business untried, during the very realization of financial success and during the very onrush of the money that flowed into his coffers, was snatched from the world!

*Graft now thy pears, Meliboeus, and set out thy vines in their order!*

But how foolish it is to set out one's life, when one is not even owner of the morrow! O what madness it is to plot out far-reaching hopes! To say: "I will buy and build, loan and call in money, win titles of honour, and then, old and full of years, I will surrender myself to a life of ease."

Believe me when I say that everything is doubtful, even for those who are prosperous. No one has any right to draw for himself upon the future. The very thing that we grasp slips through our hands, and chance cuts into the actual hour which we are crowding so full. Time does indeed roll along by fixed law, but as in darkness; and what is it to me whether Nature's course is sure, when my own is unsure?

We plan distant voyages and long-postponed home-comings after roaming over foreign shores, we plan for military service and the slow rewards of hard campaigns, we canvass for governorships and the promotions of one office after another—and all the while death stands at our side; but since we never think of it except as it affects our neighbour, instances of mortality press upon us day by day, to remain in our minds only as long as they stir our wonder.

Yet what is more foolish than to wonder that something which may happen every day has happened on any one day? There is indeed a limit fixed for us, just where the remorseless law of Fate has fixed it; but none of us knows how near he is to this limit. Therefore, let us so order our minds as if we had come to the very end. Let us postpone nothing. Let us balance life's account every day.

The greatest flaw in life is that it is always imperfect, and that a certain part of it is postponed. One who daily puts the finishing touches to his life is never in want of time. And yet, from this want arise fear and a craving for the future which eats away the mind. There is nothing more wretched than worry over the outcome of future events; as to the amount or the nature of that which remains, our troubled minds are set aflutter with unaccountable fear.

How, then, shall we avoid this vacillation? In one way only—if there be no reaching forward in our life, if it is withdrawn into itself. For he only is anxious about the future, to whom the present is unprofitable. But when I have paid my soul its due, when a soundly-balanced mind knows that a day differs not a whit from eternity—whatever days or problems the future may bring—then the soul looks forth from lofty heights and laughs heartily to itself when it thinks upon the ceaseless succession of the ages. For what disturbance can result from the changes and the instability of Chance, if you are sure in the face of that which is unsure?

Therefore, my dear Lucilius, begin at once to live, and count each separate day as a separate life. He who has thus prepared himself, he whose daily life has been a rounded whole, is easy in his mind; but those who live for hope alone find that the immediate future always slips from their grasp and that greed steals along in its place, and the fear of death, a curse which lays a curse upon everything else. Thence came that most debased of prayers, in which Maecenas does not refuse to suffer weakness, deformity, and as a climax the pain of crucifixion provided only that he may prolong the breath of life amid these sufferings:

> *Fashion me with a palsied hand,*
> *Weak of foot, and a cripple;*
> *Build upon me a crook-backed hump;*
> *Shake my teeth till they rattle;*
> *All is well, if my life remains.*
> *Save, oh, save it, I pray you,*
> *Though I sit on the piercing cross!*

There he is, praying for that which, if it had befallen him, would be the most pitiable thing in the world! And seeking a postponement of suffering, as if he were asking for life! I should deem him most despicable had he wished to live up to the very time of crucifixion: "Nay," he cries, "you may weaken my body if you will only leave the breath of life in my battered and ineffective carcass! Maim me if you will, but allow me, misshapen and deformed as I may be, just a little more time in the world! You may nail me up and set my seat upon the piercing cross!" Is it worth while to weigh down upon one's own wound, and hang impaled upon a gibbet, that one may but postpone something which is the balm of troubles, the end of punishment? Is it worth all this to possess the breath of life only to give it up?

What would you ask for Maecenas but the indulgence of Heaven? What does he mean by such womanish and indecent verse? What does he mean by making terms with panic fear? What does he mean by begging so vilely for life? He cannot ever have heard Vergil read the words:

> *Tell me, is Death so wretched as that?*

He asks for the climax of suffering, and—what is still harder to bear—prolongation and extension of suffering; and what does he gain thereby? Merely the boon of a longer existence. But what sort of life is a lingering death?

Can anyone be found who would prefer wasting away in pain, dying limb by limb, or letting out his life drop by drop, rather than expiring once for all? Can any man be found willing to be fastened to the accursed tree, long sickly, already deformed, swelling with ugly tumours on chest and shoulders, and draw the breath of life amid long-drawn-out agony? I think he would have many excuses for dying even before mounting the cross!

Deny, now, if you can, that Nature is very generous in making death inevitable.

Many men have been prepared to enter upon still more shameful bargains: to betray friends in order to live longer themselves, or voluntarily to debase their children and so enjoy the light of day which is witness of all their sins. We must get rid of this craving for life, and learn that it makes no difference when your suffering comes, because at some time you are bound to suffer. The point is, not how long you live, but how nobly you live. And often this living nobly means that you cannot live long. Farewell.

# Letter 62
# On the Intimations of our Immortality

Just as a man is annoying when he rouses a dreamer of pleasant dreams (for he is spoiling a pleasure which may be unreal but nevertheless has the appearance of reality), even so your letter has done me an injury. For it brought me back abruptly, absorbed as I was in agreeable meditation and ready to proceed still further if it had been permitted me.

I was taking pleasure in investigating the immortality of souls, nay, in believing that doctrine. For I was lending a ready car to the opinions of the great authors, who not only approve but promise this most pleasing condition. I was giving myself over to such a noble hope; for I was already weary of myself, beginning already to despise the fragments of my shattered existence, and feeling that I was destined to pass over into that infinity of time and the heritage of eternity, when I was suddenly awakened by the receipt of your letter, and lost my lovely dream. But, if I can once dispose of you, I shall reseek and rescue it.

There was a remark, at the beginning of your letter, that I had not explained the whole problem wherein I was endeavouring to prove one of the beliefs of our school, that the renown which falls to one's lot after death is a good; for I had not solved the problem with which we are usually confronted: "No good can consist of things that are distinct and separate; yet renown consists of such things."

What you are asking about, my dear Lucilius, belongs to another topic of the same subject, and that is why I had postponed the arguments, not only on this one topic, but on other topics which also covered the same ground. For, as you know, certain logical questions are mingled with ethical ones. Accordingly, I handled the essential part of my subject which has to do with conduct—as to whether it is foolish and useless to be concerned with what lies beyond our last day, or whether our goods die with us and there is nothing left of him who is no more, or whether any profit can be attained or attempted beforehand out of that which, when it comes, we shall not be capable of feeling.

All these things have a view to conduct, and therefore they have been inserted under the proper topic. But the remarks of dialecticians in opposition to this idea had to be sifted out, and were accordingly laid aside. Now that you demand an answer to them all, I shall examine all their statements, and then refute them singly.

Unless, however, I make a preliminary remark, it will be impossible to understand my rebuttals. And what is that preliminary remark? Simply this: there are certain continuous bodies, such as a man; there are certain composite bodies—as ships, houses, and everything which is the result of joining separate parts into one sum total: there are certain others made up of things that are distinct, each member remaining separate—like an army, a populace, or a senate. For the persons who go to make up such bodies are united by virtue of law or function; but by their nature they are distinct and individual. Well, what further prefatory remarks do I still wish to make?

Simply this: we believe that nothing is a good, if it be composed of things that are distinct. For a single good should be checked and controlled by a single soul; and the essential quality of each single good should be single. This can be proved of itself whenever you desire; in the meanwhile, however, it had to be laid aside, because our own weapons are being hurled at us.

Opponents speak thus: "You say, do you, that no good can be made up of things that are distinct? Yet this renown, of which you speak, is simply the favourable opinion of good men. For just as reputation does not consist of one person's remarks, and as ill repute does not consist of one person's disapproval, so renown does not mean that we have merely pleased one good person. In order to constitute renown, the agreement of many distinguished and praiseworthy men is necessary. But this results from the decision of a number—in other words, of persons who are distinct. Therefore, it is not a good.

You say, again, that renown is the praise rendered to a good man by good men. Praise means speech: now speech is utterance with a particular meaning; and utterance, even from the lips of good men, is not a good in itself. For any act of a good man is not necessarily a good; he shouts his applause and hisses his disapproval, but one does not call the shouting or the hissing good— although his entire conduct may be admired and praised—any more than one would applaud a sneeze or a cough. Therefore, renown is not a good.

Finally, tell us whether the good belongs to him who praises, or to him who is praised: if you say that the good belongs to him who is praised, you are on as foolish a quest as if you were to maintain that my neighbour's good health is my own. But to praise worthy men is an honourable action; thus the good is exclusively that of the man who does the praising, of the man who performs the action, and not of us, who are being praised. And yet this was the question under discussion."

I shall now answer the separate objections hurriedly. The first question still is, whether any good can consist of things that are distinct—and there are votes cast on both sides. Again, does renown need many votes? Renown can be satisfied with the decision of one good man: it is one good man who decides that we are good.

Then the retort is: "What! Would you define reputation as the esteem of one individual, and ill-repute as the rancorous chatter of one man? Glory, too, we take to be more widespread, for it demands the agreement of many men." But the position of the "many" is different from that of "the one." And why? Because, if the good man thinks well of me, it practically amounts to my being thought well of by all good men; for they will all think the same, if they know me. Their judgment is alike and identical; the effect of truth on it is equal. They cannot disagree, which means that they would all hold the same view, being unable to hold different views.

"One man's opinion," you say, "is not enough to create glory or reputation." In the former case, one judgment is a universal judgment, because all, if they were asked, would hold one opinion; in the other case, however, men of dissimilar character give divergent judgments. You will find perplexing emotions—everything doubtful, inconstant, untrustworthy. And can you suppose that all men are able to hold one opinion? Even an individual does not hold to a single opinion. With the good man it is truth that causes belief, and truth has but one function and one likeness; while among the second class of which I spoke, the ideas with which they agree are unsound. Moreover, those who are false are never steadfast: they are irregular and discordant.

"But praise," says the objector, "is nothing but an utterance, and an utterance is not a good." When they say that renown is praise bestowed on the good by the good, what they refer to is not an utterance but a judgment. For a good man may remain silent; but if he decides that a certain person is worthy, of praise, that person is the object of praise.

Besides, praise is one thing, and the giving of praise another; the latter demands utterance also. Hence no one speaks of "a funeral praise," but says "praise-giving"—for its function depends upon speech. And when we say that a man is worthy of praise, we assure human kindness to him, not in words, but in judgment. So the good opinion, even of one who in silence feels inward approval of a good man, is praise.

Again, as I have said, praise is a matter of the mind rather than of the speech; for speech brings out the praise that the mind has conceived, and publishes it forth to the attention of the many. To judge a man worthy of praise, is to praise him. And when our tragic poet sings to us that it is wonderful "to be praised by a well-praised hero," he means, "by one who is worthy of praise." Again, when an equally venerable bard says: "Praise nurtureth the arts," he does not mean the giving of praise, for that spoils the arts. Nothing has corrupted oratory and all other studies that depend on hearing so much as popular approval.

Reputation necessarily demands words, but renown can be content with men's judgments, and suffice without the spoken word. It is satisfied not only amid silent approval, but even in the face of open protest. There is, in my opinion, this difference between renown and glory—the latter depends upon the judgments of the many; but renown on the judgments of good men.

The retort comes: "But whose good is this renown, this praise rendered to a good man by good men? Is it of the one praised, or of the one who praises?" Of both, I say. It is my own good, in that I am praised, because I am naturally born to love all men, and I rejoice in having done good deeds and congratulate myself on having found men who express their ideas of my virtues with gratitude; that they are grateful, is a good to the many, but it is a good to me also. For my spirit is so ordered that I can regard the good of other men as my own—in any case those of whose good I am myself the cause.

This good is also the good of those who render the praise, for it is applied by means of virtue; and every act of virtue is a good. My friends could not have found this blessing if I had not been a man of the right stamp. It is therefore a good belonging to both sides—this being praised when one deserves it—just as truly as a good decision is the good of him who makes the decision and also of him in whose favour the decision was given. Do you doubt that justice is a blessing to its possessor, as well as to the man to whom the just due was paid? To praise the deserving is justice; therefore, the good belongs to both sides.

This will be a sufficient answer to such dealers in subtleties. But it should not be our purpose to discuss things cleverly and to drag Philosophy down from her majesty to such petty quibbles. How much better it is to follow the open and direct road, rather than to map out for yourself a circuitous route which you must retrace with infinite trouble! For such argumentation is nothing else than the sport of men who are skilfully juggling with each other.

Tell me rather how closely in accord with nature it is to let one's mind reach out into the boundless universe! The human soul is a great and noble thing; it permits of no limits except those which can be shared even by the gods. First of all, it does not consent to a lowly birthplace, like Ephesus or Alexandria, or any land that is even more thickly populated than these, and more richly spread with dwellings. The soul's homeland is the whole space that encircles the, height and breadth of the firmament, the whole rounded dome within which lie land and sea, within which the upper air that sunders the human from the divine also unites them, and where all the sentinel stars are taking their turn on duty.

Again, the soul will not put up with a narrow span of existence. "All the years," says the soul, "are mine; no epoch is closed to great minds; all Time is open for the progress of thought. When the day comes to separate the heavenly from its earthly blend, I shall leave the body here where I found it, and shall of my own volition betake myself to the gods. I am not apart from them now, but am merely detained in a heavy and earthly prison."

These delays of mortal existence are a prelude to the longer and better life. As the mother's womb holds us for ten months, making us ready, not for the womb itself, but for the existence into which we seem to be sent forth when at last we are fitted to draw breath and live in the open; just so, throughout the years extending between infancy and old age, we are making ourselves ready for another birth. A different beginning, a different condition, await us.

We cannot yet, except at rare intervals, endure the light of heaven; therefore, look forward without fearing to that appointed hour, —the last hour of the body but not of the soul. Survey everything that lies about you, as if it were luggage in a guest-chamber: you must travel on. Nature strips you as bare at your departure as at your entrance.

You may take away no more than you brought in; what is more, you must throw away the major portion of that which you brought with you into life: you will be stripped of the very skin which covers you—that which has been your last protection; you will be stripped of the flesh, and lose the blood which is suffuses and circulated through your body; you will be stripped of bones and sinews, the framework of these transitory and feeble parts.

That day, which you fear as being the end of all things, is the birthday of your eternity. Lay aside your burden—why delay?— just as if you had not previously left the body which was your hiding-place! You cling to your burden, you struggle; at your birth also great effort was necessary on your mother's part to set you free. You weep and wail; and yet this very weeping happens at birth also; but then it was to be excused—for you came into the world wholly ignorant and inexperienced. When you left the warm and cherishing protection of your mother's womb, a freer air breathed into your face; then you winced at the touch of a rough hand, and you looked in amaze at unfamiliar objects, still delicate and ignorant of all things.

But now it is no new thing for you to be sundered from that of which you have previously been a part; let go your already useless limbs with resignation and dispense with that body in which you have dwelt for so long. It will be torn asunder, buried out of sight, and wasted away. Why be downcast? This is what ordinarily happens: when we are born, the afterbirth always perishes. Why love such a thing as if it were your own possession? It was merely your covering. The day will come which will tear you forth and lead you away from the company of the foul and noisome womb.

Withdraw from it now too as much as you can, and withdraw from pleasure, except such as may be bound up with essential and important things; estrange yourself from it even now, and ponder on something nobler and loftier. Some day the secrets of nature shall be disclosed to you, the haze will be shaken from your eyes, and the bright light will stream in upon you from all sides.

Picture to yourself how great is the glow when all the stars mingle their fires; no shadows will disturb the clear sky. The whole expanse of heaven will shine evenly; for day and night are interchanged only in the lowest atmosphere. Then you will say that you have lived in darkness, after you have seen, in your perfect state, the perfect light—that light which now you behold darkly with vision that is cramped to the last degree. And yet, far off as it is, you already look upon it in wonder;

what do you think the heavenly light will be when you have seen it in its proper sphere?

Such thoughts permit nothing mean to settle in the soul, nothing low, nothing cruel. They maintain that the gods are witnesses of everything. They order us to meet the gods' approval, to prepare ourselves to join them at some future time, and to plan for immortality. He that has grasped this idea shrinks from no attacking army, is not terrified by the trumpet-blast, and is intimidated by no threats.

How should it not be that a man feels no fear, if he looks forward to death? He also who believes that the soul abides only as long as it is fettered in the body, scatters it abroad forthwith when dissolved, so that it may be useful even after death. For though he is taken from men's sight, still

> *Often our thoughts run back to the hero, and often the glory*
> *Won by his race recurs to the mind.*

Consider how much we are helped by good example; you will thus understand that the presence of a noble man is of no less service than his memory. Farewell.

# Letter 63
# On Care of Health and Peace of Mind

I have run off to my villa at Nomentum, for what purpose, do you suppose? To escape the city? No; to shake off a fever which was surely working its way into my system. It had already got a grip upon me. My physician kept insisting that when the circulation was upset and irregular, disturbing the natural poise, the disease was under way. I therefore ordered my carriage to be made ready at once, and insisted on departing in spite of my wife Paulina's efforts to stop me; for I remembered master Gallio's words, when he began to develop a fever in Achaia and took ship at once, insisting that the disease was not of the body but of the place.

That is what I remarked to my dear Paulina, who always urges me to take care of my health. I know that her very life-breath comes and goes with my own, and I am beginning, in my solicitude for her, to be solicitous for myself. And although old age has made me braver to bear many things, I am gradually losing this boon that old age bestows. For it comes into my mind that in this old man there is a youth also, and youth needs tenderness. Therefore, since I cannot prevail upon her to love me any more heroically, she prevails upon me to cherish myself more carefully.

For one must indulge genuine emotions; sometimes, even in spite of weighty reasons, the breath of life must be called back and kept at our very lips even at the price of great suffering, for the sake of those whom we hold dear; because the good man should not live as long as it pleases him, but as long as he ought. He who does not value his wife, or his friend, highly enough to linger longer in life—he who obstinately persists in dying is a voluptuary.

The soul should also enforce this command upon itself whenever the needs of one's relatives require; it should pause and humour those near and dear, not only when it desires, but even when it has begun, to die.

It gives proof of a great heart to return to life for the sake of others; and noble men have often done this. But this procedure also, I believe, indicates the highest type of kindness: that although the greatest advantage of old age is the opportunity to be more negligent regarding self-preservation and to use life more adventurously, one should watch over one's old age with still greater care if one knows that such action is pleasing, useful, or desirable in the eyes of a person whom one holds dear.

This is also a source of no mean joy and profit; for what is sweeter than to be so valued by one's wife that one becomes more valuable to oneself for this reason? Hence my dear Paulina is able to make me responsible, not only for her fears, but also for my own.

So you are curious to know the outcome of this prescription of travel? As soon as I escaped from the oppressive atmosphere of the city, and from that awful odour of reeking kitchens which, when in use, pour forth a ruinous mess of steam and soot, I perceived at once that my health was mending. And how much stronger do you think I felt when I reached my vineyards! Being, so to speak, let out to pasture, I regularly walked into my meals! So I am my old self again, feeling now no wavering languor in my system, and no sluggishness in my brain. I am beginning to work with all my energy.

But the mere place avails little for this purpose, unless the mind is fully master of itself, and can, at its pleasure, find seclusion even in the midst of business; the man, however, who is always selecting resorts and hunting for leisure, will find something to distract his mind in every place. Socrates is reported to have replied, when a certain person complained of having received no benefit from his travels: "It serves you right! You travelled in your own company!"

O what a blessing it would be for some men to wander away from themselves! As it is, they cause themselves vexation, worry, demoralization, and fear! What profit is there in crossing the sea and in going from one city to another? If you would escape your troubles, you need not another place but another personality. Perhaps you have reached Athens, or perhaps Rhodes; choose any state you fancy, how does it matter what its character may be? You will be bringing to it your own.

Suppose that you hold wealth to be a good: poverty will then distress you, and—which is most pitiable—it will be an imaginary poverty. For you may be rich, and nevertheless, because your neighbour is richer, you suppose yourself to be poor exactly by the same amount in which you fall short of your neighbour. You may deem official position a good; you will be vexed at another's appointment or re-appointment to the consulship; you will be jealous whenever you see a name several times in the state records. Your ambition will be so frenzied that you will regard yourself last in the race if there is anyone in front of you.

Or you may rate death as the worst of evils, although there is really no evil therein except that which precedes death's coming—fear. You will be frightened out of your wits, not only by real, but by fancied dangers, and will be tossed for ever on the sea of illusion. What benefit will it be to

> Have threaded all the towns of Argolis,
> A fugitive through midmost press of foes?

For peace itself will furnish further apprehension. Even in the midst of safety you will have no confidence if your mind has once been given a shock; once it has acquired the habit of blind panic, it is incapable of providing even for its own safety. For it does not avoid danger, but runs away. Yet we are more exposed to danger when we turn our backs.

You may judge it the most grievous of ills to lose any of those you love; while all the same this would be no less foolish than weeping because the trees which charm your eye and adorn your home lose their foliage. Regard everything that pleases you as if it were a flourishing plant; make the most of it while it is in leaf, for different plants at different seasons must fall and die. But just as the loss of leaves is a light thing, because they are born afresh, so it is with the loss of those whom you love and regard as the delight of your life; for they can be replaced even though they cannot be born afresh.

"New friends, however, will not be the same." No, nor will you yourself remain the same; you change with every day and every hour. But in other men you more readily see what time plunders; in your own case the change is hidden, because it will not take place visibly. Others are snatched from sight; we ourselves are being stealthily filched away from ourselves. You will not think about any of these problems, nor will you apply remedies to these wounds. You will of your own volition be sowing a crop of trouble by alternate hoping and despairing. If you are wise, mingle these two elements: do not hope without despair, or despair without hope.

What benefit has travel of itself ever been able to give anyone? No restraint upon pleasure, no bridling of desire, no checking of bad temper, no crushing of the wild assaults of passion, no opportunity to rid the soul of evil. Travelling cannot give us judgment, or shake off our errors; it merely holds our attention for a moment by a certain novelty, as children pause to wonder at something unfamiliar.

Besides, it irritates us, through the wavering of a mind which is suffering from an acute attack of sickness; the very motion makes it more fitful and nervous. Hence the spots we had sought most eagerly we quit still more eagerly, like birds that flit and are off as soon as they have alighted.

What travel will give is familiarity with other nations: it will reveal to you mountains of strange shape, or unfamiliar tracts of plain, or valleys that are watered by everflowing springs, or the characteristics of some river that comes to our attention. We observe how the Nile rises and swells in summer, or how the Tigris disappears, runs underground through hidden spaces, and then appears with unabated sweep; or how the Maeander, that oft-rehearsed theme and plaything of the poets, turns in frequent bendings, and often in winding comes close to its own channel before resuming its course. But this sort of information will not make better or sounder men of us.

We ought rather to spend our time in study, and to cultivate those who are masters of wisdom, learning something which has been investigated, but not settled; by this means the mind can be relieved of a most wretched serfdom, and won over to freedom. Indeed, as long as you are ignorant of what you should avoid or seek, or of what is necessary or superfluous, or of what is right or wrong, you will not be travelling, but merely wandering.

There will be no benefit to you in this hurrying to and fro; for you are travelling with your emotions and are followed by your afflictions. Would that they were indeed following you! In that case, they would be farther away; as it is, you are carrying and not leading them. Hence they press about you on all sides, continually chafing and annoying you. It is medicine, not scenery, for which the sick man must go a-searching.

Suppose that someone has broken a leg or dislocated a joint: he does not take carriage or ship for other regions, but he calls in the physician to set the fractured limb, or to move it back to its proper place in the socket. What then? When the spirit is broken or wrenched in so many places, do you think that change of place can heal it? The complaint is too deep-seated to be cured by a journey.

Travel does not make a physician or an orator; no art is acquired by merely living in a certain place.

Where lies the truth, then? Can wisdom, the greatest of all the arts, be picked up on a journey? I assure you, travel as far as you like, you can never establish yourself beyond the reach of desire, beyond the reach of bad temper, or beyond the reach of fear; had it been so, the human race would long ago have banded together and made a pilgrimage to the spot. Such ills, as long as you carry with you their causes, will load you down and worry you to skin and bone in your wanderings over land and sea.

Do you wonder that it is of no use to run away from them? That from which you are running, is within you. Accordingly, reform your own self, get the burden off your own shoulders, and keep within safe limits the cravings which ought to be removed. Wipe out from your soul all trace of sin. If you would enjoy your travels, make healthy the companion of your travels. As long as this companion is avaricious and mean, greed will stick to you; and while you consort with an overbearing man, your puffed-up ways will also stick close. Live with a hangman, and you will never be rid of your cruelty. If an adulterer be your club-mate, he will kindle the baser passions.

If you would be stripped of your faults leave far behind you the patterns of the faults. The miser, the swindler, the bully, the cheat, who will do you much harm merely by being near you, are within you.

Change therefore to better associations: live with the Catos, with Laelius, with Tubero. Or, if you enjoy living with Greeks also, spend your time with Socrates and with Zeno: the former will show you how to die if it be necessary; the latter how to die before it is necessary.

Live with Chrysippus, with Posidonius: they will make you acquainted with things earthly and things heavenly; they will bid you work hard over something more than neat turns of language and phrases mouthed forth for the entertainment of listeners; they will bid you be stout of heart and rise superior to threats. The only harbour safe from the seething storms of this life is scorn of the future, a firm stand, a readiness to receive Fortune's missiles full in the breast, neither skulking nor turning the back.

Nature has brought us forth brave of spirit, and, as she has implanted in certain animals a spirit of ferocity, in others craft, in others terror, so she has gifted us with an aspiring and lofty spirit, which prompts us to seek a life of the greatest honour, and not of the greatest security, that most resembles the soul of the universe, which it follows and imitates as far as our mortal steps permit. This spirit thrusts itself forward, confident of commendation and esteem.

It is superior to all, monarch of all it surveys; hence it should be subservient to nothing, finding no task too heavy, and nothing strong enough to weigh down the shoulders of a man.

*Shapes dread to look upon, of toil or death*

are not in the least dreadful, if one is able to look upon them with unflinching gaze, and is able to pierce the shadows. Many a sight that is held a terror in the night-time, is turned to ridicule by day. "Shapes dread to look upon, of toil or death": our Vergil has excellently said that these shapes are dread, not in reality, but only "to look upon"—in other words, they seem terrible, but are not.

And in these visions what is there, I say, as fear-inspiring as rumour has proclaimed? Why, pray, my dear Lucilius, should a man fear toil, or a mortal death? Countless cases occur to my mind of men who think that what they themselves are unable to do is impossible, who maintain that we utter words which are too big for man's nature to carry out.

But how much more highly do I think of these men! They can do these things, but decline to do them. To whom that ever tried have these tasks proved false? To what man did they not seem easier in the doing? Our lack of confidence is not the result of difficulty. The difficulty comes from our lack of confidence.

If, however, you desire a pattern, take Socrates, a long-suffering old man, who was sea-tossed amid every hardship and yet was unconquered both by poverty (which his troubles at home made more burdensome) and by toil, including the drudgery of military service. He was much tried at home, whether we think of his wife, a woman of rough manners and shrewish tongue, or of the children whose intractability showed them to be more like their mother than their father. And if you consider the facts, he lived either in time of war, or under tyrants, or under a democracy, which is more cruel than wars and tyrants.

The war lasted for twenty-seven years; then the state became the victim of the Thirty Tyrants, of whom many were his personal enemies. At the last came that climax of condemnation under the gravest of charges: they accused him of disturbing the state religion and corrupting the youth, for they declared that he had influenced the youth to defy the gods, to defy the council, and to defy the state in general. Next came the prison, and the cup of poison. But all these measures changed the soul of Socrates so little that they did not even change his features. What wonderful and rare distinction! He maintained this attitude up to the very end, and no man ever saw Socrates too much elated or too much depressed. Amid all the disturbance of Fortune, he was undisturbed.

Do you desire another case? Take that of the younger Marcus Cato, with whom Fortune dealt in a more hostile and more persistent fashion. But he withstood her, on all occasions, and in his last moments, at the point of death, showed that a brave man can live in spite of Fortune, can die in spite of her. His whole life was passed either in civil warfare, or under a political regime which was soon to breed civil war. And you may say that he, just as much as Socrates, declared allegiance to liberty in the midst of slavery—unless perchance you think that Pompey, Caesar, and Crassus were the allies of liberty!

No one ever saw Cato change, no matter how often the state changed: he kept himself the same in all circumstances—in the praetorship, in defeat, under accusation, in his province, on the platform, in the army, in death. Furthermore, when the republic was in a crisis of terror, when Caesar was on one side with ten embattled legions at his call, aided by so many foreign nations, and when Pompey was on the other, satisfied to stand alone against all comers, and when the citizens were leaning towards either Caesar or Pompey, Cato alone established a definite party for the Republic.

If you would obtain a mental picture of that period, you may imagine on one side the people and the whole proletariat eager for revolution—on the other the senators and knights, the chosen and honoured men of the commonwealth; and there were left between them but these two—the Republic and Cato.

*I tell you, you will marvel when you see*
*Atreus' son, and Priam, and Achilles, wroth at both.*

Like Achilles, he scorns and disarms each faction.

And this is the vote which he casts concerning them both: "If Caesar wins, I slay myself; if Pompey, I go into exile." What was there for a man to fear who, whether in defeat or in victory, had assigned to himself a doom which might have been assigned to him by his enemies in their utmost rage? So he died by his own decision.

You see that man can endure toil: Cato, on foot, led an army through African deserts. You see that thirst can be endured: he marched over sun-baked hills, dragging the remains of a beaten army and with no train of supplies, undergoing lack of water and wearing a heavy suit of armour; always the last to drink of the few springs which they chanced to find.

You see that honour, and dishonour too, can be despised: for they report that on the very day when Cato was defeated at the elections, he played a game of ball. You see also that man can be free from fear of those above him in rank: for Cato attacked Caesar and Pompey simultaneously, at a time when none dared fall foul of the one without endeavouring to oblige the other. You see that death can be scorned as well as exile: Cato inflicted exile upon himself and finally death, and war all the while.

And so, if only we are willing to withdraw our necks from the yoke, we can keep as stout a heart against such terrors as these. But first and foremost, we must reject pleasures; they render us weak and womanish; they make great demands upon us, and, moreover, cause us to make great demands upon Fortune. Second, we must spurn wealth: wealth is the diploma of slavery. Abandon gold and silver, and whatever else is a burden upon our richly-furnished homes; liberty cannot be gained for nothing. If you set a high value on liberty, you must set a low value on everything else. Farewell.

# Letter 64
# On Facing the World with Confidence

I shall now tell you certain things to which you should pay attention in order to live more safely. Do you however—such is my judgment—hearken to my precepts just as if I were counselling you to keep safe your health in your country-place at Ardea.

Reflect on the things which goad man into destroying man: you will find that they are hope, envy, hatred, fear, and contempt.

Now, of all these, contempt is the least harmful, so much so that many have skulked behind it as a sort of cure. When a man despises you, he works you injury, to be sure, but he passes on; and no one persistently or of set purpose does hurt to a person whom he despises. Even in battle, prostrate soldiers are neglected: men fight with those who stand their ground.

And you can avoid the envious hopes of the wicked so long as you have nothing which can stir the evil desires of others, and so long as you possess nothing remarkable. For people crave even little things, if these catch the attention or are of rare occurrence.

You will escape envy if you do not force yourself upon the public view, if you do not boast your possessions, if you understand how to enjoy things privately. Hatred comes either from running foul of others: and this can be avoided by never provoking anyone; or else it is uncalled for: and common-sense will keep you safe from it. Yet it has been dangerous to many; some people have been hated without having had an enemy.

As to not being feared, a moderate fortune and an easy disposition will guarantee you that; men should know that you are the sort of person who can be offended without danger; and your reconciliation should be easy and sure. Moreover, it is as troublesome to be feared at home as abroad; it is as bad to be feared by a slave as by a gentleman. For every one has strength enough to do you some harm. Besides, he who is feared, fears also; no one has been able to arouse terror and live in peace of mind.

Contempt remains to be discussed. He who has made this quality an adjunct of his own personality, who is despised because he wishes to be despised and not because he *must* be despised, has the measure of contempt under his control. Any inconveniences in this respect can be dispelled by honourable occupations and by friendships with men who have influence with an influential person; with these men it will profit you to engage but not to entangle yourself, lest the cure may cost you more than the risk.

Nothing, however, will help you so much as keeping still—talking very little with others, and as much as may be with yourself. For there is a sort of charm about conversation, something very subtle and coaxing, which, like intoxication or love, draws secrets from us. No man will keep to himself what he hears. No one will tell another only as much as he has heard. And he who tells tales will tell names, too. Everyone has someone to whom he entrusts exactly what has been entrusted to him. Though he checks his own garrulity, and is content with one hearer, he will bring about him a nation, if that which was a secret shortly before becomes common talk.

The most important contribution to peace of mind is never to do wrong. Those who lack self-control lead disturbed and tumultuous lives; their crimes are balanced by their fears, and they are never at ease. For they tremble after the deed, and they are embarrassed; their consciences do not allow them to busy themselves with other matters, and continually compel them to give an answer. Whoever expects punishment, receives it, but whoever deserves it, expects it.

Where there is an evil conscience something may bring safety, but nothing can bring ease; for a man imagines that, even if he is not under arrest, he may soon be arrested. His sleep is troubled; when he speaks of another man's crime, he reflects upon his own, which seems to him not sufficiently blotted out, not sufficiently hidden from view. A wrongdoer sometimes has the luck to escape notice but never the assurance thereof. Farewell.

# Letter 65
# On Obedience to the Universal Will

Where is that common-sense of yours? Where that deftness in examining things? That greatness of soul? Have you come to be tormented by a trifle? Your slaves regarded your absorption in business as an opportunity for them to run away. Well, if your friends deceived you (for by all means let them have the name which we mistakenly bestowed upon them, and so call them, that they may incur more shame by not being such friends)—if your friends, I repeat, deceived you, all your affairs would lack something; as it is, you merely lack men who damaged your own endeavours and considered you burdensome to your neighbours.

None of these things is unusual or unexpected. It is as nonsensical to be put out by such events as to complain of being spattered in the street or at getting befouled in the mud. The programme of life is the same as that of a bathing establishment, a crowd, or a journey: sometimes things will be thrown at you, and sometimes they will strike you by accident. Life is not a dainty business. You have started on a long journey; you are bound to slip, collide, fall, become weary, and cry out: "O for Death!"—or in other words, tell lies. At one stage you will leave a comrade behind you, at another you will bury someone, at another you will be apprehensive. It is amid stumblings of this sort that you must travel out this rugged journey.

Does one wish to die? Let the mind be prepared to meet everything; let it know that it has reached the heights round which the thunder plays. Let it know that it has arrived where

> Grief and avenging Care have set their couch,
> And pallid sickness dwells, and drear Old Age.

With such messmates must you spend your days. Avoid them you cannot, but despise them you can. And you will despise them, if you often take thought and anticipate the future.

Everyone approaches courageously a danger which he has prepared himself to meet long before, and withstands even hardships if he has previously practiced how to meet them. But, contrariwise, the unprepared are panic-stricken even at the most trifling things. We must see to it that nothing shall come upon us unforeseen. And since things are all the more serious when they are unfamiliar, continual reflection will give you the power, no matter what the evil may be, not to play the unschooled boy.

"My slaves have run away from me!" Yes, other men have been robbed, blackmailed, slain, betrayed, stamped under foot, attacked by poison or by slander; no matter what trouble you mention, it has happened to many. Again, there are manifold kinds of missiles which are hurled at us. Some are planted in us, some are being brandished and at this very moment are on the way, some which were destined for other men graze us instead.

We should not manifest surprise at any sort of condition into which we are born, and which should be lamented by no one, simply because it is equally ordained for all. Yes, I say, equally ordained; for a man might have experienced even that which he has escaped. And an equal law consists, not of that which all have experienced, but of that which is laid down for all. Be sure to prescribe for your mind this sense of equity; we should pay without complaint the tax of our mortality.

Winter brings on cold weather; and we must shiver. Summer returns, with its heat; and we must sweat. Unseasonable weather upsets the health; and we must fall ill. In certain places we may meet with wild beasts, or with men who are more destructive than any beasts. Floods, or fires, will cause us loss. And we cannot change this order of things; but what we can do is to acquire stout hearts, worthy of good men, thereby courageously enduring chance and placing ourselves in harmony with Nature.

And Nature moderates this world-kingdom which you see, by her changing seasons: clear weather follows cloudy; after a calm, comes the storm; the winds blow by turns; day succeeds night; some of the heavenly bodies rise, and some set. Eternity consists of opposites.

It is to this law that our souls must adjust themselves, this they should follow, this they should obey. Whatever happens, assume that it was bound to happen, and do not be willing to rail at Nature. That which you cannot reform, it is best to endure, and to attend uncomplainingly upon the God under whose guidance everything progresses; for it is a bad soldier who grumbles when following his commander.

For this reason we should welcome our orders with energy and vigour, nor should we cease to follow the natural course of this most beautiful universe, into which all our future sufferings are woven.

Let us address Jupiter, the pilot of this world-mass, as did our great Cleanthes in those most eloquent lines—lines which I shall allow myself to render in Latin, after the example of the eloquent Cicero. If you like them, make the most of them; if they displease you, you will understand that I have simply been following the practice of Cicero:

*Lead me, O Master of the lofty heavens,*
*My Father, whithersoever thou shalt wish.*
*I shall not falter, but obey with speed.*
*And though I would not, I shall go, and suffer,*
*In sin and sorrow what I might have done*
*In noble virtue. Aye, the willing soul*
*Fate leads, but the unwilling drags along.*

Let us live thus, and speak thus; let Fate find us ready and alert. Here is your great soul—the man who has given himself over to Fate; on the other hand, that man is a weakling and a degenerate who struggles and maligns the order of the universe and would rather reform the gods than reform himself. Farewell.

# Letter 66
## On the Fellowship of Wise Men

You expressed a wish to know whether a wise man can help a wise man. For we say that the wise man is completely endowed with every good, and has attained perfection; accordingly, the question arises how it is possible for anyone to help a person who possesses the Supreme Good.

Good men are mutually helpful; for each gives practice to the other's virtues and thus maintains wisdom at its proper level. Each needs someone with whom he may make comparisons and investigations.

Skilled wrestlers are kept up to the mark by practice; a musician is stirred to action by one of equal proficiency. The wise man also needs to have his virtues kept in action; and as he prompts himself to do things, so is he prompted by another wise man.

How can a wise man help another wise man? He can quicken his impulses, and point out to him opportunities for honourable action. Besides, he can develop some of his own ideas; he can impart what he has discovered. For even in the case of the wise man something will always remain to discover, something towards which his mind may make new ventures.

Evil men harm evil men; each debases the other by rousing his wrath, by approving his churlishness, and praising his pleasures; bad men are at their worst stage when their faults are most thoroughly intermingled, and their wickedness has been, so to speak, pooled in partnership. Conversely, therefore, a good man will help another good man. "How?" you ask.

Because he will bring joy to the other, he will strengthen his faith, and from the contemplation of their mutual tranquillity the delight of both will be increased. Moreover they will communicate to each other a knowledge of certain facts; for the wise man is not all-knowing. And even if he were all-knowing, someone might be able to devise and point out short cuts, by which the whole matter is more readily disseminated.

The wise will help the wise, not, mark you, because of his own strength merely, but because of the strength of the man whom he assists. The latter, it is true, can by himself develop his own parts; nevertheless, even one who is running well is helped by one who cheers him on.

"But the wise man does not really help the wise; he helps himself. Let me tell you this: strip the one of his special powers, and the other will accomplish nothing."

You might as well, on that basis, say that sweetness is not in the honey: for it is the person himself who is to eat it, that is so equipped, as to tongue and palate, for tasting this kind of food that the special flavour appeals to him, and anything else displeases. For there are certain men so affected by disease that they regard honey as bitter. Both men should be in good health, that the one may be helpful and the other a proper subject for help.

Again they say: "When the highest degree of heat has been attained, it is superfluous to apply more heat; and when the Supreme Good has been attained, it is superfluous to have a helper. Does a completely stocked farmer ask for further supplies from his neighbours? Does a soldier who is sufficiently armed for going well-equipped into action need any more weapons? Very well, neither does the wise man; for he is sufficiently equipped and sufficiently armed for life."

My answer to this is, that when one is heated to the highest degree, one must have continued heat to maintain the highest temperature. And if it be objected that heat is self-maintaining, I say that there are great distinctions among the things that you are comparing; for heat is a single thing, but helpfulness is of many kinds. Again, heat is not helped by the addition of further heat, in order to be hot; but the wise man cannot maintain his mental standard without intercourse with friends of his own kind—with whom he may share his goodness.

Moreover, there is a sort of mutual friendship among all the virtues. Thus, he who loves the virtues of certain among his peers, and in turn exhibits his own to be loved, is helpful. Like things give pleasure, especially when they are honourable and when men know that there is mutual approval.

And besides, none but a wise man can prompt another wise man's soul in an intelligent way, just as man can be prompted in a rational way by man only. As, therefore, reason is necessary for the prompting of reason, so, in order to prompt perfect reason, there is need of perfect reason.

Some say that we are helped even by those who bestow on us the so-called "indifferent" benefits, such as money, influence, security, and all the other valued or essential aids to living. If we argue in this way, the veriest fool will be said to help a wise man. Helping, however, really means prompting the soul in accordance with Nature, both by the prompter's excellence and by the excellence of him who is thus prompted. And this cannot take place without advantage to the helper also. For in training the excellence of another, a man must necessarily train his own.

But, to omit from discussion supreme goods or the things which produce them, wise men can none the less be mutually helpful. For the mere discovery of a sage by a sage is in itself a desirable event; since everything good is naturally dear to the good man, and for this reason one feels congenial with a good man as one feels congenial with oneself.

It is necessary for me to pass from this topic to another, in order to prove my point. For the question is asked, whether the wise man will weigh his opinions, or whether he will apply to others for advice. Now he is compelled to do this when he approaches state and home duties—everything, so to speak, that is mortal. He needs outside advice on such matters, as does the physician, the pilot, the attorney, or the pleader of cases. Hence, the wise will sometimes help the wise; for they will persuade each other. But in these matters of great import also—aye, of divine import, as I have termed them—the wise man can also be useful by discussing honourable things in common, and by contributing his thoughts and ideas.

Moreover, it is in accordance with Nature to show affection for our friends, and to rejoice in their advancement as if it were absolutely our own. For if we have not done this, even virtue, which grows strong only through exercising our perceptions, will not abide with us. Now virtue advises us to arrange the present well, to take thought regarding the future, to deliberate and apply our minds; and one who takes a friend into council with him, can more easily apply his mind and think out his problem.

Therefore he will seek either the perfect wise man or one who has progressed to a point bordering on perfection. The perfect wise man, moreover, will help us if he aids our counsels with ordinary good sense.

They say that men see farther in the affairs of others than in their own. A defect of character causes this in those who are blinded by self-love, and whose fear in the hour of peril takes away their clear view of that which is useful; it is when a man is more at ease and freed from fear that he will begin to be wise. Nevertheless, there are certain matters where even wise men see the facts more clearly in the case of others than in their own. Moreover, the wise man will, in company with his fellow sage, confirm the truth of that most sweet and honourable proverb—"always desiring and always refusing the same things": it will be a noble result when they draw the load "with equal yoke."

I have thus answered your demand, although it came under the head of subjects which I include in my volumes *On Moral Philosophy*. Reflect, as I am often wont to tell you, that there is nothing in such topics for us except mental gymnastics. For I return again and again to the thought: "What good does this do me? Make me more brave now, more just, more restrained! I have not yet the opportunity to make use of my training; for I still need the physician.

Why do you ask of me a useless knowledge? You have promised great things; test me, watch me! You assured me that I should be unterrified though swords were flashing round me, though the point of the blade were grazing my throat; you assured me that I should be at ease though fires were blazing round me, or though a sudden whirlwind should snatch up my ship and carry it over all the sea. Now make good for me such a course of treatment that I may despise pleasure and glory. Thereafter you shall teach me to work out complicated problems, to settle doubtful points, to see through that which is not clear; teach me now what it is necessary for me to know! Farewell.

# Letter 67
## On True and False Riches

From my villa at Nomentum I send you greeting and bid you keep a sound spirit within you—in other words, gain the blessing of all the gods, for he is assured of their grace and favour who has become a blessing to himself. Lay aside for the present the belief of certain persons—that a god is assigned to each one of us as a sort of attendant—not a god of regular rank, but one of a lower grade—one of those whom Ovid calls "plebeian gods." Yet, while laying aside this belief, I would have you remember that our ancestors, who followed such a creed, have become Stoics; for they have assigned a Genius or a Juno to every individual.

Later on we shall investigate whether the gods have enough time on their hands to care for the concerns of private individuals; in the meantime, you must know that whether we are allotted to special guardians, or whether we are neglected and consigned to Fortune, you can curse a man with no heavier curse than to pray that he may be at enmity with himself.

There is no reason, however, why you should ask the gods to be hostile to anyone whom you regard as deserving of punishment; they are hostile to such a person, I maintain, even though he seems to be advanced by their favour.

Apply careful investigation, considering how our affairs actually stand, and not what men say of them; you will then understand that evils are more likely to help us than to harm us. For how often has so-called affliction been the source and the beginning of happiness! How often have privileges which we welcomed with deep thanksgiving built steps for themselves to the top of a precipice, still uplifting men who were already distinguished—just as if they had previously stood in a position whence they could fall in safety!

But this very fall has in it nothing evil, if you consider the end, after which nature lays no man lower. The universal limit is near; yes, there is near us the point where the prosperous man is upset, and the point where the unfortunate is set free. It is we ourselves that extend both these limits, lengthening them by our hopes and by our fears.

If, however, you are wise, measure all things according to the state of man; restrict at the same time both your joys and your fears. Moreover, it is worth while not to rejoice at anything for long, so that you may not fear anything for long.

But why do I confine the scope of this evil? There is no reason why you should suppose that anything is to be feared. All these things which stir us and keep us a-flutter, are empty things. None of us has sifted out the truth; we have passed fear on to one another; none has dared to approach the object which caused his dread, and to understand the nature of his fear—aye, the good behind it. That is why falsehood and vanity still gain credit— because they are not refuted.

Let us account it worth while to look closely at the matter; then it will be clear how fleeting, how unsure, and how harmless are the things which we fear. The disturbance in our spirits is similar to that which Lucretius detected:

> *Like boys who cower frightened in the dark,*
> *So grown-ups in the light of day feel fear.*

What, then? Are we not more foolish than any child, we who "in the light of day feel fear"?

But you were wrong, Lucretius; we are not afraid in the daylight; we have turned everything into a state of darkness. We see neither what injures nor what profits us; all our lives through we blunder along, neither stopping nor treading more carefully on this account. But you see what madness it is to rush ahead in the dark. Indeed, we are bent on getting ourselves called back from a greater distance; and though we do not know our goal, yet we hasten with wild speed in the direction whither we are straining.

The light, however, may begin to shine, provided we are willing. But such a result can come about only in one way—if we acquire by knowledge this familiarity with things divine and human, if we not only flood ourselves but steep ourselves therein, if a man reviews the same principles even though he understands them and applies them again and again to himself, if he has investigated what is good, what is evil, and what has falsely been so entitled; and, finally, if he has investigated honour and baseness, and Providence.

The range of the human intelligence is not confined within these limits; it may also explore outside the universe—its destination and its source, and the ruin towards which all nature hastens so rapidly. We have withdrawn the soul from this divine contemplation and dragged it into mean and lowly tasks, so that it might be a slave to greed, so that it might forsake the universe and its confines, and, under the command of masters who try all possible schemes, pry beneath the earth and seek what evil it can dig up therefrom—discontented with that which was freely offered to it.

Now God, who is the Father of us all, has placed ready to our hands those things which he intended for our own good; he did not wait for any search on our part, and he gave them to us voluntarily. But that which would be injurious, he buried deep in the earth. We can complain of nothing but ourselves; for we have brought to light the materials for our destruction, against the will of Nature, who hid them from us. We have bound over our souls to pleasure, whose service is the source of all evil; we have surrendered ourselves to self-seeking and reputation, and to other aims which are equally idle and useless.

What, then, do I now encourage you to do? Nothing new—we are not trying to find cures for new evils—but this first of all: namely, to see clearly for yourself what is necessary and what is superfluous. What is necessary will meet you everywhere; what is superfluous has always to be hunted-out—and with great endeavour.

But there is no reason why you should flatter yourself over-much if you despise gilded couches and jewelled furniture. For what virtue lies in despising useless things? The time to admire your own conduct is when you have come to despise the necessities. You are doing no great thing if you can live without royal pomp, if you feel no craving for boars which weigh a thousand pounds, or for flamingo tongues, or for the other absurdities of a luxury that already wearies of game cooked whole, and chooses different bits from separate animals; I shall admire you only when you have learned to scorn even the common sort of bread, when you have made yourself believe that grass grows for the needs of men as well as of cattle, when you have found out that food from the treetop can fill the belly—into which we cram things of value as if it could keep what it has received. We should satisfy our stomachs without being over-nice. How does it matter what the stomach receives, since it must lose whatever it has received? You enjoy the carefully arranged dainties which are caught on land and sea; some are more pleasing if they are brought fresh to the table, others, if after long feeding and forced fattening they almost melt and can hardly retain their own grease. You like the subtly devised flavour of these dishes. But I assure you that such carefully chosen and variously seasoned dishes, once they have entered the belly, will be overtaken alike by one and the same corruption. Would you despise the pleasures of eating? Then consider its result!

I remember some words of Attalus, which elicited general applause: "Riches long deceived me. I used to be dazed when I caught some gleam of them here and there. I used to think that their hidden influence matched their visible show. But once, at a certain elaborate entertainment, I saw embossed work in silver and gold equalling the wealth of a whole city, and colours and tapestry devised to match objects which surpassed the value of gold or of silver—brought not only from beyond our own borders, but from beyond the borders of our enemies; on one side were slave-boys notable for their training and beauty, on the other were throngs of slave-women, and all the other resources that a prosperous and mighty empire could offer after reviewing its possessions.

What else is this, I said to myself, than a stirring-up of man's cravings, which are in themselves provocative of lust? What is the meaning of all this display of money? Did we gather merely to learn what greed was? For my own part I left the place with less craving than I had when I entered. I came to despise riches, not because of their uselessness, but because of their pettiness.

Have you noticed how, inside a few hours, that programme, however slow-moving and carefully arranged, was over and done? Has a business filled up this whole life of ours, which could not fill up a whole day?

I had another thought also: the riches seemed to me to be as useless to the possessors as they were to the onlookers.

Accordingly, I say to myself, whenever a show of that sort dazzles my eyes, whenever I see a splendid palace with a well-groomed corps of attendants and beautiful bearers carrying a litter: Why wonder? Why gape in astonishment? It is all show; such things are displayed, not possessed; while they please they pass away.

Turn thyself rather to the true riches. Learn to be content with little, and cry out with courage and with greatness of soul. 'We have water, we have porridge; let us compete in happiness with Jupiter himself.' And why not, I pray thee, make this challenge even without porridge and water? For it is base to make the happy life depend upon silver and gold, and just as base to make it depend upon water and porridge. 'But,' some will say, 'what could I do without such things?'

Do you ask what is the cure for want? It is to make hunger satisfy hunger; for, all else being equal, what difference is there in the smallness or the largeness of the things that force you to be a slave? What matter how little it is that Fortune can refuse to you?

Your very porridge and water can fall under another's jurisdiction; and besides, freedom comes, not to him over whom Fortune has slight power, but to him over whom she has no power at all. This is what I mean: you must crave nothing, if you would vie with Jupiter; for Jupiter craves nothing."

This is what Attalus told us. If you are willing to think often of these things, you will strive not to seem happy, but to be happy, and, in addition, to seem happy to yourself rather than to others. Farewell.

# Letter 68
# On Reforming Hardened Sinners

I am indeed anxious that your friend be moulded and trained, according to your desire. But he has been taken in a very hardened state, or rather (and this is a more difficult problem), in a very soft state, broken down by bad and inveterate habits.

I should like to give you an illustration from my own handicraft.

It is not every vine that admits the grafting process; if it be old and decayed, or if it be weak and slender, the vine either will not receive the cutting, or will not nourish it and make it a part of itself, nor will it accommodate itself to the qualities and nature of the grafted part. Hence we usually cut off the vine above ground, so that if we do not get results at first, we may try a second venture, and on a second trial graft it below the ground.

Now this person, concerning whom you have sent me your message in writing, has no strength; for he has pampered his vices. He has at one and the same time become flabby and hardened. He cannot receive reason, nor can he nourish it. "But," you say, "he desires reason of his own free will." Don't believe him. Of course I do not mean that he is lying to you; for he really thinks that he desires it. Luxury has merely upset his stomach; he will soon become reconciled to it again.

"But he says that he is put out with his former way of living." Very likely. Who is not? Men love and hate their vices at the same time. It will be the proper season to pass judgment on him when he has given us a guarantee that he really hates luxury; as it is now, luxury and he are merely not on speaking terms. Farewell.

# Letter 69
# On the Vanity of the Soul and Its Attributes

You wish me to write to you my opinion concerning this question, which has been mooted by our school—whether justice, courage, foresight, and the other virtues, are living things. By such niceties as this, my beloved Lucilius, we have made people think that we sharpen our wits on useless objects, and waste our leisure time in discussions that will be unprofitable. I shall, however, do as you ask, and shall set forth the subject as viewed by our school. For myself, I confess to another belief: I hold that there are certain things which befit a wearer of white shoes and a Greek mantle. But what the beliefs are that have stirred the ancients, or those which the ancients have stirred up for discussion, I shall explain to you.

The soul, men are agreed, is a living thing, because of itself it can make us living things, and because "living things" have derived their name therefrom. But virtue is nothing else than a soul in a certain condition; therefore it is a living thing. Again, virtue is active, and no action can take place without impulse. And if a thing has impulse, it must be a living thing; for none except a living thing possesses impulse.

A reply to this is: "If virtue is a living thing, then virtue itself possesses virtue." Of course it possesses its own self! Just as the wise man does everything by reason of virtue, so virtue accomplishes everything by reason of itself. "In that case," say they, "all the arts also are living things, and all our thoughts and all that the mind comprehends. It therefore follows that many thousands of living things dwell in man's tiny heart, and that each individual among us consists of, or at least contains, many living beings."

Are you gravelled for an answer to this remark? Each of these will be a living thing; but they will not be many separate living things. And why? I shall explain, if you will apply your subtlety and your concentration to my words.

Each living thing must have a separate substance; but since all the things mentioned above have a single soul, consequently they can be separate living things but without plurality. I myself am a living thing, and a man; but you cannot say that there are two of me for that reason. And why? Because, if that were so, they would have to be two separate existences. This is what I mean: one would have to be sundered from the other so as to produce two. But whenever you have that which is manifold in one whole, it falls into the category of a single nature, and is therefore single.

My soul is a living thing, and so am I; but we are not two separate persons. And why? Because the soul is part of myself. It will only be reckoned as a definite thing in itself when it shall exist by itself. But as long as it shall be part of another, it cannot be regarded as different. And why? I will tell you: it is because that which is different, must be personal and peculiar to itself, a whole, and complete within itself.

I myself have gone on record as being of a different opinion; for if one adopts this belief, not only the virtues will be living things, but so will their contrary vices, and the emotions, like wrath, fear, grief, and suspicion. Nay, the argument will carry us still further—all opinions and all thoughts will be living things. This is by no means admissible; since anything that man does is not necessarily the man himself.

"What is Justice?" people say. Justice is a soul that maintains itself in a certain attitude. "Then if the soul is a living being, so is Justice." By no means. For Justice is really a state, a kind of power, of the soul; and this same soul is transformed into various likenesses and does not become a different kind of living thing as often as it acts differently. Nor is the result of soul-action a living thing.

If Justice, Bravery, and the other virtues have actual life, do they cease to be living things and then begin life over again, or are they *always* living things?

But the virtues cannot cease to be. Therefore, there are many, nay countless, living things, sojourning in this one soul.

"No," is the answer, "not many, because they are all attached to the one, being parts and members of a single whole." We are then portraying for ourselves an image of the soul like that of a many-headed hydra—each separate head fighting and destroying independently. And yet there is no separate living thing to each head; it is the head of a living thing, and the hydra itself is one single living thing. No one ever believed that the Chimaera contained a living lion or a living serpent; these were merely parts of the whole Chimaera; and parts are not living things.

Then how can you infer that Justice is a living thing? "Justice," people reply, "is active and helpful; that which acts and is helpful, possesses impulse; and that which possesses impulse is a living thing." True, if the impulse is its own; (but in the case of justice it is not its own;) the impulse comes from the soul.

Every living thing exists as it began, until death; a man, until he dies, is a man, a horse is a horse, a dog a dog. They cannot change into anything else. Now let us grant that Justice—which is defined as "a soul in a certain attitude," is a living thing. Let us suppose this to be so. Then Bravery also is alive, being "a soul in a certain attitude." But which soul? That which was but now defined as Justice? The soul is kept within the first-named being, and cannot cross over into another; it must last out its existence in the medium where it had its origin.

Besides, there cannot be one soul to two living things, much less to many living things. And if Justice, Bravery, Restraint, and all the other virtues, are living things, how will they have one soul? They must possess separate souls, or else they are not living things.

Several living things cannot have one body; this is admitted by our very opponents. Now what is the "body" of justice? "The soul," they admit. And of bravery? "The soul also." And yet there cannot be one body of two living things.

"The same soul, however," they answer, "assumes the guise of Justice, or Bravery, or Restraint." This would be possible if Bravery were absent when Justice was present, and if Restraint were absent when Bravery was present; as the case stands now, all the virtues exist at the same time. Hence, how can the separate virtues be living things, if you grant that there is one single soul, which cannot create more than one single living thing?

Again, no living thing is part of another living thing. But Justice is a part of the soul; therefore Justice is not a living thing. It looks as if I were wasting time over something that is an acknowledged fact; for one ought to decry such a topic rather than debate it. And no two living things are equal. Consider the bodies of all beings: every one has its particular colour, shape, and size.

And among the other reasons for marvelling at the genius of the Divine Creator is, I believe, this—that amid all this abundance there is no repetition; even seemingly similar things are, on comparison, unlike. God has created all the great number of leaves that we behold: each, however, is stamped with its special pattern. All the many animals: none resembles another in size—always some difference! The Creator has set himself the task of making unlike and unequal things that are different; but all the virtues, as your argument states, are equal. Therefore, they are not living things.

Every living thing acts of itself; but virtue does nothing of itself; it must act in conjunction with man. All living things either are gifted with reason, like men and gods, or else are irrational, like beasts and cattle. Virtues, in any case, are rational; and yet they are neither men nor gods; therefore they are not living things.

Every living thing possessed of reason is inactive if it is not first stirred by some external impression; then the impulse comes, and finally assent confirms the impulse. Now what *assent* is, I shall explain. Suppose that I ought to take a walk: I *do* walk, but only after uttering the command to myself and approving this opinion of mine. Or suppose that I ought to seat myself; I *do* seat myself, but only after the same process. This assent is not a part of virtue.

For let us suppose that it is Prudence; how will Prudence assent to the opinion: "I must take a walk"? Nature does not allow this. For Prudence looks after the interests of its possessor, and not of its own self. Prudence cannot walk or be seated. Accordingly, it does not possess the power of assent, and it is not a living thing possessed of reason. But if virtue is a living thing, it is rational. But it is not rational; therefore it is not a living thing.

If virtue is a living thing, and virtue is a Good—is not, then, every Good a living thing? It is. Our school professes it.

Now to save a father's life is a Good; it is also a Good to pronounce one's opinion judiciously in the senate, and it is a Good to hand down just opinions; therefore the act of saving a father's life is a living thing, also the act of pronouncing judicious opinions. We have carried this absurd argument so far that you cannot keep from laughing outright: wise silence is a Good, and so is a frugal dinner; therefore silence and dining are living things.

Indeed I shall never cease to tickle my mind and to make sport for myself by means of this nice nonsense. Justice and Bravery, if they are living things, are certainly of the earth. Now every earthly living thing gets cold or hungry or thirsty; therefore, Justice goes a-cold, Bravery is hungry, and Kindness craves a drink!

And what next? Should I not ask our honourable opponents what shape these living beings have? Is it that of man, or horse, or wild beast? If they are given a round shape, like that of a god, I shall ask whether greed and luxury and madness are equally round. For these, too, are "living things." If I find that they give a rounded shape to these also, I shall go so far as to ask whether a modest gait is a living thing; they must admit it, according to their argument, and proceed to say that a gait is a living thing, and a rounded living thing, at that!

Now do not imagine that I am the first one of our school who does not speak from rules but has his own opinion: Cleanthes and his pupil Chrysippus could not agree in defining the act of walking. Cleanthes held that it was spirit transmitted to the feet from the primal essence, while Chrysippus maintained that it was the primal essence in itself. Why, then, following the example of Chrysippus himself, should not every man claim his own freedom, and laugh down all these "living things," so numerous that the universe itself cannot contain them?

One might say: "The virtues are not many living things, and yet they are living things. For just as an individual may be both poet and orator in one, even so these virtues are living things, but they are not many. The soul is the same; it can be at the same time just and prudent and brave, maintaining itself in a certain attitude towards each virtue."

The dispute is settled, and we are therefore agreed. For I shall admit, meanwhile, that the soul is a living thing with the proviso that later on I may cast my final vote; but I deny that the acts of the soul are living beings. Otherwise, all words and all verses would be alive; for if prudent speech is a Good, and every Good a living thing, then speech is a living thing. A prudent line of poetry is a Good; everything alive is a Good; therefore, the line of poetry is a living thing. And so "Arms and the man I sing," is a living thing; but they cannot call it rounded, because it has six feet!

"This whole proposition," you say, "which we are at this moment discussing, is a puzzling fabric." I split with laughter whenever I reflect that solecisms and barbarisms and syllogisms are living things, and, like an artist, I give to each a fitting likeness. Is this what we discuss with contracted brow and wrinkled forehead? I cannot say now, after Caelius, "What melancholy trifling!" It is more than this; it is absurd. Why do we not rather discuss something which is useful and wholesome to ourselves, seeking how we may attain the virtues, and finding the path which will take us in that direction?

Teach me, not whether Bravery be a living thing, but prove that no living thing is happy without bravery, that is, unless it has grown strong to oppose hazards and has overcome all the strokes of chance by rehearsing and anticipating their attack. And what is Bravery? It is the impregnable fortress for our mortal weakness; when a man has surrounded himself therewith, he can hold out free from anxiety during life's siege; for he is using his own strength and his own weapons.

At this point I would quote you a saying of our philosopher Posidonius: "There are never any occasions when you need think yourself safe because you wield the weapons of Fortune; fight with your own! Fortune does not furnish arms against herself; hence men equipped against their foes are unarmed against Fortune herself."

Alexander, to be sure, harried and put to flight the Persians, the Hyrcanians, the Indians, and all the other races that the Orient spreads even to the Ocean; but he himself, as he slew one friend or lost another, would lie in the darkness lamenting sometimes his crime, and sometimes his loss; he, the conqueror of so many kings and nations, was laid low by anger and grief! For he had made it his aim to win control over everything except his emotions.

Oh with what great mistakes are men obsessed, who desire to push their limits of empire beyond the seas, who judge themselves most prosperous when they occupy many provinces with their soldiery and join new territory to the old! Little do they know of that kingdom which is on an equality with the heavens in greatness!

Self-Command is the greatest command of all. Let her teach me what a hallowed thing is the Justice which ever regards another's good and seeks nothing for itself except its own employment. It should have nothing to do with ambition and reputation; it should satisfy itself.

Let each man convince himself of this before all else—"I must be just without reward." And that is not enough; let him convince himself also of this: "May I take pleasure in devoting myself of my own free will to uphold this noblest of virtues." Let all his thoughts be turned as far as possible from personal interests. You need not look about for the reward of a just deed; a just deed in itself offers a still greater return.

Fasten deep in your mind that which I remarked a short space above: that it makes no difference how many persons are acquainted with your uprightness. Those who wish their virtue to be advertised are not striving for virtue but for renown. Are you not willing to be just without being renowned? Nay, indeed you must often be just and be at the same time disgraced. And then, if you are wise, let ill repute, well won, be a delight. Farewell.

# Letter 70
# On Style as a Mirror of Character

You have been asking me why, during certain periods, a degenerate style of speech comes to the fore, and how it is that men's wits have gone downhill into certain vices—in such a way that exposition at one time has taken on a kind of puffed-up strength, and at another has become mincing and modulated like the music of a concert piece. You wonder why sometimes bold ideas—bolder than one could believe—have been held in favour, and why at other times one meets with phrases that are disconnected and full of innuendo, into which one must read more meaning than was intended to meet the ear. Or why there have been epochs which maintained the right to a shameless use of metaphor. For answer, here is a phrase which you are wont to notice in the popular speech—one which the Greeks have made into a proverb: "Man's speech is just like his life."

Exactly as each individual man's actions seem to speak, so people's style of speaking often reproduces the general character of the time, if the morale of the public has relaxed and has given itself over to effeminacy. Wantonness in speech is proof of public luxury, if it is popular and fashionable, and not confined to one or two individual instances.

A man's ability cannot possibly be of one sort and his soul of another. If his soul be wholesome, well-ordered, serious, and restrained, his ability also is sound and sober. Conversely, when the one degenerates, the other is also contaminated. Do you not see that if a man's soul has become sluggish, his limbs drag and his feet move indolently? If it is womanish, that one can detect the effeminacy by his very gait? That a keen and confident soul quickens the step? That madness in the soul, or anger (which resembles madness), hastens our bodily movements from walking to rushing?

And how much more do you think that this affects one's ability, which is entirely interwoven with the soul—being moulded.

How Maecenas lived is too well-known for present comment. We know how he walked, how effeminate he was, and how he desired to display himself; also, how unwilling he was that his vices should escape notice. What, then? Does not the looseness of his speech match his ungirt attire? Are his habits, his attendants, his house, his wife, any less clearly marked than his words? He would have been a man of great powers, had he set himself to his task by a straight path, had he not shrunk from making himself understood, had he not been so loose in his style of speech also. You will therefore see that his eloquence was that of an intoxicated man—twisting, turning, unlimited in its slackness.

What is more unbecoming than the words: "A stream and a bank covered with long-tressed woods"? And see how "men plough the channel with boats and, turning up the shallows, leave gardens behind them." Or, "He curls his lady-locks, and bills and coos, and starts a-sighing, like a forest lord who offers prayers with down-bent neck." Or, "An unregenerate crew, they search out people at feasts and assail households with the wine-cup, and, by hope, exact death." Or, "A Genius could hardly bear witness to his own festival"; or "threads of tiny tapers and crackling meal"; "mothers or wives clothing the hearth."

Can you not at once imagine, on reading through these words, that this was the man who always paraded through the city with a flowing tunic? For even if he was discharging the absent emperor's duties, he was always in undress when they asked him for the countersign. Or that this was the man who, as judge on the bench, or as an orator, or at any public function, appeared with his cloak wrapped about his head, leaving only the ears exposed, like the millionaire's runaway slaves in the farce? Or that this was the man who, at the very time when the state was embroiled in civil strife, when the city was in difficulties and under martial law, was attended in public by two eunuchs—both of them more men than himself? Or that this was the man who had but one wife, and yet was married countless times?

These words of his, put together so faultily, thrown off so carelessly, and arranged in such marked contrast to the usual practice, declare that the character of their writer was equally unusual, unsound, and eccentric. To be sure, we bestow upon him the highest praise for his humanity; he was sparing with the sword and refrained from bloodshed; and he made a show of his power only in the course of his loose living; but he spoiled, by such preposterous finickiness of style, this genuine praise, which was his due.

For it is evident that he was not really gentle, but effeminate, as is proved by his misleading word-order, his inverted expressions, and the surprising thoughts which frequently contain something great, but in finding expression have become nerveless. One would say that his head was turned by too great success.

This fault is due sometimes to the man, and sometimes to his epoch.

When prosperity has spread luxury far and wide, men begin by paying closer attention to their personal appearance. Then they go crazy over furniture. Next, they devote attention to their houses—how to take up more space with them, as if they were country-houses, how to make the walls glitter with marble that has been imported over seas, how to adorn a roof with gold, so that it may match the brightness of the inlaid floors. After that, they transfer their exquisite taste to the dinner-table, attempting to court approval by novelty and by departures from the customary order of dishes, so that the courses which we are accustomed to serve at the end of the meal may be served first, and so that the departing guests may partake of the kind of food which in former days was set before them on their arrival.

When the mind has acquired the habit of scorning the usual things of life, and regarding as mean that which was once customary, it begins to hunt for novelties in speech also; now it summons and displays obsolete and old-fashioned words; now it coins even unknown words or misshapes them; and now a bold and frequent metaphorical usage is made a special feature of style, according to the fashion which has just become prevalent.

Some cut the thoughts short, hoping to make a good impression by leaving the meaning in doubt and causing the hearer to suspect his own lack of wit. Some dwell upon them and lengthen them out. Others, too, approach just short of a fault—for a man must really do this if he hopes to attain an imposing effect—but actually love the fault for its own sake. In short, whenever you notice that a degenerate style pleases the critics, you may be sure that character also has deviated from the right standard.

Just as luxurious banquets and elaborate dress are indications of disease in the state, similarly a lax style, if it be popular, shows that the mind (which is the source of the word) has lost its balance. Indeed you ought not to wonder that corrupt speech is welcomed not merely by the more squalid mob but also by our more cultured throng; for it is only in their dress and not in their judgments that they differ.

You may rather wonder that not only the effects of vices, but even vices themselves, meet with approval. For it has ever been thus: no man's ability has ever been approved without something being pardoned. Show me any man, however famous; I can tell you what it was that his age forgave in him, and what it was that his age purposely overlooked. I can show you many men whose vices have caused them no harm, and not a few who have been even helped by these vices. Yes, I will show you persons of the highest reputation, set up as models for our admiration; and yet if you seek to correct their errors, you destroy them; for vices are so intertwined with virtues that they drag the virtues along with them.

Moreover, style has no fixed laws; it is changed by the usage of the people, never the same for any length of time. Many orators hark back to earlier epochs for their vocabulary, speaking in the language of the Twelve Tables. Gracchus, Crassus, and Curio, in their eyes, are too refined and too modern; so back to Appius and Coruncanius! Conversely, certain men, in their endeavour to maintain nothing but well-worn and common usages, fall into a humdrum style.

These two classes, each in its own way, are degenerate; and it is no less degenerate to use no words except those which are conspicuous, high-sounding, and poetical, avoiding what is familiar and in ordinary usage. One is, I believe, as faulty as the other: the one class are unreasonably elaborate, the other are unreasonably negligent; the former depilate the leg, the latter not even the armpit.

Let us now turn to the arrangement of words. In this department, what countless varieties of fault I can show you! Some are all for abruptness and unevenness of style, purposely disarranging anything which seems to have a smooth flow of language. They would have jolts in all their transitions; they regard as strong and manly whatever makes an uneven impression on the ear. With some others it is not so much an "arrangement" of words as it is a setting to music; so wheedling and soft is their gliding style.

And what shall I say of that arrangement in which words are put off and, after being long waited for, just manage to come in at the end of a period? Or again of that softly-concluding style, Cicero-fashion, with a gradual and gently poised descent always the same and always with the customary arrangement of the rhythm! Nor is the fault only in the style of the sentences, if they are either petty and childish, or debasing, with more daring than modesty should allow, or if they are flowery and cloying, or if they end in emptiness, accomplishing mere sound and nothing more.

Some individual makes these vices fashionable—some person who controls the eloquence of the day; the rest follow his lead and communicate the habit to each other. Thus when Sallust was in his glory, phrases were lopped off, words came to a close unexpectedly, and obscure conciseness was equivalent to elegance. L. Arruntius, a man of rare simplicity, author of a historical work on the Punic War, was a member and a strong supporter of the Sallust school. There is a phrase in Sallust: *exercitum argento fecit*, meaning thereby that he *recruited* an army by means of money. Arruntius began to like this idea; he therefore inserted the verb *facio* all through his book. Hence, in one passage, *fugam nostris fecere*; in another, *Hiero, rex Syracusanorum, bellum fecit*; and in another, *quae audita Panhormitanos dedere Romanis fecere*.

I merely desired to give you a taste; his whole book is interwoven with such stuff as this. What Sallust reserved for occasional use, Arruntius makes into a frequent and almost continual habit— and there was a reason: for Sallust used the words as they occurred to his mind, while the other writer went afield in search of them. So you see the results of copying another man's vices.

Again, Sallust said: *aquis hiemantibus*. Arruntius, in his first book on the Punic War, uses the words: *repente hiemavit tempestas*. And elsewhere, wishing to describe an exceptionally cold year, he says: *totus hiemavit annus*. And in another passage: *inde sexaginta onerarias leves praeter militem et necessarios nautarum hiemante aquilone misit*; and he continues to bolster many passages with this metaphor. In a certain place, Sallust gives the words: *inter arma civilia aequi bonique famas petit*; and Arruntius cannot restrain himself from mentioning at once, in the first book, that there were extensive "reminders" concerning Regulus.

These and similar faults, which imitation stamps upon one's style, are not necessarily indications of loose standards or of debased mind; for they are bound to be personal and peculiar to the writer, enabling one to judge thereby of a particular author's temperament; just as an angry man will talk in an angry way, an excitable man in a flurried way, and an effeminate man in a style that is soft and unresisting.

You note this tendency in those who pluck out, or thin out, their beards, or who closely shear and shave the upper lip while preserving the rest of the hair and allowing it to grow, or in those who wear cloaks of outlandish colours, who wear transparent togas, and who never deign to do anything which will escape general notice; they endeavour to excite and attract men's attention, and they put up even with censure, provided that they can advertise themselves. That is the style of Maecenas and all the others who stray from the path, not by hazard, but consciously and voluntarily.

This is the result of great evil in the soul. As in the case of drink, the tongue does not trip until the mind is overcome beneath its load and gives way or betrays itself; so that intoxication of style—for what else than this can I call it?—never gives trouble to anyone unless the soul begins to totter. Therefore, I say, take care of the soul; for from the soul issue our thoughts, from the soul our words, from the soul our dispositions, our expressions, and our very gait. When the soul is sound and strong, the style too is vigorous, energetic, manly; but if the soul lose its balance, down comes all the rest in ruins.

> *If but the king be safe, your swarm will live*
> *Harmonious; if he die, the bees revolt.*

The soul is our king. If it be safe, the other functions remain on duty and serve with obedience; but the slightest lack of equilibrium in the soul causes them to waver along with it. And when the soul has yielded to pleasure, its functions and actions grow weak, and any undertaking comes from a nerveless and unsteady source.

To persist in my use of this simile—our soul is at one time a king, at another a tyrant. The king, in that he respects things honourable, watches over the welfare of the body which is entrusted to his charge, and gives that body no base, no ignoble commands. But an uncontrolled, passionate, and effeminate soul changes kingship into that most dread and detestable quality—tyranny; then it becomes a prey to the uncontrolled emotions, which dog its steps, elated at first, to be sure, like a populace idly sated with a largess which will ultimately be its undoing, and spoiling what it cannot consume.

But when the disease has gradually eaten away the strength, and luxurious habits have penetrated the marrow and the sinews, such a soul exults at the sight of limbs which, through its overindulgence, it has made useless; instead of its own pleasures, it views those of others; it becomes the go-between and witness of the passions which, as the result of self-gratification, it can no longer feel. Abundance of delights is not so pleasing a thing to that soul as it is bitter, because it cannot send all the dainties of yore down through the over-worked throat and stomach, because it can no longer whirl in the maze of eunuchs and mistresses, and it is melancholy because a great part of its happiness is shut off, through the limitations of the body.

Now is it not madness, Lucilius, for none of us to reflect that he is mortal? Or frail? Or again that he is but one individual? Look at our kitchens, and the cooks, who bustle about over so many fires; is it, think you, for a single belly that all this bustle and preparation of food takes place? Look at the old brands of wine and store-houses filled with the vintages of many ages; is it, think you, a single belly that is to receive the stored wine, sealed with the names of so many consuls, and gathered from so many vineyards? Look, and mark in how many regions men plough the earth, and how many thousands of farmers are tilling and digging; is it, think you, for a single belly that crops are planted in Sicily and Africa?

We should be sensible, and our wants more reasonable, if each of us were to take stock of himself, and to measure his bodily needs also, and understand how little he can consume, and for how short a time! But nothing will give you so much help toward moderation as the frequent thought that life is short and uncertain here below; whatever you are doing, have regard to death. Farewell.

# Letter 71
# On Self-Control

The question has often been raised whether it is better to have moderate emotions, or none at all. Philosophers of our school reject the emotions; the Peripatetics keep them in check. I, however, do not understand how any half-way disease can be either wholesome or helpful. Do not fear; I am not robbing you of any privileges which you are unwilling to lose! I shall be kindly and indulgent towards the objects for which you strive—those which you hold to be necessary to our existence, or useful, or pleasant; I shall simply strip away the vice. For after I have issued my prohibitions against the desires, I shall still allow you to wish that you may do the same things fearlessly and with greater accuracy of judgment, and to feel even the pleasures more than before; and how can these pleasures help coming more readily to your call, if you are their lord rather than their slave!

"But," you object, "it is natural for me to suffer when I am bereaved of a friend; grant some privileges to tears which have the right to flow! It is also natural to be affected by men's opinions and to be cast down when they are unfavourable; so why should you not allow me such an honourable aversion to bad opinion?"

There is no vice which lacks some plea; there is no vice that at the start is not modest and easily entreated; but afterwards the trouble spreads more widely. If you allow it to begin, you cannot make sure of its ceasing.

Every emotion at the start is weak. Afterwards, it rouses itself and gains strength by progress; it is more easy to forestall it than to forgo it. Who does not admit that all the emotions flow as it were from a certain natural source? We are endowed by Nature with an interest in our own well-being; but this very interest, when overindulged, becomes a vice. Nature has intermingled pleasure with necessary things—not in order that we should seek pleasure, but in order that the addition of pleasure may make the indispensable means of existence attractive to our eyes. Should it claim rights of its own, it is luxury.

Let us therefore resist these faults when they are demanding entrance, because, as I have said, it is easier to deny them admittance than to make them depart.

And if you cry: "One should be allowed a certain amount of grieving, and a certain amount of fear." I reply that the "certain amount" can be too long-drawn-out, and that it will refuse to stop short when you so desire. The wise man can safely control himself without becoming over-anxious; he can halt his tears and his pleasures at will; but in our case, because it is not easy to retrace our steps, it is best not to push ahead at all.

I think that Panaetius gave a very neat answer to a certain youth who asked him whether the wise man should become a lover: "As to the wise man, we shall see later; but you and I, who are as yet far removed from wisdom, should not trust ourselves to fall into a state that is disordered, uncontrolled, enslaved to another, contemptible to itself. If our love be not spurned, we are excited by its kindness; if it be scorned, we are kindled by our pride. An easily won love hurts us as much as one which is difficult to win; we are captured by that which is compliant, and we struggle with that which is hard. Therefore, knowing our weakness, let us remain quiet. Let us not expose this unstable spirit to the temptations of drink, or beauty, or flattery, or anything that coaxes and allures."

Now that which Panaetius replied to the question about love may be applied, I believe, to all the emotions. In so far as we are able, let us step back from slippery places; even on dry ground it is hard enough to take a sturdy stand.

At this point, I know, you will confront me with that common complaint against the Stoics: "Your promises are too great, and your counsels too hard. We are mere manikins, unable to deny ourselves everything. We shall sorrow, but not to any great extent; we shall feel desires, but in moderation; we shall give way to anger, but we shall be appeased."

And do you know why we have not the power to attain this Stoic ideal? It is because we refuse to believe in our power. Nay, of a surety, there is something else which plays a part: it is because we are in love with our vices; we uphold them and prefer to make excuses for them rather than shake them off. We mortals have been endowed with sufficient strength by nature, if only we use this strength, if only we concentrate our powers and rouse them all to help us or at least not to hinder us. The reason is unwillingness, the excuse, inability. Farewell.